TAKEN ABACK

Deborah Tuite

Author's Note

The anthropological importance of the Caribbean colonies, their economic impact on European nations, and influence on other burgeoning states, cannot be underestimated. The incredible prosperity of those islands during the seventeenth and eighteenth centuries started industrial and political revolutions, developed a middle class, and spurred the largest exchange of wealth the world had ever known.

Touted the "most wickedest city", Jamaica's Port Royal was the largest English-speaking town in the new world. It was the hub of Caribbean wealth and activity, but that elated status ended abruptly when a large section of the city fell almost vertically into the harbor during the earthquake of 1692.

Today, the ruins lie beneath three to four hundred feet of murky water in Kingston Harbor. Hurricanes, weathering, fires, construction, and removal of artifacts nearly always compromise the historic integrity of ancient archeological sites. However, the sunken city of Port Royal remains relatively unmolested, frozen in its tragic final moment and protected by the soft sediments of the harbor. The ruins are a time capsule and most likely the world's best example of seventeenth century living. Past explorations, excavations, and scientific studies of the site revealed a treasure of knowledge and a wealth of history.

I would like to thank the underwater explorers, their supporters, the faculty and students who analyze the discoveries of the Port Royal ruins, and the many keepers of Caribbean antiquities, both private and public, who work to record and preserve this special heritage. There is so much more to learn from the Port Royal site and other ruins throughout the Caribbean Islands and I wish future expeditions, research, and preservation endeavors my heartfelt success.

taken aback

definition source: Wikipedia, Glossary of Nautical Terms, 2009

. . . an inattentive helmsmen might allow the dangerous situation to arise where the wind is blowing into the sails 'backwards', causing a sudden (and possibly dangerous) shift in the position of the sails.

Dedication

Many thanks to Tom and Jon and to my family and friends who contributed patience and knowledge in the writing of this book and to John and Ginger Garrison who introduced me to the Caribbean and to Ian Hart who taught me its history. Most of all, I want to thank my husband, Chris, and dedicate this book to him.

Table Of Contents

CHAPTER 1

Wrapped in a shroud that was once his hammock, the corpse of William Montague lay at the shoeless feet of the *Rosa*'s crew. His wife, pale and statuesque, stood over the body while the captain mumbled dispassionate words, something about the mortality of a man born of woman.

Huddled beside the widow were the dead man's children. The oldest child, Sally, a pretty girl and nearly a woman at fifteen, found the scene on deck morbidly irresistible. She fixed her eyes on the tightly sewn bundle of soiled canvas. It was not difficult to imagine it a sack of potatoes or some heap of refuse ready for disposal. Yet, within that grisly package, her father lay. That man resembled nothing of her strong protector. A fortnight of fever followed by sporadic attacks of crippling cramps and excessive vomiting left her beloved Papa shriveled and wasted with blistered lips and cracked bleeding skin. Worse, the flesh of his face seemed to shrink away leaving him gaunt with gaping mouth and grotesque stare. He died in the night with his knees drawn up close to his chest and by morning's discovery, had stiffened in that indignant stature. Fearing the unidentified sickness, the crew of the morning watch hurriedly prepared the body for funeral without cleaning him or making an effort to correct his position.

A gust of wind from bow to stern delivered an acrid smell of death and stirred panic in Sally. "We should not be here," she whispered to her mother. Receiving no response, Sally closed her eyes and tried to swallow a growing angst. She shook her head in disbelief. *This was not the plan Papa had designed for our future*, she thought. Her father had always possessed a cautious and practical sagacity that, for many years, kept his troubled family from financial ruin. So it seemed odd to Sally that he would then take such a risk and submit all of them, along with the remainder of the family's fortune, to such a dangerous endeavor. *Why Papa, why?* She thought for a moment and finally concluded, *Uncle Robert!*

It was her uncle's careless extravagancies and debts that left the family to make such despairing choices. Sally grimaced. She could still hear the harsh shameful threats of those who came to their door demanding their money. The taste of that humiliation lingered. *Such a price my father paid,* she thought, *for one so . . . unworthy.* She scowled at her mother. *Had Mama been stronger*, Sally supposed, *and more forceful in her protests, Papa might have aborted this desperate scheme of running a sugar plantation in the Caribbean and still be alive this day!*

The wind freshened. It caught the edge of Sally's cape and whipped it across the face of her brother, James. Any other time, he would have retaliated in some playful manner, but his fearful eyes remained set on that bundle balanced atop a polished plank. The young boy with straw-colored hair and an abundance of freckles was half the age of his sister. He explored the folds of his mother's skirts to search for a comforting hand, but she clenched them fast to a tattered bible she held close to her chest. Tears stained the ruddy glow of his youth as he looked up at her. She did not respond. The crew suddenly snapped to attention. The captain finished. The eulogy was complete.

"He should have said more," Sally whispered to no one in particular, then louder, "He should have said more!" Her objection went unanswered.

Two seamen lifted the plank from the deck and carried it to the gangway. With a nod from the captain, they tilted one end high over their shoulders. William

Montague slid off the board and splashed quietly into the contentious morning sea.

James bolted from his mother's side to climb the rails. He stretched out in time to see the gray waters swiftly swallow the canvas coffin leaving nothing but the dull morning light dancing on the disrupted water.

"Mr. Tibbs was right," James shouted to Sally recalling that the *Rosa*'s benevolent seaman and ship's cook, Mr. Barnaby Tibbs, had hastily sewn some bricks inside the hammock to give it weight.

"No worries, lad!" James remembered Mr. Tibbs saying. "He be sunk afore the first fish takes its nibble. Tis our secret, now," the cook had warned. "Captain Blake would 'ave me hide and dock me wages if he knew I 'ad these here Nettlebed bricks. Worth money, they are. Ship's ballast now, but they'll soon be pavin' them streets of Bridgetown in Barbados, eh lad?"

James was grateful for the care and kindness Mr. Tibbs had shown in his effort and design. For a moment, he pondered the fate of his father's body. Would sharks molest him? Would the sea preserve the body, or rot it as quickly as a beast on land?

"Are maggots in the sea?" he asked Sally as the sailors around them bustled about and returned to their chores of the forenoon watch.

"Mr. Tibbs said there were all manner of creatures in the sea. I suppose there is something like maggots," Sally reasoned, grabbing the back of the boy's breeches. "I do not believe it is a bad thing, James, to be buried at sea. No worse than on land, just different."

"But, people put stones on graves and carve names into them, don't they . . . so they can find them again to offer them prayers. How will we ever find Papa?" James asked in a quivering tone.

"True," Sally explained. "We leave no stone to mark his resting place, but untrue that there is no marker." Sally thought for a moment. Her effort to suppress her tears left a painful lump in her throat. She swallowed hard. "Do you remember what happens when you throw a stone in the water, how it forms ripples that travel away from the spot where the stone struck? Whenever you want to send a message to Papa, you need only touch your hand upon the sea and create ripples. Those ripples will carry your prayers to this exact place. Soon, the whole sea will hear you James, and the waves will carry the tale of William Montague. All will know of our Papa, the birds that fly above, the creatures below, and all those who sail upon her surface. And the wind will listen to the sea and take that tale to every land. The sea is his marker, James, and as long as there is a sea, he will never be forgotten."

James gave his sister a half smile as he jumped down from the rails. He did not believe her story. He wanted to, for it was a good one, but he was too old now for such fantasies. While Sally tended their mother, James wandered off toward the stern to study the water. He had no love for this cranky, relentless sea. From the start, it made him terribly ill and he spent most of the voyage cross-legged on his hammock with a bucket between his knees. The *Rosa* was a merchant ship well fitted for cargo, not passengers. Their cramped quarters was merely part of the lower deck partitioned from the other passengers and crew by a wall of spare canvas. It was an airless and dark stinking place. Below, without a view of the horizon, the rolling and pitching of the ship and the swinging of his hammock compounded his sickness. Though he gave in often to the persistent hunger of his youth, food barely reached his stomach before rising again. It was not until they reached the Canary Islands that he began to feel better. "Gettin' them sea legs, ya are!" Mr. Tibbs had told him. But just as he rallied, his poor father became ill. It was difficult for James to endure the sounds and smells of his father's sickness without reacting in sympathy.

Aside from the captain's elaborately carved bedstead, a wooden pallet, hinged to the bulkhead, was the only other bed on the ship. It was reserved for Mrs. Montague. Everyone else, crew and passengers alike, slept in hammocks made of canvas or woven hemp. By day, the hard narrow pallet was folded up, mattress and all, and clamped to the bulkhead. On sunny days, at least at the beginning of the journey, Mr. Tibbs would take the mattress topside for an airing. "Why, jist da smell of salt air encourages them fleas to jump ship!" he had claimed. Tibbs called the thin mattress "the donkey's breakfast" for he took its stuffing straight from the rations of the livestock on board. To better manage the needs of the ailing man and for his safety, the crew moved William Montague from his hammock to the pallet. After that, replacing the stuffing or even turning the soiled mattress became a futile practice and the odor forced James and the others to sleep on the weather deck when winds were fair. However, this past night, the weather turned cold and drizzly and they were all forced to return below.

As he looked out to sea, James tried to piece together sporadic flashes of memories and feared he might have heard the exact moment when his Papa breathed his last. During that dreadful night, James swung in his hammock just above his father's bed and watched shadows dance as the flame of the wall lamp responded to the rush of a rising wind. Intensifying air currents squeezed through the tiniest cracks in the ship's upper bulkhead making a wheezy, whistling sound nearly indistinguishable to that made by his father as he grappled to fill his lungs. Time between the man's breaths lengthened and each inhalation was softer than the one before. Finally, his Papa turned over on his side and the struggles for air abated. Interpreting this change as a sign of recovery, James precariously dangled over the edge of the hammock and reached down to feel his father's forehead. It was dry and his brow cool. He remembered thinking, *the fever is gone! At last he sleeps!* He wanted to wake his mother but she seemed so peaceful, slumped on a cask next to the pallet and mildly snoring with her chin on her chest. James decided to leave them both to their gentle rest. Feeling much relieved and believing the crisis was over, he snuggled back into his hammock and fell asleep to the melodious moans of calmer breezes.

He closed his eyes from the twinge of guilt that now pierced his heart. He remembered his mother's harsh shrill that ruined the peace of the early dawn and heralded this fateful change for the family. Pushing such thoughts aside, James climbed between the ship's belaying pins and leaned over the rails to watch the choppy waters pass the stern. Again his sister clutched the waistband of his breeches to pull him back but this time he broke free from her hold and ran off to embrace his mother.

Again, and most uncharacteristically, the Widow Montague made no effort to comfort her son. She stared straight out to sea with expressionless puffy eyes and slouched shoulders. A strange glow from the sun, now rising higher and deeper behind thickening clouds, cast an eerie hue on her pallid face.

"Mama? It will be all right, Mama," James assured. "I will look after us now."

Having finished his duty to his deceased passenger, Captain Wallace Blake went about his business without acknowledging the bereaved family or the two other passengers of the *Rosa*. Through a stained stubby beard that covered his long supercilious chin, the captain shouted orders to his sailing master.

"Heave the yard, Mr. Cane, bring her into the wind!" Anxious to deliver the comforting sweet tangy wetness of his cup to his lips, the captain retreated to his quarters. Since leaving Bristol Port, he lost much sleep to the awful memories that churned in the deep boughs of his troubled soul. Insomnia, brought on by nighttime apparitions, so palpable and real, left him crotchety and depressed by day. At least here, in the quiet refuge of his cabin, Captain Blake could wash away the webs of those nightmares with copious flagons of wine.

Blake had been ambitious in his youth and he knew that for a person of his poor standing, crewing on Dutch slavers would be one of very few opportunities for promotion. Sure enough, through the trade of human cargo, he quickly gained a reputation as a fine seaman and rose fast through the ranks until finally he was appointed Master of the *Rosa*. It was an empty prize for the price had been too high. He was haunted by images of despicable acts committed by ruffian crews gathered from the world's insalubrious seaports. Beseeching cries of the slaves still echoed in his brain causing him to suffer from paralyzing headaches, a diminished appetite, and dozens of sleepless nights. The poor diet led to decaying teeth and painful rancid boils on his neck, back, and buttocks. He grew to abhor his life at sea and swore each voyage would be his last but since childhood, the sea was all he knew. He tried but failed to earn like wages on land so, like a hopeless addict, he returned to the sea again and again. With each passage, he became less of a gentleman, less of a scholar of the oceans and skies, intolerant, cantankerous, and lacking compassion. And now . . . now, he must deal with this heavy burden of the Montague family.

For the passage of the entire family and for the purchase and transport of the new sugar press, boiler, and other equipment stored below the *Rosa*'s decks, William Montague borrowed heavily from the ship's company. *Family and goods are now the company's possessions*, the captain surmised. *Cargo. No different from the oxen, bricks, or barrels of flour*. As if to sanction his conclusion, the captain downed a flagon, and then another.

Still on deck, Quartermaster Edward Waller nervously adjusted the sleeves of his coat and cleared his throat several times before he was able to utter awkward words to Montague's daughter.

"I must apologize for my captain's sudden departure, Miss Montague," he explained as he bowed before Sally. "He . . . we must all be away to our duties."

Sally smirked and raised a single eyebrow. "I fear your captain is insulting, Mr. Waller," she retorted. "That his demeanor could have changed so, puzzles me. Before leaving Bristol, he seemed quite civil . . . at least well mannered. But now, the crew of the *Rosa* skirts around him as one does a barking dog. Their respect seems to center on you, Mr. Waller. It is to you that they look for protection from the sea and each other. Why is that?"

Edward said nothing in reply for he could neither disagree nor offer plausible excuses for his captain's bad behavior.

"Forgive me," Sally injected when she saw his uneasiness. "I am grateful for what you have done for us, Mr. Waller. You certainly won Papa's admiration. Before he became ill, he talked at length about how you and he had shared interests in plantations and commerce. He admitted to me that you expressed misgivings over this endeavor . . . to go to the West Indies. Papa had an unshakable resolve. Too late have the risks of this adventure come to my understanding, Mr. Waller. Might I enquire, what will become of us?"

Edward looked aft to where the widow and her son stood. "Look to your family, Miss Montague. I will speak with my captain. The . . . death of your father has tested the captain's temperament. I beg for time to speak with him later, when his disposition improves." He bowed again and pivoted away from her before she could respond.

The ship's bell rang twice, paused, rang twice again, paused, and then rang once more. Edward took mental note of the crew remaining topside before leaving the weather deck. The funeral service was a distraction for which some might take advantage and skip the second half of their watch. Satisfied that all on the Forenoon Watch were still present and working, he turned his attention to his captain. As if bracing himself for battle, Edward paused and inhaled deeply before knocking on the captain's door.

"Come!" Capt. Blake groused. "Ah, Mr. Waller! More's the pity," he complained to Edward, "that Montague did not have the courtesy to die before we left Gomera in the Canaries. Then, at least, I could have unloaded this unlucky family onto that island for the next ship sailing for England and profited by the cargo he left below." The captain fell roughly onto the chair at the table that served as his desk between meals. "Ah, the foolish man, playing out this dangerous folly," he sighed. "And to expose his family so! I question my own judgment for granting passage to such a desperate man, but then one cannot question the ship's company, eh, Mr. Waller? They obviously thought the investment was to their advantage." The captain removed his wig with hat still attached and carelessly put it on its stand. He scratched his sweaty graying head vigorously. "If not my ship, the eager fool would have found another. There's no fury as a man after a lost fortune, eh Mr. Waller? No fury! Especially when there is a need to keep him and his out of a debtors' prison." He grabbed his flagon of Madeira and threw his head back. A thin dark red line trickled down the corner of his mouth onto his beard. He wiped it with the back of his hand, adding another stain to the sleeve of his coat, and drank more. When the cobalt blue onion-shaped bottle was empty, he corked it, turned it upside down, and carefully slipped its neck through an iron ring on the side of the cask lashed beside his bed. Before the day was through, his scrawny cabin boy would fill it several times more.

Edward had heard the story many times about how Blake, as a younger wiser seaman, steered clear of drink, seeing how it poisoned the souls of many good mariners. His captain obviously found deep solace in it now.

Blake removed a small knife he stored with its tip imbedded in a crack on the surface of the table and used it to sharpen his quill and to pry open the lid of the ink well. He dipped his quill, and entered into the *Rosa*'s log with remarkably clear penmanship:

Buried at sea William Montague, passenger, by Wallace Blake, Captain of the *Rosa* this 4 March 1663

"You know now what must be done, Mr. Waller?" the captain questioned.

"Aye, sir, I do. Tis why I stand before you, sir, to appeal their case. This family . . . they are still caught in the fog of uncertainty. Perhaps, if I might have a word with Montague's widow, some arrangement may yet be made to counter this procedure of rule and yet satisfy the company's requirements, sir," Edward pleaded.

Captain Blake squinted and sighed, but gave the benefit to his young quartermaster. "The man was a penniless fool with a greedy disposition, Mr. Waller. He debited himself, his woman, and his children to gain riches slackly promised by some distant accountant on a minuscule island in the Caribbean. Nevis! Humph! 'Come,' they promise. 'Come! For our island shores be lined with silver and gold. Land aplenty! Wealth galore! Why, a mere thimble full of its rich soil is enough to grow a tree!' It's claptrap! Fools that make such claims and bigger fools that believe them, eh Mr. Waller? Oh, and let us not forget the growing cry of freedom that belches so forcefully from the colonies. Freedom from the perceived shackles of suppressing aristocratic demands . . . the very manacles that, no doubt, set this poor man on his reckless and lethal course. Our Mr. Montague was not unlike the many others, Mr. Waller. Second sons. Desperate sons. A family's last hope to recover squandered fortunes. So why, pray tell, do you think *this* case requires special consideration?" Expecting no reply, the captain sighed again, "Ah, Montague has left me a great charge. I understand his only relative was a brother who would not give a farthing's value to note what became of his family." The captain sighed again. He tugged at his waistcoat the way he always did before giving a command. "We are more than halfway and it is well within the rights of the ship's company to demand compensation for their transport. I am an agent of that company as are you, sir, and must, therefore, do *their* bidding however unpleasant. Understood, sir?"

"Aye, aye, Captain, understood," Waller replied softly.

Captain Blake opened a tin box, removed a rolled parchment, broke the seal and, shaking his head, read the details of the promissory note. "William Montague's considerable debt to this ship's company will be paid," he declared. "It is my duty as captain of the company's vessel and yours, Mr. Waller," he repeated. "No doubt, the Widow Montague will quickly find another husband to see to her needs and those of her children, perhaps one of substance this time. And the girl, surely she must be . . . ripe for the picking." Edward stiffened to restrain his rage and cap his desire to challenge his superior for such callous words.

The captain made note and signed a document, blotted, examined it once more and satisfied, returned it to the tin. "In payment, Montague, in payment. Now, Mr. Waller, you are dismissed! See to the rigs and shorten the sails. I feel a change in the wind," he said to the quartermaster, waving him out the door. Looking at the empty bottle he shouted for his boy, "Where are you, you little wart! Come see to your duties, blast you!"

Edward maneuvered sideways to allow the frantic cabin boy access to the captain's quarters. He could see through the companionway doors that Mrs. Montague was still on deck and he wondered how much of the captain's boisterous rant the grieving widow overheard. Once on the main deck, he commanded, "Secure aloft, Mr. Cane."

"Aye, sir!" came the reply.

"Trim the sails, Mr. Cane. Secure the rigs," Mr. Waller ordered. "Prepare for weather."

"Aye, aye sir!"

For all his misgivings, Edward respected his captain's uncanny mariner instincts. Studying the sky, he tried to identify the clues Captain Blake might have seen that tipped him into believing foul weather was afoot. Edward saw nothing. He felt, smelled, and heard no change in the air. The sea looked the same. He smiled and nodded in appreciation. There was something . . . some illusive character that his inexperienced senses missed. Drunk or sober, Captain Blake could read the sea and Edward was not about to doubt his predictions. Satisfied the crew was following Mr. Cane's commands, he went off to pay his respects to Mrs. Montague.

Edward did not share all of his captain's sentiments regarding the nature of William Montague, though, like many pilgrims to the new world, thought him naïve and overly optimistic in matters of finance, too trusting in transport across the seas, and unknowledgeable of colonial affairs and law. Even so, he considered Montague a man of honor and a gentleman who possessed extraordinary initiative and a dangerous, unrelenting enthusiasm. He enjoyed Montague's company and was surprised at the interests they shared, including an unyielding desire to dote over his only daughter.

Sally Montague enchanted Edward from the first he saw her on the docks at Bristol Port. She was vibrant with innocent but curious eyes, taking in all and flashing with the wonder of her first sea voyage. She was bright and quick, witty and out-spoken, and her style was dashingly bold. She was a breath of fresh air. After so many crossings with the reserved Puritans, dressed in their plain and simple manner of drab gray woolens and stiff white collars, Sally was a visual relief to Edward. The trading of textiles and dyes from the East was finally beginning to show in the fashion of ladies and Sally wore her colorful frocks most daringly. At the start of the voyage, her shiny black hair had been pulled up to the crown and wound in a neat top knot with curled and wired locks tied with silk ribbons above her ears. The curls bounced flirtatiously as she moved with her youthful zest but they soon paid a toll to the elements. It did not take long before the salt, wind, and sun bleached and matted her hair. Her locks unfurled and tangled mercilessly. Edward laughed the day she surrendered and tucked her disheveled hair beneath a simple white gathered bonnet. He had seen it before. Improper washing, full exposure to weather, rations of scrapple and hardtack, foul water, and the dank stale air of the ship's lower decks tarnished the beauty of the finest of ladies within days of leaving port. Even through this rough and challenging voyage, Sally retained her exquisiteness in her energetic blue eyes and her unflappable positive attitude. Now, however, Edward saw her beauty burdened by the shadow of uncertainty and sorrow. He squeezed his eyes shut in an involuntary grimace as he remembered his own childhood lessons of how quickly the tide of fate can turn.

Edward knew that towards the end of William Montague's life he showed great remorse over the risks to which he subjected his family. Before fever clouded his thoughts, Montague confided that he agonized over the possible fate of his wife and children if he died. Several evenings ago, Edward visited the ailing man as he lay below the deck so near to death. Montague struggled to speak.

"I lay, these nights past, awake with the knowledge and the gravity of my error, sir!" the dying man confessed. Edward protested and assured Montague of his recovery, an act he now regretted for it might have been better for his family if Edward had allowed Montague to speak on and perhaps reveal some way to avoid this pending outcome. It's done now, Edward thought, and the prospect for this family is indeed cruel. He debated whether to share Montague's confession with his grieving widow, but decided against it believing the admission was uttered in confidence and would now serve no value.

He went across the deck to rescue the distraught widow from James. Although the boy's attire was that of an adult in miniature, his round cherub face and missing front teeth gave hint to his tender age. A sad, lost boy was now before him and Edward knew too well the magnitude of a grief so great at an age so young.

"You best take your mother down below, Master James, out of this freshening wind. It appears we are in for another storm," Edward ordered in a low voice as he would in commanding his seamen. James nodded and obeyed willingly. The boy turned to his mother who swayed gently in an unconscious effort to correct her balance as the ship rolled. She said not a word and had not since discovering her dead husband. James hesitated and flashed a pleading glance to the quartermaster. Edward cleared his throat, removed his hat, and approached the widow.

"I deeply regret your loss, my lady," Edward offered and bowed. While his head was still down, he cocked it slightly in the direction of the companionway. The boy dutifully responded by taking his mother's hand, pulling her gently to lead the way.

Edward stood upright, replaced his hat, and looked at Sally. Exchanging thoughts without words, they stared at each other for a long while. He was about to say something when the captain shouted a command.

"Aye, aye, sir!" he replied keeping his eyes fixed on Sally. "You must go to attend to your mother, Miss Montague," he said softly. Sally curtseyed, lowered her head, and departed. Before descending the narrow steps, she gathered up her skirts in her arms, turned with tears in her eyes and asked, "We are in a desperate way, are we not, Mr. Waller?"

Edward's eyes dropped quickly to the deck, an involuntary gesture he immediately regretted. There was no hiding the facts. He raised his head and with a deep intake of breath replied, "I will speak again with the captain on your family's behalf, Miss Montague. Do not trouble yourself so. I will do all within my power to protect you . . . and your family." It was a shallow answer for he knew his captain's resolve, but the words spoken were from his heart and he vowed to keep that promise.

Still on the weather deck were the *Rosa's* other two passengers, Ned Haywood and his wife, Belle, planters from Barbados. They stared intently into Edward's eyes, waiting for an answer to Sally's question. Edward glanced nervously at the Haywoods. They were seasoned voyagers and had lived on Barbados for many years. He knew they understood the social and legal demands of the sea and the landing rules that governed the colonies by necessity, not compassion, and certainly with little mercy. Before the Haywoods could say a word, Edward bowed and quickly excused himself as he went about his tasks. The Haywoods exchanged a grim look before following the Montagues to their shared quarters below.

CHAPTER 2

A rush of nausea hit Belle Haywood as she pulled back the curtain of the passenger's sleeping quarters. The odor of death lingered. She swooned and looked at the frail widow sitting in the same spot where she kept vigilance over her sick husband.

"Ah, ya poor, poor soul," Belle pitied as she tried to comfort the widow. "I suspect nothing in yer good and gentle breedin' prepared ya for such misery as this."

The bed lay barren, freshly scrubbed and stripped of its foul mattress and soiled blankets. Ned got to work knitting and stitching together bits of torn sailcloth for replacement bedding.

"Reckon this here will do for now, Mrs. Montague," Ned said. "Mr. Tibbs, he washed them blankets for ya. Up top they are. Don't' think they'll dry much afore this next rain, though."

"Perhaps, it would be better to rest yourself in Sally's hammock, my lady," Belle whispered, "whilst we remake this here bed." The widow remained pensive and silent.

"Thank you Mrs. Haywood," Sally offered, "but I think you have forgotten how terribly difficult Mama found mounting these hanging cradles. I doubt she can manage it. I've only recently got the hang of it myself."

It was difficult for Belle not to smile for she so loved a good pun, even an unintended one. Giving the hammock an arrogant swing and adjusting Ned's handy-work of sailcloth she said, "Ah, perhaps not, then. Suppose this bed will 'ave to do as it is." Whispering comforting words and assurances, Belle guided the distraught woman to the bed. She received only an empty stare in return.

"Not to worry, dear lady, we'll see to them blankets, though it's not likely they'll dry before reaching land, will they Ned? Nothin' ever seems to dry at sea, now does it Mrs. Montague? Perhaps Mr. Tibbs will show us a mercy and place 'em near his fire." Belle tucked the sailcloth over the widow's shoulders. "There, that should offer thee some comfort."

The passenger and crew quarters were close enough for all to have suffered the worst manifestations of Montague's illness but throughout the ordeal most remained compassionate and charitable. Several of the crew forfeited their rest to help the family. Even so, Belle knew there were a few scoundrels on board who harbored ill feelings towards the likes of Montague, not the man himself, but his kind . . . the type who would enslave and master. *Those sour few*, Belle worried, *would not think twice about taking advantage of this vulnerable family. But they might not be so keen if I'm about!*

Turning to Sally, Belle said, "Though there be more hours of daylight left to this sad day, tis not worth of savin'. It'd be a mercy to sleep right through it, I say. Best we all pray this tragic journey be done and the shores of Barbados shine clear in our eyes."

Sally smiled and grasped Belle's hands and she returned the gesture by drawing the girl deep into her ample bosom and patting her gently on the back.

"Ah, there now lass. Tis a bad thing, this. Ain't it so, Ned?"

"Aye, luv, tis indeed," Ned agreed.

"But fate . . ." Belle continued. "Well, fate has a way of turnin' about difficult times. You must be strong for James and your mother." Belle hesitated before breaking the embrace. She felt obliged to give the young girl the kind of love and assurance denied by her grieving mother.

"Ah, Sweets, I wish I could tell ye, all will be made right by the morn. There be powers greater than us poor mortals lookin' after this here ship and we must rely on faith that God knows what he's on about, eh Sally? Rest easy now, pretty thing, till the morrow," Belle whispered as she pulled the partition that separated the families.

Sally jumped up into her hammock and skillfully twisted until she managed an upright position. She instinctively adjusted her skirts symmetrically around her folded legs, and wrapped her long thin arms tightly around her knees. She stretched and arched her back, and slowly exhaled. She was grateful for the company of the Haywoods. Throughout the voyage, they offered valuable counsel to her when her mother seemed unable to cope. Leaning over the hammock, she stared at the prostrate figure of her mother. It annoyed Sally that her mother was strangely distant to these kind people and angrily recalled the day they boarded the *Rosa*. Gracious and polite initially, her mother checked her cordiality after Belle uttered her first words in the dialect and manner of a commoner. Sally objected to her mother's haughty demeanor. *If it is wealth that determines class*, Sally wondered, *then who now has more?* Sally rolled back out of the hammock and then turned her attention to a small cask at the foot of the pallet. She opened it and took out a crock of honey and two thick, hardtack biscuits. She brushed her hand over the biscuits to check for mealy worms, and then placed the biscuits and honey in James's lap.

"Be sure to secure the lid and return the honey to the cask when you have finished. Mind your crumbs, James; we do not want them stuck in the honey. No sticky fingers and drop nothing for the rats!"

"What, no supper, Sally?" he asked. Not waiting for an answer he added, "Are we going home, sister . . . to England? Will we have to live with Uncle Robert? Or are we going on to the plantation alone . . . without Papa?"

"James, do not to worry yourself so with these questions. I am sure Mama has a plan. Eat now, and then rest dear brother, otherwise you will be sick again."

Sally looked down at her mother and eased her anger. *I cannot blame Mama for this*, she thought. *She could not have anticipated the predicament Uncle Robert would set for the family. She was brave to follow Papa. But now what?* Her mother rested on her back with her mouth slightly opened. She breathed deeply as if in a heavy sleep. A tiny tear gathered in the corner of her eye, trickled down across her temple, and got lost in the tumble of her hair. Sally pulled the sailcloth up under her mother's chin and bent low to leave a gentle kiss on her forehead.

"Sleep well, Mama," she whispered softly before trundling back into her hammock. After many bungled and embarrassing attempts at mounting the sling during the first week of the voyage, she now maneuvered in and out of it with a natural grace. A rope, used to tie up the hammock during the day, dangled from the bulkhead. She grabbed it and pulled on it to create a gentle sway but the tragic occurrences of recent days kept her from relaxing. She played her normal trick of counting the different sounds of the ship to send her off to sleep: the scurrying of the barefooted sailors on the deck above, the creaking of the boards, the stretching of the ropes, the whipping of a loose sail, the ringing of the ship's bells, the slapping of the water against the bulkhead, the commands of the sailing master and the echoing acknowledgements of the crew.

Something fell and clanged across the deck as the ship suddenly shifted. Sally woke with a start. She tumbled from the hammock and landed hard on the deck. It was dark and she was confused. There was a fresh smell of rain in the air. A storm had picked up. The ship pitched sharply and Sally groped in the darkness for support. With a flash of lightning, she was able to get her bearings. It was the third storm of the journey. Sally could sense the helmsman struggling to steer the ship into the wind, but the seas shifted and the *Rosa* rolled from side to side as the waves approached from abeam. Through the darkness, Sally felt her way to James's hammock.

"What is it?" he stirred.

"Tis nothing, just another storm. Sleep James, while you can." Sally groped beneath his hammock to feel for the empty bucket and once found, she wedged it between his feet. She then went to her mother's bed and felt along the pallet, but found only empty sailcloth. Sally waited for another flash of lightning. It was just enough light to confirm the bed was empty.

"Mama?" she whispered. For a moment, she froze with fear. She turned abruptly to the direction of the lightning flashes, the narrow steps of the companionway. Squinting in the dull light, she noticed the candles were unlit, a precaution in a storm. "Mama?" she shouted, unable to conceal her growing panic. "Mrs. Haywood?"

"What is it, Sally?" Belle jumped down from her hammock with a thud. Ned did not stir.

"Where is Mama?" Sally asked as she grabbed a hammock for support.

"She's not here? Ah lass, she probably went topside. Stay here with James. I'll check on her."

"No. I'll go," Sally insisted. In her sternest tone she commanded to James, "You are not to leave your hammock. Please watch after him, Mrs. Haywood."

Belle was fussing. "Would it not be better if Ned went? I think you should stay, Sally."

"I will return quickly. No sense in waking him."

Sally turned her ear toward the crew's quarters and heard nothing. She made her way around the mast to the sail locker, and then felt around its walls to the galley. The bricks of the stove were cold and the pots secured. *Topside*, Sally thought, *they have all gone topside.*

One oil lamp, securely fastened to a post below the hatch, was still lit. Thin streams of water trickled down the steep steps as the ship continued to rise and crash. Sally looked up. The lightning flashed continuously, one strike after another. She thought it strange that the door of the companion way was still open because in storms calmer than this, the sailors always slammed the hatch door tight. Sally climbed through the hatch to the half deck. It was dark. She had never known such darkness. Heavy clouds obscured all traces of moonlight and a fierce chilling wind drove the rain against her in an almost horizontal direction.

An insecure sail flapped wildly and some bit of metal clanged against an iron fixture. Several seamen rushed about while the sailing master cried out his orders. "Ease the jib, Mr. Stokes! All hands stand by for high seas and heavy rolls! Watch the helm! Keep it as close to the wind as she'll lie!"

Lightning lit the sky again followed quickly by a loud clap of thunder that reverberated in her bones. As Sally started across the main deck, a thick dark arm grabbed her. It was Tommy Bett, the black seaman from Africa. He pressed his bare wet heavily tattooed torso hard against Sally, pinning her alongside the windlass as the ship rolled. She let out a scream as a cold salty wave crashed over them. Edward was at the scene in an instant.

The seaman corrected his posture and retreated once the quartermaster had a firm grip on Sally's arm.

"Miss Montague, it's safer down below!" he shouted.

"My mother, Mr. Waller!" Sally choked on the seawater. "Have you seen her? She is not below."

"Mr. Waller!" shouted the captain over the wind. "Get that woman below and secure those hatches."

"Aye-aye, sir!" Edward held tight as he carefully eased Sally back towards the hatch to the decks below. "Where is James?"

"He is with the Haywoods. Please, sir," Sally begged, grabbing his wet sleeve. "My Mother!"

"Mr. Strangeway!" Edward caught the ship's cooper as he was ascending the steps. "Have you seen the widow Montague?"

"Aye, Mr. Waller," Twiggy Strangeway shouted. "I did. Amidships she was, sir, abaft the fore hatch, storm brewin' and all!"

"Take Miss Montague below and find the woman." The ship rolled and Edward tightened his grip as he transferred her arm to Mr. Strangeway. "You'll be safe with Twiggy. The cooper will find your mother," he shouted over the wind.

"Where could she be? She must be found. The storm . . ." Sally was beside herself with worry. The cooper guided her down the narrow steps to the waiting arms of Ned Haywood.

"Goodness, child! You're soaking wet!" Belle cried.

"Please, Mr. Strangeway!" Sally begged as she looked up at the cooper.

"Ya be worryin' too much now, Miss," Twiggy bellowed. "We'll find 'er all right. 'Tis a small enough vessel, this. Now sees ya stays below, and ya best put on somethin' dry."

Twiggy Strangeway, hesitated a moment then slammed the hatch door. He did not lock it while there were souls below, but it would keep the worst of the sea from tumbling down into the lower decks. Just then, the ship pitched high, knocking the cooper flat on the deck. The ship heaved up on a wave's crest then plummeted quickly down its backside. For a second, the cooper clung to the molding of the hatch, but lost his grip and began to slide. With fingers splayed, he tried to grasp a strong hold on the deck boards. The flesh from his fingertips tore as he slid further towards the bow until the toes of his right foot caught something. Cursing, he scrambled to his feet and grasped a lifeline before the ship slipped sideways over another crest. He rubbed his fingertips against his tongue and tasted the salty rust in his blood. They were raw and if they festered, he would find it difficult to do his duty. Assured no one would hear him over the wind, he cursed again.

The ship's bell clanged steadily and urgently as the sailing master shouted the command for all hands on deck. The call for the entire ship's company of men meant that lives and cargo were threatened and Twiggy instinctively turned to his trade and the business of securing the ship. The search for the lost widow would have to wait until this new danger ended. Though small for a merchantman, great ships as the *Rosa* did not respond quickly to steerage and could only sail seventy degrees to the wind at best. Whether a ship would turn topside or ride a storm with grace was often due to the work and skill of its cooper. Careful balance of the ship's ballast and faultless lashing of the cargo helped to keep the *Rosa* even-keeled with the angry waves.

The storm raged on and grew furiously with a hard rain but the cooper gleamed heartily as he minded the cargo. The challenge and the excitement of the storm this night confirmed that his decision to go to sea was right and true to his spirit. This was the adventure he sought! Never on land did he feel so alive, so valuable, and considered so necessary. At home, he was a cobbler by trade. It earned him a modest living, but there was always a relentless stirring in him. He grew tired of fitting feet with cowhide and longed for a taste of adventure at sea.

"Am I to die without ever 'aving lived?" he once complained to his wife. "I feel it in me very bones, dear wife, I was meant to do more than put together shoe leather." As Twiggy remembered his wife he felt a pang of guilt. She suffered cruelly from his absences. When they were first married, their home in the little village in south Warwickshire was about as far from the sea as anywhere in England. But the sea called to him. It acted like a magnet, drawing him down the Avon to the Severn River and on to the shores of the Bristol Channel and beyond. Though his wife frequently lost her battle against the force it had on him, she retained a faith that one day he would return to her, settle, and be satisfied to be the gentle cobbler she married. "Go then, Twiggy," she had said to him, "and ya sees to it, ya come back to me!"

"Aye," he laughed aloud through the wind of the storm, "I will return to thee, my pretty wife, but with memories of a life worth lived; and if not with a pot of gold, with thoughts of adventure that will surely see me through to me dyin' day."

In the deck below, Belle fussed over Sally. "Ned!" she shouted through the dark. "Come and unlash that cask. This poor child needs to have dry clothes afore she catches her death!" Ned dragged the cask across the deck and opened it. Belle gestured with her finger for Ned to turn around as she struggled to rid Sally of her drenched frock.

"I cannot find Mama!" Sally shivered as the ship pitched fiercely. They all three tumbled and waited on the floor until it was safe to right themselves again.

"She'll be found, Sally!" Ned insisted. Ignoring the need for modesty, he pulled the women to the hammocks for safety.

"Yes, fear not, dear," Belle tried to comfort, "I am sure they will find her and keep your Mama from harm's way." Belle shooed her husband away again to allow Sally to dress.

Sally turned at the sound of someone retching. "James!"

"Not to worry, Sally," Ned comforted as he cradled James's head over a bucket, "Just the motion. Poor lad fares badly with even the slightest sea." With his stomach empty, James moaned, fell back into his hammock, and quickly entered the delirious stupor brought on by seasickness. Removing the bucket, Ned covered it with its wooden lid and grimaced as the contents sloshed about with every roll of the ship.

"She's gone, isn't she?" Sally whispered frantically to Belle. "Mama is not on board. She's been swept to sea, otherwise she'd be found by now. What terrible evil is this that has befallen my family? Pray, what fate awaits us now?"

"Shhh, my child. You despair for no reason. She's found, I tell you. She's found! It is too rough to put her through the hatch. That's it, isn't it Ned?" Belle responded nervously.

"Aye, they probably have her holed up somewhere, safe, till the wind dies down and this ship stops knockin' about." Ned assured, but it was difficult to hide the fear in his voice.

Horrid visions raced through Sally's mind. "Whatever was on Mama's mind to be above in such weather?" she asked. To herself she thought, *would Mama really have abandoned us to the mercy of this uncivil captain?*

"Ya put yer worries aside, Sally," Belle continued. "Now let us rest our bones, pray, and wait this out. 'Tis all we can do for now."

But Sally could not rest nor would she pray. Instead she paced about the small sleeping quarters. A confusion of jumbled thoughts and speculations made her all the more nauseous. She sat on the pallet.

"There now, lie ye down, Sally," Belle comforted. "They'll bring her along."

The storm raged for hours. Sometime during the night, the movements of the ship eventually settled to a slow but unpleasant bob and an hour after that, the winds calmed. Edward opened the hatch and slid down along the edge of the steps. He lit two candles, placed one on the sconce and carried the other to the partition.

"Miss Montague?" he whispered. With no reply, he gently pulled the curtain to one side and lifted the candle above his eyes. He could see two women sleeping fast on the pallet and, for just an instant, rejoiced that Mrs. Montague was found. But slowly his eyes adjusted to the poor light and he saw that it was Sally and Mrs. Haywood. James, on his hammock, did not stir.

Edward was relieved to find them sleeping. The tragic news he bore could wait until dawn. They had been through enough this night and would need the rest. Ned intercepted him as he made a retreat to the hatch. For a moment, the two men stared at each other in dull light.

"It was a bad storm," Edward finally said. It was a redundant statement, but he didn't know how else to reveal his news. "Three storms, all bad! Too much for a ship in one crossing, wouldn't you say, Mr. Haywood? This was the worst of them. We needed all hands to save the *Rosa*. Still, we all kept an eye for the Widow Montague and we searched every inch of the decks, the hold, even the bilge. There's no sign of the lady, I fear. If she was on the weather deck . . ." Edward did not need to finish.

"Dear God. What fate awaits these children now?" Ned whispered.

Edward's eyes turned dark as he looked toward the partition. He pressed his lips tightly and inhaled sharply. "The sky is clearing, but it's still an unpredictable sea, Mr. Haywood. Please stay below, sir, and I beg you, mind the children."

"As they were my own, Mr. Waller."

CHAPTER 3

The morning sun painted the tips of scant clouds with bright crimson and orange. Sally admired the brilliant splendor of sun's rise while she pretended to listen to the captain's awkward and stoic explanations of her mother's disappearance. A memorial service was hastily called and as before, the ceremony was brief, even more so without a body.

Deeply moved, Barnaby Tibbs whispered words of condolences to the children during his captain's dry oration. James said nothing. Sally reached down to take his hand but found it tightly clenched in a fist. She bent slightly and saw a distorted and angry face. "*He should be angry,*" Sally thought as she tightened her grip on his hand. "*Our father dead, our mother gone – disappeared. We are orphans. Orphans!*"

James narrowed his eyes as he stared coldly at the captain. He choked with rage and before Sally could stop him, he suddenly lunged at Captain Blake.

"You will pay for this deed!" the boy screamed.

Sally stood frozen with surprise as Tibbs and Edward Waller restrained the boy. The captain glared down at James and as before heralded the end to the ceremony by slapping his bible shut.

"Mr. Waller," he ordered still eyeing James, "I will see this . . . this *boy* and the girl in my quarters. Dismiss the company." He turned and left without further word.

Sally stiffened. She bent down to calm her brother, took his hand, raised her head and followed the captain's tracks. She could feel the eyes of the crew upon her.

"If we may be permitted to accompany you . . .," Ned offered, running after her.

"Oh, yes please, Mr. Haywood," Sally replied. "Stand with us, sir, for I know not what wicked plans this captain has for us."

Sally became breathless as she tried to check her anxiety. "Captain Blake!" she blurted as she entered his quarters. "I trust you will arrange for our return passage to England as soon as possible."

The captain, already busily writing in his log, looked up at the girl with surprise. He puffed his cheeks as his face turned scarlet. He paused for a moment to regain his composure and then slowly rose from his desk.

"My dear young lady," he started in a hoarse but controlled tone. "Your father did not secure your fare for a return passage on this ship or any other. In fact, he did not pay for your outward passage. He is, or more to the point, *was* in debt to this ship's company for the passage of your family, and for the purchase of a sugar press, the boiler, and the transportation and delivery of said items."

Mr. Waller and the Haywoods crammed into the small quarters and stood behind Sally.

"Ah good. A complete audience, I see!" The captain continued, "We are, by my calculations, a few days from Bridgetown Harbor of Barbados. The Laws of Navigation are quite clear concerning entry to that harbor. The Governor will not permit me to release passengers who are, shall we say, unable to provide for themselves. This ship's company would suffer a penalty for landing persons without a proper license. What is the penalty now, Mr. Waller? I believe it is over 10,000 pounds of sugar, is it not? And this ship's company needs to be compensated for your passage. I am not a heartless man, Miss Montague. These papers provide the best way . . . nay, the only way for you and your brother to disembark and perhaps find your passage back to England. With these, your debts to this company will be been satisfied."

"Bondage, Sir?" Ned blurted. He cringed at his indiscretion, even as the words fell from his lips. He gave a quick glance at Belle who returned a disapproving glare sharper than the blade of a knife.

Sally gasped and instinctively pulled James closer to her. "Bondage? There must be some mistake, Captain Blake. Our circumstances are greatly distressed, sir, I grant you, but we are not without means." The notion of servitude seemed unimaginable and the growing panic that welled within Sally was now desperate to escape.

"Yes, well . . ." the captain hesitated. "Miss Montague, the fact is you have no means and are short on options. I cannot act against the mission of this ship's company nor will I encroach upon the laws of the King or the Governor of Barbados. Such an act would cause the Governor to revoke the company's trading license. I cannot permit that to happen. Once we drop anchor, good citizens of Bridgetown who are in need of service will negotiate with me as the agent of the company. It is but a formality, is it not Mr. Waller? Mr. Haywood, you have lived on the island for years. Is this not the correct procedure?" The room was silent.

"This is an outrage, sir," Sally protested. "My father would not have permitted this!"

The captain sighed deeply. With exaggerated animation, he unrolled the papers and turned them around on the table to face Sally.

"Your father was quite aware of the risks and the extreme consequences if he failed in his endeavor. That is his hand, is it not?" the captain asked.

Sally examined the signature. "This is signed by my father's hand," she replied softly and turned to Edward. "What papers are these, sir?"

"Agreements" the captain interceded "between your late father and the company. My dear Miss Montague, may I assume that you are a clever young woman capable of penning letters?" The captain extended his arm, quill in hand, to Sally. "I give to you my desk, pen, and paper. I urge you to read the agreements your father made on behalf of your family and write what letters are necessary for your hasty return to England. On the next ship passing under the King's flag, I will personally put your letters upon that vessel." Turning to Mr. Waller he added, "N'er be it said that I did not do all within my powers to assist these children, Mr. Waller. Mr. Lee will take your watch, sir, until you relieve him. Stay here and assist Miss Montague as she may require."

"Captain?" Sally inquired. "Why not put my brother and me on the next ship that sails for England?"

The captain smiled at her wit, "Alas, I cannot, madam. The laws are clear. I understand you have an uncle . . . in Gloucestershire, I believe? Perhaps he can honor your father's debts."

"If it is fare you require, sir, then what of the possessions my father has stored below? Surely that is enough to compensate this ship's company," Sally reasoned. From the corner of her eye, Sally noticed Edward Waller stiffen.

Captain Blake glanced at Waller, pressed his lips together, and inhaled sharply. "Your father owns nothing on this ship, Miss. The ship's company bought that equipment. It represents part of an investment, albeit an unfortunate one, in your father's sugar plantation. The compensation hoped for was from a share of the profits generated by the sugar mill for the next three years. A quick sale of the equipment to which you refer will not begin to settle the considerable debts your father has incurred to the company." Captain Blake waited for someone to speak. The room remained silent. The captain bowed and opened his cabin door. He hesitated in the doorway, and then turned to Sally. His expression showed an uncommon softness and he seemed to struggle to find the correct words. "The sea . . . it can be . . . most unforgiving. Your father may not have known the full extent of that when he signed those papers, Miss Montague. Few do. He acted like so many who seek to take their fortunes from this new world. He imagined the magnitude of his dreams and the sincerity of his hopes would somehow protect him from the mundane habits of sickness and death. Your mother must have . . ."

"I don't understand," James interrupted. "Sally, what is he on about? What is this about Papa," James cried. "What has happened to Mama? Is he to blame?"

The boy's interruption snapped the captain's mood. He raised his voice slightly in his irritation, "I have no time to debate this subject. In short, your father gambled your security and lost. You will be permitted to secure a few personal items from your sea chests when the cooper can spare the effort and I his time. Again, I advise you to write the letters you deem necessary as I will not present this opportunity again." With this, the captain left his cabin and began shouting orders to his men.

Sally turned gray. "Can this be true, Mr. Waller?"

"Though my captain is no gentleman, Miss, I believe he means you no harm and does speak the truth. These measures may seem extreme, but he cannot put you onto another vessel and it is true that entry to the islands is strictly controlled. It prevents captains from offloading infected persons or scallywags onto land or other ships." Edward picked up the papers Captain Blake left on the table. "Your father confessed to me his . . . financial difficulties. He died with your future greatly burdened on his heart. I have no doubt, Miss Montague, that had your father made it to Nevis, he would have quickly recovered his pride, his wealth, and your family's reputation. The company knew that, or they would not have invested so heavily. But fate has deprived him the opportunity and in your unlucky case, it appears that all that could go wrong has."

"Aye," Ned agreed. "To be orphaned at sea . . . but all is not lost, Sally. This sour, quarrelsome captain may indeed have the best plan. 'ave ya family left in England or an attorney, perhaps? Do ya know anyone on Nevis?"

Sally groaned and sank into the captain's chair. James came up to her and gently took her hand. "Are we orphans, Sally?" he asked in a whisper. Sally sighed deeply and placed her hand on his cheek. Ned glanced at Edward.

Sally dropped her head and closed her eyes. "Before this day, Mr. Haywood, I was an impractical girl who paid little attention to my father's affairs." With a look of resolve, she sat upright and inhaled deeply. "My father carried papers in his sea chest. Perhaps that is where we might find some answers."

"I know the one you mean – the little one, beside the bed!" James shouted. "I'll fetch it, Sally," he said and made a dash for the door. Sally tried to grab for his shirt, but missed.

"I will go after 'im. He'll not leave me sight," Belle insisted.

"In my simplistic childish manner I seek someone to blame for this, as does my brother," Sally said after James left the room. "My uncle comes to mind. He is Papa's eldest and only surviving brother and heir to the estate . . . property given to our family in 1417 by the Duke of Bedford, brother of King Henry V," Sally recited. She closed her eyes and slowly shook her head. "Good old Uncle Robert. He earned well his reputation for opulent generosity for he entertained the whole of West Country society with parties, hunts, balls, and grand feasts. An endless stream of royal guests came, ate, and bedded at the great house. And of course they brought their servants and horses . . . all needing quarters. The many beeves, sheep, pigs and a great deal of our stock of pork in the smokehouse it took to keep our 'guests' happy! The cost to us in flour, vegetables, milk, butter, fish and game from the marshes! Why, in candles alone, a fortune was lost and it seemed that after every one of his illustrious affairs, our cellars were cleaned of claret, Madeira, and spirits. They paid him nothing for his hospitality. There seemed to be no shortage of those willing to take advantage of his generosity and my uncle suffered from a chronic need to out-do himself. No one ever doubted that the family Montague was well suited and financially secure!" Sally's eyes welled. She bowed her head and the tears fell. Edward removed a linen handkerchief from his coat pocket and offered it to her. She took it, raised her head again and dabbed her swelling eyes. "Forgive me. I weep in anger at my own foolishness. I gave little concern as to *how* Uncle Robert paid for those lavish events. My business was to be the best dressed and enjoy the pleasures of the moment while pretending to ignore the attentions of handsome suitors."

"Ah, lass, how could ya have known?" Ned asked.

"But that is the tragedy, Mr. Haywood." Sally stood up from the chair and paced the small quarters. "I *did* know. I heard my parents argue often on the matter of Uncle Robert. A thousand times my father protested the behavior of his brother. His flamboyant life was a complete ruse – a lie. Uncle Robert had no sense of accounting. He could neither calculate his troubles nor predict the doom. There was no money. Though the estate is well over a thousand acres of the finest West Country soil, my uncle's debts exceeded all profits and values of the property. He turned to gambling to recover his losses, but he gambled recklessly on dishonest enterprises and continued to borrow money incessantly. The land, the house, and all the family's investments could not possibly cover the debts incurred by the hapless man!" She stopped and sighed deeply. "At first, no one, outside the family, suspected. Uncle's façade of wealth was so faultless that it afforded him even more credit, much beyond his means . . . and ours. He seemed unable to stop." Sally dropped her head. "A few creditors, suffering financial difficulties themselves, called his loans. Poor Papa! His efforts and earnings kept the family from debtor's prison more than once, but even he could not keep up. Once the word was out that my uncle could not pay his creditors, they all came calling . . . demanding payment, making threats." Sally dabbed her eyes again before continuing. "Uncle Robert had only one surviving son, Clive. I did not know my cousin well for he was much older. He lived in London when I was a child and later went off to Nevis. It was Clive who petitioned for a land grant and created a sugar plantation in Nevis. He convinced Papa that it was the only way to save our family from ruin."

James stumbled into the cabin followed by a breathless Mrs. Haywood. She carried a small but heavy chest.

"James, me lad, what have ya brought us, then?" Taking the chest, Ned looked to Sally for approval before opening it.

"Please, sir, open it and let us piece together this mystery," Sally said.

James bit his lip in anticipation as Ned removed a fist full of documents. Ned smiled sheepishly, shrugged, and handed the papers over to Edward. Sally blushed with embarrassment, for she had not considered that Ned could not read. While Edward shuffled through the papers, Sally continued with her account. "We gave little thought to the plantation in Nevis until word came of Clive's death. A ship carrying a pestilence anchored at Charlestown and spread pox throughout the Island of Nevis. My cousin died of it. So you see, I do have some understanding of the dangers of off-loading passengers, Mr. Waller. The manager of the estate on Nevis wrote to my uncle demanding instructions for the plantation and the mill that Clive had started. Papa intercepted the letter. He studied the manager's accounts and declared that if only half the figures reported were true; the plantation had great potential to produce fast wealth and would restore our family's good graces. Mama was against the idea of going to Nevis. They argued fiercely over it until she finally agreed to accompany Papa, but insisted that James and I remained in England. Papa wouldn't have any of it, refusing to put our care into the hands of his reckless brother." Sally chuckled at the irony and looked at Edward. "He entrusted his family to this dangerous and inconstant sea over his own brother! It was all just another gamble, this time executed by my father with a much greater risk and cost than any taken by my careless uncle."

After studying William Montague's papers and the contract with the ship's company, Edward reluctantly agreed with his captain. "I would recommend that you leave the ship at Barbados" he concluded, "under whatever circumstances the captain provides. You will be in a better position in Barbados to inquire about the plantation in Nevis. The ship's company has no claim to that property, only profits from the mill. I have trustworthy acquaintances in Barbados, Miss Montague, and I will see to it that your papers are secured by my friends, Thomas Modyford and his wife, Elizabeth." The Haywoods gestured their approval at hearing the name. Edward continued, "They are kind, respected people. Sir Thomas was once governor of Barbados. He is politically astute, well associated, and the most successful planter in the West Indies. I would trust your care to them."

"*Secure* our papers, Mr. Waller?" the words choked Sally with fear. "You mean purchased, do you not? We are to be sold . . . as slaves? Dear God!"

Belle rushed over to assure the girl. "There, there. It is but a formality, Sally. The captain was truthful in that. Just a quirky business of port. A quick agreement of attachment to someone on the island who is able to sponsor you and James."

"With your permission, Miss Montague," Edward added, "while in St. Kitts, I will look into your father's affairs in Nevis and send word to you."

"St. Kitts! The *Rosa* sails for St. Christopher Island?" Sally's mind raced with possibilities.

"No. She docks in Barbados, then sails on to the colony in Virginia. I leave the *Rosa* in Bridgetown to take delivery of a ship in St. Kitts. I have accepted a commission to sail her to Boston," Edward acknowledged humbly.

"*Captain* Waller! You are to be congratulated, sir," Ned declared.

Edward tipped his head shyly. "Captain Blake is aware of my intent, but the crew is not. If you please, I would request that they remain ignorant of this for now," Edward pleaded.

"Oh, aye, Mr. Waller, we understand. Must retain discipline, eh? Not a word will we breathe of this matter, will we lad?" Ned said poking James's back with his finger and causing the boy to wiggle.

After some time examining Montague's papers and the captain's maps, the party was able to establish the location, acreage, and assets of the Nevis plantation. Edward made notes, while Sally began the task of writing just one letter to the only soul who could possibly help. Uncle Robert.

"Captain Blake is correct, Miss Sally. The press and the boiler are not yours. The ship's company is on this bill of sale." Edward rubbed his hand through his hair as he hunched over the papers.

"Tis likely Blake will sell the press and boiler at auction in Barbados," Ned surmised.

"Then we have nothing?" Sally whispered the question so James would not hear. "And without the equipment, the plantation will be useless?"

"No, not useless," Edward assured. "You might be able to sell the land or if it is planted, keep the land and sell the cane to someone who has a press. The profits will be less, but if we can establish you as a landowner . . ." Edward began to pace and rub the back of his head as if in great thought. He looked at Sally. "You will please forgive me, but I must return to my duties before my captain's patience runs aground. I have tapped Mr. Lee's generosity enough this day," Edward declared. "And to be honest, it will give me time to sort some ideas." He bowed deeply.

"You have been most courteous, Mr. Waller, and helpful," Sally smiled as she gathered her papers. "I am indebted to you for the kindness and counsel you have given to my brother and me."

"Mr. Waller, sir?" James asked with a single tear streaming down his fat rosy cheek as he followed Edward to the top deck. "*Are* we going to be sold as slaves?" Edward spun around with solemn face and stared down at James.

"Master   Montague,   no   poorer   set   of circumstances could ever make you a slave to any man." Edward squatted down to be face to face with the little boy. "Sometimes, we are challenged by circumstances not of our making. It hardens the heart a bit, but each time we learn and are better suited for the next blow and, my dear James, life throws us many blows. But through it all, you must never forget *who* you are, no matter your destiny. You are and will always be a gentleman, sir. Your father had a high esteem of you. See that you honor his trust!" Edward smiled and rubbed the top of James's head. "I must leave you now, but I will come as I can. In the meantime, Mr. Tibbs will see to your needs. He is a scruffy old heap, our Mr. Tibbs, but there is not a man on board with as many talents or a kinder soul."

"Mr. Waller!" Mr. Lee shouted from somewhere above. "The main topsail yard suffered damage by the storm, sir!"

"I come along, Mr. Lee!" Edward replied as he left the captain's quarters.

The party returned to the decks below where Belle set to tidying the small sleeping quarters. Though the straw rations were greatly diminished now that they neared the end of their voyage, Mr. Tibbs managed to replace the mattress for the pallet. Atop the bed, Belle laid a bundle containing the remains of Mrs. Montague's possessions. Ned returned the sea chest by the bed while Belle searched his eyes for answers.

Ned smiled at his wife, "Tis an ugly mess, Belle, but not a hopeless one. Mr. Waller will see that their papers fall into the right hands in Barbados. Them Modyfords are good people, they are, and will look after 'em, Belle." Ned turned to Sally. "We know them well. Influential people are them Modyfords, he being governor and all. And a good planter, he be, wouldn't you agree, Belle?"

"Oh, aye. That Mr. Waller, if he can pull this off, he will have done right by you and the lad, Sally. We would take those papers ourselves, we would, had we not spent every penny on our . . . visit to England. Anyways, ya be having good friends in us on the island, Sally, we'll sees that yer looked after proper." Belle said.

"Thank you. Thank you both for extending your kindness at a time when we are in such need." Sally hugged the Haywoods and gave in to her sorrow with streams of tears. She had so many questions, so many fears. She glanced in the direction of the bed where her mother and father had lain only days ago and she looked at James who sat with wide-eyes, cross-legged on his hammock. How was she to cope alone, she wondered? How would she care for James?

"I was so foolish in Bristol," Sally confessed to Belle. "Had I shown the least bit of maturity, Papa might have included me in their discussions and shared their concerns. But I preferred to spend that time minding my precious wardrobe and planning those last important social engagements."

"Best not to think of that, now, Sally. Don't see how revisiting the past will change the present. Yer time now be best spent thinking through the difficult days ahead lest ya make errors of judgment. Rest here on this bed, Sally. I will bring thee food later. We'll takes young James up top deck for now."

Sally welcomed a moment to herself. She opened a small cask at the foot of the pallet and as she placed her mother's belongings into it, something slid off the top of the pile and onto the deck. It was her mother's silver brooch. Sally picked it up and clasped it in her hand. *Why is this here*, she wondered, *Mama always kept it on her cape.* She opened her hand and ran her fingers along the smooth twists of the filigree. Sally shuffled through the pile and looked around the bed for the cape. It wasn't there. She didn't expect it to be there. Her Mama wouldn't have gone on the top deck in a storm without her cape. Sally held the brooch a moment longer questioning why her mother had removed it. *Well*, she thought, *this is one thing the ship's company will never own!* She wrapped it in a handkerchief and tucked it deep within the cask. She used the heel of her hand to pound the lid firmly in place. She scurried onto the pallet, curled up tight, and wrapped herself in the blanket. Compared to her conforming hammock, she found the pallet hard and wondered if she would ever get used to, or even have, a proper bed again. Her thoughts drifted, jumping from the past to the future in an instant. How could her father not have made allowances for such a disaster? As she closed her eyes and tried to reconfigure recent events, she heard a scratching noise by her ear. She opened her eyes in time to see a rat scurry across the floor.

"Thought you were alone, did you?" she asked the rat while grabbing a book that lay beside the bed. She hurled it at the rat. The book slammed right into the side of its head. The rat squealed, twitched once, and then fell silent. Sally gasped. Surprise at the accuracy of her aim, she suffered immediate remorse at taking a life. In the dark corner, she focused on her timely weapon and recognized its familiar form. She scrambled from the pallet, crawled to the corner and, ignoring the rat, retrieved the book. It was her mother's bible. She wiped its cover with her skirts and retreated to the pallet. Sally opened the book and in the dull light she could make out the names and dates penned by various hands on the inside cover . . . Montagues that lived and died throughout the centuries. Further back in time, names were recorded, but the dates of births and deaths were scant. Later, they were more precise and included the day and month as well as the year. *A long lineage, a proud line*, she thought. Sally noted that she would have to enter three more dates of death for her cousin Clive and her father and mother.

It was evening when Belle returned to Sally. While balancing a steaming pewter porringer in one hand, Belle gently shook Sally with the other.

"Wake up, my dear. Mr. Tibbs, God bless 'im, was particularly cooperative this eve. He made a huge pot of steaming porridge. Already the sailors have had their fill and want for more, but he set aside this one for you. Don't know what's got into our Mr. Tibbs, putting out the way he has. Tis a blessing for us all." Below, it was difficult to tell night from day, but Sally saw from the opened hatch that the light of day had already faded. She sat up right on the pallet and took the hot porringer by its shell-shaped handle. She blew over the bowl to cool it before tasting it.

"Hmmm. This goes down well. Thank you, Belle. I did not think me so hungry, nor so in need of such a heavy sleep. Where is James?" she asked.

"With Ned, he is, and enjoying the attention of Mr. Tibbs." Belle sat down beside Sally.

"Belle, tell me how you first came to Barbados."

"Ah, sweet, the beginning . . . well, it is not a good tale, but I suspect no different from many. Me Da, he looked after the horses on a lovely farm just outside of Stratford. I grew up there, along the River Avon. Ah, Sally, it was a good time and me Da, he be a good and proper horseman, he was. Raised them, groomed them, trained them. But a mare kicked him badly about the ribs and he bled inside. Naught could be done for 'im, God bless his soul. The master of that land, he evicted me ma and sisters from our house. Ah, I cannot blame the man. He were good enough to us, and a right Christian, he was. Saw to it that me Da had a proper burial. But he needed the house for his new groom, the one he hired to replace me Da. We moved about after that, trying to find what work we could. Agnes, me oldest sister, she married a man from Worcester and took in the youngest of our brood, me sister, Kathryn. Kathryn was still a young thing, then. That left just ma and me. Ma took in laundry but she got the cough. It wouldn't go away, that cough. It got worse and she became so weak she could scarcely put one foot afore the other. She stopped working so I took in laundry. Just a wee thing then, Sally. Couldn't earn enough to pay the rent. Then we run out of food." Belle took a long breath in and held it for a moment. "I can still remember them pains in me belly. Ma, she was afraid for me, so she took me down to the Bristol docks and signed me over for transport to Bridgetown. It was the best she could do for me. I don't rightly know how old I was, but I know I was not yet a woman." Belle stopped and stared at nothing in particular. She blinked and looked at Sally. "That is how I came to Barbados, Sally, as an indentured servant. I was bonded . . . to respectable people, mind. They never done me no harm. But I was theirs for seven years."

"What did you do?" Sally asked.

"I was too young to do much of anything 'cept cleanin' and plantin' the kitchen garden. Later I learnt to cook and my mistress, she taught me to sew. Ned's story is much the same. He worked his years, then worked years more to buy the last two years of my servitude. We married, and then worked another five years afore we had enough to buy our farm. Governor Modyford issued the land grant himself, he did, and he sold us our first cow. It wasn't much, our land. But we managed to catch enough water to grow some grazin' for a couple of milkin' cows and a few goats. Why, every butcher in Bridgetown trusts the quality of our cheese and the governor won't buy any save for ours alone. We farmed and took on other jobs. We saved up and bought more land and more cows. Done well for ourselves, we have. Ah, but the troubles we had! The pox, insects, too much rain, not enough rain, storms that pushed the sea into our pastures, and winds that tore at everything higher than an ox . . . But, I would do it all again, with my Ned, I would. Had seven children together. All boys! Three are still on the island; one went off to St. Kitts. The Lord saw fit to take the rest." Belle sighed and then slapped her hands on her knees to push off the pallet. "Now, see ya finish that porridge. Only the angels know when Mr. Tibbs will be so generous again with his fire. Ya be lucky for the efforts of that Mr. Waller, Sally. Good to have him as your friend. If it is your will to go back to England, then he or them Modyfords will find a way for ya do just that. But with no good family back there, no one 'cept that gamblin' debtor of an uncle, these fair West Indies may offer a better life for thee and James. Had me ma not sent me off to Barbados; I would surely be dead of hunger. Do ya understand what I am telling ya, Sally? There be many a good and wealthy gentlemen on Barbados and too few women of culture, like yerself."

Sally studied the face of Belle and nodded slowly. She listened closely to her words and understood the implications. A quick marriage to someone of means had already crossed her mind as she pondered her options, particularly when thinking about the welfare of James.

"Belle, why did you and Ned go back to England?" Sally asked.

Belle seemed surprised and uneasy by the question. She thought for a moment about the answer then chuckled, "Vanity, I suppose, or pride. Or, perhaps it was just plain swagger. With our children all grow'd and after so many years, we thought perhaps England might have changed, with the likes of Cromwell, the commonwealth, and all. We thought we might be . . . accepted . . . for what we had become, and not judged by who we once were. Thought that was what the fight was all about. Imagine!" she gave a little laugh, then shivered. She shook her head in disappointment. "Money alone is not enough to step across . . . a certain line. Not in England. In Barbados, it's possible for criminals and former slaves to live like nobles. But England . . ." she gave a long sigh, "Ah, it's an *old* place with *old* ideas."

"Did you find your family, Belle?"

"My sisters, but not me ma. No, I never found her. Even me sisters had no word of her fate. I pray she did not suffer to die alone. I said me proper farewells to my sisters this time. I'll not go back there. Me and Ned, we have a good life in Barbados. The island is home now. It's where we want to spend our days . . . in the warmth of the Barbadian sun with our lads and their families."

"Belle?" Sally stood and reached out to take the woman's rough hands. "What do *you* think happened to my mother?"

Belle stiffened and reacted by slowly retracting her hands from Sally's. She turned slightly and lowered her voice, "It was a boisterous storm, Sally, a terrible storm. Why, even Mr. Strangeway nearly got himself washed away. Your mother was . . . so frail and out of her mind with grief. I doubt that she had the strength to match that force of wind and water. The sea took her, lass. A sad, sad loss to thee and James, but there it is. She's lost to that sea, Sally." Belle put her arms around the girl and patted her back, not so much as to comfort Sally, but to keep the girl from looking directly into her eyes and detecting the lie she struggled to hide. Only an hour before, she and Ned had speculated about the circumstances of Mrs. Montague's disappearance and had both concluded it was not likely an accident.

CHAPTER 4

Sally spent the next days interrogating all who would tolerate her incessant questioning. Even the hard and distant captain was intrigued by the girl's strange eagerness to learn about the sea, classes of vessels, and trading in the colonies. Though he pretended to be annoyed, the captain was flattered yet perplexed.

"What does the girl intend to do with such information, build a fleet?" Captain Blake asked Edward. "I mean to say, the boy, he could at least benefit from knowing the lines and sheets perhaps to secure a position on a ship one day as did you and I. But this young woman, it is unbecoming of her to inquire so, Mr. Waller. She needs to mind her place and confine her thoughts to her predicament."

"I believe Miss Montague merely gathers the intelligence she thinks she needs, sir, for the purpose of managing . . . her situation."

"Well, I find it irritating. Do see that she does not get underfoot, Mr. Waller."

"Aye, aye, sir."

Sally sensed a knowledgeable ally in Ned Haywood and pumped him relentlessly of his intelligence. She wanted to know the steps to planting and processing cane and other crops, the strange and wondrous customs of the Arawak and Carib Indians, and of every threat . . . all the furies from God and nature and man.

"Ah, when it comes to sugar, I can tell ye a thing or two," Ned proudly explained. "It were me own oxen that helped English planters clear their first cane fields and it were me own steers that drove their first grinding mills!" He scrambled about the deck collecting small bits of scrap before coming back to Sally. He took her hand and motioned for her to sit on the deck. He sat beside her and placed the collected items before them in orderly groupings.

"Let's sees . . . first," Ned explained "the land is made ready by hoeing troughs 'bout a yard square." He pointed to the rope strands laid out in a checkerboard fashion. "The troughs are filled with water to moisten the soil in each square and make it soft for plantin'. The cane cuttings are jammed down into that soft soil for the roots to grow." Ned demonstrated with long slivers of straw that he jammed down into the fine cracks between the deck boards. "Then when the cane's grow'd taller than a man sometime between January and May, it's cut, stacked on the backs of donkeys, and taken to the crushers." Ned gathered up the hay slivers. "Two large steers, tied to a shaft, circle round the wheel that turns them heavy presses." Ned squeezed several bits of straw between the heels of his pressing hands. "It's a woman's job, both slave and free, to pass the cane through the press. Beggin' yer pardon, Miss Sally," Ned said in a low voice, "but it's reckoned that if'n a woman gets her arm caught in them crushers, it's less of a loss to the planter. The foreman, he hangs about with his cutlass made ready in case the worst happens. Ya sees, by the time ya stops the steers, well, I suppose losing an arm to the cutlass is a sight better than dyin' crushed to a pulp."

Sensing that he said too much, Ned stopped for a moment and waited for permission to continue. Though Sally made a face and had turned quite pale, she nodded for him to go on. "The juice is then squeezed out of them canes and falls into a hogshead where it's mixed with lime." Ned used a water ladle to demonstrate the process. "That was my job, Sally. I'd crush up the limestone and heat it in a kiln to produce the lime. Ya needs to add the lime to clean up the juice, keeps it from goin' off. That's a problem with sugar makin'. Once the cane is cut, it's no time at all afore its rotten and unfit for sugar. Once the juice has been squeezed out, them stalks become the bagasse. When the bagasse is dry, it's used to fire up the boilers. The lime and impurities are skimmed off and the juice is ready for processin'." Ned sat upright, caught his breath, and paused. He leaned close to Sally and pointed with his finger to emphasize the importance of his next statement. "The man who boils the sugar juice down, now he's the most important man in the whole works. He's got know just how long and how hot that juice needs to cook. If he does his job right, when the juice cools it hardens into crystals, some big, some small. The juice has to drain off them crystals, so they put the lot into a tall cone-shaped funnel that hangs from the ceiling." Somewhere, Ned found a funnel for his demonstration. "That's when the molasses drips down off the sugar crystals, right into a waiting hogshead where it's stored until it's needed to make the rum. And them big brown sugar crystals, they're shipped off to England." Ned smiled and rubbed his hands together to signal the conclusion of his lesson. He raised his eyebrows in anticipation of questions.

"Who ever dreamt this complicated process in the first place?" Sally asked.

Ned was somewhat disappointed with the question, but he knew the answer. "Ah, I heard tale once, that it was the Moors that brought their sugar-makin' skills to Spain. Don't rightly know when, but some time after that, them Jews in Spain learnt it and they brought it to Brazil. They must 'ave taught it to the Dutch. Then the Dutch kicked them Jews out of Brazil. Their loss, the crown's gain! Some three hundred of them Jews come to

Barbados!" Ned shook his head and pursed his lips. "Those Dutch in Brazil, they're trying to put me out of business!"

"How so? I thought you raised cattle." Sally said, confused.

"Aye. That's the truth! Them sugar planters need me steers to drive them presses. But the Dutchies, they want to put up windmills to replace the steers. They say their windmills can turn more presses faster and feed off nothin' but the wind."

"Is it true?"

Ned rubbed his chin and replied softly, "Aye, so long as the wind blows."

"How often must the cane be planted? How long does it take before it can be cut?" Sally asked.

"Oh, I reckon that all depends on the field and the weather. A planter can leave the stubble from the last cut to grow back, maybe three years, afore he needs to replant it again. It takes about a year and a bit to ripen."

"You mean, you cut a field, and it grows back?"

"Aye, it does. Like grass in a pasture," Ned explained.

Sally's questions soon became too complicated for Ned to answer: how many barrels of molasses can one acre of cane land produce? How many men are needed to cut one acre of cane? How much does a planter get for one hogshead of molasses? That night, Sally's dreams tangled with the steps of sugar making and she caught herself waking startled, only to fall off again and dream of more sugar.

By morning, she decided sugar was much too complicated. When she learned that Belle had a special interest in trade and even fancied herself as a merchant one day, Sally focused her research on the shops in Bridgetown and which items traded well. She learned about the lace work of the Dutch, the ones that Ned mentioned who recently immigrated to Barbados from Brazil. Most interesting to Sally was hearing about a fabric dye extracted from a bush called logwood. Belle taught her how to identify the plant, the steps taken to extract the blood red dye, and where to find the valuable resource.

While Sally learned the art of lace-making from Belle, James fought boredom and loneliness by shadowing Twiggy Strangeway and Barnaby Tibbs who gave him the honor of slush detail. During the day, Barney would set James down on the weather deck with half a dozen greasy pans.

"Now, the whole crew of the *Rosa*, they be dependin' on how much slush you collect, James. Here's what you do, lad. You scrapes these here pans clean of the grease and ye puts that grease in this here crock. That there grease is the slush. Scrapes them pots clean so they whistle, mind. The more grease we collect, the more slush we can sell," Barney instructed.

"Yuk! Who wants to buy this . . . slush?" James asked while making a face.

"Why, these here saltys on the *Rosa*, mate! All kinds of uses for slush. Greasin' the running rigging, or blisters on their hands, covering cuts so's the salt water don't burn, and I knows some who use it in their hair . . . them nits don't stick to greasy hair now do they? And whatever's left over, I trade on shore and puts the money in a pot. That be the crew's slush fund!" Barney explained.

"For what?"

"Never ye mind, about that!" Barney exclaimed, trying to cover his smile.

Quartermaster Waller offered the most useful advice to Sally and James. His frankness and familiarity of the politics of the West Indian Islands gave them a simple, uncluttered view of the challenges of colonial life.

Sally treasured her moments with Edward for it was not just his knowledge that attracted her so. Every time he came near her, however innocent or brief the encounter, she lost her concentration, her stomach tingled, her breathing became shallow and rapid, and her face burned with heat. Though an unfamiliar and strange feeling, she craved it and wanted more.

Unlike Ned and Belle, Edward seemed reluctant to speak about himself. Even so, his passion heightened when he spoke of the young Massachusetts Bay Colony, particularly when he described his wooded land along the Charles River. Through his words, Sally came to know Massachusetts with its sheltered harbors, wide beaches, kettle ponds and salt marshes, its rich soil, and thick woods, streams inhabited by beaver, and meadows full of turkey and whitetail deer.

Sally learned, through her skillful interrogation, that Edward eventually wanted to settle in Massachusetts and build his fledging shipping business. He obtained a grant for 300 acres of forested land northwest of Boston where he harvested lumber for the building of casks and barrels. He wanted to start a cooperage in Cape Cod where his barrels and hogsheads would be packed full of salt-cured codfish bound for Britain and the Caribbean. His profession at sea was the means to finance his warehouse in Boston.

"It's not all a bed of roses, Miss Montague," Edward warned. "The land of Massachusetts is a good deal unsettled. It is hostile and plagued with much sickness. The climate is extreme and unforgiving. The river can freeze in the winter, drop low in the summer, and flood viciously in the spring. And offshore, storms can brew in an instant.

The bay, however, is a wondrous thing! It's full of all sorts of creatures with oysters as wide as your two hands put side-by-side. In summer the bay is so full of fish, you can walk across it, from Boston to the Cape! And those fish, they bring the whales. Have you ever seen a whale, Miss Montague? Magnificent monsters!"

Sally was pleased that Edward released his inhibitions and shared with her the dreams for his future. She kept him talking for as long as Captain Blake would allow. She was genuinely happy for his good fortune but at the same time felt a twinge of envy. He seemed so set on his course while hers was so full of uncertainty. *He* was close to having the life of his dreams while she and James were now so far from theirs. Once, while they were alone on the half deck, Sally boldly asked about his personal plans, whether he intended to marry.

Edward hesitated, and then forced a crooked smiled, "Is there no cap to your curiosity, Miss Montague?" Sally blushed and was about to apologize when Edward raised his hand. "As a matter of fact, there is a young lady who has quite stolen my heart forever. She has the finest face in the whole of Massachusetts and causes me to spin!" Edward closed his eyes and inhaled slowly as he imagined his sweet Anani's laughter. A deck swab dropped his bucket and the cracking clatter spoiled the moment.

"My apologies, Miss Montague, but I must return to my duties." Edward bowed.

Sally curtsied and smiled. She was intrigued yet so very disappointed for in the past days, she enjoyed a fantasy that the *Rosa's* quartermaster might sweep her off her feet to rescue her and James from their frightful and uncertain fate.

So, she thought, *he has a sweetheart in Massachusetts!* She wondered what the woman was like. *Did she come to the colonies by her own means, or was she a stowaway or slave? Perhaps she's a convict or an indentured servant and waits for Edward to release her from her bondage. Or perhaps she took refuge from an abusive husband. No,* Sally thought, *she escaped to the colonies after her father promised to marry her off to a horrid man many times her age, a fat, poxy-faced ogre. Edward must have freed her from that awful fate.* Sally spent some time musing over the possibilities. She queried Belle about Edward's mysterious lover, but she knew nothing. She shamelessly tried to shake down the details from Mr. Tibbs and Mr. Strangeway, but after all her digging and probing, Edward Waller's elusive mistress remained a secret.

Once, when she and Belle were alone in their quarters, Sally confessed her attraction to the handsome Mr. Waller. Belle laughed till the tears ran down her rosy cheeks. Sally was, at first, slighted by Belle's reaction but her laughter was so infectious, it was difficult not to join in, especially as she was convinced that she might never laugh again.

Belle lifted her skirt to wipe her eyes. "Ah, forgive me, dear Sally, for it is too soon to be in a humorous mood. You poor dear thing! You *are* exploring every prospect. No one can fault ya for that, Sally. Such a handsome man, Mr. Waller is! Ambitious and hard working, too. He'd make a fine husband, to be sure, he'd be a good catch."

"Belle! You make it sound as if . . . I was fishing for a mate." Sally protested and glanced about to be certain no one was within earshot of that remark! She felt uneasy, as if this was a forbidden conversation. Sally was about to end it. She tried to hide her grin behind her hand. "Yes," she whispered, "I suppose, that is exactly how it must appear. How embarrassing! If he had the slightest inkling of returning my affection, I surely now have chased him away with my brazen inquiries."

"Do not act in haste, lass," Belle said in a serious tone. "You must first test what fate holds for thee in Barbados."

"It matters not, for Mr. Waller is promised to another!" Sally replied.

Belle looked puzzled for a moment, and then shrugged. "I am aware of no such mistress, but perhaps Mr. Waller is not the right man for you. He is capital rich, but penny poor." Belle picked up a comb and walked behind Sally who seemed happy for the grooming ritual and removed her bonnet and hairpins.

"No, lass, tis someone who jingles gold in his purse while sitting in a grand house, that's what you and Master James need now," Belle started as she unfurled the long curls. "Back in England, there is a certain way, a certain . . . tradition in which a gentleman pursues a young lady. It is a time-honored game with carefully crafted rules governing flirtation and courtship, even proposal. Rules that favor the gentlemen. Do you agree?"

Sally thought for a moment and shrugged. "No" she simply said.

"No? Think ye of this, Sally. A young lady may be free to display signs of interest, but who makes the first call? In the grand parties you attended, have you ever known a young lady who chose not to follow the correct sequence of courtship?"

"Yes, oh yes. Rachel Brown. She gave her heart to an insufferably shy weasel of a lad. His lack of attention tried her patience, so she took matters in her control. Ah,

Belle, how the tongues did wag! Poor Rachel. None of us truly knew the full extent of her mischief, but mere rumors made her life quite miserable. When the unkind words fell upon her father's ears, there was the devil to pay! He sent her off, some say, to a convent in Scotland. A *convent*, do you believe it? And they were not even Catholic. I never saw Rachel again."

"And the gentleman . . . the object of her affection, what of him in this affair? How was *he* punished?" Belle asked.

Sally thought for a moment then declared in surprise, "Nothing! Peter Small was his name and I am quite certain he suffered not at all from the scandal. In fact, after the incident, he seemed more boisterous and obnoxious than ever."

"Ah-ha!" Belle triumphed. "Tis my point taken. You must be very clever when playing this game, Sally. Barbados plays by different rules. There, your friend Rachel would be applauded for her initiatives and young Peter Small would have been ousted for his stupidity."

Sally was shocked and turned to face Belle whose head was nodding and grin was wide.

"Yes, tis a fact that every colony in the west is short of our farer sex, dear Sally, and that gives *us* the advantage. And you, my dear, carry a dowry coveted by many . . . your youth, your looks, and of course, your land! I believe I reversed the order of importance. And that land is already planted to sugar with the start of a sugar works! That adds value to your significant worth. A young girl, especially a maiden of refined upbringing like you dear Sally, could snag a handsome catch in an instant, and on *your* terms. Mind that you keep a firm grip on your fishing line until ya knows what fish it is you want to yank!" Sally dropped her jaw again.

"Am I to sell myself to the highest bidder, Belle? How is that different from a woman of the night?"

"Child, the bidding for Sally Montague has already begun. You said yourself that you played with the affections of men in your pursuit. And don't ya be thinking for a moment that it's just a woman's game. Men play it too. I can think of a dozen penniless men who sought after a woman of substantial means, married a rich widow or a homely spinster for personal gain or some distant relation to keep wealth within the family. Fortune hunters! Lovers! The line between them is blurred."

"I believe my uncle did just that . . . marry for money, I mean. Twice!" Sally mused. "And what of marrying for love?"

"Ah," Belle dismissed. "Whims of a young girl's heart! Who among us ever has the luxury or luck to marry for love? If it were different and you be in England this moment," Belle continued, "do ya not think thy own father would be arranging your courtships with the most desirable men of the county?"

"Was your match with Ned one of . . . convenience?" Sally asked.

"Yes. I had two more years to serve on my contract. He had the money to buy my freedom. Love came later," she replied bluntly.

"Is it likely, Belle, someone other than the Modyfords will try to purchase our papers with . . . such thoughts in mind?"

"Oh, indeed, that is why our Mr. Waller will take steps to see that does not happen!"

That night, Sally could not sleep. She felt every fold in the mattress and heard every creaking, stretching sound on the ship. "A husband of substance," she thought. "I will keep that option open and will not hesitate to use it to advantage myself and protect my brother." Sally made a promised to herself, and pledged on her mother's tattered bible, that she would strengthen her resolve. She would react through logic, not emotion. She would accept her responsibilities to James and guard their welfare better than her parents had done.

Edward noticed the change in Sally's demeanor immediately. As the days progressed, she eased off her questioning and took on a determined look. She spent more time seeing to the needs of James, observing the skills of Mr. Tibbs, and trying to master the quiet art of lace-making.

Edward found himself longing too much for her company, but as they approached land, his duties were more demanding and she seemed to make herself less accessible. It annoyed him that she occupied so much of his thoughts. Her image interrupted even his deepest sleep. No woman had affected him so. He was almost relieved by her remoteness. Perhaps now he might better concentrate on his duties. It would not bode well for a future captain to act heartsick over a girl so young. And he was firmly committed to his goals. With the influx of settlers, there would soon be an increase in enterprise and trading and with that, a greater demand for barrels and lumber. His land in Massachusetts was blessed with hardwoods. White and red oaks for barrels, casks, and ships' keels. Hickory for fencing, maples for furniture, elms for decking, and chestnuts for houses. And once he cleared the forest of its timber, there was the farm to plan. In addition, it was time to consider a proper education for his adopted daughter. The Puritans of Boston had a high regard for the schooling of young ladies and Anani was now old enough. He had no time for serious romance and could not afford to split his attentions in so many directions. It would be impractical and disruptive to take on the responsibilities of a young wife and her orphaned brother. "No," he whispered while alone on night watch. "This will not do. Not now." He would stick to his plan.

"Land ahoy!" came a shout from above on a bright clear morning. "Land ho!"

"Clear all decks!" ordered Mr. Waller. Men scurried to tie up the hammocks, bedding, and tables on the lower decks. Gun crews set out to move the ship's four demi-culverin cannons into position and lay out their tools, shot, wadding, and buckets of seawater and sand.

On the upper decks, Mr. Strangeway attached several prepared T-posts to the rails. On the top of the posts, he tied neatly braided wigs made from whitewashed rope ends and over the cross posts, he draped old tattered moth-eaten coats cinched around the middle with a blackened rope. The four painted tree trunks that once made up the sides of the pigpen on the weather deck were rolled over to the rails. Mr. Strangeway pushed the narrow ends through gun ports in the railings.

"These be me Quaker Guns," he winked at James as the boy watched in wonder. "And these here," he laughed as he patted a dusty coat, "These be me wooden mates. Don't eat much and stays sober, they do! Even through a lookin' glass, they look real enough. Gives them pirates, shall we say, *pause*. They'll 'ave second thoughts afore they attacks such a well-armed merchant ship as the *Rosa*."

Mr. Tibbs extinguished the fire in the brick-lined galley and secured his pots while Mr. Strangeway adjusted the barrels and casks below decks and tightened the ropes that held the cargo fast. On the raised decks sailors were busy trimming the sails and securing the yards while others scurried about catching tethered goats and pigs and locking them in their crates below. Soundings were taken and the depths shouted with regular timing. All stood ready for action.

During the commotion of making the ship ready, James slipped away from Mr. Tibbs's guardianship and climbed to the quarterdeck where Mr. Waller was busy eyeing the horizon through his spyglass. "It seems we prepare for battle, Mr. Waller," James observed.

"Aye, James, it is what we do. Evil forces linger in and about these islands for which we must be ready," Edward answered, not taking his eye from his spyglass.

"Do you mean pirates?" James asked.

"Aye!" Edward assured the boy by letting him take a quick look through the spyglass. "Pirates, privateers, buccaneers. It is now that we are most vulnerable to attack. Whether England is at peace with Spain, France or Holland does not seem to matter in these waters. Commissioned to harass a particular nation's fleet, buccaneers are oft times conveniently blinded to the flag of the ship they attack. The seas are full of pirates, mariners from many nations who show their allegiance to none. Mr. Haywood!" he shouted. "Watch after the lad, will you, sir?"

Edward rubbed the hair on James's head. "I would not like to see you tangled in the ropes." Once Edward turned over the boy to Ned's care and in a single leap supported by the rails, he jumped down to the half deck to give orders to the men.

Several minutes passed before Sally could focus her untrained eye on the faded blue outline just above the horizon. She last saw land five weeks ago when they left the shores of the Canaries. Now, this bittersweet vision brought both excitement and fear to her heart. She huddled close to James.

In the distance, Barbados seemed a beautiful paradise and the closer the ship sailed to its shore, the more enchanting it became. Deep-water rollers crashed against the northeastern shore but as the ship sailed slowly around to the leeward side, calmer waters prevailed. Softer waves brushed against the reefs guarding the azure shallows of the broad white-sand beaches and narrow coves. Soon the pale pink coral stone buildings of Bridgetown came into view and the crew relaxed.

The Haywoods scurried around the deck trying to recognize some structure or another. They were home and their faces took on a peaceful glow. Belle playfully nudged her husband and he responded by laughing and drawing her nearer. The happy outcome of their convenient union was unmistakable to Sally.

Captain Blake briefly came to Sally and James to remind them that they were to remain on the ship until he cleared their debarkation arrangements with the proper port authorities. Sally suddenly regretted her aloofness to Edward and she feared it might cause him to forget his promise to mediate the sale of their papers to the Modyfords. Making an effort to capture his attention from across the ship's deck, she gestured her gratitude to him and beamed a heartfelt smile. He acknowledged by tipping his hat and returning the smile.

CHAPTER 5

Once ashore, Edward kept his word and searched for Thomas Modyford. He knew that what he had to offer was not the best of sale, a boy too young and a girl too beautifully delicate, both orphaned with some questionable relative who likely had no means to fiscally respond to their needs. He checked the usual haunts in Bridgetown before riding out to Modyford's Great House.

Considered one of the finest plantations in Barbados, it was a short journey from Bridgetown. The horse he rented from the blacksmith in town was a fine breed and he enjoyed the ride that took him past acres of cane lands, coconut palms, and fields of tobacco, cotton and ginger. Modyford was a leader in experimental agriculture and over the years Edward fuelled his curiosity by collecting various exotic crops from other islands. An avid horticulturalist, Modyford kept copious records of his investigative cultures and of those of other planters throughout the West Indies and the American colonies. When it came to planting, he was competitive and not at all above dabbling in agricultural espionage. He delighted in botanical gossip, and would send a covert group of his field hands out to test the successes and even the failures of his challengers. With the anticipation and fun of a keen player, Modyford looked forward to Edward's introductions and clandestine intelligence reports.

It was mid afternoon when Edward arrived at the small valley spring below the great house. He dismounted to take in the view, refresh himself, and lead his horse to water. Whenever he visited, he made a habit of stopping here for not only did he feel it was necessary for the horse after riding uphill in such heat, but it also provided the time for one of the field hands to scurry up to the house to announce his arrival.

Unlike most great houses that mimicked the English country houses the planters had left behind, Modyford's plantation house incorporated a clever blend of Spanish, Dutch, Moorish, and local Indian designs that offered structural advantages for living in the tropics. Perched high on a gently sloped hillside, the panoramic view was not so much for the appealing nature of the vista as for defense. There was a clear vision of everything within the range of musket fire and the house stood far from potential fuel that might threaten the structure in a brush fire or raid. The windows at ground level were large, protected by heavy bullet wood shutters hinged at the sides, and shaded by the roof of the large verandah that extended the entire length of the house. The second story had smaller square windows with shutters hinged at the top to provided shade when fully opened. With a low profile to guard against storms, the house was open and airy yet defensible, for the threats were many: slave revolts, pirates, Caribs, buccaneers, and raids from countrymen of nations warring with England. Strategically cut into the masonry were several vertical slits, narrow on the outside and wider on the inside, to provide pivot for muskets. Aside from their defensive role, the slits were well placed to capture the evening sea breeze that not only cooled the house, but also discouraged mosquitoes.

With his horse sufficiently watered, Edward reluctantly put on his heavy wool coat and adjusted his chemise. He beat the dust from his felt hat and adjusted its feather and rim before displaying it to his horse. "Impractical clothing for this temperature, would you not agree?" he chuckled. Whereas most newcomers to the tropics quickly adapted their clothing for the oppressive heat, the hard-set gentry refused to relax their code of dress. When greeting the Modyfords, it would not be proper to dress in anything less than his best so Edward wiped his brow and surrendered to this illogical custom, He mounted his horse and headed for the house.

Having been alerted, Thomas Modyford and his wife, Elizabeth, waited in the yard to greet Edward.

"My good fellow, it is so wonderful to see you again. Good voyage, this time?" questions flowed from Modyford as he reached out in a friendly gesture. Edward dismounted and removed a package of sailcloth containing several spindly plants dangling loosely from a single clay pot. He left his horse to the hands of the stable boy and then turned his attentions to Elizabeth Modyford.

"By my troth, mine eyes are blessed by your very visage, my lady, and I am happy to see you so well!" Edward took her slender hand and bowed deeply with his nose nearly touching her delicate fingers. She giggled.

"You are looking quite fit yourself, Edward. I am so pleased that you came to see us," she blushed.

"The pleasure is always mine, my lady!" Edward flattered. "The voyage was satisfactory, this time, Thomas. Rough seas, a top crew, no conflicts on the ship or the seas, and the cargo remain intact."

"Praise be, Edward!" Elizabeth Modyford declared. "The seas around these islands have been plagued by pirates. Unscrupulous characters lacking virtue of any sort! Tis dangerous times!" She shivered at the thought and went about calling for sweetened lemon water to be served on a prepared table on the covered porch.

"And we suffered a ferocious storm, did we not dear Lizzy?" Thomas added. "A fortnight or so ago, now. Some of the islands did not fare as well as ours, I understand. And following that, a horrific plague of locust!

The little blighters ate everything . . . even the tobacco! That resulted in the death of many, but imagine! Tobacco! Ah, but tell me, what exciting flora have you brought to me this time?" Modyford slid to the edge of his seat and rubbed his hands in anticipation.

As if to guard some secret, Edward leaned forward, "I have four interesting vines from Madagascar. Orchids. The French call them vanille. The flowers are exquisite, but it is within the dried less attractive beans where you find its true treasure. Tiny seeds, when crushed produce a delightfully scented flavor. I fear these plants did poorly on the voyage, Thomas, and may require much effort to restore them back to good health. They like neither the cold March air nor the salty sea spray."

"Orchids! Lizzy, did you hear that? From Madagascar! Does that island share our hot and steamy climate?" Thomas was already commercializing the offspring of his gift and seemed thrilled by a new challenge. "Lizzy, bring some chocolate for Edward," he shouted, then turned to Edward and said in a lower voice, "The chocolate does not go well with her lemon drink, she will tell you that, but it is quite the treat when you add just a spot of milk and sugar."

"Oh, Thomas, I am sure Edward does not want a hot drink after his long ride." Elizabeth protested.

"No, actually," Edward said, "I do not mind. Though I find chocolate rather bitter, the thoughts of adding sugar and milk to it, well, how could I ever refuse an experiment like that?"

"You have been to Madagascar?" Thomas asked.

"No. I bought the plants from a Moor in a market in the Canaries. The Moor warned me that they need shade and a moist mossy tree to climb upon. I was thinking of the forest where the spring – "

"Yes, yes! Perfect!" Thomas interrupted. "But they will have to be protected from the monkeys. Pesky things, they are. A bad day when the sailors brought those awful creatures from Africa to our island! They come through the fields in droves now. Worse than locusts and they, too, eat anything. Everything! They succeeded in doing what the Spanish had hoped to do . . . raid every garden on the island. Horridly prolific! Bouncing and strutting about the bushes, flashing their bright blue balls! No barrier seems to keep them at bay. Whatever we construct, they can figure out a way around or through it."

Thomas started on the natural breeding habits of the monkeys, but Elizabeth tactfully placed a jug of hot chocolate between the gentlemen and began to pour. Edward suddenly remembered the last time he drank the dark bitter chocolate and approached the steaming mug with some trepidation.

"I find the smell is more alluring than the taste," Edward complained before sipping the drink.

"Hold your opinion, until you test this mixture," Thomas politely requested as he stirred into Edward's mug a bit of sugar and scalded milk.

Edward swallowed. His eyebrows shot up and he beamed a smile. "Hmmm. This is quite tasty," he said as he gulped. "Lovely! Have you circulated this formula to others?"

"Ugh," Thomas grumbled, "I *did* and the innkeepers in Bridgetown won't have any of it. They are bent on serving their bitter chocolate unaltered. Sour men serving a bitter drink!"

"Give it time, Thomas. I think this will catch on. Extraordinary taste! The milk tames the bitters and the sugar transforms this drink into something . . . well, more palatable than tea. Speaking of which, how have the tea plants taken?" Edward inquired over his last botanical gift to Thomas.

"As a matter of fact, they have not. I fear the soil is not right. Too sandy, perhaps. Too salty? Or the sun too intense. The weather on Barbados is not consistent. One season it will be dry and windy and the next, torrents of rain flood the island. I fear it is our lack of tall mountains to conciliate the climate. We need proper mountains to carry the clouds higher and thus forcing them to surrender their rains gently. The tea's tender leaves shrivel in the dry winds and the plant suffered from mildew after our sudden downpours. I believe what they need is shelter, some elevation and shady nooks in the hillsides."

"Tell us of Anani, Edward. How fares she?" Elizabeth asked, purposefully changing the topic for had she not, Thomas would carry on about his tea for the whole of the afternoon.

"She fares very well, my lady, and grows faster than I had reckoned. She is a fine young lass," Edward boasted as he spoke of his adopted daughter. He removed a small bejeweled disc from his coat pocket and handed it to Elizabeth. "This is a painting of her. It's a good likeness. The artist caught well the blush of her cheeks. I have it in my mind to send her to school. There is a reputable establishment for young ladies in Boston and with good fortune, it is my hope to place her there."

"How exciting for her!" Elizabeth said as she handed the miniature to Thomas.

"Ah, lovely girl, Edward, lovely!" he responded as he held the miniature portrait at arm's length to focus on the image.

"Aye," Edward agreed, "and a handful! She has a tendency for wildness and has, at times, been difficult to manage. She enjoys canoeing about the salt marshes, and has been known to climb a tree or two. She is not afraid to go out to fish on the water by herself for hours at a time. On her own, my lady! It is dangerous! A harsh tide, a sudden storm, not to mention that fishing is not an acceptable activity for a young lady."

Elizabeth smiled behind her fan. "Is she still under the care of your housekeeper, Mrs. Hourglass was it?" she inquired.

"Mrs. Watchit," Edward corrected with a laugh. "Yes, it was a tremendous stroke of luck finding her. Not much gets past her roving eyes nor escapes her keen ears. Without her vigilance, I would be quite lost."

They all laughed and Edward took the advantage of the light moment to approach the reason for his visit.

"Thomas, there is a matter of business that I must discuss, with your permission my lady." Edward squirmed.

Sensing his uneasiness, Elizabeth gave an approving smile, "As long as it is not politics. Thomas loves to maul that topic, but it does sour his stomach so, and his disposition! Shall I go off and see to some task whilst you natter?"

"No!" Edward replied abruptly. "It involves you, too, my lady." He shifted in his chair, took a deep breath and began. "The *Rosa* carried onboard passengers . . . two families . . . one headed for Nevis. The head of that family contracted a fatal illness just after we left the Canaries. He was an educated gentleman of quality and I believed him to be a most honorable man. He planned to run a mill and sugar plantation and saw it as an opportunity to pay off his brother's substantial debts. Unfortunately for his family, he borrowed heavily from the ship's company to refurbish the mill and signed over the better part of the profits for the next three years. He even borrowed to transport his family."

"Oh dear. Why is it so that debt begets more debt? It is a sticky and tangled rope from which, once grasped, few escape," Elizabeth asked, placing her fan upon her chest. "I fear the ending of this tale, Edward."

"Indeed, my lady," Edward continued. "Your fears are not unfounded. His widow was quite beside herself. The very night of his burial, she walked upon the upper decks in the middle of a terrible storm, perhaps the very storm that struck Barbados. She was lost. Swept away. At least, that is what we have determined. That unfortunate man and his wife left behind two orphans, a girl, well, a young woman actually. She is fifteen and her brother is seven."

"Oh, pity the children," Elizabeth cried waving the fan frantically. "A devastating fate, poor things! No doubt this affected you greatly, Edward, having been orphaned yourself at such a young age."

"Yes, yes," Thomas agreed. "Terrible thing. Swept from the ship, you say? Odd."

Edward hesitated before beginning again so that the full thrust of the tragedy would play heavily on their hearts. His silence also left open the speculation of other possibilities for the widow Montague's demise. He could sense from the change in her face that Elizabeth understood. She stopped her fanning.

"Oh dear!" she whispered as she caught her husband's eyes.

Edward continued, "Captain Blake has signed papers on the children and I have requested that you be given first option to purchase those papers. I have brought with me an amount that I believe my captain will find more than adequate to settle Montague's account with the ship's company and to provide for their sponsorship." Edward handed over a significant bundle of pieces of eight.

Thomas took the bundle and showed surprise by the weight. He squinted at Edward, looked quickly to Elizabeth, then back to Edward.

"They are good respectable Christian children," Edward added nervously. "Both educated and healthy. The girl, Sally . . ." He groped for a way to describe her without uncovering his affection. "She is most refined and would be an asset to your house. The lad is young, but quick and clever. They need a worthy guardian until they settle their father's estate in Nevis and arrange passage back to England. You once rescued me as a stray, I thought perhaps . . ."

Thomas picked up his long clay pipe, dipped it into a crock and scooped a bowl full of freshly cut tobacco leaves. He gently tamped the leaves down into the tiny bowl with his index finger. Thomas frantically searched his pockets and the tables around his chair. Elizabeth reached in the pocket of her apron and pulled out a long narrow set of tweezers.

"Would this be what you are looking for?" she said slyly.

"You are a dear!" Thomas replied and disappeared into the house. He returned with an ember firmly caught in the tweezers and carefully used it to light his pipe. He took several puffs and offered an empty pipe to Edward. Edward repeated the packing procedure. Thomas blew on the still captured ember and placed it over the leaves while Edward drew in the fire. He took a moment to enjoy the taste and smell of the weed before continuing with his request.

"I suspect the pecuniary status of these orphans is not the best," he said. "Until I investigate their holdings in Nevis, I cannot tell you what is theirs. The children have no one left in England save an uncle who would most likely land them all in a debtors' prison, or worse." Edward stopped to study Thomas's reaction.

Thomas rose from his chair and began to pace the veranda. He cleared his burning throat, turned his pipe upside-down, and was about to tap it across his palm to release the spent tobacco, but catching his wife's disapproving stare, opted instead to knock it gently against a post and allowed the ash to fall upon the flowerbed.

"It is a sad situation for the children and one might be quick to judge the father for acting with reckless regard, but any one of us in these colonies can understand the temptations and desperate states that drive a man. It is that vitality, nay, the *fear* of what might happen and the seemingly careless motivation to jeopardize everything to act anyway that I seek in a man! Ah, *that* is the quality necessary for settlement. Too often I see ships land with spiritless souls, those who do not want to take risks and lack innovation."

"Thomas," Elizabeth softly interrupted to redirect the conversation, "The children."

"Ah, quite right. Lizzy, what do you think? Could you stand the company of two little ones?"

"Oh, Thomas, you need not ask. It would be wonderful!" she stood up and gave her husband a quick embrace of approval. She winked at Edward, "I so long for the company of another female!"

Edward smiled and expelled an audible sigh of relief. "They are presently in the care of Ned and Belle Haywood who refused to disembark until the fate of the children was secured."

"The Haywoods!" Elizabeth exclaimed in surprise. "But I thought . . ."

"Their return to England did not give them the satisfaction they desired," Edward explained simply.

"I am not surprised," Thomas replied. "I have seen it before. Through hard work, good common people like the Haywoods rise, gain respect, wealth, and position here in these islands only to learn that their new status is not transferable. Back home, their peers are lowly and miserable, and the close ranks of high society will never let them enter. They are lost between two diabolical worlds. Some day, I fear these worlds will clash!" Thomas slapped his hands on his knees and rose quickly. "Well, Edward, let us go to this captain of yours and relieve the Haywoods of their charge. Lizzy, dear, we will be needing three beds."

"Your kindness is most appreciated, dear lady, but I fear that my time in Barbados is short and I have much business in Bridgetown."

"Oh, that is a pity, Edward. Will you have time, at least, to come to supper, perhaps tomorrow?" pleaded Elizabeth.

"It would be an honor, my lady." Again, he bowed and took the woman's hand.

"I will be a moment, Edward. Shelby!" Thomas shouted to the stable boy, "Shelby! My horse! And Mr. Waller's mount, too." Thomas disappeared into the house with his wife following and giving him a verbal list of things she required from town.

As they rode slowly back to Bridgetown, Edward shared news of England and the progress he had made on his shipping business in Boston and the cooperage on Cape Cod.

"Now, Edward," Thomas suddenly changed the subject. "What of this girl?"

Edward smiled. There was no pulling the wool over his old friend's eyes. "Sally Montague is . . . special, Thomas, and if she were older or my ambitions less taxing on my purse, I would not be asking this favor of you," Edward confessed.

"Then lad, why not have her and settle here in the Caribbean?"

"The thought crossed my mind and when you see her, you will understand what a tempting prospect that is to me. But she is still a girl, just three years older than Anani. Besides, I leave soon to take delivery of a merchantman in St. Kitts."

"Ah! So, it's *Captain* Waller, is it? You have worked long and hard for your own commission, Edward. I do wish you all the best, but I fear you are too much locked onto this course you have set for yourself. It is harmful if it denies you a bid for companionship. And think of Anani. She's coming on to being a grown woman, Edward. She'll marry someday and be gone. Who then will keep you company on those long cold nights in New England? Property and success can bring a man a measure of happiness and power, but only a woman can fill his heart and keep him warm at night." Modyford remained silent for a moment for he suddenly sensed a tiny version of his wife sitting on his shoulder and shouting into his ear, "stop preaching to the boy, Thomas!" He finally added, "We'll look after this girl and the boy for as long as it takes and treat them as our own. If the situation changes, we will get word to you, Edward. Now, I must tell you *my* news, for it may affect your decision to place their care into our hands. I have petitioned the King for the governorship of Jamaica."

"Jamaica! That is wonderful news, Thomas!" Edward exclaimed, and then realizing how it might affect Sally and James asked, "When will you know of the appointment?"

"Oh, I suspect there is a scramble among the young, hot-blooded Baronets of England for this rare chance to conquer new territory. But the colony is struggling and the previous governor, Sir Charles Littleton, strongly recommended to the King that an *experienced* planter be its next governor. Poor broken man, he lost his wife and infant son to fever just months after he arrived in Jamaica. Those whom he is charged to govern are not farmers. CAPTAIN Waller!" he suddenly changed the subject. "Ha! Oh, I do like the sound of that! Your own ship! Splendid, Edward, splendid. Such an accomplishment for one so young! Lizzy will be so pleased to hear this news. Well done, lad, well done! If word of the governorship arrives before we hear from you, would you have concerns if the children come with us to Jamaica?"

"Not if they remain in your capable hands, sir. I cannot tell you how grateful I am that . . ."

"Please, Edward." Modyford brushed the mention aside.

"With regards to the charge to secure their papers, I must insist the burden be mine, and mine alone. It must be a condition of our agreement," Edward responded.

"I hesitated to ask about the money, for fear there might be some . . . indiscretion too sensitive for Elizabeth's ears," Thomas explained awkwardly.

"No, sir, you misunderstand my intentions. Forgive me! I do not mean to suggest there is any impropriety to my actions, Thomas." Edward pulled back on the reins and hesitated for quite some time. Thomas turned his horse around to face Edward and waited. Finally, Edward managed, "I can see that there is no clear way to explain my intentions and see how others might think the same as you. To be frank, I am not sure of my intentions."

Thomas laughed. "There is no need to explain, Edward. You have our complete trust. However, I think it prudent to keep this our secret. I hope that you will tolerate the precautions of an old man, but I would feel better if *my* name appears on those papers. Few on this island or any other, under the King's flag, would challenge my signature or question my motives. It would be infinitely less complicated if you leave this transaction to me. You must trust *me* on this, Edward," Thomas warned.

"In your name only, sir, but the price . . . I wish that to be my responsibility. *I* buy their freedom, Thomas," Edward demanded.

"It is obviously important to you and I shall not press you further to explain to me why this weighs heavy on your mind. Though I do suspect that it is your *heart* that motivates you. I will accept this, as it is. Their first step they take on Barbadian land shall be as free citizens, on that you have my word, sir!" Thomas dipped his head in a gesture of agreement.

"Please, Thomas, I would prefer them never to know how this came to be," Edward pleaded.

"Agreed." Thomas bowed his head again, then arched his eyebrows and shrugged. "Mysterious, but I will honor your request."

That being settled, Edward smiled as they continued their journey. "Governor of Jamaica? Why would you leave all that you started here for that untamed, rowdy settlement in Jamaica?"

"Ah, Barbados is too small for my ambitions, Edward. Too crowded! Jamaica is huge and it has properly forested mountains. If I am right, those highlands should provide rich soil, plenty of free flowing but controllable water that can be sequestered, and a stable climate more agreeable to a variety of crops. I need not tell you the difficulties that Jamaica has encountered in establishing a productive population. I sent letters to the king identifying the possible causes. It is full of the wrong mix of people, drunken sailors and prissy aristocrats who both came looking for instant wealth and were shocked to find that they actually had to work for it. Why, they could not drive a plough if their lives depended upon it. And it does! Jamaica needs experienced planters, hungry farmers with vision and stable families who know how to handle the adversities of the Caribbean. From Barbados and other islands, I have been collecting such souls for the past year now. If the king grants me the governorship, I am taking them with me, hundreds of them! They trust me as a farmer and as a governor. They will follow me, Edward."

"I hear *your* incentive, but what of those who promise to follow you?" Edward asked.

"Ah, quite right. They're not coming for the sheer adventure of it. Land, Edward, land is what they're after and there is plenty of it in Jamaica! Thirty acres for every freeman and freedom from taxation for twenty one years!" Modyford declared. "Mind you, they have to improve the land, not just sit and watch the grass grow. And they have to live on it and make it produce! And none of this 'planters in absentia' business!"

"For every freeman? Man and woman? Light man and dark man? What happens if a Frenchie wants to go with you?" Edward asked.

"He'd be welcome! Every free man, woman, and child! And yes, Edward, even those two children who wait for us on the *Rosa*. That is sixty acres between them! Not a bad way to start a life, I'd say. They can take it or sell it for passage back to England or anywhere they have a mind to go. And yes, I do plan to take as many slaves as I can. That has been the problem with that colony, you see, it lacks a large labor force to help with the burden of hard work in a hot climate. Coming from Africa, those negroes have a higher tolerance of heat. Why, an Englishman, even with good intent, merely wilts in the tropics. Not the negroes. The sun revitalizes them. They convert it somehow to pure stamina and fortitude," Thomas explained. "I envy them for that!"

Edward did not engage for he disagreed with that popular notion and witnessed, too often, evidence that a black man had no more ability to withstand the abuses of climate than a man of lighter skin. He chose instead to think about the ramifications of Thomas's news for Sally and James. If Thomas were appointed Governor of Jamaica, their odds would improve significantly.

CHAPTER 6

"Ah, we'll see thee again, tis small enough, this island," Belle said as she bade farewell to James and Sally.

Ned braced the young boy's shoulders. "See after yer sister, lad, and remember yer upbringin'. Wouldn't do to be less than a gentleman, now would it?" He turned to collect their few bundles and held out his elbow for Belle.

"Mrs. Haywood, my dear, we are home!" he declared. Belle cocked her head, flashed a flirtatious smile, and took her husband's arm. With the help of the seamen, they climbed down the ropes and into the small dinghy. Several people on the docks were waving and shouting to them.

"Must be their family," Sally whispered to James as they leaned over the rails.

"Will we see them again?" James asked. Sally did not answer. Once the Haywoods clambered up onto the jetty, they never again turned in the direction of the ship. Sally lowered her eyes and stroked the curly blond hair of her brother. "Let us go down below and gather our goods." The boy seemed no longer interested in the scene on shore and readily obeyed.

Covering the western sky with a shocking crimson, the sun was setting when Edward and Modyford left the captain's cabin and came to the children.

"Thomas Modyford, I would like to present Miss Sally and Master James Montague," Edward introduced with a sense of accomplishment.

Modyford bowed. "Miss Montague, Master Montague, I am most happy to make your acquaintance. My wife, Elizabeth, and I would like to express our deepest sorrow for your most tragic loss. We would be honored if you were to share our home while you settle your affairs."

"We understand our position, sir, and are prepared to serve you," Sally said as she curtsied.

"Serve us?" Modyford stepped back. "No, no Miss Montague. You misunderstand. You and your brother will not *serve* us in any manner. It is *I* who wish to serve *you*. We want you to be our guests."

Sally looked to Edward who beamed a smile at her.

"It's all right now, Sally. The Modyfords will look after you."

Sally grasped James's hand. "I do not understand, sir. I thought . . . We have not been sold into servitude?"

"No, no, Miss Montague, not at all. You both leave this ship free and clear," Thomas explained. "Your debt to this ship's company has been satisfied."

Her lip quivered, but Sally managed, "Thank you, sir! We are . . . eternally grateful."

Thomas felt uneasy accepting credit for the act and glanced at Edward who surreptitiously shook his head. Thomas pursed his lips, but honored his friend's request.

James pulled away from Sally and ran to Barnaby Tibbs who was listening from a respectable distance. The cook squatted down in time to receive James's embrace. Sally had not realized how close the two had become during the final weeks of the voyage. Tears streamed down the cook's ruddy face and disappeared in his long curly red mustache. The two exchanged a few tender words before their final farewell.

James returned to Modyford, bowed politely, and declared, "Sir, I thank you for your kindness." Modyford was visibly moved. Laying a hand on his shoulder he replied, "Let's go see what Lizzy has for our supper, eh?"

Twiggy Strangeway helped Sally collect her sea chests, a few bundles of what remained of their clothes, and other possessions the captain would allow her to take. "Will you be coming with us, Mr. Waller," she asked.

"Alas, I cannot, Miss Montague. Business keeps me in Bridgetown. But I will be joining you tomorrow for supper."

"I look forward to tomorrow then." She started to climb down to the dinghy but paused. "Mr. Waller. God bless you, sir."

Edward said nothing. Once the dinghy was away, Sally Montague looked back once. Standing alone on the quarterdeck, she caught a glimpse of Captain Blake. The captain forced a half grin and gave a quick nod before turning away. James waved wildly and shouted to Barnaby and Twiggy who, with careless regard to their station, waved back.

Edward leaned against the rails long after the party in the dinghy had gone ashore. Barnaby came by his side and interrupted his thoughts. "Will ye be joinin' the capt'n for some supper aboard, Mr. Waller?" Edward gave a tired sigh and glanced again towards the shore. The lights of Bridgetown were just beginning to sparkle in the twilight and he could hear the faint sound of a fiddle.

"No, I will be going ashore this night. For now, I will be in the captain's quarters. When the dinghy returns, Mr. Tibbs, see that it is made ready for my departure."

"Aye, aye sir."

Edward knocked quietly on the door of the captain's quarters.

"Come!" was the rough cry from within. The captain was shuffling parchment and maps. "Ah, Mr.

Waller, this matter of the children, the outcome meets with your approval?" Not waiting for an answer, the captain continued. "The problem is solved, then, and it is well out of our hands, is it not? Yes, well, I must prepare for the unloading of the cargo at first light."

"Yes, sir."

Edward was about to leave, when the captain added, "One more bit of business, Mr. Waller." Blake walked across the cabin to his quartermaster. "Edward, you have been a fine officer and have seen to your duties well. The best. Yes, the best who ever served under my command! I congratulate you on your commission and wish you well. I have said so in this letter." The captain held out a letter, folded, and sealed.

Edward was surprised. He expected hostility. It was not uncommon for an officer to resign for a chance at advancement with another company, but such endeavors were not usually accepted with such grace by the captain of the vessel on which the officer served.

"Thank you, sir." Edward accepted the letter and then added, "Captain Blake, may I say that it was an honor to serve under your command and . . ."

"Stop!" Blake suddenly turned ugly. "Do not ruin the moment with patronizing dribble, Mr. Waller. Go! I command you to leave this ship at once . . . you are hereby relieved of further duties, sir and free to leave this ship this night. Go!"

Edward, puzzled for a moment over the behavior of his captain, surrendered to his command. He gave a final tribute by bowing deeply, and left.

Alone in his cabin, Captain Blake filled his glass with Madeira. "Go!" he said softly to himself, "Go, before . . ." He drowned the words with his drink and quickly guzzled another.

Edward went below to pack his locker and a duffle. He left orders for his possessions to be delivered to The Pelican Tavern in Bridgeport and said farewell to the crew still on board, particularly to the cook and the ship's cooper with whom he sailed on previous crossings.

"Ye be off a-pirating, no doubt?" asked Edward.

"Nay, Mr. Waller, we 'ave no desire to dance the hempen jig." Barnaby laughed, making a gesture of a noose pulling around his neck.

They watched at the rails while Edward climbed down the ropes and boarded the dinghy. Barnaby lowered the duffle down to him. Still leaning over the rails, he said to his friend when the dinghy was off, "That Mr. Waller, now there goes an 'onorable man, Twiggy."

"Aye, ye be right about that, mate. Be good to serve under a capt'n like that, eh Barnaby?"

A thought flashed across the minds of both men in the same instant. They looked at each other with a twinkle of understanding in their eyes. Plotting without words, they winked at each other.

Barnaby twirled his mustache, raised his bushy eyebrows, and gave a low breathy laugh. "Aye, mate. Where'd ya say he was goin' to pick up that there ship of 'is?" knowing that Twiggy always kept a close ear to the captain's door.

"St. Kitts, Barnaby," Twiggy replied with an impish laugh. "St. Christopher's Island, I believe the gentleman said."

"Aye . . ."

On shore, Edward strode along the sandy road to The Pelican. He knew the innkeeper from past years and was confident that he'd be able to rest and find a safe place to stash his belongings until he searched for a ketch bound for St. Kitts.

That night, as he lay in a cot listening to the disharmonious snores of four others who shared his room at the Pelican, he couldn't get his mind to settle. When he finally drifted off to a restless sleep he dreamt he was a boy again, running after rats that would feed himself and his sisters. The rats ran into a field of stinging nettles. "What do ya think you doin', lad," the man in his dream asked. It was Jon Trappit! "The rats! They're getting away!" Edward replied, running into the nettles. Edward felt the stings and woke in a sweat. He had lain on his arm and was now suffering from pins and needles. He rubbed his arm vigorously, causing the others in the room to stir. Edward tried to sleep again, but it was no use. Transitioning to a world that did not move affected him with queasiness. He rolled from the cot, reached for his waistcoat, and tiptoed from the room.

The air outside was fresh from the sea and Edward contemplated sleeping on the beach until he saw that it was already littered with mariners unsuccessful or too poor to secure a bed for the night, or those who had collapsed there after a good time in the taverns. *No mind,* Edward chuckled to himself, *the desire for sleep is gone.*

Seeing a hint of light in the eastern horizon, Edward strolled inland from The Wharf Street up High Street towards the town center. A slight elevation in the road gave him a better view of the garrison below and the bay beyond. He turned and slowly walked backwards for a bit while he watched the sun's first rays color the sea in silver and pink stripes.

"It's Sally," he whispered aloud. "She is the cause of this insomnia!" *I have found the right woman,* he thought, *at the wrong time. This course I chose was set years ago and I cannot see a way to accommodate such a weighty change. Not now. Not when I have, at last, my own command.*

Though the shop keepers of Bridgetown were beginning to stir at first light, there was still no traffic on the road and Edward decided it was as good a place as any to sit, watch the sunrise, and sort his muddled thoughts of duty, desire, and destiny. It was not too late. He could still go to her and make his affections known or to at least explain why he could not. But then, recalling the searing events that changed his own life, he remembered the lethal consequences of decisions made in fervor not logic, with passion not sensibility. Edward would not make those same mistakes. He carefully calculated the options that would lead him and Anani to a lucrative, comfortable life. A young bride and her orphaned brother . . . No! *She is too young,* he determined, *and I am not ready.*

"No," he declared aloud. "I cannot change my course, now. Not now."

CHAPTER 7

It was not in Elizabeth Modyford's nature to do anything mundane. Every event at the great house was an elaborate affair not soon forgotten, and this . . . the first occasion to impress her two young charges would be no exception. Elizabeth fussed over every detail and conducted her army of slaves like a general. Suppers were her specialty. The crystal sparkled, the silver glimmered, and the china spread with precision and design. Fresh flowers, carefully arranged by size and color, adorned every corner of the dining room. She rose early to direct the preparations, including the tailoring of fresh clothes for the children who, taking advantage of their soft feather beds, slept soundly until midday.

When Sally finally opened her eyes, it was to a bright breezy room. She was confused at first, but the smell of fresh linens, dried in the sunlight and ironed to perfection, reminded her where she was. She buried herself in the soft cushions to savor the happiness a moment longer before sitting upright. After her long luxurious bath last night, Mrs. Modyford provided her a sleeveless nightdress. She rubbed her hands over her arms, grateful that they were once again smooth and no longer sticky from the salt air. James, who slept in a bed near the window, had covered his head with the linens to hide from the bright light now streaming through the window. Even from across the room, Sally could feel the heat radiating from the opened window.

"James! Wake up. We've slept too long. The sun is already high in the sky. We don't want to give our guardians the impression we are lull-abuts. Get up!" Sally demanded. She leaped from her bed to give her brother a shake, but was startled by the image of another person in the room. It was *her* image in a large toe-to-head reflecting glass. Sally gasped. She hadn't seen herself since leaving England and although the mirror had its flaws, the changes she observed were not the reflections of an imperfect glass. She had, indeed, transformed. She was much thinner. The skin that had been exposed to the sun contrasted starkly with her usual paleness. Her flesh was peppered with bruises, scratches, and scabby sores. Her dark black curly hair was now lighter, straighter, and dull.

"My stars! Look at me! What has become of me?" she cried.

"Nothing!" James moaned still buried in the sheets. "You're still the same nagging sister."

Out of a horrible fascination, Sally stared a little longer at her scrawny reflection until she heard the sound of the door opening. Startled, she turned around and tried to cover her exposed flesh. A small black woman dressed in a white frock and headscarf entered the room and bowed.

"Come to help you dress, miss," she said softly and immediately went about the room as one familiar with her duties. "Madam expects you both dressed for supper."

Sally could not imagine such an exquisite meal so far from home. Oyster rolls, turtle steak pie, baked fish, a pompetone, and so many puddings! Beggar's pudding, trifle made with jellyrolls and thick custard, and wine jelly served on a platter surrounded by soft fruits rolled in powdered sugar. But her sweetest surprise was the pleasure of being seated across the table from Edward Waller. He looked so stunning that he quite took her breath away. Her tongue refused to cooperate with what she wanted to say to him. Several times Elizabeth interrupted her husband's dominance of the conversation to direct a question to

Edward, then to Sally, in an obvious effort to seed a conversation between the two. Try as she might, Sally could utter not more than just a few words.

Too soon, the dinner was finished. James took no heed to the warnings of eating such rich food in moderation and had to retire to his room with stomach pains. The rest of the dinner party retreated to the breezier verandah to enjoy a glass of port.

"How did you meet?" Sally asked boldly.

This time it was Elizabeth who hesitated.

"I meant to say, how did you meet Mr. Waller?" Sally clarified.

"Ah," Thomas volunteered, "now that is a story! One that I remember like it was yesterday. It was '51. Yes, October of 1651. Edward came to Barbados with the General-at-Sea, Sir George Ayscue."

"Touchy times after the execution of King Charles," Edward explained. "Barbados was enjoying a bit of autonomy while Parliament was distracted with civil war."

"What! More like the mother country was wringing us dry!" Thomas injected.

"Was there no fighting here on the island during those troubled times?" Sally asked.

"No! Well, not until they . . . disposed of the king. Until then, we had too much to lose to squabble amongst ourselves. We needed to preserve our rather lucrative trading status and our freedoms of self-governance. We even passed a law against disparaging name-calling. Anyone caught attributing a person as Roundhead or Royalist was punished severely!" Thomas huffed.

Edward chuckled. "They paid a fine by having to purchase a round of drinks to all within the local public house where the offending names were spoken," he enlightened.

"It maintained a light-hearted and delicate neutrality," Thomas defended and then sighed. "That changed after the execution. Farmers, who were not as successful as some, allowed themselves to be driven by jealousy. One thing led to another . . . you know how it goes." Elizabeth looked to Sally, then to her husband. She shook her head, certain that Sally knew nothing about those particular faults of men.

"The assembly here favored the son of our dead king, Charles II. Parliament didn't take kindly to that," Edward sneered, "and they sent Asycue and the fleet to Barbados to quell the Dutch."

"The Dutch?" Sally was confused. "How were Dutch involved?"

"Ah. That lucrative trading I mentioned . . . it was with the Dutch," Thomas added.

"And you were the governor at that time?" Sally asked, now intrigued with the story.

"Good gracious, no! Lord Willoughby. Shady character, that man! Sent by Charles II. And Asycue's fleet, I suspect, was supposed to be nothing more than sabre rattling. Parliament's show of force," Thomas conjectured.

"The fleet was sent to enforce the embargo," Edward corrected.

"Imagine, Sally, a country enforcing an embargo on its own colony!" Thomas stated fervently. "Was it a wonder that Barbadians were ready to take up arms?"

"We had over a thousand men. There was no hope of rebellion," Edward declared. "While Asycue tried to parley with the unhappy Barbadians, we captured as many Dutch ships as we could. We had 27 by count."

"But that still does not account for how you met," Sally reminded.

"Ah," Edward continued. "A Dutch ship attacked us and a chain-ball tore into our ship. It's a terrible sound, Sally, the sound of a ship tearing apart. It shattered the main spar, splitting that tall pine into tiny shards and splinters that flew across the decks. One such splinter ripped into my left shoulder like a spear. As it is during battle, the dead and wounded are tended only after the guns are silent. I was dragged to the side rails so my body would absorb further debris in case we were hit by a broadside." Edward stopped when, judging from the look of horror on Sally's face, he realized his tale was too graphic.

"I saw him there, on his ship," Thomas picked up the story. "He was dying. The ship's surgeon did his best, but conditions were abysmal. Not a place for healing. I was sent to parley peace and as a sign of goodwill, agreed to take the wounded to shore."

"He was in a dreadful state!" Elizabeth recalled. "The wound was dirty and crawling with maggots. Our physician suggested we leave the maggots to clean the wound of dead flesh. Of course I was against this, but it did seem to work. Though I cannot imagine . . ." She stopped short. It was obvious that Elizabeth did not want to imagine it, even now.

"As you see," Edward laughed to soften the moment. He stood with his arms straight out, "I am completely healed, much to the generosity of these fine people!"

"Did you go back to your ship?" Sally asked.

"No. The navy deemed me unfit for service and I was discharged. I stayed on Barbados for nearly a year," Edward remembered.

"And you, sir, were the hero in all of this?" Sally asked Thomas.

"Hero? No hero came from that conflagration. To his credit, Asycue showed much restraint and pursued no retributions for what were surely treasonous acts. Is he the hero? I think not. His liberal treatment of our Barbadian malcontents added fuel their insatiable craving for more independence. He has planted a dangerous seed. The rising disparity between the colonies and Britain is problematic throughout the colonies. One day, the children of England will grow beyond the call of their mother. And as for me . . . my interest was to put an end to the conflict quickly, so that we might return to the minding our crops and making our fortunes. I cared deeply that a cane field was allowed to remain fallow while its workers went off to throw stones at a giant!"

There was a pause in the conversation as they all took time to ponder the gravity of Thomas's prediction. Edward took the opportunity for a graceful exit.

"My dear lady," he bowed before Elizabeth, "you have once again honored me with a feast! The day grows short and I must prepare for my sail to St. Kitts. It has been my pleasure to see you again." Edward took her hand and kissed it gently. Thomas shouted for the stable boys to bring Edward's mount and went off to supervise.

Edward declared, "I cannot leave without saying goodbye to James." He gave a quick bow and went inside the house to find the boy.

"He's a good man, do you not find him so, Sally?" Elizabeth inquired.

"I do, madam. I do. Excuse me." Sally rose to follow Edward and came to the bedroom door just in time to hear Edward's tender farewell to her brother.

"Will we see you again?" James asked innocently.

"I trade in these waters, James. With luck, we *will* meet again. Do you think I will recognize you as a grown lad? I mean, you might look quite different when you have those front teeth back."

James thought for a moment. He rolled up his shirtsleeve and bent his elbow. "Do you see this scar? I got it while climbing a tree. I am told that it will be there when I am an old man."

Edward laughed and ended with a familiar rub on the head. When he turned, he came close enough to Sally to brush against her skirts.

"I do hope that is true . . . what you said about meeting again one day," she whispered. Her heart was beating so fast, she worried he would hear it.

"You can count on it, Miss Montague," he promised laying his hand gently on her shoulder. She wanted him to stay longer, but he smiled and then left.

Later, as the sun dipped low in western sky a gentle breeze wrapped around the house of Modyford. Elizabeth and Sally sat alone on the verandah to enjoy the sunset.

"I must confess, I am quite taken by Mr. Waller," Sally suddenly admitted.

"It is obvious he feels the same way," Elizabeth answered.

Sally looked surprised at Elizabeth. "But, he cannot. I mean . . . he is promised to another."

Elizabeth looked confused.

Sally explained, "He told me so. There is another woman in his life."

It took a minute for Elizabeth to make sense of what Sally was saying and when she realized the cause of the confusion, she put her hand on her bosom and laughed. Then sensing the gravity of the misunderstanding she explained, "Ah yes, you poor dear, there is another. And she has, indeed, quite stolen his heart. Edward has a daughter, Sally. Anani. She stays at their home in Massachusetts."

Sally jumped from her chair. "A daughter?" She looked in the direction where the road meandered away from the house, where she saw Edward ride away. "It was his daughter! There is no other? No wife?" Sally asked in despair.

"No. I don't believe there is any other in his life other than Anani." Elizabeth was slowly putting the pieces of this melodrama together. "He didn't tell you?"

"Mrs. Modyford, please, I must see him!" she pleaded. "When did he say he was leaving Barbados?"

Elizabeth placed her hand over her mouth, sat back in her chair, and sighed with disappointment. "Oh my dear, he would be leaving this very hour. The ships slip out to sea under the cover of darkness. You believed him to be attached? That is why . . . Oh, you poor, poor girl."

Sally turned away from Elizabeth and walked slowly to the edge of the verandah. As the last of the sun's light disappeared below the horizon, she whispered, "I didn't know." Elizabeth followed her, put her arm around her shoulder and led her back to the house. Neither woman spoke of this again.

CHAPTER 8

Captain Edward Waller took delivery of the *Gloucester* in St. Kitts at the end of August 1663. Before sailing her to Boston, he went to Nevis in a small sloop to investigate the Montague land holdings. He was lucky to have pinched two able seamen from the *Rosa*'s crew, Twiggy Strangeway and Barnaby Tibbs. They traveled with him to the little island off the eastern shore of St. Kitts. Nevis, just seven miles long and five wide, had one tall mountain in its center and was blessed with rich volcanic soil. Edward met the manager of the sugar plantation in Charlestown and found him to be honest, capable and genuinely shaken by the news of the Montague family.

"What happened to the press and boiler?" the manager asked.

"It is likely the captain of the *Rosa* sold them in Barbados," Edward replied.

"Pity. We surely needed that equipment here, Captain Waller." The manager showed the men a map of the estate. "Here, along the southern slope of the mountains is where the cane lands are. The soil there is good with plenty of water. The last couple of years saw high yields throughout the cane lands. There are only a few presses in the south and they cannot keep up with the yield. Harvesting is time-critical Captain Waller, and the millers here on Nevis have defined a pecking order favoring the bigger well-established farms, those that are occupied by their owners and with permanent work forces of slaves. And there be another problem," The manager shifted about and dropped his head. "You see, Captain Waller, I haven't been paid a proper compensation since the death of Clive Montague. Getting that mill up and running, well, that might have turned things around on this estate. Without it, profits will always be marginal and vulnerable to the whims of the millers. I've got a family, Mr. Waller," the manager related.

Having spent most of his money on the security of Sally and James, Edward was not in a position to negotiate the manager's back pay. However, he did his best to persuade him to stay on. He wrangled a deal with a promise to carve five acres off the estate for the manager to keep for his own in exchange for staying one more year while arrangements were to be made to sell the land.

"Make it ten, sir, and I will bring in the cane you see growing," the manager proposed.

"Agreed!"

A contract was drawn and the manager seemed satisfied.

"Another year then, sir," the manager agreed.

"Let's hope it be a profitable year," Edward replied. With the transaction completed, they returned to St. Kitts. Before his departure, Edward wrote a letter to Sally Montague and a separate one to Thomas Modyford reporting on the developments of the sugar plantation. Twiggy delivered the letters to a Dutch fluyt sailing directly to Jamaica.

"She'll be getting' the news afore the week is through, Capt'n!" Twiggy announced.

"Then, let us haul anchor and be on the way, Mr. Strangeway! Our first port of call – Virgin Gorda!" Edward commanded.

One of the roughest fractions of the *Gloucester*'s long journey to Boston was the slender strip of waters between the islands of Tortola and St. John known as Sir Francis Drake's Channel. Not two miles wide in places, the normally calm channel suddenly spawned a squall. The unruly waters and unpredictable shearing winds left several of the *Gloucester*'s wide sails torn and the ship had to turn about and anchor in Coral Bay, St. John for repairs.

When they set sail again, it was on smoother seas to Virgin Gorda to pick up a shipment of logwood, and then onto the Turks Islands, past Virginia and New Amsterdam. As they approached Nantucket, the weather once more turned foul. As the crew struggled with a faulty bilge pump, the wild nor'easter threatened to swamp the *Gloucester*. Were it not for the skills of Twiggy and Barnaby, the ship might have joined the many other wrecks along the shallow banks of Cape Cod.

Edward delivered the *Gloucester* and ship's log to the much-relieved owners in Boston Harbor on September 14th. 1663. Thankful to see the ship, its cargo, and crew in good order, the new owners complimented Edward on his ability to sail through two storms relatively unscathed.

"Some were not as fortunate," they claimed. "A small ketch and two fishing vessels were lost in that nor'easter. For your skills and speedy delivery of the *Gloucester*, we have added a bonus to your pay, Captain Waller, and trust you and your crew will continue your service with us."

"Perhaps in the future, good sirs, but for now I must attend to my businesses here in Boston," Edward replied.

Edward gladly compensated his deserved crew their wages plus a generous share of the bonus. Barnaby and Twiggy, wanting a respite from the rigors of another winter at sea, agreed to stay on in Boston to help Edward build his cooperage. He gave them each a significant portion of his wages to purchase supplies, two large wagons, and a couple of strong mules for hauling.

The process of his barrel-making began two winters before when he cut the trees from his wooded property near Watertown. Of the white oak logs, he selected the best for the barrel staves and with a team of draft horses, dragged the logs over the frozen ground to the Charles River. There, Edward tied them together to form 3 connecting rafts, and floated them down to the mill.

To prevent tearing the veins in the wood, the millers split and planed each log by hand. The method was expensive and labor-intensive but necessary to make his barrels as impenetrable as possible.

Stacked loosely in tiers to fully expose the lumber to the air and rain, weathering the newly planed wood helped to purge odors and impurities from the wood and decrease the harsher tannins that might affect the taste of the barrel's contents.

Now, nearly two years after the trees were felled, it was time for Barnaby and Twiggy to load the pre-cut timber onto the wagons and drive south along the muddy track to Edward's unfinished warehouse in Roxbury. The men arrived just as a cold rain began to fall.

"Whoa, there, hold up!" Barnaby called to the horses as he pulled back on the reins of the lead wagon. He turned around and laughed at Twiggy. Before them stood the shell of a building with only half a roof. A stray goat came out of the doorless entry and bleated a warning.

"Well, it ain't no palace," Twiggy shouted from the wagon, "but it'll keep us out of this rain."

They unloaded the boards and stacked them again under the shelter. The boards would remain in the warehouse until they aged enough to become staves. The large thick rays of white oak wood provided just the right amount of porosity to allow bend-ability and resiliency during dry shrinkage and wet swelling. White oak was also strong and weighty, perfect for surviving the rough treatment of portage and transportation by sea.

The light of day was disappearing by the time they got around to building a makeshift lean-to for the wagons. The two men and the mules slept inside the sheltered end of the unfinished warehouse. In the morning, still cold and rainy, Barnaby hitched one wagon to return to Boston to search for an ironmonger who would make the right kind of hoops for the barrels while Twiggy stayed on at Roxbury to supervise the completion of the warehouse.

With his business in Boston finished, Edward was anxious to see Anani and took a seat in a carriage headed for Dorchester. Whenever he was away at sea or up in the highlands harvesting timber, Anani and his housekeeper, Mrs. Watchit, boarded in the grand house of his friend, Richard Tucker. It was a perfect arrangement. Richard, a widower, received the help of an additional housekeeper while his only daughter, Alicia, had the friendship and company of Anani. An added bonus was the income Edward received from renting his house in Boston.

By the time Edward reached Dorchester, it was late afternoon. His giddy excitement was soon dashed by the news that Anani was in Boston with Alicia and Mrs. Watchit.

"They've gone for a tea party, old boy," Richard explained. "What they do at such an affair is anyone's guess. It's the done thing now, these tea events. It took them a week to agree upon what manner of dress was appropriate for a tea party. I expect them back before dark. Tis soon enough, Edward. In the meantime, this will give us the opportunity to talk for I know I have no hope of winning your ear once Anani is present. Allow me to compensate your disappointment with a stein of good beer from somewhere in the southern states within the Holy

Roman Empire. I know not where. I won a keg of the drink playing cards."

"I thought you did poorly in cards," Edward laughed and after a long sip, looked up in surprise. "This is cold!"

Richard laughed, "It's contraband, Edward! Isn't it delightful? The Huns truly have this down to perfection. I think they let me win to be rid of it. I am hiding it down in that chilly spring house."

Edward smiled, but decided he did not like chilled beer, believing that it somehow masked its flavors. "So Richard," he mused while trying to warm the beer by cupping his hands around the stein, "tell me of your exploits and high adventures as a great civic leader of the fair town of Dorchester."

"Ugh. The duties of selectmen bore me to tears, my friend. The paramount function seems to be chasing after farmers who do not properly mend fences. And I mean that in everyway possible. Here, a broken fence is a crime, a great offence! *Offence* . . . do you suppose the word originated from that very crime? Off-fence . . . The fence is off . . . The other day I had to go after a gentleman for the twenty pounds his father left him. Someone challenged him on it, claiming he loaned that money to the deceased old man to build a fence, a fence that never materialized. What is even more *offensive*, please forgive me, is that some knobby-kneed, spotty-faced clerk actually keeps watch on who inherits what. I ask you! These petty civil servants are in every corner of our lives, Edward!" Richard complained. He finished his stein before continuing. "The most excitement I had all year was giving permission to the constable to arrest an interloper for carrying away stones from Squantums Neck. Yes, stones! He had a mind to build a simple shelter for his poor family and committed the great crime of neglecting to solicit the town's permission before taking said stones from the riverbed. Nor did he properly compensate the damages incurred to the proprietors of land along the banks of Squantums Neck for removing the stones." Richard raised his hands up. "I had a man arrested for stealing stones, Edward. Stones!"

"Yet, surely, these minor trials will put you in good practice for the higher offices you seek," Edward suggested.

"*Sought*, Edward, sought. This undertaking has left me with a sour taste and I have little desire to extend my services to Dorchester. I had hoped, rather than adopt the same pattern of British rule; this colony might lead brave men to forge a new promise of government with a greater *collective* responsibility. Instead, we accept the unimaginative status quo. Parishes, counties, and townships! They are all tiny insular chiefdoms run by small-minded incompetent chiefs! They have inflated opinions of themselves, these power-hungry players! This system of imported government does not serve the colonies well and is oft times taken over by fanatics and bigots. North of Boston . . . ah well, we must not spend our time dribbling such petty politics!"

"Cynicism! Hmmm . . . this is new," Edward mocked. "When last here, I saw before me an ambitious man with many hopes. What has changed you so, Richard?"

"Aye, I *was* bent on conquering the evils of our fair colony, was I not? But now I fear this growing trend of too much power falling into too few opportunistic hands, untrained in the rule of law and doing little to represent fairly the citizens who so earnestly gave them their trust. They but advance their own self-interests. As a selectman,

I like least the task of deciding who may and or may not live within Dorchester. Prime example: the Widow Hill, poor woman! Since her husband died, there is no one to keep her company or help her to maintain her house and garden save her son-in-law, now a childless widower himself. At the mere suggestion that the acquaintance may seem improper, our wise council voted nay to her motion that he inhabit here amongst us. Worse, the selectmen gave her strict instructions that she must turn him away, should he decide to grace her abode again. What rights have we to do that? And the Widow Higgins from Boston! She could winter with her daughter here in Dorchester, but *only* if the good widow provided a letter from the selectmen of Boston promising that her winter accommodation here would not disoblige them of the duties which they owe unto her. Is this the way of it in colonies of the Caribbean?"

"No. Not at all!" Edward chuckled. "No one monitors the movements of freemen and settlement is encouraged by all, through generous incentives if need be. Different classes, races, and nationalities, even those with whom England has declared war, settle the islands. However, Richard, there is a consequence to this liberal tolerance. There is scant order to that society. Crime occurs at such a rate as to be quite unimaginable to someone of Dorchester. And, I dare say," he laughed, "the good citizens of Massachusetts would find the loose establishments within the Caribbean towns quite . . . objectionable! The colonies of New England are, for the most part, inhabited by those who might consider themselves godly, while the Caribbean seems to have attracted the godless."

"Godless, but happy, no doubt! If it were not for the incessant heat, I might consider transporting my lot to some feisty little tropical island! And you have met no one there worth redemption?" Richard asked.

Edward replied with a broad grin and a cheeky but involuntary rising of his left eyebrow.

"Oh, now, there is a look! Do tell. Who *is* she?" Richard surmised. "And pray, why is she not here by your side?"

"She is but a child, Richard. In years, only a few more than Anani."

"Ah, how deliciously scandalous! And selfish! You deny our Council of Selectmen such superior gossip for discussion. And I do hate to be the bearer of news that you, sir, are determined to ignore, but in a few years our daughters will soon enough be young ladies! No, come now, this is not sufficient. Details! There must be more to this and I'm all ears," Richard tested.

"I could not take advantage of her . . . circumstances," Edward confessed quietly.

"Ah. Now this does sound intriguing. Do go on!" Richard mused while adjusting his seat for an anticipated lengthy tale.

"She, and her young brother, became orphaned on the crossing," Edward started.

"Dreadful!" Richard murmured with sudden remorse for his flippant behavior.

"I . . . bought their papers to secure their entry to Bridgetown, Richard, and left them in the care of friends. She will soon, most likely, be sailing back to England or on her way to Jamaica under the guardianship of its future governor. I left them in capable hands."

"And what, pray, is the matter with *your* good hands? Oh, Edward, really! It is hardly ungentlemanly to attempt to rescue her from a fate! What charms has she that won your heart so?"

Edward recounted the details of their tragic voyage and remarked on her many endearing features. When he stopped talking, Richard seemed stunned.

"You must go to Jamaica and fetch her immediately! How many years have I known you? And in those years, I have never seen you so smitten. Go back, Edward, for surely this will profit your heart. Find this young woman before she is lost to you, and to Anani."

"How would that be? A mother and a daughter, practically the same age?" Edward protested.

"*Adopted* daughter, Edward. Anani is adopted and therefore offers legitimate leniency towards such rules of protocol. And look how our two daughters, the same age, have become good friends . . . sisters really," Richard suggested.

Edward forced the subject to change. "You must tell me the news of Anani. How fares she, Richard? And Alicia, is she well?"

"Prepare yourself, dear friend, for in the months of your absence, she did grow into a beauty. Thy dearest, and mine, have turned many heads. Mrs. Watchit, so aptly named, God love her, must now keep one eye on each girl. Especially in Boston! Only a dozen years are they! I fear to think what it will be like in a few more years, my friend. We will, too soon, be chasing off their suitors with the flat of our swords," Richard warned. He leaned closer to Edward and in low voice, "They are growing breasts, Edward! Breasts!"

"And her wild streak?"

"Gone! Well . . . somewhat. Alicia's quiet demeanor has had an affect on Anani and she is now quite the lady. She'll be surprised and so pleased to see you. She misses you, Edward," Richard said softly. "Will you be staying with us in Dorchester?"

"For the winter, if you can accommodate me. I have taken on two shipmates as partners. Mr. Strangeway is a cooper and Mr. Tibbs is an ironmonger who is also a fine cook and as jolly a man you'd ever have on the high seas. Mr. Tibbs will manage the warehouse and Mr. Strangeway will build the cooperage on the Cape."

"Still intent on building the warehouse in Roxbury?" Richard asked.

"Indeed, I have started its construction and now have the funds to complete it," Edward replied. "Everything is in place, the wood, the metal, the know-how, and the labor. Everything, that is, except the salt from Cape Cod. I just hope production has improved significantly these past months; otherwise the demand for salt-cured cod will greatly exceed their yield of salt. I fear it is too wet and humid on the Cape to dry the pans of salt water by wind and sun alone. While in Boston, I heard they have taken to boiling sea water in huge vats. Boiling the brine, Richard! Such a process cannot be sustained."

"It sounds much faster than waiting for the inconstant New England sun to do the job," Richard replied, not understanding Edward's objection.

"To fuel the fires necessary to reduce seawater to salt, they would have to strip the land of every tree. Those stunted trees on the Cape cannot produce logs sufficient for such an enterprise. It seems a rather drastic measure and a waste of wood for such short-term gains. When they run out of trees, what then?"

"Ah, now, you see!" Richard raged. "That is what I am on about! Greed! Why can we not comprehend that today's greed will surely produce tomorrow's poverty? I have just the solution, Edward. The islands of the Caribbean, are they not surrounded by saltwater for the harvesting? And is the climate there more conducive to the drying of salt? Why not produce the salt there? You could fill your barrels with something they want from here, wool for instance. There is a new woolen mill just built on the Charles. In the Caribbean, you fill the barrels with their bounty of salt and bring them back to Massachusetts to be packed with cod for England. And in England, you could use the same salt and barrels to ship us some pork? Now you'd have your barrels and the salt for your cod and I would have my pork!

Edward raised his eyebrows. Richard had an instinctive, if not comical, way of simplifying complexities. It was the very quality that made him a top-notch barrister and convinced Edward that his friend would make a talented politician.

"Now, to get back to the girls," Richard continued.

"Yes, as our house is still occupied by our tenant, I thought of taking the girls to Cape Cod."

"Hmmm. They have grown rather fond of the social scene in Boston and might find the Cape a bit . . . provincial," Richard cautioned.

"Richard, you have been so generous to take Anani into your home. The girls are good for one another. They'll enjoy the water and the village. It's harvest time. I'm sure they will find the festivities amusing and it will provide you a much-deserved rest. Are you still courting . . ." Edward searched for her name.

"Mary," Richard finished. "Since last we met, dear boy, the relationship has . . . escalated." He hesitated. Edward raised his palms and cocked his head to one side to jest for more detail. "I *may* present her with a proposal," Richard admitted. "Perhaps . . . I am still thinking on the matter."

"And Alicia, she is happy with this?" Edward inquired.

"Of course! Alicia loves her dearly, and so will you my dear friend. Besides, I suspect that too soon my daughter will be seeking to wed some character or another and then up and leave her poor old Papa. I would then be quite alone. I have been alone before, Edward, and I have decided it is not to my liking. Mary is kind, good humored, and works hard to keep me happy. You must know how difficult a task that is. She will make a good wife and a good friend to Alicia."

"I am happy for you, Richard, and pray you have many good years together. I hope I am here for the wedding."

"Wedding? I have yet to propose! I am thinking of taking a law student into my practice. He's a Jew, but damned good at letters. I have yet to decide if I can handle him as well as a wife. When and where do you go next, Edward?"

"There is a rather ancient Dutch fluyt in Boston's harbor. She is quite a prize! Three hundred ton, eighty feet long. She can hold more cargo than any English ship of similar size. She's got a flat bottom, broad beams, and a round stern. More importantly, she can be manned with a short crew of just twelve men. Twelve, Richard! Such a savings in both aggravation and wages, I can scarcely imagine. She's being refitted and should be done in about a year's time. I've been asked to sail her to Portsmouth to join the naval fleet there." Edward replied with a glint in his eye.

"The navy? You're not . . ."

"No. No. The *ship* joins the navy, not I. I just deliver her. I merely take the opportunity of the admiralty's shortage of captains in Boston. No, Richard, I am through with the navy, though fortunately for my purse they have not completely cut their ties with me."

"Will not the Dutch be anxious to win their fluyt back?" Richard asked.

"No doubt, good friend, but then she'll have a keen English captain at her helm. After Portsmouth, I'll be off to Bristol where I pick up a merchantman full of goods bound for Barbados."

"Ah, so it is back to the Caribbean, then, where I suspect you will find the time to visit this . . . Island of Jamaica?" Richard slyly asked.

Edward only laughed, but beneath the laughter was determination to do just that. This time, he thought, he should be better placed financially to offer Sally more than promises of a future, and she might be better positioned to consider his proposal.

CHAPTER 9

When the official documents arrived from London in February 1664 appointing Thomas Modyford the Governor of Jamaica, he had already amassed over seven hundred freemen with promises of free passage, land, and a generation of no taxation. Among them were Sally and James Montague.

The preparations for the emigration kept Sir Thomas away from home leaving Lady Modyford the task of managing the plantation. Always, Sally was by her side studying the accounting and processes necessary to administer such a vast estate. Elizabeth was grateful for the company and enjoyed a sense of pride in sharing her knowledge. Her husband rarely acknowledged the work she contributed and her efforts were often taken for granted, part of the burden of being the wife of a planter *and* a statesman.

"What's to become of these lands when you leave Barbados, Lady Modyford?" Sally asked as they rode on horseback to the indigo fields.

Elizabeth bit her lower lip, an immediate reaction to stop the words from revealing her heart's desire. She had often wished that she could stay behind and do exactly what she was contented to do, but Thomas would never tolerate even the suggestion.

"Please, won't you call me Elizabeth? It will take my ears time to respond to this new title and my soul even longer. We intend to keep this place running in absentia. Thomas complains often about the deteriorating states of many good farms whose owners remain in England, and here we are, joining the ranks of other absentee landlords. However, Jacob Wallenberg is a good overseer. We can only put our trust in his honesty and good management."

Elizabeth explained. "We may just get one good cutting of the indigo before we leave," she added looking over the field.

"It's beautiful!" Sally declared as she dismounted. She ran through the field of minty green plants with lavender colored flowers, did a girlish twirl, and laughed, "There is a delicious scent, like sweet peas."

"Some are still with their flowers, but most are now spent. If you look at them, they do resemble tiny versions of the sweet pea. But the dye does not come from that small purple flower, Sally. It's in the leaves."

"These tiny leaves? But they are green."

"Come along. I'll show you how it is done." Lady Elizabeth went off at a trot.

On a gentle rise above the field, the processing area was alive with the activity of about one hundred workers. The day before, ox-driven carts full of leaf-covered branches were unloaded into a large coral stone trough half filled with water.

"The leaves want to float," Elizabeth instructed. "That is why they must be weighed down with those heavy logs. Yesterday, before the leaves were first put into this trough, the water was treated with pig fat, crushed seed, and wood ash to start the fermentation process. There is something in the fat that helps to break down the leaves into the dye and sugar. See the bubbles? A gas is produced, not too unlike the process used to make ale. This slurry is now ready for the next step, Sally, over here," she said descending stone steps to a second trough, longer, shallower, and at lower elevation.

"You see," Elizabeth pointed to a pipe at the bottom of the first trough, "the water now contains the dye and is drained from there into this trough. The fat, the seed hauls, and the leaves remain behind." As if on cue, four scantily clothed men jumped into the second tank. They positioned themselves shoulder-to-shoulder, grabbed a log attached to the rim of the trough for support, and started to sing. As they sang, each lifted their left leg back and then trusted it forward, creating a synchronized stir to the rhythm of their song. Squatting at the edges, two other men dumped handfuls of gray powder into the churning bluish green water while a third scooped up a handful of water. He rubbed it in his hand several times and bent over to taste and smell it.

"At this stage, we need to get as much air into the mixture as possible," Elizabeth yelled. "The air makes the dye settle out at the bottom of the tank."

"What is that gray powder?" Sally shouted over the measured rhythmic cha-chung, cha-chung, cha-chung sounds of the mixing water and singing.

"Slake lime. It helps stop the fermentation process."

"Why is that man tasting the water?"

"We know when it is ready for the final stage when this mixture has neither a bitter taste nor slippery feel. At that point, the liquid on the top is siphoned off, the pigment is scooped out of the trough, rinsed to remove the impurities, and then it's shoveled into these sacks," she explained as she led Sally to a thatch-covered shelter where at least a dozen tear-shaped canvas sacks hung from the rafters. The draining liquid was collected in wooden buckets placed under each sack. "We reserve that liquid for our own needs. It has just enough dye to color cotton a pale shade of blue." With a cheeky grin, Elizabeth lifted her skirt slightly to reveal a blue petticoat the color of a robin's egg. She shouted instructions to several women who were minding the sacks. One climbed a ladder to untie a sack while the others reached up to bring it down. They carefully opened the sack to reveal a gooey wet blue paste.

"This is the indigo dye," Elizabeth simply said. "It's too sticky right now, but once most of the water has drained, the paste is flattened out like pastry, cut into squares and sun dried, just like making bricks. And it's those bricks that get shipped to England. We have to be very careful that they are completely dry, for if they are not, the fermentation process may continue and produce gas. Seeing that the bricks are stored in the confines of a ship's hull, gas is something we don't want to produce!"

"And this a profitable enterprise?" Sally asked.

"Oh, like harvesting gold, Sally!"

"Do you think this indigo plant will grow in Jamaica?"

Elizabeth laughed. "Ah, I see I have given away my secrets to a new competitor!"

It was a long hot but relaxing ride back to the great house and Sally took advantage of the peace to pry.

"Elizabeth, how is it that Edward Waller has adopted a child?"

Elizabeth smiled. She expected the question long before now and was quite prepared to relate that story and more, still hoping to rekindle the relationship and create a match worthy of her reputation.

"Thomas and I came to Barbados to escape the ravishes of England's civil strife. We were fortunate to be able to make such a choice. Edward's family was caught up in that dreadful siege of Colchester Castle. He was only twelve years old, the same age that Anani is now. I don't know the horrific extent of his ordeal, Sally. I am not sure I could bear to know for within those walls most died horribly. He lost his entire family. His father went down on the first day of battle and, sadly, his mother and two sisters died later, of starvation I believe. Hunger does not discriminate." Elizabeth stuttered, but continued. "On the night before the final battle, two noblemen, in the hopes that their final letters be delivered to a woman they both loved, sister to one and fiancée of the other, commanded Edward to escape and make his way to London where she lived. While the rest were distracted by that fateful battle, Edward shimmied through the walls and made his way to the forest. He was half dead when he stumbled into the path of a deserter, a man allied with the Roundheads by the name of Jonathan Trappit."

"Did they fight?" Sally asked.

Elizabeth shook her head. "In a crisis, the strangest and most unlikely alliances do occur. Out of necessity, they saved each other. The trials they endured together on that treacherous journey bonded them closer than brothers. But when they finally came to where the road split east to west, Jon Trappit went to Bristol. Edward wanted to follow, but his duty was in London."

"What happened to the two nobles?"

"They were murdered. Lord Fairfax had those two brave Cavaliers, Sir Charles Lucas and Sir George Lisle, executed as an example to other Royalists who had a mind to challenge Cromwell and his 'model' army." Elizabeth thought for a moment, as if dwelling in her own sad memories. She shook her head and said quietly, "Can it have been so long ago now? It does not seem so." Her thoughts were interrupted by Sally's insistence.

"What of Edward? Did he deliver the letters? You still have not told me how he came to adopt a child."

"Patience!" Elizabeth retorted. "I'm coming to that. Their escape from Colchester was an arduous journey and Jon Trappit and Edward developed a close relationship in that short time they were together. Jon went to sea and

Edward, well, he ended up staying with Sir George's family in London. They took him in as one of their own, healed him, educated him, and saw to it that he was well appointed when he expressed a desire to serve in the navy.

"That's when he came to Barbados?" Sally asked.

"Yes, that much of the story you know. But, when he left us, finally, he met up with Jon Trappit again, in Bridgetown. Trappit had given up his life at sea to become an apprentice to a German silversmith right here in Barbados. He married a Taino woman and had a child by her."

"A . . . Taino?" Sally asked.

"A native girl, a West Indian. Her kind is practically all gone now. Slaughtered, killed off by disease, enslaved. Edward stayed with Jon and his wife for quite some time . . . until Cromwell's fleet arrived in Barbados in '55 with nearly empty ships!" Elizabeth's tone was disapproving. It was obvious to Sally that Elizabeth had no love for England's Lord Protector. "Cromwell had in mind to take back from Spain the islands formally claimed by Drake. Promising release from servitude and shares of plunder, that fool governor, Searle, recruited indentured servants and freemen, including Edward, to man the ships of *Army* General Robert Venables and *Navy* Admiral Sir William Penn. As if an army general and a navy admiral would ever succeed in sharing a command! Too many cooks in the kitchen! Over three-quarters of their crew were young, inexperienced, and completely undisciplined farm boys from the islands. The expedition was doomed from the start." Elizabeth thought for a moment, shrugged and said, "In hindsight, it was probably a blessing that Barbados, Nevis, Montserrat and the other islands rid themselves of so many lack-lusters. I can tell you from personal experience, the slaves we acquired to replace them are so much more . . . controllable. Not all volunteered for the folly. Some of our best men were stolen, taken right off the streets by the press gangs. Unbeknownst to Edward, Jon Trappit was one such man. Witnesses claimed later that he resisted and in the process suffered a mortal injury. He died at sea before the battles began. When his wife heard that he was dead, she put a knife through her own neck."

Sally gasped and pulled back on the reins, "She killed herself?"

Elizabeth continued on her way and simply replied, "It is their way, Sally. However, it was a miracle that the silversmith's wife had taken the child to the beach, for it is also their way to kill their own children. The Trappit's little orphaned daughter, Anani, was saved and the old German and his wife looked after her. The grand naval mission failed, of course. Eventually, the leaders, once championed heroes during the civil battles, were stripped of their commands and sent to the Tower. The Spanish islands, Hispaniola and the others so desired by Cromwell, were too well defended . . . except for one."

"Jamaica?" Sally guessed.

"Jamaica!" Elizabeth confirmed. "After the battles, Edward did not come back to Barbados, at least not immediately. He stayed with the fleet on its return to England where he resigned his commission and found a ship bound for Boston."

"That was his first trip there?" Sally asked.

"Yes, and he was quite taken with the colony. He invested his small pension in land, but continued his journey to the Caribbean. It was quite the adventure. He made several stops, cutting logwood, I believe. Eventually, he made his way back to Bridgetown carrying quite an assortment of plants for Thomas's collection." Elizabeth stopped and dismounted. She pointed up the hill where the great house could be seen through the trees. "I like to walk it from here," she said, "Gives the horses time to cool down before we put them up."

Sally followed Elizabeth's lead but leaned against the horse while her stiffness abated.

"What happened next?" she asked.

"Ah, well, because of the plants for Thomas, he came directly to us. Edward was devastated when we broke the news to him about his friend and immediately went to Bridgetown to inquire about Trappit's little girl. The silversmith produced a will, stating that it was Jon Trappit's wish that Edward look after his wife and child should he die. And that, Sally, is how Anani became Edward's little girl."

There was a long period of silence as the women finally arrived at the great house. Sally looked at Elizabeth with a mournful stare and declared, "He is truly every bit the honorable man that I believed him to be."

Elizabeth smiled back and agreed, but was uneasy by the tone of Sally's remark. It had such an air of . . . finality.

In June, the eager settlers with their families and slaves set sail for the southern Jamaican fortifications at the end of Palisades, a port that the English called The Point.

The rough and tangled founding settlement of Port Royal, started by the remnant crew of Penn and Venables, was in poor condition. However, within months, Modyford refurbished the governor's mansion, Customs House, the docks, and built the King's Warehouse. He formed a governing council and divided the island into parishes. Six months after their arrival and after the lines were drawn; Modyford presented Sally and James their land grants as a Christmas gift.

"These credentials profit my heart more than my purse, Sir Thomas. A declaration that my brother and I arrive in Jamaica free, beholden to no man and these," she exclaimed waving the papers in the air, "give title to thirty acres each, bordering the Milk River along the south coast in the Parish of Clarendon."

"And no taxation!" James added, reciting without understanding the reason why that would cause others to rejoice.

"Whatever will you do with this land, my dear?" Elizabeth asked while musing over Sally's exhilaration.

"Do?" bawled Modyford. "Why it's land, woman! The question should be what would this land do for *them*? And in Jamaica's warm sweet air and its productive ground, a safe answer would be . . . anything, my dears! With a bit of hard work, anything!"

"Oh Thomas, for pity's sake. They are but children, still!" Elizabeth protested.

"Cacao! Sally, you must first plant a walk to cacao," Modyford advised. "It will be five years before you see your first crop, and by then, you two will be children no longer." He playfully rubbed the top of James's head before continuing. "James will see to the management of the trees and I shall share with you the secrets of chocolate. Ah, chocolate! There is not a nobler gift from the Heavens. What will you call this cacao walk of yours, Master James?"

"Moon Walk!" James answered abruptly.

"Moon Walk? Why Moon Walk?" Elizabeth inquired.

"Sir Thomas said when viewed from the bluffs above, the rapids on the Milk River are as white as the full moon," James answered.

"Clever boy! You see, Elizabeth, what a clever planter he is already. Sally, I have arranged for the two of you to visit the land behind that piece of paper you grasp so tightly. My very kind and close friend, Sir Gregor Cranston will accompany you. He owns the property adjacent to your . . . your *Moon Walk*. He arrived in Jamaica before us and has enjoyed much progress on the building of his estate."

"Wonderful! That is very kind of you to make such an arrangement so quickly . . . and provide us the opportunity to meet our neighbor. Where is his land? Can you show me on the map?" Sally asked.

Modyford unrolled three maps before he found one suitable. They all laid a hand on the corners of the map to keep it flat and hunched over to follow Sir Thomas's finger. "Now, let me see. Here is the Milk and . . . we follow it up from the sea and yes, here are your plots. Moon Walk is just there." The two circles drawn to represent the land of Moon Walk disappeared easily under a single digit of his hand. "See how the river flows northeast from the shore, then turns sharply west? This plain from the river east is the property of Sir Gregor." As his hand began to sweep over a large area of the map, Sally and James looked to one another with wide eyes. Modyford responded, "Yes, Sir Gregor holds a rather . . . significant piece of land in the Parrish of Clarendon. Like me, he was dissatisfied with the limitations in Barbados and came to this island with grander expectations and greatly expanded hopes. You will enjoy him, Sally. His manner is . . ." Thomas looked to his wife for the right word.

"Reserved?" she offered.

"Yes, that's it. Reserved. So much so as to make him appear morose to those that know him but slightly. Though, not so! He is a deep thinking man with a primitive sense of wonder. He sees the indifferent Earth in a mystical light beyond my understanding." Modyford paused, and then shook his head to refocus. "Sir Gregor has an ancient lineage and an eye for a somewhat quirky manner of fashion, though I truly think he is perfectly unconscious of it, wouldn't you agree, Elizabeth?"

Lady Modyford covered her mouth to hide a giggle and nodded. "There is certainly something about him . . . something distinct and separate from other men. He spent some time in Paris, so I think we can forgive him for his odd manner of personal décor. I am sure he will delight in looking after your investments." To her husband she said, "Why are their lands so far from Port Royal, dear? Could you not have secured a piece somewhere closer?"

"There was no property close by. Those lands had already been taken, and in some cases, snatched!" Thomas looked nervous. "I'm sorry. It was the best I could do. I had . . . promises to keep."

Sally focused on Elizabeth's comment. "What do you mean, Elizabeth? I am comforted to learn that Sir Gregor is to be my neighbor, my lady, but I am determined that we shall look after our own interests. We intend to live there, James and I. It may be a small holding, compared to many in Jamaica, but I believe it will provide for us."

"Oh my dear," Elizabeth chuckled dismissively, taking her hand away from the map and letting her corner roll. "You cannot possibly live in the wilderness on your own. The island is far from secure. This property is miles from Port Royal. You would have no protection." Seeing that her words had no impact on the girl, she looked to her husband for reinforcement. "Tell her Thomas!"

"It is not possible, Sally." Thomas used the placated tone when he did not wish to cross his wife. "At least, not now," he added quickly. "The Spanish are still quite put out for having lost the island. Even more disturbing are the reports of the slaves they abandoned with a promise of freedom if they continue to harass us. These renegades shelter in the highlands, here and here to the north of your land," he indicated on the map "and here in these mountains to the east. They are proving to be an intolerable menace to our settlers. Give me time, and I shall put this right. But for now, this first venture is a scouting expedition only. Now, on another matter, after receiving Edward Waller's recommendation on your holdings in Nevis, do you still have in mind to sell that property?"

"Yes, Sir Thomas. My brother and I have talked through each option thoroughly. Neither of us wishes to go to Nevis. We know no one there and would rather sell the property and have the money to invest here in Jamaica." Sally replied confidently.

"I believe you have made an excellent decision, the two of you! What do you think, Elizabeth?" Sir Thomas asked his wife, and then not waiting for her reply said, "I might have just the buyer."

Elizabeth stepped in front of her husband to gain his full attention. "*Will* they have enough from the sale to return to England, comfortably, if they choose?"

"Oh, heavens yes," Sir Thomas replied. "Edward said the cane lands alone have much value. Though the sugar works is quite derelict, it is partially built and retains some worth. I cannot say whether the sale would cover your uncle's debts, Sally, for I know not their extent, but you will receive a fair profit. I will lay a wager on that."

Modyford was instantly aware of his poor choice of words and quickly glanced at his wife. Her look told him that his inappropriateness had not missed her ears.

"I can only speak for myself, I no longer wish to return to England, Elizabeth," Sally declared. "I have nothing there and my memories of home are fading. At least here, in the Caribbees, James and I own property, landowners by our own rights. I understand that, someday, we may have to forfeit our land to those with whom my uncle owes money. They may have a legal right to it, but I will not surrender Moon Walk without a fight! And until they lay claim, we will reap its profits."

"There's the spirit, Sally!" Modyford proudly applauded. "If half the men have but a fraction of that high spirit, Jamaica will soon be the gem in the British crown!"

Sally took Modyford's arm and said, "Come, Sir Thomas, show me again on the maps the property for which I have such high hopes!"

Within a fortnight, Elizabeth introduced Sally and James to Sir Gregor Cranston. The extraordinary man triggered Sally's curiosity immediately. Rather than a colonial planter about to board a sloop headed for the island's untamed interior, he looked as if he had been summoned to attend the king's court. On his head, Sir Gregor wore a curled blond, powdered, and much-perfumed periwig. From his neck to his knees, he was bundled in a bright baggy coat made of fine gold brocade with breeches to match. Bleached-white boot hoses distinguished his highly polished black square-toed shoes. Stuffed into a plain wide leather belt loosely cinched around his middle were a cutlass and a pistol. In contrast to the rest of Sir Gregor's genteel appearance, his weapons looked worn and slightly tarnished . . . as if they had had many unhappy encounters.

Sally glanced at James and covertly reached out to shut the opened jaw of the astonished boy. She caught his eye, pursed her lips, raised her eyebrows, and gently shook her head to show her disapproval of his rude stares.

The party, along with four marines and a pilot departed The Point in two shallow-bottomed single-mast sloops, ideal for exploring the shoals along the coast. They carried several guns, powder, a week's supply of food and water, and each sloop towed a canoe for navigating the river.

Enamored at first by the adventure, by midday Sally grew restless as the shade, provided by the sails, narrowed. She was relieved when the pilot ordered the small boats to put into shore on a narrow sandy beach. Though quiet and reserved, Sir Gregor's manners were faultless and he displayed a genuine interest in seeing after Sally's needs. He also proved tactful and apt at pulling in the reins on James's incessant enthusiasm for exploration.

The party dined on a surprisingly civil meal and after dealing with other necessities boarded again, heading west with a wind that ran parallel to the southern shore. Sally watched the position of the sun and surmised that the craggy and convoluted coast was not at all straight, but heading slightly in a northwest direction and was distinguished by at least one large bay.

She had difficulty at first in engaging Sir Gregor in conversation. He seemed intent on taking notes and gathering navigational information. Finally, at the risk of being too forward, she boldly asked if she might have a look through his spyglass. Surprised, Gregor obliged and pointed out the larger landmarks that piqued his interests. He removed a folded map from his waistcoat pocket, a small vial of ink, and a much-shortened quill. Together they added annotations to the map as they sailed along the shore.

The sun was setting when they reached the mouth of the Milk. They dropped anchor away from shore and the navy seamen took one canoe to look for a suitable camp along the riverbank. Returning to the light from the lamps on the sloops, they reported that crocodiles and mosquitoes occupied the banks. With that account, everyone agreed to spend an uncomfortable but breezy night at sea and postponed their exploration until the dawn's first light.

The reconnaissance party of six left in the morning in two canoes, navigating only about a mile up the Milk before the rapids and falls forced them to tie up. As they continued their journey heading northeast on foot, James found a limestone outcrop that offered a far-reaching vista over the treetops and across the sloping plain of the parish that Thomas Modyford called Clarendon. It seemed to roll as far as the horizon. Gregor and Sally imagined the boundaries of their properties and satisfied, returned to the sloops before nightfall. That evening, with the two sloops tied together, the crews celebrated their journey with shanty songs and stories of privateering. James sat and listened with large round eyes and opened mouth. Gregor and Sally settled at the bow of the lighter sloop and ignored the music and laughter. They shared a bottle of wine, bread and goats cheese while they talked of the dreams they had for their plantations. Finally, they fell asleep with Sally tucked into his great yellow coat.

At first light, they set sail for The Point. Sally noticed an air of apprehension about Sir Gregor. Several times, he gestured as if to make some inquiry and then backed away. Just as they did on the outward journey, but much later in the day, they stopped along the same sheltered beach for their meal and relief. It wasn't until then that Gregor finally came out with what was on his mind.

"Miss Montague," he tried as they boarded the sloop, "that is to say, with the permission of my friend, Sir Thomas . . . Governor Thomas. I would like, that is . . . might I be permitted to call upon you . . . again . . . in Port Royal?" Gregor struggled.

Sally was shocked. Given his reputation for coyness, she did not expect him to react so boldly and so soon after their first acquaintance. She noticed the sudden silence around her and looked about to see the eyes of the sloop's mariners, all within easy earshot of Sir Gregor's plea, were upon her, waiting for her reply. However, when Sally's eyes met theirs, they quickly turned away and, pretending a complete lack of interest, fell back to their chores. Sally felt her face blush. She lowered her head, smiled, and replied in a faint whisper, "Yes, Sir Gregor, I would . . . like that." Sir Gregor was a happy man and made little attempt to disguise his elation for the rest of the journey.

It was a short but blissful courtship. Amid much construction and renovation, Sally Montague and Sir Gregor Cranston wed at the Governor's Mansion in Port Royal just before Christmas 1664. Sir Thomas Modyford presented the bride and James Montague stood beside the groom. Elizabeth cried for Sally's happiness. The match was not her first choice, but it was a good one, profitable and stable . . . a safe choice for Sally.

At thirty-one, Gregor had imagined himself to be unwed forever. In the past, his shyness and caution cost him the possibility of two engagements, once in England and the other on Barbados. The two women were both delightful in every way but one. They did not ignite his spirit and he could not imagine committing to a dispassionate relationship. After his second failure at romance, he gave up the tedious task of courting and instead dedicated his energies to his skill as a planter and cartographer. He was good at both and that satisfaction seemed enough to neutralize the loneliness, until he met Sally.

Being near Gregor did not give Sally the same intense tummy-flutters that she had in the presence of Edward. Whatever she felt for Edward would be tucked away in a secret place within her heart. She had a different kind of passion for Gregor, one spawned from the feeling of being safe and loved, and she was determined to return his affection with loyalty, affection, and humor. Gregor was there for her and willing, without hesitation, to give to her and James his protection, his love, and his home.

After the wedding, the family of three went off to Spanish Town where they rented a small cottage while they built their house and their dreams in Clarendon on a site beside a sheltered wood they called Windhaven.

CHAPTER 10

By the summer of 1664, Edward Waller's cooperage outside the little village of Sandwich on Cape Cod was finished and ready to start production. Before sailing the refitted fluyt to Portsmouth, he made one more visit to the Cape to check on the progress of the workshop.

"You are further along than I had hoped, Mr. Strangeway," Edward complimented.

"Aye, Capt'n Waller. Should be ready to roll out the first barrels in about a fortnight or two, dependin' on how long it takes for them apprentices I've taken on to figure out what they're doin'. How fares the salt?" Barnaby inquired.

"Not well. Their quota fell short . . . again. There is no shortage of cod, just the salt in which to preserve them. I am scouting for other goods to stuff into our barrels. There's quite a demand for barrels in Boston, so just keep them coming, Mr. Strangeway, and I will find a way to fill them. In the meantime, keep an eye out for opportunities while I'm gone."

"Aye, I will do just that."

"Any word on your family?" Edward asked.

"They be comin' soon enough, Capt'n Waller, they will. They'll be here afore you return. Might I ask after Miss Anani?"

"She's well, thank you for asking. I suspect she'll miss coming out to the Cape while I'm gone, but lately she seems more preoccupied with other things. I will miss her. And, I look forward to the pleasure of meeting your good wife and sons. My best to them until I return, and to you, Mr. Strangeway."

"Aye, Capt'n. We'll keep it runnin' for ya. Good sailin', sir."

Boosted by Waller's compliments, Twiggy looked forward to his first lesson with his apprentices. He took on three young lads to train in the ancient art of coopering. Two were living at the cooperage in rooms at the back of the workshop, next to Barnaby's temporary accommodation. The youngest was living with his family in the village.

In the morning, Twiggy slid the large door of the workshop open to find three shiny and eager, anticipating, and wanting faces.

"Right now lads," Twiggy started, "this here be a complicated and skilled process. Startin' with the pick of timber and careful selection of the best wood for them there staves. It makes the difference when formin' the bilge," he instructed.

"Sir?" one of boys interrupted. "What's a bilge?"

"That bulgin' shape of them barrels, that's the bilge and it serves two purposes. Imagine if this here was a cask, full to top with heavy molasses. How would ya move her, then?" The boys looked at one another.

"Don't know, sir. Would be a chore, that!" one of them dared to answer.

"Aye, and an impossible one at that, ya knuckle-head!" Twiggy replied, giving the two who didn't answer a quick slap to their heads. "Ya couldn't move it. Not with the three of ya's. So that's why they have this bulge in 'em, makes these heavy barrels a mite easier to roll. See, ya can pivot them quickly to control the direction of the roll," he demonstrated. "A watertight barrel made of heavy hardwoods can weigh nearly ten stones!"

"Now, it's my job to hand-pick them staves. Maybe one day, one of ya will be good enough to do what I do, but for now, I picks 'em. Then I hands them over to the lucky one who'll position them within this metal jig here to raise the barrel and create the 'rose'."

"A rose, sir?"

"Aye," Twiggy confirmed. "That's what we calls them staves when they are poking out in all directions, like a bloomin' rose! The maker of the rose, he has to force these three metal hoops into place to create a strong hold on them staves. That's the tricky part, lads. May take more than the rose-maker to get a hold on it and hammer them in least 'til ya skinny tadpoles puts some meat on ya!" Twiggy scoffed. "Once them staves are braced by them hoops, he hands it off to the next cooper who dampens the barrel and places it over the fire to char the insides. We calls this, toastin' the barrel."

The boys looked at one another with trepidation. Twiggy had already warned them that this is the trickiest part because the char can affect the taste of whatever is stored within the barrel. Much care had to be made to achieve the right amount of toasting.

"Heat from the fire," Twiggy continued, "dampness in the air, how much water is in the wood . . . all that helps to keep the wood flexible. Using this here winch, ya all three work together to arch them staves while moving these hoops in place to tighten the hold."

"And all this while the barrel is still over the fire?" asked one of the apprentices.

"Oh, aye! It stays over the fire 'til I says it comes off. I tells ya when the arc of the bilge is right. I tells ya when I think the staves are stable. Only then do I say the toast is right!"

"What about the top and the bottom?" the youngest asked.

"Ah, now that's your job, little mate!" Twiggy replied with a wink. "Whilst we work on the barrel, lad, you'll be preparin' them barrel heads for us. Ya be carvin' out them round disks of wood to twenty-three inches in diameter. Twenty-three mind, not a sliver larger or smaller. Once the barrel has toasted, these other lads here will trim the stave and carve a groove into the two ends. You then must measure each head to fit. Every barrel is different. We fits your bottom head in first, fill the barrel, then fits the top head. That's it, lads! One completed barrel for the shippin' of Capt'n Waller's goods!"

"What about the brand?" the smartest of the lot asked.

"That be good thinkin', lad. Good thinkin'! We burn Capt'n Waller's mark into the top head, once it's fitted proper."

It wasn't long, with Twiggy's good tutelage, before the best of the three young coopers-in-training could assemble one barrel in an about eight hours. It was a good return for the labor, but Twiggy discovered that by rotating, combining, and dividing the jobs assigned to each cooper, the team could collectively work on several barrels at a time and complete five barrels during that same eight-hour period.

"I want five a day, mates," Twiggy announced to his workers. "If you give me five good barrels in eight hours or less, then the rest of day is yours. Good barrels, mind! Nothin' sloppy for Capt'n Waller."

It was a good arrangement and the time incentive was precious to everyone. It gave the young coopers the opportunity to fish for their supper and Twiggy time to work on his cottage. When there was enough daylight left after working and fishing, the lads pitched in to help Twiggy build the home he would soon share with his wife and two sons.

Since leaving the *Gloucester*, Barnaby Tibbs enjoyed much success working for Edward Waller. He collected wood from the mill along the Charles River, oversaw the precutting of the staves, managed the warehouse at Roxbury, and ferried the wood, iron strapping, and hardware across the Bay to Twiggy's workshop on Cape Cod. However, the small café in Roxbury was his personal enterprise.

Barnaby didn't set out to open the café. Using the wages he earned serving on the *Rosa* and the *Gloucester*, he bought the cozy two-up, two-down cottage on Center Street as an investment. While living in the lower rooms, he rented the upstairs rooms to a freed black man that everyone called Fisherman Henry. In addition to rent, which was dutifully paid in full and on time each month, Henry also supplied Barnaby with fresh fish. Every morning, before Barnaby would get out of bed, Henry would row down to the mouth of the Charles and into the harbor to fish, then row back in late afternoon with the hopes of selling his catch in the market. It was Barnaby who first discovered the demand for *cooked* fish.

Rather than Henry selling his fish at market, Barnaby used his culinary talents to cook it and sell it to the steady stream of hungry people who, while traveling to Boston, stopped for the night in Roxbury. As an alternative to the more mundane food served at the boarding houses and taverns, Barnaby served up tasty spiced pan-seared fish from his home. Even with splitting the profits between them, Henry earned more in a week's time, than a month of selling his catch at market. Without the need to go to market, Henry extended his time at sea to snag greater catches.

As Barnaby's culinary reputation grew, residents of Roxbury and visitors to town began to congregate every night in the ground floor rooms of his house, forcing Barnaby to cook outside and sleep in a room upstairs. They could only accommodate two small tables in each room, but Barnby's café soon boasted a large loyal patronage. With standing room only, they crowded in to enjoy the food, to pass on gossip, and chatter about politics, the weather, and crops.

Some townsmen, unable to fit into the café, or too busy to take the time to chat with neighbors and strangers, bought Barnaby's fish directly from his make-do kitchen in the cottage's small garden. Henry managed the rooms while Barnaby did the cooking and served the backyard customers. Unable to resist the smell of the spiced fish and risking the charge of being too lazy to do their own cooking, Barnaby's neighbors, and even the owners of nearby boarding houses, surrendered to temptation and bought their supper from the café.

Having an ingrained disdain for civic constraints, Barnaby neither gave his establishment a proper name, nor secured the legal permits to run it. But the illicit café was soon so popular among the citizens of Roxbury that no one wished to challenge its validity. Everyone loved it, including the constable and the vicar. Soon the café was simply known as, Barnaby's Place.

Refusing to pay taxes on what was now clearly a business, albeit illicit, Barnaby instead paid a substantial "donation" to the Town of Roxbury. The amount was actually higher than the assessed taxes would have been and for that generous and profitable reason; authorities ignored official complaints and forgave Barnaby's delinquencies.

Some of the complaints did have merit. As the demand for his spicy fish grew, Barnaby took to cooking the fish in a large open barbeque pit, Caribbean style.

Every morning, Barnaby filled a pit with wood scraps from the mill, kindled it, covered it with a flat iron plate, and left it to smolder for most of the day. By evening, the glowing charred wood provided a perfect even heat for frying about a dozen fish at one time in rich duck fat. He and Henry built a high and sturdy thatched roof over the pit to keep it dry from the rain and snow and to reflect back some of the heat to help warm them during the chilly evenings. More than once a stray spark from the pit danced its way up to the thatch and set it afire. The newly hired town clerk noted that Barnaby's Place was precariously close to a house where the majority of the town's magazine of twenty or more barrels of powder was stored. That young clerk ran a short, but unsuccessful, campaign to shut down the café.

Barnaby did, however, make one concession to the town. The town's selectmen requested that Barnaby's Place not serve customers on the eve before and on the day of the Sabbath. He agreed, feigning that he respected the Puritan nature of the populous, when in reality, it provided the perfect excuse to spend good-weather weekends on Cape Cod with Twiggy. The two men enjoyed rowing through the salt marshes, crabbing, and fishing for cod. Occasionally, a ship would sail past the peninsula on its way to Boston's port and the scene would cause them to reminisce about their sea-going adventures.

"Ever wish ye were back at sea, then, Barnaby?" Twiggy asked.

"Nah, been 'aving a good time on shore, Twiggy, and would like to keep these here ways for awhile longer," Barnaby replied, studying his friend. "Thought ya were going to bring yer family here and settle down a bit?"

"Aye," Twiggy agreed. "Aye, they be comin' soon enough. Oh, aye. I was just askin' . . . 'bout the sea, I mean. With Capt'n Waller sailing off to England last week, well, it sort of stirred me inners a bit. Had a notion to follow him, I did."

Barnaby said no more. He knew his friend well and recognized the rising of his wanderlust. Barnaby narrowed his eyes and thought, *"This time, old friend, I ain't goin'!"*

CHAPTER 11

Just before Christmas, Edward Waller delivered the Dutch fluyt to Portsmouth and its cargo of massive oak boards from Massachusetts, most over sixteen inches in width. Though the voyage went without incident, there were rumors in Portsmouth that the plague that had ravished Holland the year before had now spread to England. Edward stayed long enough to do business with traders, and retreated from England's shores on a merchantman from Bristol Port to Bridgetown, Barbados by way of the Azores.

The ship carried a load of pig iron, linens, dyed cloth, crockery, and other finished goods. While the merchantman docked in Bridgetown to be loaded with Barbadian products of logwood, rum, and molasses, Edward found passage on a small yacht bound for Jamaica with the intent of finding his bride, Sally. He first called on his friend, Sir Thomas Modyford at the governor's house in Port Royal. Once again, the Modyfords had to break sad news to Edward.

"Sir Gregor Cranston is a good man, Edward," Thomas explained nervously. "A worthy man of honest means with a substantial plantation along the Milk River. Sally is well looked after, as is the boy." Thomas could see plainly that the news had crushed his friend. He waited for Edward to speak and when no words came, he looked to Elizabeth to ease the moment.

"They are quite well, Edward. Would you . . . like to visit them? We can go together. I would like that and you could see for yourself. James, I am sure would love to see you again," Elizabeth suggested.

"No. No, thank you, my lady. Your offer is most kind, but . . . my ship. She sails soon from Barbados. I . . .

should go there . . . to resume my duties," he answered trying to disguise his disappointment.

"Will you not stay with us, Edward?" Elizabeth asked.

"Thank you, both, you have been most generous, but I cannot. I have a prior engagement this night." It was a poor excuse and a lie, so he tried to change the subject. "I have brought more tea plants, Thomas. I will have them sent tomorrow, if that is convenient."

"Edward, I . . ." Thomas started but words failed him.

"No," Edward said putting his hand up in an apologetic manner. "I am happy for Miss Montague . . . Lady Cranston. And for James. Truly, I am. Relieved, actually, and grateful that you took such good care of them. Please, convey my congratulations."

"Why not deliver that message yourself, Edward?" Elizabeth tried once more and seeing no reaction added, "Or, perhaps a letter?"

"Yes, that might be . . . Yes, I will send it . . . with the tea plants. Thank you." And with that, Edward bowed deeply and left the governor's house. Though he tried to pen some semblance of words that expressed his happiness for the woman with whom he had hoped to spend his life, he just couldn't bring himself to lie. Not to her.

The tea plants arrived at the governor's house without a letter.

"Why do I feel we betrayed him, Thomas?" Elizabeth asked.

"We didn't know he'd be back, nor understand the extent of his affection. More importantly, *she* didn't know," Thomas reasoned.

"Nor will she. We mustn't tell her, Thomas. Not in her condition. It would only complicate things. She's happy with Gregor. Once the baby comes, she will have forgotten all about Edward Waller. Let it be."

CHAPTER 12

The contentment enjoyed by Sally and Gregor was short lived for there was a fierce urgency to clear fields, construct buildings and fences, plough, and plant. It was tough work and failures outnumbered the successes in every endeavor.

When the workload became greater than Gregor could manage, he hired a quiet but capable Welshman, Mr. Watt, to oversee the plantation and direct the building of the great house. His most challenging job was supervising the two-dozen indentured farm workers who were prone to heat exhaustion and malaise.

"Ye be better to replace this lot with half as many slaves, Sir Gregor, and ye be getting' double the work for it," Mr. Watt advised.

"No, Mr. Watt. You'll not see a slave at Windhaven," Gregor replied with a firm sense of conviction.

Mr. Watt and his wife, both devout Puritans, came to Jamaica from Barbados on one of Modyford's ships and as such were given grants to thirty acres of land each. They combined their properties at the foothills of the Blue Mountains in the eastern part of the island and presented the land as a gift to their only son who arrived with his bride from England in the autumn. Until his son's crops turned a profit, Mr. Watt thought it prudent to work another man's land for hard currency. There was also the need to keep Mrs. Watt far from their contentious and exasperating daughter-in-law. The arrangement worked well; close enough to visit occasionally yet far enough to quell the constantly sparring women and earn a good wage for themselves.

In the early days of settlement, the administration in Port Royal offered little in the way of support to the new planters of Jamaica. Modyford was determined to change that. He struggled to organize a government and to define the rights of privilege to those who served on the House of Assembly. Unlike the House of Commons in England, on which Jamaica based its elected governing body, the assembly took on additional responsibilities of administering revenues and authorizing the Governor to draw funds. The assembly was often at odds with the appointed council members over privilege and limits of their respective powers.

Due to the construction in Port Royal, the location of Jamaica's first assembly was Spanish Town. Rich in vulgarity and excessive drinking, the meeting was quite jovial in nature. Though it failed to pass a single piece of legislation, the council members were surprisingly congenial.

However, the second assembly, convened in Port Royal, proved to have none of the flavor of the first. Its members threw hostile words and combative gestures at one another. An argument over taxation grew so violent that Captain Ritter of the assembly engaged Major Joy of the council in a mortal altercation. Modyford immediately dissolved the assembly . . . indefinitely.

To add to the uncertainty and angst of established rule in the colony, word of a rampant plague in London reached the islands in the summer of 1665. The fear of spreading the disease to the colonies and disarray in London brought commerce to a standstill and that started a long period of deep recession throughout the Caribbean.

By autumn, the dreaded Bills of Mortality arrived from England listing the names of over sixty-eight thousand dead. There was hardly an Englishman in

Jamaica who did not know or was not related to someone on the list of the dead. The sadness conflicted sharply with one of the happiest events at Windhaven, the birth of Molly Cranston.

Nearly a year after the news of the plague, a letter from London addressed to Sally and James arrived at Windhaven. It was covered with sooty fingerprints and smelled heavily from the acrid smoke used to treat documents suspected of being touched by the afflicted. Sally broke the seal, cautiously unfolded the letter, and read it aloud.

July 1665, London
To Sally and James Montague –

My dearest children of William my sweet dead brother I write this letter to inform you that by the charity of our Lord I will soon once more be with him, your dear mother, my two blessed wives and our children. Though by God's good grace I still breathe I am shut up in this inn where seven others have already died of this wretched and horrible malady. The doors are nailed shut and only opened again by a paid guard who allows the passage of a woman, a kind poorly paid nurse who crosses the painted red X at great risk to herself to bring porridge and beer to the wretched few of us who yet draw breath. I suspect her official purpose is to count the dead inside. There is no milk for the porridge for alas there is no one left to milk the cows. It does not matter for I have lost the desire to eat. The innkeeper seems to have retained his health and has shown us nothing but great kindness though he is locked in this same prison of death. The summer's heat is harsh and thousands have taken to living on boats on the Thames believing isolation on the water will spare them from the miasmas of poisonous air. Nearly as bad as the sound of good people suffering are the screams and yelps of wretched dogs and cats. Men with clubs roam the streets to kill any on sight believing them to be agents of this pestilence. This cruel campaign to eradicate the beasts has not stopped the spread among people and has only caused an increase in the vermin they eat. Rats scurry about feeding on the dead. Fires are lit each night and day trusting the fumes will counter the mal air. God has shown us no mercy and yet I pray for your forgiveness. Forgive me, dear children. Forgive a foolish man who in his dealings with the devil has condemned thee to great hardships.

The letter ended abruptly without closure or signature. Added to the bottom of the letter and written in a different and untrained hand were the words:

Robert Montague gest Swan Inn ded and takn to pleg pit west wol. St. Giles-in-the-Fields London 10 of Augest 1665

"Uncle Robert!" Sally was surprised and confused.

"What does this mean, Sally?" James asked. "What is a plague pit? I do not understand, I thought Uncle Robert lived in Gloucestershire. Why was he in London? Where is his wife? What does he mean by asking forgiveness? What for? Is he dead? Have we no family now?"

"No mention was made of his wife," Sally replied patiently, re-reading the letter. "Odd, I have quite forgotten her name. We must assume that providence has spared her. I do forgive Uncle Robert his indiscretions for he is the very reason why we are here. It is I who should be forgiven for I never wrote to him to tell him how happy this accident of fate has made us. And we do have family, James. Our family is here. You, Gregor, Molly and me . . . and soon another!"

James showed no signs of comprehending. He continued to play war games with his little tin soldiers.

"Do you not understand what I said? I am going to have another baby, James." Sally declared softly.

"Already?" James blurted, still rather disengaged.

Sally was surprised for a moment. She raised an eyebrow and asked, "Are you not happy by this news, brother?"

"Yes. Do you know what I heard this morning? I met an old seaman who went pirating with Henry Morgan to Grenada. He said . . ."

"Hush!" Sally was irritated. "I wish not to hear those wretched stories, James. It is a sinful thing they do. Buccaneers, pirates, privateers! It matters not what they call themselves, or what Letters of Marque they carry. They steal and hurt people. Do you understand that? They are criminals who profit from sin!"

"Thomas Modyford said," James continued, ignoring his sister, "it's the pirates who are keeping *us* alive, Sally. Nothing comes from England, now. Everyone is afraid of the Black Death and the war with the Dutch. Down at the Three Turtles, the sailors are saying the Dutch are to blame for the plague. They filled a ship with slaves, all dead from the plague, and sailed it up the Thames, right into the heart of London. Thomas said it is the pirates that keep the Spanish from taking back this island. What is a plague pit?"

"I suspect it is a common grave. When too many poor unfortunate souls die at once, it overwhelms the gravediggers and becomes necessary to dig one large grave. I told you to stay away from the taverns, James. Those old thieves fill you ears with untruths and romanticize the evils of their unholy ventures. Now go fetch your Latin book. I fear you are a good deal behind in your studies." Sally knew that much of what James said was straight from the lips of Thomas Modyford or Gregor, subjects dropped from the conversation when she was present due to her delicate condition. James returned with his Latin grammar book.

"Sally," he asked thoughtfully "Is the sea a common grave pit?"

She was surprised by the question. "Yes, I suppose it is. Latin!" she answered pointing to the book.

"Why must I learn this language? No one but priests speak it. Might it be better to learn Spanish or French? Then, if I am ever captured by them, I would understand their evil plots."

"And so, dear James, you shall. Latin is the mother of both languages. Master it, and the others will be easier," Sally proposed.

Later that evening, when Gregor returned from Windhaven, Sally showed him the letter.

"This and another letter were delivered this morning by our kind neighbor, Mr. Weatherstone. Wasn't that thoughtful of him, Gregor? This letter . . . I am not sure what to make of it." Sally stopped for a moment to allow Gregor time to read.

"Your uncle is dead," Gregor said in such a way that Sally could not decide if he was asking or declaring it a fact.

"How sad" Sally remarked, "to have died in such a horrible manner. When last I saw my dear uncle, he was one step from debtors' prison and I thought poorly of him. I am sorry for that now. Apparently, he managed to avoid prison for a more gruesome end. Do you suppose his debtors will continue to pursue their quest and seek compensation through you or me?"

Gregor chuckled. "These islands are populated with gentlemen . . . and women . . . who escaped the long reach of a British magistrate's arm, Sally. No, the holders of those loans no doubt find the colonies much too profitable to chase after the very ones who keep their pockets filled. But this letter is puzzling. On what matter of business was he in London and St. Giles-in-the-Fields of all places – hardly a place for a gentleman. Why did he not leave whilst he could? How is that this letter took a year to reach you?" Gregor asked, not expecting an answer. He read the letter again. "I have a friend who works at the Royal Exchange, not far from St. Giles-in-the-Fields. I trust him to be discrete. Would you permit me to write to him regarding the circumstances of your uncle's death?" Gregor asked.

"Ah, yes please, Gregor. That would greatly ease my mind. I am most concerned about the fate of his third wife. I do not consider her my aunt, or the wife before her. However, that does not diminish my concern for her well being," Sally replied. "The letter speaks nothing of her welfare."

"I will make inquiries to her whereabouts and nature."

"I am ashamed to say this, dear husband, though I have committed much thought to remembering, I cannot recall her name. I hardly knew her before we sailed . . ."

Gregor laughed. "I will write the letter in such a manner as to disguise that deficiency. Do not trouble yourself so," he glanced around the room to make sure they were alone and came close to his wife. He gently put his hand on her belly.

"There is little to feel. I have barely a bump," Sally whispered.

"He will grow soon enough!" Gregor replied with a broad grin.

"He?"

"Or she." Gregor corrected. "It matters not to me, Sally. Though I confess, it would be good to carry the Baronetcy onto another generation of Cranstons, but it seems to me providence has already provided us with perfect issue in our Molly and I will not tempt fate by wishing for a boy. Whatever God has provided us, I am thankful."

Gregor wrote the letter of inquiry to Mister John Applethorpe at the Royal Exchange and delivered it in person to the captain of *HMS Assistance*, a 40-gun fourth rate frigate of the Royal Navy that was sailing from The Point in a week's time. The letter made its way to St. Kitts where the captain of the *Assistance* transferred it to the captain of the *Patience*, a merchant ship that sailed more directly to England. The *Patience* arrived at Portsmouth harbor five weeks later where the letter, with many others, was taken by barge to London. A courier took it on its final journey to the Royal Exchange. They received Sir Gregor's letter late Saturday. It sat in the letter room until early Monday, the 3rd of September 1666, when a young lanky clerk with an awkward gait and foolish grin took up the letter and read its addressee. Normally, his job would be to pass the letter onto to the appropriate senior clerk who would then deliver it directly to the hands of its beneficiary, Mister John Applethorpe on the second floor. However, that Monday was not a typical day. The senior clerk in charge of the second floor mail was absent from his station. In fact, many workers, from lowly clerks to the top management of the Royal Exchange did not come to work that day. A fire, started in the King's bakery on Pudding Lane just after midnight on Sunday, flared and threatened many houses along the Thames. By dawn Monday morning, Londoners woke to see the clouds tinged with orange, not from the rising sun, but from the flames consuming a sizable area around London Bridge. As the air along the waterfront blackened with smoke, there were rising concerns that the fire might spread beyond the ability of authorities to contain it. Many Londoners opted to stay close to their families and homes to pack their treasures in case there was a need to quickly abandon their property.

The young clerk at the Royal Exchange, however, was not about to jeopardize his new position as dispatcher over a contentious fire. Eager to impress his employers, he arrived to work early and was soon rewarded with this rare opportunity to demonstrate his competency at the more challenging endeavor of delivering the mail. The clerk took the letter up the winding steps to the second floor. The intended recipient was not at his desk, so the clerk carefully positioned the letter towards the center of the desk, propped up slightly so that the addressee would not fail to see it upon his return.

From the corner of his eye, the clerk caught the unusual movement of people running. Considered vulgar and disruptive, the act of running in the Exchange was strictly forbidden. As he turned to inquire about the commotion, he saw through the windows on the south side of the building ominous orange and yellow flames dancing high above the skyline. The clerk froze in a stupor of disbelief. London was burning. A man, frightened and quite breathless, ran through the halls shouting for everyone to evacuate the Exchange. The few employees left in the building rushed around gathering important papers and shoving them into satchels. The clerk looked wildly about the desks and wondered what he should save. Deciding the best option was to save himself, the redheaded lad snatched the letter he had just delivered and scrambled frantically down the stairs and out onto the street now full of people screaming and running in panic.

Kindled by dilapidated wooden houses, bone dry from the long summer's drought, the fire was hopelessly out of control. Winds carried droplets of flames and hot embers along the river, west, and north in the direction of the Royal Exchange and by Tuesday, all that was left of the building was a smoking shell.

CHAPTER 13

In the Caribbean, the crushing economic impact of London's losses to the fire aggravated an already serious recession brought on by the plague and made worse by several devastating hurricanes. Crashing through the islands, the storms sunk ships, shredded vegetation, and flooded low-lying fields of cane and cotton. By the winter of 1666, Jamaica suffered shortages of food and other supplies.

Severely damaged by the great winds of the late summer storms, Sir Gregor scrapped the unfinished house at Windhaven and began to rebuild it from the foundation. Blight destroyed most of the first cacao saplings at Moon Walk and in an effort to contain the infestation Mr. Watt burned the remaining trees.

"We'll plant new trees over on the bluff, here behind the house away from the diseased ground," Gregor instructed Mr. Watt while studying the map of his property.

"May be difficult finding them saplings, Sir Gregor," Mr. Watt warned. "Seems like this here blight has affected the whole island, despite measures to stop it."

"Then we'll have to trade for them from Barbados or Nevis. Has it affected their trees?"

"Haven't heard. I'll ask about down at the Three Turtles, sir," Mr. Watt replied. "Somebody will know."

"Tis a rotten year, Mr. Watt. Even if we take in a harvest of cotton this year, the port lacks the ships to transport it to England or any other country," Gregor fretted.

"Aye, but at least we are all in the same boat as the other planters, Sir Gregor," Mr. Watt retorted.

Gregor stared at his foreman trying to determine whether this Puritan was, in fact, attempting humor. "See what you can find out at the Three Turtles, Mr. Watt. And if you see young James there, do pull the lad out by his ears!"

"Aye, sir. And, might I ask how the lady fares?" Mr. Watt inquired.

"I wish I could say she is doing well, but Lady Cranston has not had an easy time with this pregnancy, not as the first. She has been quite ill for the last four months. The ladies who attend her, they keep telling me that all is well, but . . ."

"If God permits it, all will be well," assured Mr. Watt.

"Yes, I suppose," Gregor replied vaguely.

The great house at Windhaven received its final structural addition in January. Still a diamond in the rough, at least the rooms were done and just in time for Sally to give birth to a tiny baby boy much earlier than expected. The baby was not well. He seemed to struggle to breathe and had an alarming blue hue to his skin that in the following days faded to a sickly yellow. Fearing she might lose the baby, Sally refused to allow herself a close attachment. It was an impossible feat. Every time Sally held the baby to her breast, she surrendered her love to him completely.

Christened, Michael, the tiny baby lost his struggle to live. Sally was inconsolable. Even during the sickness of her pregnancy, she rose at the crack of dawn to meet the challenges of the day, but now she moped in her bed until well into the afternoon. She barely showed an interest in Molly. If she ate at all it was the evening meal, alone in her bedroom. Gregor did his best to mend his wife's broken heart, but found it difficult to mask his own grief over the loss of his son and heir. Recognizing the need for each to be alone, Gregor invented some pretense of business in Port Royal and left immediately following the hasty burial.

Eventually Sally pulled herself from the confines of her bedroom and began the slow pace of recovery. She could no longer ignore the needs of her daughter, Windhaven's perishable inventories, James's education, and the mundane decisions related to the workings of the plantation. Yet, her physical care and appearance lagged.

One day, about a week after Gregor had left, Sally sat with Molly on her lap on the verandah. Still dressed in her nightdress and robe, they were enjoying a gentle morning breeze that caught the spent petals of a nearby tree, sending them high into the air. The wind suddenly cut and the white petals fluttered back to the ground like falling snow causing Molly to shriek with laughter. Sally followed the petals with her eyes until she notice two figures on the horizon riding toward the house. Though their pace was slow and not threatening, she shouted for her house servant, Lucy. By the time Lucy arrived on the verandah, Sally had recognized the smaller rider as James.

"It looks like James has brought visitor, Lucy. See to Molly, and bring some refreshments for our guest, whoever he is."

It was an effort for Sally to rise from her chair, as if some horrible force kept pushing against her struggles to return to the land of living. She tightened the belt of the loosely knitted robe and walked down the steps of the verandah to greet them.

"Look who I found fumbling around the property, Sally!" James cried with delight. The gentleman removed his wide brimmed straw hat and bowed while still in the saddle.

"Edward!" Sally exclaimed, now embarrassed by her attire.

"I met Sir Gregor at governor's house in Port Royal, Sally," Edward Waller explained as he dismounted. "He told me you were not well, so I thought I would come to jostle you back to happiness."

James led the horses away and Edward took the moment to express his sympathies.

"Thank you, Edward. It isn't just the loss of our son, you understand," she searched for all the ills bestowed upon her in an effort to give credence to her extended period of mourning. "We have had such a horrific year. All our hopes, our dreams! How much worse can it be?"

"Self-pity does not become you, Sally. I've come from England and I assure you, for so many it is worse, much worse."

"You shock me, sir. I expected your understanding, or at least a thin thread of compassion."

"And you have that, madam, but it's time to put away your tears. Look what you have, Sally! A family, this land, your youth and, I pray, your good health. You can rebuild, start again. Have more children."

"What brings you to Jamaica?" Sally tried to change the subject.

"Indigo. I pick up a shipment from Port Royal and wanted to visit Jamaica's distinguished governor and his wife."

"With no plans to visit us?"

Edward squirmed at the question. He wasn't sure if Sally knew that he had been to these shores three times since her marriage. He was grateful to be interrupted by Lucy arriving with a tray full of jingling cups and a steaming kettle. "Chocolate," she announced with a grin.

"Lucy, please show Captain Waller the guest room. I am certain he will want to freshen before his drink," Sally said without taking her eyes from Edward. He bowed and followed Lucy into the house. When James returned to the verandah from the stables, Sally grabbed his shirtsleeve. "Where did you find him?" she asked excitedly.

"Down by the creek. He was riding one of Mr. Simpson's old nags and the beast was leading him the wrong way. I think it would have been night time before he located us," James chuckled. Sally did not see the humor and waited for more. "He was coming to see you, dear sister. He said Gregor was concerned about your well-being and thought a visit might be in order. Are you not pleased to see him again, after all these years?" James was teasing Sally, an art he had perfected in his dozen years. "You know, I hardly recognized him. He seems . . . shorter than the captain of my memories." James shrugged and proceeded to eat the biscuits Lucy had put out for Edward. "Anyway, at least he got you up out of that chair. Where's Molly?"

"Thank you for your hospitality, Lady Cranston," Edward interrupted as he returned looking less dusty. "I sailed to the Milk on a small sloop belonging to a turtler from Port Royal. I believe the man wishes to create a pen for his turtles. He's exploring the seas around the mouth of the river and plans to return to the Point tomorrow, so my visit is, unfortunately, short. I hope you don't mind, your daughter was crying. I entered her room and settled her. She's beautiful, Sally. She has your hair and eyes."

"Good thing," James laughed. "You've seen Gregor's or was he wearing his wig?"

"James!" Sally scolded.

"Forgive me, do I hear Lucy calling?" he replied mockingly and ran into the house.

"He becomes more incorrigible by the day," Sally excused. "I am glad you met my daughter. Her name is Molly. And tell me, Captain Waller, how is *yours*?"

Unaware of Sally's misunderstandings, now so many years ago, he answered in the tone of a proud father. "Ah, Anani has become . . . a beauty! She still attends school, though this is her last year as there does not seem to be a school for young women beyond her age."

"How old would that be?"

"Fifteen."

Sally shot him a look, recalling that *she* was fifteen when she first met Edward on the *Rosa*. They both sat down and she was about to inquire about the mysterious Anani further when Mr. Watt ran towards the verandah breathless and shaken. Lucy, ever patrolling what she considered her turf, placed her hands on her hips and challenged Mr. Watt's intentions.

"Now, Mr. Watt, you knows you ain't comin' dis close wit' Miss Sally not fully dressed," Lucy complained.

"Miss Lucy, I gotta see her. I need her. She has to tell me what to do," Mr. Watt insisted.

"Hmmm! I tolds the man, madam, he has no business being here on this verandah. I tolds him that, but here he is!" Lucy protested, but allowed Mr. Watt access. Sally shook her head and rolled her eyes. She grew wary of their constant sparring.

"Lady Cranston!" Mr. Watt beckoned from the steps. "Lady Cranston, there is a matter of urgency in the barn. It requires your immediate assistance."

Sally looked at Edward puzzled and surprised. "In the barn? What is it, Mr. Watt?" she asked rising from her chair and pulling the robe up around her neck. "Cannot this 'urgency' await Sir Gregor's return?"

"Madam, I would not ask you to come if it were not of immediate importance," Mr. Watt declared. "We must deal with the matter . . . now!"

Seeing that her foreman was determined to keep the matter a mystery, Sally relented, "I'll come along, Mr. Watt. Edward, do you mind?"

"Yes, perhaps I had better accompany you, Lady Cranston," he agreed.

"Now, Mr. Watt, what matter is so urgent?" Sally demanded, regretting even more that she was not properly dressed.

He said nothing, but pointed and went off in the direction of the barn. The door of the barn was closed and Mr. Watt moved his face along its surface, peering through the cracks in the wood. Satisfied, he pulled the door back slowly and defensively.

There on the straw-covered floor, a negro man lay bleeding and breathless. His lower leg was bent at a sickening angle and his face, covered with sweat, was greatly distorted with pain. Sally concealed her mouth in an effort to stifle her loud gasp. She looked shocked at Mr. Watt.

"Ah, no, my lady! I had no part in this! Tis how I found him," Mr. Watt defended.

Edward took command immediately. He removed his coat, rolled his sleeves up to his elbows, and knelt beside the wounded man. "Get Miss Lucy, Lady Cranston. Tell her to bring some linens and water. And bring the lye soap. And tell her I need needles and thread," Edward kept adding. Sally stood frozen, her hand still covering her mouth. Hearing no motion, Edward turned and stood to position himself between the injured man and

Sally to gain her attention. "He'll be be fine, Sally. It looks like he has broken his leg. Mr. Watt, have you whiskey?"

"I abstain from the drink of the devil, sir, but I know where Sir Gregor keeps his flasks."

"Then take Lady Cranston and fetch it." As the two ran back to the house, Edward remembered to shout after them, "And have Miss Lucy put water on the fire!"

Sally returned to the barn breathless, carrying a basket of implements and potions to mend the man's torn flesh. She approached cautiously.

"Who are you?" Sally asked the man. He did not answer, but panted heavily, and looked wildly about. "Are you a slave? Do you speak English?"

He responded in a raspy low voice. "I am no slave! I am a free man!"

"Can you prove that?" Sally felt immediately foolish asking such a question, but her worries concerned the slave hunters who might be after the man.

"No, madam, I carry nothin' to prove I am freed."

Sally hesitated, and then guardedly knelt beside Edward to help him dress the wounds. He carefully removed the torn leggings to examine his broken leg. Sally gasped again. Through the large gash along the front of his calf, the cream colored jagged ends of two bones poked through the bloody pulp. Along side the bone was a vessel that pulsed with blood.

Edward declared, "It is a miracle that these broken bones have not severed that vessel. You must restrain your movements," he whispered to the man. He looked up to see a puffing and pale Mr. Watt carrying a large jug of rum. "Good job, Mr. Watt. We must set these bones back to their correct position and cauterize this wound. He will need the assistance of those spirits." Lucy arrived with a repair kit in hand and a bucket of steaming water.

"Do you know this man?" Sally looked to both Lucy and Mr. Watt. They shook their heads. "Who are you? What is your name?" Sally asked the man again.

"I am Nero. I am a freed man," he claimed, and then fell back unconscious.

"Now, that's a mercy! I'll heat up the rod, sir," Mr. Watt said to Edward.

For the remainder of the afternoon, the four of them worked tirelessly to mend the bones and flesh of Nero. When at last they were satisfied that their patient was stable, they left Mr. Watt in the barn to attend to Nero's needs through the night.

On the way back to the house, Edward looked at his bloody hands and asked, "Is it always this dramatic at Windhaven?"

Combining an exhausted sigh with a nervous laugh, Sally replied simply, "Yes!"

James was peacefully playing with Molly and Lucy was frantically instructing the kitchen staff on the details for a quick evening meal. Sally and Edward went to their respective bedrooms to clean up for dinner. It was only then that Sally looked long and hard at her face in the reflection glass. A stranger stared back, haggard and old looking. Her hair was a mess. It was pulled back in a tight braid carelessly wrapped at the crown of her head with flyaway stragglers that dangled across her forehead and cheekbones. She slowly removed her nightdress, soiled with Nero's blood and dust from the barn. Aside from darkened places where her flesh was exposed to raw sunlight, the rest of her was in good order. Childbirth had barely distorted her figure. She retained her feminine curves and her breasts, though no longer swollen with milk, stood upright and firm. "Salvageable," she mused, "with a bit of care."

It was over an hour before Sally descended the stairs to the gaping mouths of James and Edward. She wore a salmon-colored satin dress trimmed in blue cotton lace that she herself had dyed and crocheted. The dress reflected the prevailing style of voluminous elbow-length pleated sleeves and a long bodice front that ended in a point over a plain blue-dyed cotton shift. Her dark hair, oiled and shiny, was parted down the middle and held back behind her ears with two silver combs. Soft ringlets, resting on her shoulders, framed the pearl choker around her neck.

"My lady," Edward announced with a deep bow. Taking her hand as she managed the last steps, Edward beamed, "You are a vision!"

"It was good of you to come, Edward. You have jolted me from my doldrums!" she replied.

"I can take no credit for your beauty, madam. And as for my visit, it seems it has been over-shadowed by the strange circumstances of this day. I hope you will soon solve its mysteries."

"Finally, she's dressed!" James snarled.

They had, at last, time for a lengthy conversation and had only just started the second course of the meal when there came a shout from the front door.

"I'm home!" It was Gregor. Sally immediately felt a flush of deep contradictions. She was, of course, happy at the sound of her husband's voice, but at the same time she felt as if she had just been caught committing an act of impropriety. She was profoundly disappointed that she would not have that conversation with Edward and feared she might never again have the opportunity.

After cordial greetings by all, Gregor joined the feast and announced, "My dearest Sally, you look splendid!

Splendid! And, no doubt, your spirits will be lifted higher when I tell you the welcoming news from Port Royal. Shops are full and the House of Assembly meets once again. It is proving to be more progressive than ever before. And best of all, there appears to be a complete recovery of commerce. Port Royal is bustling. Yours is not the only ship anchored off the Point, Edward." Gregor sat down at the table and borrowed James's bread plate to fill for his dinner. "Forgive me, I am famished! Of course," he continued between mouthfuls, "once again, we have the Dutch to thank for this new prosperity. They are trying to snatch Suriname from England's grasp. Forgive me, but England's loss will be Jamaica's gain! It can only mean higher demand and thus, higher prices for our Jamaican goods! Now, what's happened here in my absence?" Gregor stopped eating and waited for a reply.

There was an uneasy silence. Eyes flashed to one another and for a moment, and only a moment, Gregor wondered how Edward had managed to return the spark to his wife's eye. And just as quickly as the thought had risen, he dismissed his flare of jealousy.

James smacked his hand on the table and snatched the advantage. Completely unrestrained, he took great delight in telling Gregor about the mysterious man in the barn. Sally harped in occasionally to dampen James's exaggerated account and Edward offered what assurances and facts as he could.

"Well!" Gregor pushed back his chair. "I suppose I should investigate this, but perhaps it would be better to leave our . . . unexpected guest to his recovery and will see to him in the morning. My word! I am indebted to you, Captain Edward. Your presence, I am sure, provided some measure of comfort to Sally. I do not possess the knowledge to repair such a severe wound. How is it you do?"

"Survival aboard His Majesty's vessels necessitates such learning, Sir Gregor," Edward replied.

"Aye. I suppose so. Indeed . . ."

For the rest of the meal, the discussion turned to a lively blend of politics, commerce, and fashion. When the pudding was finished and the plates removed, the party retreated to the comforts of the reception room. Lucy brought Molly down to be cuddled before her sleep. It was Sally's custom to sing to her daughter after dinner, but in her grief, she had stopped the practice.

"I feel that I have neglected you, my poor girl," Sally whispered to Molly as she began to sing a soft melodious tune. The two men puffed on their pipes contently and James relaxed as they all enjoyed the song.

'Well!" Gregor suddenly announced, "I have suffered an exhausting journey and must beg your forgiveness, Edward, for retiring so early. James, it may be wise for you to do the same. I will need your assistance tomorrow. I'll take Molly, Sally." Gregor scooped the baby into his arms.

"I will follow, shortly, my dear, after I've made sure Edward is comfortable."

"No, please my darling. Stay. No doubt you two have much to catch-up on. Good night Edward. I will see you at breakfast."

They were alone at last. It was what she wanted. Why then would the words that burned in her heart for so many years not come?

The silence was long and awkward, broken only when Edward spoke of the humorous misadventures of Twiggy and Barnaby. Her laughter eased the tension. Edward began to share with her his dreams and all the wonders he had seen and heard on his adventures. As the hours ticked by, Sally, too, loosened her inhibitions enough to divulge the happy times she had with Gregor, of the successes and failures at Windhaven, the pleasures of Molly, her frustrations with James, and even the strange letter she received from her uncle. They reminisced of their time on the *Rosa* and for a moment, it seemed she was that young girl again . . . on the decks of the *Rosa*, hanging on Edward's every word.

"I wonder what happened to that awful captain?" Sally asked.

"The day I left him in Bridgewater was the last I saw or heard of Captain Blake," Edward replied. "He wasn't all that bad, Sally. A tough old goat, but I think there was something there, deep in his nature . . ." The room went silent again until he said in a low nearly inaudible voice, "I came back for you, Sally."

"Sorry?"

"But, I was . . . too late."

"When?"

Edward rose from his chair and paced. He said nothing.

"I didn't know, Edward."

"Sally, you've done well – your family, this plantation. You and James are . . . thriving and I am . . . most relieved and happy for you. I want you to believe that."

Sally stood, but did not approach. "Edward, I . . ."

Edward raised his hand to stop her words. He swallowed hard. "It is late, Lady Cranston, and a proper time for me to retire." He came to her, took her hand, and for a long while held it tight while he stared into her soft eyes. Finally, he bowed low. His lips came within a hair of her tender hand. Sally felt his warm breath and reached out to touch his cheek, but he rose suddenly and in an instant, he was gone.

Sally stood in that empty room for quite some time. She brought her hand, the one he had taken, pressed it against her cheek and kept it there until a tear rolled onto it. "Oh Edward," she whispered.

In the morning, Mr. Watt introduced Gregor to the prostate and feverish Nero. Sally, fully dressed and eager to fall into her routine again, joined her husband in the barn. Together they were able to ascertain the story of Nero's circumstance. He came to Windhaven to steal a cow so that he might present a dowry worthy of a woman he intended to marry. Thinking it would be easier to steal one from the barn, Nero risked slipping through the open door. When he saw there were no cows in the barn, he climbed up to the loft to get a better look over the fields. A loose floorboard in the loft resulted in his nearly fatal fall. After hearing Nero's story, the three retreated outside the barn to discuss the matter.

"Can he be moved to quarters better than the barn's floor Mr. Watt? Perhaps, with our new demands on the land, we might consider hiring this man," Gregor suggested.

"Aye," he replied with reservation, "we'll be needing more hands for the plantin'. There's work aplenty. But, Sir Gregor, we have much reason to doubt this man's integrity. After all, he did come to the barn to steal a cow!"

To purchase a wife," Sally defended.

"Beggin' yer pardon, Lady Cranston, but stealin' is stealin'," Mr. Watt argued. "And this here negro . . . he'd be a cripple for some time. Don't know how good he'd be as a hand. But . . . ah . . . "

Gregor knew Mr. Watt enough to recognize when he was holding back. "Speak up, Mr. Watt, what's on your mind," he demanded.

"Aye. There is something about him, Sir Gregor. Last night, talkin' with him, well . . . He's like no other slave I've come across. He talks . . . well, like a gentleman who's had some learnin', sir."

"What?"

"Aye, Sir Gregor, and he can read. And he shows much remorse for what he'd plan to steal. I believe that is a man who should be forgiven his sins."

Gregor rubbed the back of his neck, cocked his head to one side, and studied his wife. He was momentarily distracted by her beauty and so relieved to see the return of her high spirits. "And we are certain that he is not a runaway," he continued.

"As certain as we can be, by his word, Sir Gregor," Mr. Watt replied. "Captain Waller and me, we discovered his back has met a whip before, but them scars are old. He said he was once a slave to the A-Rabs and then to a Greek who freed him for saving his life. That's what he claimed, Sir Gregor. Captain Waller, he spoke to Nero in Greek and Nero answered, enough to satisfy the captain that his story be true."

"Hmmm. Extraordinary. Mr. Watt, I see no reason to keep us from adding him to the payroll and see to it that he is quickly on his feet or he may never walk again! Oh, and Captain Waller will be leaving after breakfast. Have Simpson's nag saddled and ready."

"Beggin' yer pardon, Sir Gregor, but the captain, he rode out just after dawn on that old horse. He left a letter . . . with Miss Lucy."

Sally said nothing. She was, to some extent relieved for she knew neither what she would say to him nor how she might react at another parting.

As they walked together back to the house, in that rare quiet moment to themselves before the rest of the household awoke, Gregor spun Sally around and pulled her into his chest. He put his arms around her and gave her a long unrestrained embrace.

"It's good to be back, Sally," he whispered. "It's good to have my Sally back."

CHAPTER 14

The ambush was set. Two boys muffled their breathy giggles in the crooks of their elbows while another watched their intended victim approach by poking his head around the wall just far enough to get a good view down Port Royal's High Street.

"Shhh! He's coming!" whispered the watch as he pulled his body in to hide fully behind the wall with the others. Across the street, a baker struggled to roll a heavy barrel through his shop's doorway. He stopped for a moment, shielding his eyes with his hand to focus on the boys. He glanced down the road to identify their target. The baker shook his head and moved his lips. He turned his back to the street and continued to push the barrel.

The drunk, unaware of the looming attack, stumbled about on the muddy street now steaming in the sun after a short morning rain. He muttered an old sea chant waving his arms to lay emphasis on a story only he understood. As he approached the corner, the boys jumped out to pelt the unstable man with mud pies and fresh horse dung. The drunkard fell, but the attack continued with more ferociousness. The timeworn man cursed as he fought to right himself. People near him stopped briefly then, ignoring the mayhem, went about their business. Encouraged by the lack of adult interference, the boys escalated the attack using their bare feet to inflict further cruelty. The man mustered enough energy and rage to let out a horrific roar. He struggled to his knees and threw his clenched fists high above his head. The boys stopped. Another roar accompanied by putrid spittle sent them running. Bruised and fouled, the man slowly dropped his hands to his side. A cloud darkened the street as another gentle drizzle of rain fell. Still on his knees, the drunkard raised his face skyward and began to sob while tiny droplets washed over his face, carrying the red mud in thin narrow streaks through his long knotted gray hair. The dampness heightened the odor of the dung. He tried to wash it from his face and in doing so, revealed something to the woman who had stopped to stare.

"Captain Blake?" Sally challenged. "It is you, Captain Wallace Blake, is it not?"

The old man said nothing. Still on his knees, he gazed up at Sally, twisting his head back and forth trying to identify her. Unsuccessful, he raised his arms again. This time the roar caught in his throat and choked. He coughed, retched, and finally vomited. Sally jumped back in time to spare her skirts. The baker renewed his attention from his doorstep.

"He be giving ye trouble, me lady?"

"No. No, sir, there is no trouble here. I believe I know this man," she shouted back.

"Stay clear of that poxy trash, me lady, for fear he do ye harm."

Ignoring the baker, Sally bent low over the man. "Can you get up?" The old man answered with another bout of vomiting. "You, sir!" Sally shouted to the baker. "Can you help me?"

"I'll not touch 'im, me lady. No one would buy me goods if I laid a hand on that filth."

"Sir, please. He needs to come off the road, at least out of this rain. Can you spare some charity to help me?"

"I say leave 'im! How came ye to know a maggot like that?" the baker shouted.

"I believe this man is Captain Blake. Please, can you help?" Sally was annoyed when she saw the baker ignore her pleas and step back into his shop. She wanted to curse him – loudly!

"I will help, Miss," offered one of the boys who participated in the attack.

Sally glared for a moment at the boy. She knew the lad, Penelope Hugh's youngest child.

"Willy Hugh! Why would you taunt this man, so? Never mind. I am grateful for your change of heart for I am in need of your kind assistance."

Together, they managed to drag the distraught captain to the street's edge. She gave the boy a coin from her purse with instructions to fetch her driver and wagon from the smith's shop. Willy Hugh took the coin with a half grin and a glint in his eye, then seeing the state of the man, handed it back to Sally.

"I'll fetch Nero for ya, Lady Cranston, but not for money I don't deserve," Willy said and ran down the street to McNicol's blacksmith's shop.

Sally smiled at Willy's sudden redemption. The rain stopped again, the clouds parted, and a hot sun quickly filled the air again with a sticky steamy dampness. She removed her bonnet and shaking it vigorously, looked down at the barely breathing heap. Though his face had egregiously changed, his deep dark intense eyes gave her an unmistakable clue to his identity. Indeed, this horrible little man before her was once the captain of the *Rosa*. She swooned at his stench and fought off the awful memories of that fateful voyage five years ago. Twice she felt it right to leave this man to the gutter and the third notion had an even stronger resolve. She was about to step away, when a woman with a heavy scent of lavender touched her arm.

"Do you need some help with this one?" she asked.

"Thank you. I was just trying to get him off the road. There is a wagon coming," Sally replied.

"This your man, then?" the woman asked as they struggled to drag him under a portico.

"Oh, good heavens, no! He's a ship's captain. I knew him, once. A long time ago."

"Kind of you, to show this heap some attention. My name is Jaclyn de Witt."

"Thank you for helping me, Mrs. de Witt. I'm Lady Cranston. Sally Cranston. Do you live in town?"

Jaclyn laughed. "I do. And it is just Madame, my lady. Madame de Witt. That's my establishment, over there," she pointed to the whorehouse across the street. "It is a pleasure to meet a real lady in this town."

"Likewise!" Sally heard the wagon approach and turned to wave to Nero. When she turned back, Jaclyn de Witt was gone. Sally looked up and down the road and saw only the baker who stood outside his door with his hands on his hips and shaking his head.

Nero jumped down from the driver's seat before the horses came to a full stop.

"This here man, he hurt you, madam?"

"This here man captained the ship that brought James and I to the Indies, Nero. He is vile and most evil, but for all his faults, I find I cannot, though tempted, find it within my heart to leave him to die in the street like some mad dog. Help me get him into the wagon."

Nero hesitated and looked at Sally in disbelief.

"Well, come on. I wish to leave Port Royal before the rains worsen and flood our passage home," Sally demanded. She bent over Capt. Blake, but Nero gently nudged her out of the way. In what appeared to be one smooth effortless motion, he hoisted the barely conscious man over his shoulder and dropped him like a sack onto the bed of the wagon. The force released the air from the captain's lungs and Nero reeled from the smell. He pulled his collar above his nose and mumbled, "This here man, Lady Cranston, he smells like he died days ago."

"Yes," Sally agreed as Nero helped her onto the wagon. "He will make our journey . . . challenging."

"We need vanilla for this."

Sally laughed at his reference. The last time Nero used his vanilla formulation was when he helped remove a dead beached whale near the mouth of the Milk River. The smell of that carcass made fishing near the Milk's estuary impossible. It took days to cut up and drag the rotted carcass out to sea.

"What do you want with this man, madam? I believe I know this captain. He is not a good man. This man was once a slaver. You know this?"

"Yes, I do. It was a long time ago. I can't imagine that he has captained a boat recently, do you? I know not whether this is the devil's work or if this man's guardian angel drives me to such foolishness. I just know I could not leave him there in the mud to face the wrath of those misguided children.

"He is lost to rum. All rum, no soul. Lost to demons, this one, madam."

Sally raised an eyebrow. "Yes, I can see that, Nero. And smell it! But I am not so certain he is without a soul. As for his demons, I want you to take him to those who can help him be rid of them."

Nero quickly looked away.

"It's no good, Nero. I know about the others, in worse state than this man. I know you've taken them to the hills, to those demon-chasers up in the mountains. I want you to take Capt. Blake to them. If he has any chance of regaining his life, he must first deal with those demons that pulled him across into his sad and dark world."

"It is too dangerous for a white man, madam. 'Tis for black people, not whites."

"Nero, look at that." Sally gestured to the back of the wagon. "That is no longer a man, white or black. I challenge your African ways to rid that . . . that heap of flesh of his demons. Only then can the white man's religion restore the man's soul."

"I do not like this, madam. It is difficult for such a man to give up his vices. He will be trouble for you. For me. And for the demon chasers." Nero grumbled.

"If this man betrays you or your demon chasers, I will shoot him myself. You have my word on that." Sally glanced back at their groaning passenger. "I think he started out like any other man, but took a wrong path. Oh, do let's put these horses to work and head this wagon into the wind, Nero. I need to breathe. My head is light from holding my breath so."

Sally had two acquaintances conveniently placed for her occasional forays to Port Royal. Their first stop was in Kingston where Sally was a good friend to a young woman named Haddie. Haddie was always tickled to host Sally when she passed through Kingston and both women delighted in the opportunity to exchange gossip and critique the latest fashion. Outside Spanish Town, Sally stayed with Nall, a sweet kindhearted widower who befriended her and Gregor just after their wedding. Nall, recently retired from his various enterprises in Port Royal, enjoyed a quiet life on his small plantation. While Sally slept comfortably in the houses of her friends, Nero and the contentious captain slept in the stables. Both Haddie and Nall tried in vein to dissuade Sally from taking on the drunken old captain. "If I abandon him now, it would be on my conscience," Sally reasoned.

By the third day, the captain recovered enough to sit upright in the back of the wagon. During the entire trip, he spoke not a word and Sally wondered whether he was capable of remembering who she was. She was certainly surprised that he did not try to leave them, even when they insisted that he bathe in a warm spring they passed along the way. In fact, they had a hard time dragging him out of the soothing waters.

Once home, Nero unloaded the wagon of goods and unhitched the horses to water, feed, and brush them. Sally insisted that the captain strip from his smelly old flea-infested rags, which Nero quickly burned. Mr. Watt and Lucy dragged the pathetic man to the bathhouse, scrubbed his flesh with lye soap until he was nearly raw and coated his wrinkly skin with oil of lilac. Lucy dressed the man in a clean shirt and britches. An hour before dusk, Nero saddled two horses and prepared to head north to the Maroon camps. Sally wrote a letter explaining that her servant, a freeman called Nero, had permission to take the horses and the feverish captain to a cool mineral spring in the mountains to relieve his ailment. It was a good cover. If slave hunters stopped Nero, fear of contracting the sickness would most likely cease any further inquiry. Slave hunters used to avoid the hidden dangerous mountain paths, but as runaways from the plantations increased, so did the tenacity of their hunters. Competition for bounty pushed them to take greater risks and travel further into the mountains.

"Tis more likely," Gregor worried, "that renegade Maroons will steal our good horses or do harm to Nero and the captain." He tried to talk sense into Sally and begged her to abandon the folly.

"And what would you have me do with this man, Gregor?" she asked.

"Sally, I have seen the results of years of rum and bad living in Port Royal. It breaks the soul and pays irreparable harm to the body. Remember the vicar's bill? The one he circulated when he called for temperance to spirit drinking? It claimed the inners of persons poisoned by excessive drinking shrunk, turned black, and ceased to function, leading to agony and death," Gregor reminded her.

"Oh, Gregor, I do understand any hopeful treatment issued upon him may be too late, but my heart compels me to proceed, however unreasonable."

Gregor's concerns were not directed solely at the captain. Without Nero, he and Mr. Watt would have the burden of managing the farm's labor. He gave orders for Nero to return with the horses in one month, with or without a sober Captain Blake.

Nero went to the back of the Great House to the two large rooms that he built adjoining the summer kitchen. It was the most comfortable home he ever had. There, Nero said farewell to his wife, Ruth, and their baby boy, Bo. He mounted his horse, took the other by the reins, and disappeared down the lane just as the rains started up again.

CHAPTER 15

Nero yanked the old captain's head up by the hair and held the knife against his neck so tight that a narrow trickle of blood flowed from the wound. Driven by emerging memories long ago forgotten, it was the second time since leaving Windhaven that Nero suffered a fitful rage with the intent to kill the man. Each time the broken captain made no effort to stop him and each time Nero stopped short of killing the man.

I could easily kill this drunken waste of a man and bury him here. No one would doubt my story that the old man died of drink. I could hide among the Maroons and wait until the whites stopped looking for me, he thought. *Then make my way back to Windhaven to collect Ruth and Bo.* Bo! It was the thought of Bo that kept the knife from hitting its mark.

"You, devil, deserve to die!" Nero spat at the captain. "Killing you, however pleasing to my soul, would only rob me and my family the freedom I worked so hard to earn. I fancy not a noose around my neck. Even if I could escape and get my family to the Maroons, this living would be too hard for Bo and Ruth." He knew enough about these thorny elusive Maroons to know that living in the mountainous hideouts would be tenuous, difficult, and violent. "No!" he said, "I carved out a good life at Windhaven, for myself and my family. Too good to let this temptation ruin it." Nero released his grip on the contemptuous captain's head and pushed him to the ground.

"You are not worth the high price I would pay for this indulgence, slaver!" Nero declared as he grabbed his horse's reins. The animal responded with a snort as Nero once again navigated on foot the narrow path through the thick forest. The bedraggled captain struggled to mount his horse and followed, head down to cover the trail of tears that fell into his beard.

Though it had stopped raining, water cascaded from the leaves above in a steady cool drizzle. The forest carried the sweet pungent odor of mold. For Nero, it was an unpleasant smell for it reminded him of the river bank where he had been hiding the day the Arabs stole him away from his village.

Unlike the majority of negroes in Jamaica, both freemen and slaves, Nero came from a village in *east* Africa. His people, the Wapokomo, lived a quiet communal existence along the silted shores of the great Tana River.

He remembered his mother's laughter as she gossiped with the other women gathered to wash clothes at the river. His father was a fisherman and hunter of hippopotamus and crocodiles. Though politics and the affairs of other villages were often the topics of heated discussions at tribal gatherings, the Wapokomo prized peace and favored the art of careful negotiation rather than resorting to confrontations. The Wapokomo were masters of arbitration and were often called upon by other tribes to settle disputes.

During the summer of Nero's tenth season, word reached his village about a brutal attack by Arab slavers on another Wapokomo village further south and nearer the coast. The young men of the tribe called for war, but the elders, thinking war would be too costly for all the Wapokomos, thought it more prudent to parley a peace. Among the emissaries sent to negotiate, was Nero's father.

With two camels loaded with rice, skins, and four large elephant teeth, his father and three other elders went off to make treaty with the Arabs. They did not return.

Early one morning, before the villagers arose, the Arabs circled the small enclave and attacked with sudden and violent surprise. They systematically killed the very young, piling their bodies in a heap at the center of the village. They killed the old, assaulted the women, and burned the houses. Few escaped the terror.

Nero grabbed his younger brother and ran with many others to the river, but the Arabs were waiting there and trapped the lot of them. Wooden yokes were attached to the necks of the men while women and girls, his mother and two sisters included, were tied in groups with sisal rope so rough, it tore their flesh when they struggled. The Arabs tied his brother and other young boys with one end of a rope around their necks and the other end tied to a goat or a cow. Whips cracked as the Arabs herded the surviving captives and livestock away from the ruins of the village and started them on their long and bloody trek to the coast.

Suffering from exhaustion and thirst, many, including his mother, died by the second day. Each day more succumbed until the caravan of bedraggled humans arrived at the island city the Arabs called Manbasa. The Wapokomo knew it as Kisiwa Cha Mvita – City of War.

As they marched through the town, Nero was both fascinated and terrified of the sights and sounds of the streets of Mvita. He had never smelled such sweetness from the spices piled high in front of the brilliantly colored tents of the markets. As the shackled, bleeding, emaciated Wapokomo stumbled down the narrow streets of Mvita on their way to the coastal Portuguese stronghold called Fort Jesus, no one took notice of them nor expressed pity at their plight.

At the entrance of the fort, a tall thin naked man hung limply from an archway of coral stone. He hung by a large hook embedded deep under his ribs. As Nero passed beneath him, he was startled to hear the man moan softly and was surprised to see him still alive with such heinous wounds. He noticed the man's skin was much lighter than his own – the color of the Tana after a heavy rain. Nero wondered what offense the man had committed to warrant such cruel punishment.

Inside the fort, African strong men, working alongside Arab slavers, freed the young boys from their livestock burdens. The beasts were herded back towards Mvita while the boys were taken away from the main group. It was the last time Nero saw his brother. For Nero and the others long heavy chains, clamped tight around the ankles, replaced the ropes and yokes. They were pushed into dark, stuffy stone cells, women in one, men in the other. Those that resisted were clubbed to death and their bloodied bodies left on the chains for the others to pull along.

During the first night, Nero was startled awake by heart-stopping screams from the direction where the Arabs took the young boys.

"What are they doing to them?" Nero whispered in terror.

"I have only heard, not seen." An older Wapokomo man, not from his village and who was already a prisoner when Nero arrived whispered back. "It is said that the Arabs cut off the penises of boys destined to become warriors of an army. They believe if a boy is deprived his manhood, he becomes more aggressive. Boys tendered to serve in a household have their testicles removed. They believe this barbaric practice will produce a more passive slave and more importantly, no longer a threat to the female members of a house. It is said, many do not survive this butchery."

Nero screamed. The tribesman tied next to him vomited. The screams continued. Nero and many others shouted out the names of their family and friends, offering comforting words and prayers. No one slept and several more men died during that long night.

At the break of day, Nero and others in his group were herded down a long tunnel the other prisoners called The Tunnel of No Return. Each was given a ladle of water, and then pushed to the end of the tunnel that opened to the seashore. Two large dhows were anchored just off shore. At the sight of the ocean, Nero saw terror in the faces of many prisoners. To board the dhows, they were forced to wade chest-high in water. Two captives gave in to their fears of the water and refused to enter. They fought fiercely with the slavers, but a swift cut to their ankles ended the combat and severed them from their chains. The slaves had barely time to scream before the next swing of the cutlass removed their heads. The water turned crimson and choppy from the frenzy brought on by the sharks. The predators were distracted long enough for the others to scramble up the Jacob's ladder without further incident. Shaking from the ordeal, Nero made a promise to himself – live. Just live.

With little water and no food, the dhow sailed north and followed the coastline for many days until they came to the island of Lamu. There they disembarked and were given rancid goat milk mixed with over-ripe fruit. Not knowing where or when he would be offered sustenance again, Nero wafted down the slurry, bugs and all. Separated from his tribesmen and chained to a small group of strangers, Nero was loaded onto a larger Portuguese merchantman along with a cargo of ivory, ebony, spices, cloth and grains. Though there were many black people on the ship, some slaves others not, no one spoke the language of the Wapokomo. Nero felt alone in a ship awash with human suffering.

The merchantman sailed around the Arab nations and north up the long, salty Red Sea. From Suez, the slaves joined a massive camel caravan and crossed the great eastern desert to Cairo. Forced to carry heavy ivory, it was during this part of Nero's long journey that he lost faith and decided to break the promise he made to himself. Because he was so far from his home, he believed that he was destined to be nothing more than a beast of burden to the Arabs, valued less than a camel. It was a destiny he would not allow and decided to end his life as he had seen others do. He fell to his knees, dropped the end of the ivory tusk, and refused to get up. He closed his eyes and waited for the swift and welcomed action of slaver's cutlass. *Strike well*, Nero prayed, *and end my misery quickly*!

A slender Arab stood over Nero, his ample robes shadowing the prostrate figure in the sand. The Arab shouted a command to the boy who tended the camel that carried water and bent low to help Nero to his feet. Nero was stunned as he watched the Arab lift the heavy ivory and carefully positioned it back onto Nero's shoulder. The Arab said in a soft voice, "as-salaamu 'alaykum" and raised his hand slowly to his forehead while bowing slightly. He dipped a ladle in the water bucket and gave it Nero who gulped it all. It was an unmistakable gesture of kindness and it was enough to see Nero through another day.

In Cairo, he was sold to a Greek master of a large trading sloop. The Greek was as benevolent to Nero as he was to the two others who crewed his ship. Neither of them was African and Nero did not understand their language, but each patiently helped Nero learn the ropes and chores. Not only did the Greek teach them navigation and other skills of a mariner, but also the languages spoken along the trade routes – Greek, Spanish, and Portuguese. Most importantly, the Greek taught Nero how to read, write and do simple mathematics. He spent many years with the Greek sailing and trading along the Mediterranean's shores. In a loose alliance, they often traveled in convoy with other ships for protection from attacks by the Barbary corsairs. They traded in the dangerous North African ports of Algiers, Tunis, Tripoli, Sal and Mamora. Once, they ran into a terrible storm off the coast of Tangier. The sloop, picked up and dashed against the rocks by ferocious waves, ripped its hull and she heeled hard to starboard. All on board were thrown into the sea. The unending waves broke the sloop to pieces. Nero dove below the surface of the pounding waves to retrieve his drowning master. Barely conscious the Greek clung to Nero's back as he swam for two hours before they washed ashore.

For that, the kind Greek gave Nero his freedom. With no ship to sail, Nero reluctantly left the Greek in Tangier and joined the black Moors. He converted to Islam, married the daughter of a half Spanish, half Moor inventor from Gibraltar, and signed on with a Portuguese ship bound for Brazil.

While nearing the island of Fernando do Noronha, a Spanish warship fired upon and captured the Portuguese merchantman. The Spanish privateers scuttled the badly damaged ship after transferring her goods and prisoners. Once again, Nero suffered the shackles of captivity. They sailed on to Jamaica and careened the warship for repairs at Cayo de Carena. The ship was still heaved-over when the English navy, commanded by Penn and Venables, attacked the harbor. The Spaniards and all their captives ran and hid in the mountains and along the north shore. Though outnumbered, they acted as a single force – slaves, prisoners, and masters – to harass the English invaders. Most of the Spaniards escaped to Hispaniola, but Nero was still held by a small well-armed militia of ten Spanish farmers along with their slaves and other captives from the Portuguese merchantman. Weakened by sickness and malnutrition, the Spanish subjugators soon showed little interest in keeping their captives. Nero mustered his remaining strength to desert the party. He wandered in a delirious state through the thick forest until, on the third day, he collapsed.

Los Marrones, the Maroons, found Nero nearly dead from hunger and fever. This fierce, though loosely organized group, defended themselves from their former Spanish masters. They profited most by raiding plantations to the south, but they also established small settlements based on family units or trusted alliances. They kept cattle and cleared small tracks for farming. Nero recovered and for the first time in years, he enjoyed a period of peace living among the Maroons. He slowly surrendered to the realization that he would never again return to his wife in Gibraltar and, in time, he fell in love again.

Ruth was a young mulatto woman from a maroon settlement in the mountains to the east and after a short courtship; Nero began the arduous and delicate task of negotiating marriage with her family. Her lighter skin made Ruth more valuable and the price for her was high. Her family demanded two bulls but Nero was a Wapokomo and no tribe in Africa was better adept at the art of finding the middle ground. He managed to talk them into accepting one cow and a half-barrel of rum. The family accepted. As Nero had neither a cow nor rum, he would need to go south to raid an English plantation.

It was during the raid on Windhaven that Nero stepped on a loose board and fell through the loft of the barn. He landed hard and seeing his shattered bones, he was certain he would die there in that barn, until Mr. Watt found him.

Mr. Watt built an elaborate brace for the broken leg enabling Nero to hobble about with the aid of two sticks, everyday a little further. After two months, the brace was removed, and though he would forever walk with a limp, Nero's fortune, once again, changed for the better when Mr. Watt offered to hire him as a farm hand. He saved enough from his wages to purchase a fine cow and a full barrel of rum. Nero returned to the mountains to purchase his wife and felt a great sense of pride knowing that Ruth was won by honest means. He married his beloved who, shortly thereafter, bore him a son, Bo.

Nero looked at the broken man before him with distain. "Aye," he said to the old captain as he thought of his wife and son. "Life was good until Lady Cranston ordered me back to these mountains for your sake, you filthy old slaver."

After traveling for two days through the steaming hot forests, Captain Blake showed signs of distress from the sudden and complete cessation of alcohol. His tremors worsened, he could not sleep, and his eyelids twitched uncontrollably. The old man endured a loss of appetite, sweated profusely, was pale, and nauseated. Though it seemed impossible that anything could be left in the man's stomach, the long suffering captain continued to vomit a foul dark liquid. At times, he appeared lucid and could stay upright in the saddle, and other times he was so violent and difficult Nero had to tie and gag him to suppress the loud incomprehensible ranting. His charge must surely have alerted the Maroons of their approach and Nero worried that their presence might not be interpreted as friendly.

That night, two half-naked dark-skinned and ornately scarred men entered Nero's camp. Their quiet mumbling as they squatted before the trussed white man awakened Nero with a start. He spoke with them in a combination of Spanish and English languages. One of the men left the camp while the other took some dried leaves from a pouch that dangled from his neck. He squatted next to the fire and seeing a cup that Nero used for his supper, placed the leaves at the bottom of the cup. He used a stick to crush the leaves and then added a milky substance from a gourd hanging from his waist. He stirred the infusion by swirling the cup for several minutes. The odor it gave off was pleasant and sweet.

The Maroon rolled the captain on his back, lifted his head slightly and forced the liquid down his throat. From the small of his back, the Maroon retrieved a long curved knife with a narrow blade. It startled Nero until he understood that Maroon intended to cut the ropes that bound the captain. Nero protested and raised his hands. Carefully, Nero reached over the captain and untied the ropes.

"I may need these again and wish to spare myself the need to splice them," he explained.

The Maroon elucidated to Nero that the infusion of chili powder, ginger, cinnamon, and sugar would control the captain's delirium and tremors. Later, when they reached the Maroon's compound, a shaman administered 15 drops of tincture of capsicum in beef broth. Each day the number of drops would increase by 15 until the seventh day. By that time, the broth would contain the maximum amount of capsicum. Any more than that, the shaman explained, would burn the captain's insides. Nero expressed his appreciation for the administration of the captain's treatment and surreptitiously inquired about the charges for such care.

"¿Es este hombre un amigo suyo?" a Maroon asked.

"A friend? No. No amigo. No. El es mi enemigo." Nero replied.

"Enemigo! You want kill?" the Maroon asked, confused.

"No. I want him cured. No kill. Yo lo deseo que curara."

"Ah . . ." the Maroon answered in a knowing tone. "Ah . . . comprendo. Comprendo!" Nero smiled and thought, *At least someone understands this mission because I am still having difficulty comprehending the reasons why Lady Cranston thought this man was worth saving.*

Over the course of the treatment of potions, liniments, brews, herbal remedies and incantations, the captain suffered terribly. There were times when he looked as if he might be cured. This excited Nero with thoughts of returning home but found, by next morning, the captain relapsed into a restless delirium complaining of foul smells or persistent and loud noises. He endured profound confusion, hallucinations, and a heavy pounding of his heart. As his symptoms slowly abated, so did his anger and suspicion, until the captain took on a quieter and more reflective demeanor. The recovery, though quite dramatic, was not rapid. However, only days before the allotted time constraint, he suddenly announced that he was ready to go home.

"And where might that be, your home?" asked Nero.

Captain Blake looked surprised at first, as if he had not been confronted by that question before. His jowls sank and his eyes drooped. He cleared his throat and said, "I have none."

"No people?"

Again, he hesitated before saying in a soft voice, "I have . . . No. Not a soul."

Nero's instinct told him that the old captain was lying, but it was not his concern. On the day they departed from the settlement, Captain Blake asked how he might repay the Maroons for their kindness whereupon they produced a prepared document listing items they needed. Not all the items listed were material in nature, some were in-kind actions, favors, and services. The captain promised to provide for them as much and as often as he could but in return, the Maroons had to promise that the Windhaven Plantation would be off-limits to all future raids. The sacrifice of a chicken sealed the deal.

Captain Blake decided not to return to Port Royal, but instead asked Sir Gregor if he might work at Windhaven, offering the pact made with the Maroons as collateral. Mr. Watt was delighted for the extra hand, but did not wholly share the confidence of the captain's complete cure. He ordered all barrels of rum and wine locked in the fruit cellar and insisted that Captain Blake accompany him and his wife to their Sunday church meetings on a regular basis.

CHAPTER 16

The spring of 1669 was warm for Cape Cod and it caused Maggie Strangeway to break into a sweat. She was particularly aggressive in the beating of her rag-woven rug and took full swings at it. Grunting loudly, she released a cloud of billowy dust with each strike. Tears welled in her eyes and her jaw locked in an angry scowl.

"You *said* you were happy here!" she challenged her husband who was sitting on a stump watching the attacks. He was smoking his pipe, puffing in synchronous rhythm to the harsh beating of the rug.

"Aye, wife, indeed I have been all these years quite a happy man, yes" he replied.

"You *said* you would not go to sea again!" she continued her litany of perceived promises.

"No, now, I never said that, me luv. I said merely that I was happy here as a landlubber," he refuted calmly.

Maggie stopped her thrashing and with one firm blink, she released her tears. She turned to face her husband. "I left me home to come fer ya, and sailed our young'uns across that sea fer ya, Twiggy. Now yer wantin' to leave me. Again. Here, in this strange land, with n'er friends or family about."

"Cape Cod is hardly strange to ya, Maggie. Ya been livin' here nigh on a couple of years now and enjoying this better life, I'd say. There's this here house. Better than we've ever 'ad, and own it outright, now, don't we? And the boys, they be goin' to school for their learnin', jist like ya wanted. They likes it here, Maggie. And workin' for Capt'n Waller, we're doin' all right, the four of us. Couldn't 'ave done as well in England, now, could we?"

"Exactly my point, Twiggy. Why would ya even think of goin' back to sea and leavin' all this – what we 'ave worked so hard fer?" Maggie snorted like an angry bull as she bent over to pick up the cane to give the rug a few more whacks. "What does Capt'n Waller say about ye jist up and leavin' 'im?"

"Ah, he's a good man, Capt'n Waller. A generous man. He said, there be a job for me when I gets back. He understands. He knows the cooperage will run well without me. The lads can 'andle it now, Maggie. I trained them well enough, I did. Too well. Some days, I feels like a square dowel trying to squeeze me through a round 'ole," Twiggy explained as he watched the swings deteriorate to reckless flailing. "Maggie, Maggie, luv! You'll soon 'ave that rug in shreds. Leave it and come on over 'ere and talks to me." Twiggy got off the stump and wiped it clean with his handkerchief. He carefully disarmed his wife of her cane, took her hand, and led her to the stump. As she sat down, Maggie gave him a look that made him rethink his strategy. Perhaps it would be more prudent, he thought, to approach the subject when cooler minds prevailed. Too late! He was in for it.

"Look at me, Maggie!" he said struggling to get down on one knee beside her. "Me days are numbered, they are. Might I 'ave this one last adventure before me time's up? And if I gets me treasure this time, we'd be sittin' pretty fer the rest of our lives, Maggie."

"You said those very words to me ten years back!" Maggie confronted. "Say what you really mean, Twiggy Strangeway. I no longer please thee."

"Ah Maggie, tis no truth to that. Never! Why the fire between us, it grows with every season!"

Maggie turned away, folded her arms across her ample chest, and pouted. "If ye thinks we do so well, why go and risk it all?" she cried.

Twiggy hesitated. He didn't have an answer. It was a question that plagued him on many sleepless nights. His knees were beginning to ache and it took him two tries to stand up, and even then, with the help of his wife.

"Look at you!" Maggie noted. "You are right to say thy days are numbered. Ya not be a young buck anymore, Twiggy. This venture you seek, it's a young man's undertakin'. Why not leave it to 'em and stay 'ere to watch yer sons grow?"

Twiggy sighed. "Ya always were the practical one, Maggie. I don't know why I 'ave an itch to seek out more than what I 'ave right 'ere. It's jist part of me. It's who I am. Take the widow Alexander across the way there. She keeps that mockin' bird in a cage. It sings and she likes that. It keeps her company. She thinks it sings for her but that bird don't sing for her pleasure. It's cryin', it is. Cryin' because it ain't free, Maggie. But old Mrs. Alexander, she'll keep that bird locked up in that there cage 'til it dies." Twiggy explained, nodding his head.

Maggie looked back at him, confused and bewildered. She heard clear enough what he said, but had not the slightest understanding of his meaning. "It's Barnaby, ain't it?" she finally said. "This is *his* idea. Barnaby Tibbs has no wife or family to look after. You do!"

"Aye, Barnaby is goin', but it was *me* who asked 'im," Twiggy clarified.

With that, Maggie pressed her lips together, "Right then, seems it's already decided. Have ya told the boys?" Maggie asked with tears flowing again.

"I will this night," he promised, trying to stifle his excitement.

"Where will ya go?" she asked more tenderly.

"Jamaica."

Maggie gestured as if she wanted to say more, but instead she shrugged, picked up the cane, and went about beating the rug to shreds.

CHAPTER 17

In the early months of 1670, Governor Sir Thomas Modyford's fragile peace with Spain was once again shattered when a Spanish man-of-war attacked Jamaica's northern coast, burning plantations and taking several planters and their slaves as hostages. The tight group of buccaneers of Port Royal, who called themselves The Brethren of the Coast, wanted to retaliate. They grew restless and were ready to react to the slightest rumor. In a deliberate taunt, the Spanish Captain Pardal nailed a placard to a tree in the western part of the Jamaica. On it was written a challenge for Henry Morgan, the notorious leader of Brethren, to come out to sea so the English could witness the valor of the Spaniards. Modyford restrained the angry Morgan, trusting the boastful rants of the cowardly raider were not sufficient to instigate war.

However, while caught in a spring gale, a ship captained by one of Morgan's most trusted friends blew into a bay off the east coast of Hispaniola. Pardal's man-of-war caught up with the ship, attacked, and killed its captain. Henry Morgan could hold back no longer. He sought and received from Modyford and the council a letter of marque to seek not only Spanish ships at sea, but to land on the enemy's country and quell further threats to Jamaica.

Port Royal flooded with men eager to join the Brethren for treasure, for revenge, and just adventure. Among them were two old sea salts from Massachusetts.

"Gentlemen, may I present my services to you?" the young man bowed quickly before pulling a chair to the table in the Port Royal Ale House where Twiggy and Barnaby enjoyed their third flagon. The well-dressed man introduced himself as an attorney who offered legal services to the sailors of Henry Morgan. "My colleagues tell me you sail tomorrow to meet up with Morgan and the Brethren."

"Aye, perhaps we are and perhaps we won't. What business of that be yours, sir?" Barney Tibbs groused.

"Have you drawn up your wills, gentlemen?" asked the attorney.

"Wills?" Barnaby retorted. "I ain't got much to decree and I surly 'ave no one to take up what I 'ave, mate."

"And how about you, good sir?" the gentleman asked Twiggy. "Have you no loved ones you want to protect?"

Twiggy looked at Barnaby. "Aye, as a matter of fact I do, but none here in Jamaica. Would this here document be honored in the Bay Colony of Massachusetts?"

"Oh, indeed, sir. It would. I represent the King's law, sir, and last I heard Massachusetts is a colony of the crown." With that cue, the gentleman pressed out a tightly rolled scroll onto the table and moved Barnaby's flagon to weigh down a corner of the paper. He pulled from his coat a tiny flask of ink and from his hat he plucked a small feather quill. He dipped his quill and asked, "And your name sir?"

"Theodore Strangeway of Sandwich, Massachusetts. That be on Cape Cod," Twiggy replied.

"Theodore! Theodore?" Barnaby laughed. "Why, I never knew that!"

The attorney kept writing. "And who is the beneficiary?" he asked. Twiggy looked to Barnaby for translation.

"That would be Maggie and yer sons, Twiggy. Hey, there. What's this will gonna cost 'im?"

"Four shillings," replied the attorney. "That is a bargain to pay for such peace of mind before a great battle at sea, wouldn't you say?"

"Go on, mate, we all 'ave 'em," shouted a young sailor at another table. He had two whores, one on each knee. "I just can't decide which one of these lovelies gets me gold tooth!" All those within earshot of the remark laughed. Twiggy however, seemed solemn.

"You say, whatever I command on that there paper, that's the way it'll be?" Twiggy asked.

"Yes, sir, by the law, your final wishes will be granted," the attorney explained.

"Then I wants me wife, Margaret Strangeway, to 'ave all me riches and the house and the land on Cape Cod. It ain't much, but I would like her to 'ave what's mine. And if'n she dies or can't forgive me fer leavin' her again, then it all goes to me boys, Thomas and John Strangeway."

"Here, now. If I pay ya four shillings, can I 'ave me one of them wills?" Barney asked.

"Who ya going to leave yer riches to, Barnaby? You ain't got kin," Twiggy asked.

"I want to leave what I 'ave to yer missus, Twiggy. Maggie, she done bake me the finest pies! And to yer boys. Seems I owe them that for making me laugh so hard. I would like 'em to 'ave me fishing rods and me skiff. Oh, and me traps. And I 'ave me a fish shop in Roxbury. It's really me house. I'd like that to go to the negro, Henry. Don't reckon Henry has any other name. That fishing boat he uses, that'd be mine, too. I guess he can't run the fish shop without me boat, so he might as well 'ave that as well," Barnaby stated.

Twiggy was touched by his friend's generosity. They both reached into their money sacks and laid eight shillings on the table.

When the attorney was finished, Twiggy and Barnaby made their mark. He blotted the paper, rolled it, sealed it, placed everything back into his coat pockets and moved onto the next table.

"Here," Barnaby whispered, "how do we know he is a real lawyer and that he'll do right by us, Twiggy?"

"No worries, mate, he's good." the young man with the whores declared. "He's been doing it for years. But you're right to ask. There are some sticky thieves about, taking advantage of them that's running off to fight the Spaniards. Those slimy gents, they talk all fancy, takes your particulars, and your money, then uses the paper to wipe their arses." Again he drew laughter. "What ship ye be sailing?"

"Don't rightly know. Heard of any that need a cooper and a cook?" Barnaby inquired.

"I reckon 'bout half dozen around the Point be needing your good services. Been to sea much?" he asked. Twiggy and Barnaby laughed.

"Aye!" Twiggy answered. "Been several years, now, off and on."

"Been in battle at sea?" the young man asked.

"Aye!" Barnaby answered. "Seen a bit, we 'ave, ain't we Twiggy?"

With that, the young man stood up suddenly, sending his whores to the floor. "Sorry, my dears, but business calls. When you have finished that ale, I can take you to a ship that might sign you up."

Barnaby and Twiggy exchanged a thought the way two old friends can do with just a look. They decided to trust the man, put down their cups and rose from the table.

"We'd be obliged to ya, Master . . ."

"Haywood, Peter Haywood from Barbados, at your service," the man replied with a bow.

Twiggy and Barnaby looked at each other then eyed the young man.

"Used to know some Haywoods from Barbados. Belle and Ned Haywood, that were their names," Barnaby said scratching his head.

"That's my father and my mother. How came you to know of them?" Peter Haywood asked.

"We sailed with them on the *Rosa* from Bristol," Barnaby replied.

"Of course! You're the cooper, and you sir, Mr. Tibbs, the cook!" Peter supposed in surprise. "My mother spoke often of that voyage. I grew up hearing the tales of the mysterious widow who went by the board."

"Aye, that be a sad tale, indeed. Left behind two orphans. But they do well, now. Land owners, they are, right here in Jamaica. We've just come back from a visit with them. Yer parents, they are well?" asked Twiggy.

"Yes, and still farming. Come, I will sign you up myself aboard the *Rover*. I'm its First Mate. She's a fine ship, not as fast as some, but she's wide and more shallow bottomed. She'll hold more cargo that most. Responds well in rough seas and carries 16 guns," Peter boasted.

By the end of June, two thousand men in thirty-eight ships, the largest army of buccaneers ever assembled, rendezvoused with Morgan's flagship off the coast of Hispaniola. Their goal: to attack the Isthmus of Panama and capture the city for the safety and good of Jamaica and for the wealth it surely held.

One month after the fleet sailed, Thomas Modyford received word of the Godolphin Treaty between England and Spain. Signed on the 18th of July in Madrid, the Spanish agreed to recognize English control of Jamaica and other colonies in the Americas and both countries agreed to suppress piracy in the Caribbean.

"They have given us the peace I sought too late!" Thomas lamented.

"Can you not recall Morgan, Thomas?" Elizabeth asked sensing the impending disaster.

"It's too late. No vessel would be able to reach them in time. And even if I could stop Morgan, I am not certain I would," he replied. "We've signed treaties before and still they attack our shores."

"Be careful, Thomas, there are those who might consider taking no action to stop Morgan a seditious act."

"No doubt!" Thomas looked at his wife long and hard. "There may be . . . unexpected consequences, Elizabeth. I cannot see how I might right this."

"Surely, you cannot be held responsible for the actions taken before your knowledge of this treaty," Elizabeth protested, trying to suppress her growing concern.

"That's just it. The action has not occurred yet and the raid will certainly be seen as a violation of the treaty, an act of war. Either way, it appears by my orders, I have started a war. The most I can hope for is support from those who may do not favor the terms of the treaty. But read the terms, Elizabeth, what is there not to like? The Spanish have given us all that we asked. And what colony does not now support the repression of pirating, Spanish or English? No, no. I fear that this will end badly for me, Elizabeth. We must . . . prepare for the worst."

"Thomas, you frighten me so. What will happen to us?"

"Two kings – both Charles II – one of England, one of Spain. They will most likely parlay tit for tat and our English Charles II may well offer my head as amends to Spain's Charles II."

Elizabeth was wild-eyed with panic. "What if Morgan fails?" she asked.

Thomas shook his head. "I'd still be in trouble. It was my hand that signed the marque. Perhaps the best outcome will be if he is victorious. His popularity and a triumphant and profitable outcome may prevent the king from taking harsher treatment against us."

Elizabeth snuggled into her husband's chest. They remained embraced like that for some time, sensing the fall that was surely to come.

Morgan's fleet sailed for Chagres and captured the heavily fortified town on the east coast of the Isthmus. A land corridor to Panama was now open, but not so easy to transverse. The tropical forest was nearly impenetrable. Leaving some men behind to mind the ships, 1,200 men trekked across the ruthless jungle. They struggled against the heat, swarms of biting flies and mosquitoes, torrential rain, and surreptitious attacks by Indians who seemed to disappear into the jungle before a single shot was fired.

Thinking the lush forest would be rich in game and fruit, Morgan had ordered his men to pack light on provisions. It was a fatal miscalculation. Hunting proved to be a challenge. Hacking the vegetation back just to get near the wildlife alerted not only the game, but also the enemy.

Morgan's advantage of a surprise attack was foiled and the Spaniards rushed out to meet them, not to confront them, but to strip everything edible from the villages that lay in the path of the English. After a week, the men were so desperate for food they began to eat leather softened in boiling water. Only Morgan's charismatic leadership held the hapless buccaneers together, that and the promise of riches from the finest prize of the Spanish settlements.

"I think I am dying," declared Barnaby. "My head throbs so and leeches have sucked the life from my balls."

"Stand fast, Barnaby. There is no hope for those left behind. If you falter, the Indians will have your balls dangling from their belts," Peter Haywood warned.

"We signed on for sea duty," Barnaby reminded his friends.

"Aye, this might be a sad ending for us, old friend," Twiggy added.

On the ninth day of their march across the Isthmus, the bearded dirty rag-tag group, numbering just over half their original force, stumbled from the jungle onto the plains outside the city. Across the fields, the aged Spanish governor and his impressive defense of cavalry, infantry, and artillery lined up in perfect formation, well prepared for battle. They clearly outnumbered the buccaneers, but Morgan's keen sense of offensive strategy was superior even on land. He outflanked the enemy, broke their ranks, and sent them running over a hill. Just as the buccaneers thought they had the lead, a horrible rumbling filled the air. The ground beneath their feet shook.

"Earthquake?" Peter asked as he looked to his friends.

"I don't think . . ." Twiggy had barely time to finish when the horizon along the hill filled with a dark movement.

"Holy Mother, what . . .?" Barnaby was about to ask.

"Cattle! Stampede!" came the cry. But the Spanish failed to know their enemy – buccaneers! Buccaneers were cattlemen! Instead of running, some of the men moved up to position themselves before the crushing herd of over a thousand cattle and oxen. They held fast and fired well-placed shots from their muskets. A few cattle at the front of the herd went down. Seeing the fallen, the panicked herd turned, regrouped, and charged uphill towards the surprised Spaniards. The heavily armed and burdened Spanish infantry and artillerymen were overwhelmed. The horses of the cavalry bucked and scattered when confronted with frantic bulls followed by the yelling and screaming buccaneers. The horses reared and sent their riders to the ground. The governor's men were defeated and the city of Panama was doomed.

When the victors breached the walls of the fallen city, Morgan either lost control of his men or chose to disregard all sense of decency. The result was an orgy of reckless torturing, raping, and killing of the residents of Panama. Alerted well in advance of the approaching raid, the citizens of Panama loaded their treasures aboard the *La Santissima Trinidad*. The ship slipped out of the port days before the buccaneers reached Panama. Though the Spaniards left several careened ships that could easily have been righted to chase after the *La Santissima Trinidad*, by the time Morgan discovered the news, his men were too drunk or too obsessed with finding easier treasure to bother with a pursuit on water.

The loss of the treasury was not the only disaster. A fire, possibly started when the Governor ordered the city's powder magazine to be blown, spread quickly and destroyed much of the remaining fortune and buildings.

Morgan, fearing the captured booty was not sufficient to appease his men, made the unwise decision to stay in the city for nearly two weeks in the hopes of uncovering more. He sent groups of buccaneers on excursions outside the city to search for buried loot, but found none. Finally, in February 1671, Morgan gave the order to return to the ships. With horses laden with loot and a collection of over 500 hostages, the exhausted ramble of buccaneers took twice as long to return to the east coast. All the while they were constantly harassed and ambushed by Indians and surviving Spaniards.

On the beach, the loot was hastily divided and after all the cuts, each buccaneer received a paltry 200 pieces of eight. Morgan, fearing their displeasure might lead to mutiny, ordered barrels of rum to be taken from the ships and opened on the beach to celebrate their victory. Again, Morgan lost control of his men. Drunk and unruly, they abandoned their hostages, fought over shares, and committed all sorts of debauchery.

"Where is Barnaby?" Peter Haywood asked after finding Twiggy well away from the others.

Not entirely sober Twiggy replied, "He is lost to his rum and happiness!"

"I have just heard a rumor," Peter whispered, "and we may be in grave danger. This rum is a distraction, Twiggy. Morgan told his most trusted men to take not a drop of it. He plans to sail his best ships this night without the rest of us."

"Ah, come about, mate. Why would he do something like that?" Twiggy asked disbelieving.

"Because he is afraid. He worries that having received such small awards; the men may see fit to take the king's share and take their anger out on Morgan. I tell you, Twiggy, he's taking the soundest of the ships and leaving the broken ones for this lot left on the beach. Morgan intends to leave us behind, Twiggy. The Spanish and the

Indians, they're there in the jungle just waiting for the advantage. And the hostages we allowed to escape will fortify them. They'll trap us here on the beach."

"These be tittle-tattles, Peter. They say, he says . . . Rumors! I heard them all before."

"I found three of Morgan's crew who are willing to swap places with us. They're Spanish, the three of them, and are willing to take their chances here. They'll sign us on board as Morgan's crew, for a dear price," Peter said, looking around to be sure that no others heard.

"It's a sham, Peter! They mean to rob us!" Twiggy insisted. He looked about, then asked with suspicion, "And what might that price be?"

"A hundred," Peter whispered.

"A hundred!" Twiggy protested loudly, drawing the attention of those around him. "That's half our loot! Don't ya see, Peter? They will takes our money and come morning all them ships will still be anchored out there. They're 'aving us on, mate!"

"Shhh! I would rather give a hundred than my life, Twiggy. I'm going. The choice is yours if you want it," Peter said.

"Let me think on it while I goes and finds Barnaby. Last I saw, he be passed out up the beach, there." With great effort, Twiggy rolled up from the sand and stumbled on to find his friend. To his irritation, the three Spaniards followed. One of them had a devilish grin that annoyed Twiggy. He did not trust them but he was unwilling to completely ignore the instincts of Peter.

Barnaby was lying on his back with an empty jug by his side. With his eyes half opened and a stream of bubbling drool flowing from his lips, he was clearly lost in a stupor of rum. Twiggy got down on his knees next to his friend, slapped his face several times with no response.

"Barnaby! Barnaby Tibbs, up with ya, man!" Twiggy shook him by the shoulders.

"Twiggy, we have to go. They've loaded the ship and are about to pull anchor. These men want their money now or the deal is off!" Peter pleaded.

Twiggy looked off to the horizon and squinted. In the moon's faint light could see silhouetted figures moving about on Morgan's ship preparing the sails. He looked down at Barnaby, then to Peter. "I cannot just up and leave me mate."

Both men tried to rouse Barnaby. They succeeded in lifting him, but their attempts to drag him across the soft sand failed. Morgan's men were now impatient and threatened to end the deal. With great effort, Twiggy hoisted the robust Barnaby over his shoulder but sailors claimed that would not do. He'd not be allowed on the ship in such a state, they said, and began to walk away.

"Wait! Espere – por favor!" Peter pleaded. He took Twiggy by the arm. "We have to go without him."

"I can't leave 'im." Twiggy roughly shook Barnaby who responded with a moan, but little else.

"Twiggy, we have to go. Trust me on this. You must consider your family . . . your boys. Barnaby is clever and lucky. He'll to find a way to follow, but to stay with him, my friend, is a risk too high for the likes of you and me." Peter pulled Twiggy away from the unconscious Barnaby. Money exchanged. An argument ensued among the three Spaniards, but in the end they agreed to take Peter and Barnaby to Morgan's ship.

Twiggy looked at his friend lying in the sand once more. "Forgive me, Barnaby. Forgive me, old friend," he cried.

At first, Morgan's early arrival in Port Royal was jubilant and festive. But slowly facts about the foibles of the invasion, the harsh treatment of the residents of Panama, and the abandonment of crew on the Isthmus darkened the celebratory mood. Families and friends of the seamen left behind became anxious and openly challenged the behavior of Morgan. Claiming the charges against him were preposterous, Morgan defended his actions by explaining that the fleet officially disbanded once the booty was fairly and openly distributed, according to the rules of the Brethren. However, neither Morgan nor Modyford could so easily explain the atrocities.

In London, Spain's ambassador demanded recompense and satisfaction for the assault on its citizens and the destruction by fire of their finest city. It came in the form of Sir Thomas Lynch. In June 1671, Lynch was sent from London to replace Thomas Modyford as governor of Jamaica and to arrest Modyford and Morgan for their part in the raid on Panama. Fearing Modyford's power and the strength of his advocacies, Lynch remained anchored in Kingston Harbor and invited Modyford to dine aboard his ship.

"It's a trap!" Elizabeth warned.

"My dear, you worry too much. If he wanted me in chains, he would have sent his marines to have me arrested. No, I believe he merely wants assurances that he will not be harmed or undermined in his take over of the governorship. I'll be back late. Don't wait up for me and for my sake, do not worry."

Thomas enjoyed a magnificent meal, but decided he thoroughly disliked Lynch. He seemed to radiate an air of mistrust. After the meal, Lynch filled several glasses of port and gave an elaborate, if not overly loquacious, toast to the king. Thomas lifted his glass, but the other officers at the table did not imitate the gesture, as was the custom. They set their full glasses down upon the table and removed their swords. For a moment, Thomas felt his wife clearly on his shoulder.

Thomas Modyford was taken captive and was immediately sent back to England in chains where he was banished to the Tower of London. Though confined, for the most part, within the walls of the great Tower complex, he was not treated as an ordinary prisoner. At his own expense, Modyford was allowed all the conveniences a gentleman might have in his home – fine furnishings, excellent food, superb wines, servants, and limitless entertainment and visitors. He did not, however, have the freedom to broker his own price for such luxuries and relied on the mercies of the King's men. They, of course, tacked on a handsome surcharge for their services.

Peter Haywood stayed in Jamaica with Twiggy. Upon hearing their plight, Sir Gregor and Lady Cranston invited them to come and stay at Windhaven until they fully recovered from their ordeal. Peter accepted the offer, but Twiggy remained in Port Royal.

"No, thank ya kindly. But, I couldn't face your brother, Lady Cranston. I knows how fond the lad was of Mr. Tibbs," he lamented. "No. I'll wait here in Port Royal. Tis a better place to be if any news comes of old Barnaby."

After several false leads and even an attempted swindle, Twiggy spent every penny on the purchase of information of the fate of Barnaby. He finally can across one story that seemed to have a measure of credibility. The pirate claimed that after Morgan left, those that were left behind scrambled to make ready the remaining ships for the homeward journey. Provisions were low. He and others, including Barnaby, went into the forest to forage. The Spaniards surrounded and captured the hunting party, treated them with much brutality, and marched them back to Panama City to be exchanged for Spanish hostages held by the French. According to the pirate's account, Barnaby died of fever before reaching the city. It took another week before Twiggy found two others who corroborated the story.

Twiggy was a broken man, both in his heart and his pockets. Much grieved and racked with guilt, he wanted to go home. Wallace Blake asked Sally if he might go to Port Royal to see his old crewman. Sally agreed, but only if she and James would be permitted to accompany him for his safekeeping. It was a heartfelt reunion. The old captain handed over a purse to Twiggy to help with his passage home on the promise that he would not take to the sea again. James did his best to exonerate Twiggy for the loss of Barnaby.

It took some time, but Twiggy eventually found a place on a ship headed for the northern colonies. Before leaving Jamaica, however, he made an effort to find the attorney who had drafted Barnaby's will.

Nearly a year after Modyford was sent to the Tower, Henry Morgan was finally arrested and transported to London in April 1672. Although considered a prisoner of state, Morgan was never incarcerated and spent most of his "punishment" consulting with the high admiralty and cavorting with the aristocracy in London.

Two years seemed a sufficient penance to pay for the sacking of Panama and with no charges against them; King Charles II of England finally released the two Jamaicans from their bondage. He praised the loyalty of both by rewarding Morgan with a knighthood and by making him Lieutenant-Governor of Jamaica and Modyford, the Chief Justice. Both were ordered back to Jamaica.

CHAPTER 18

"Light the bloody thing!" the chubby boy with the runny nose shouted.

Molly gathered the hem of her dress, twisted it and tucked it between her knees. She knelt on the ground and struck the flint close to the fuse.

"It's the wind!" she complained. "It's blowing it out." Undaunted, she struck the flint harder and this time succeeded in igniting the fuse. "There!" she said. "I've got it!"

"Well throw it then, you stupid girl!" another boy sputtered dumb-founded as he cautiously stepped back. "Throw it!" he screamed.

"Not yet. Not yet. We've got to . . ." Bam! The flash blinded Molly. Her nostrils stung from the sulfur. It took a second before she realized the firecracker exploded before she was able to throw it. Her eyes cleared enough to see blood squirt from her finger with the pulsating rhythm of her heartbeat. She looked up to see her friends shouting and running towards her, but she heard nothing. Blackness covered her eyes once again.

"Molly? Molly, dear?" Following the physician's request, Sally tried to arouse her daughter. She brushed a cool wet cloth over Molly's forehead until she opened her eyes. "That's better. You've had an accident, but you are fine now, Molly. Can you understand me?" Gregor nervously paced the room behind her.

Molly lifted her left hand. It was wrapped in soft white linen from the wrist to the end of her fingers. "Oh, thank the Lord,' she struggled. "I thought I had blown it right off. It is . . . still there, is it not?"

Sally inhaled deeply. She was relieved that her daughter, at least for the moment, had forgotten the agony of the amputation and cauterization. "Yes, my darling, you can see your hand is still there, but it has suffered a grievous injury. You have . . . you have lost your little finger of that hand," Sally began to cry despite her obvious efforts to preserve an air of composure. She wiped her tears and continued, "The doctor is much assured that if you take the very best of care and allow your hand to heal properly, you will be able to do everything you did before, Molly."

"Not everything!" Gregor groused. "There will be no more fire sticks, young lady! Where did you get such a thing, daughter?"

"I gave it to her," a deep voice came from the doorway. James stood as if waiting for an invitation to enter.

"Oh, James! She is a child! And a girl!" Sally scolded her brother.

"And she can shoot a pistol better than me. I thought she would be more responsible with it," James reasoned.

"Don't blame him, mother. It was my fault. I held it for too long," Molly pleaded.

James came close to the bed where his young niece lay. He said nothing, but nodded his head, smiled, and reached out to flick Molly's nose in a teasing yet tender manner. He turned and left the room. Gregor was anxious to follow him.

"Rest up now, sweet Molly!" Gregor awkwardly bellowed and slipped out of the room.

Molly grabbed her mother's arm. "Please don't let father blame James. It really was my fault, mother. We were playing a foolish game of dare."

"Molly, what have I told you about playing with the boys? It is not becoming! And look where this foolishness has led you."

"James's fire stick was nothing, mother. We have made worse devices using gunpowder. It wasn't his fault! Why must father and James constantly quarrel so?"

"Shhh. Do not fret, Molly. We will talk of this later. The doctor said complete bed rest after such a shock. So, rest, easy now!" she commanded. Sally adjusted Molly's bedding, and then left the room, closing the door to keep Molly from hearing her father's raised voice as he admonished James.

"This time Molly was fortunate," Gregor scolded. "Your injudicious influence might have cost her much more than a finger. Why, that young George Manning said that only seconds before, while lighting the damned thing, she had her face right up against it!" Gregor steamed as he paced in front of James. "Her face!"

"It was foolish to have trusted her so. I am sorry," James sulked.

"Trusted her! What were *you* doing with such a thing?" Gregor demanded.

"A Dutch ship from China has come to port and the sailors at the Three Turtles were . . ."

"I have asked you repeatedly to stay clear of those wicked ale houses," Sally interjected as she entered the room, carrying the youngest and newest member of the Cranston clan, Thomas. "Now see what has come of your patronage there."

James exhaled rudely. "Sally, for pity's sake, I am sixteen and I . . ."

"Before we take up this rather old and tired argument James, your sister and I have a proposal we wish to discuss. And now is an appropriate time! We are aware of your . . . discontentment as a planter."

James raised his hand to protest. "It's not the planter's life I . . ."

"No, now, please let me finish," Gregor insisted, trying to keep calm. "You are of an age, as you just reminded us . . . *again*, and are free to follow your own ambitions. However, your sister and I would like to offer you the opportunity to extend your education," Gregor proposed, crafting his words carefully. He did not expect enthusiasm or even gratitude, but still, James's inimical reaction did surprise him.

"So, you wish to pack me off to London?" James huffed.

"Actually, no. Boston." Sally stepped in to tender calmer tones. "We have written to Ezekiel Cheever, headmaster at Boston's Latin Grammar School. He is prepared to take you as a student of preparatory studies. If you do well, he may recommend you for a place at Harvard College, James. We have also arranged with Captain Waller that you board with him, at least at the week's end, while you complete your studies there."

"Edward Waller? You've plotted this with him? When?" James thought for a moment then said, "I see. You made these . . . arrangements while he was here during his last visit with us and chose not to include me in those discussions?" He pulled his lower lip in and clamped it between his teeth as if to try to keep further words captive.

Gregor cleared his throat and then said, ignoring the protests, "Well, that is it. How think you on this matter, James? Does such a proposal . . . interest you?"

James sighed. "It is a generous offer, Gregor. One designed with much hope for me and presented in haste, I suspect, to keep me from corrupting my niece further and from pursuing my true desires – to go pirating."

"Oh mercy, James, not this again!" Sally said exasperated. She sat her three year-old toddler on the floor along with several playthings to keep him occupied. "Why are you stuck on this ambition? Do you not understand Governor Lynch's resolve to put an end to this illicit practice? Have you not seen how many he's hung at Gallows Point?"

"Morgan's men have . . ." James started.

"Henry Morgan was taken from this island! In chains!" Gregor shouted.

"But in England he remains a hero. He's coming back, they say, this time with the king's appointment. Both he and Thomas Modyford have been vindicated." James declared.

Sally could see the sizzling acrimony growing between her husband and her brother, a state that was becoming all too frequent and increasingly difficult to soften.

"I pray often" she said quietly "that the next wind will carry Thomas home to Jamaica, back to his long-suffering wife, Elizabeth. However, I do believe that privateering is a practice that is no longer accepted, James. And Thomas will certainly not sanction the very activity that put him in the Tower. To stay afloat, these islands, no matter to which country they owe their allegiance, must have free commerce. That cannot happen if the seas are full of thieves." James sat down in a chair and, as he had done since he was a boy, respectfully listened to his sister. Seizing the opportunity, Sally pulled up a chair close to his, and took his hand in hers. "The time has come, dear brother, when you must prepare for your situation in life."

James rose suddenly from his chair and went over to Thomas, sat down on the floor cross-legged and teased the child with a rattle. He declared in a more civil, though not convincing, tone, "I had hoped to be a planter one day." He looked at Gregor. "Have you not prepared me for that enterprise?"

"Aye," Gregor agreed. "Tis a fine livelihood, James. But you'll need more than you have now to become the best." Gregor tapped his index finger to the side of his head to make his point. "Take not my word on this. Think of the best planters on Jamaica, all gentlemen with proper schooling. It is right that a young man's heart be full of adventure, but it is not right that he wants to become a thief!" Gregor could not help himself from raising his objections and his volume again.

Sally threw her hand up to silence her husband. He obeyed and retreated to the far side of the room and looked out the window. "The Latin School . . . it's a good prospect, James. Take it. Give it two years. If it does not satisfy you, then you'll be of an age to chart your own course, and I promise, God willing, we will assist you in whatever path you choose. Will we not, Gregor?"

Gregor looked surprised. Her statement was too open, too vague to give such a promise, but seeing her imploring eyes said, "Of course we will, James. Despite what you may think, I . . . we care much for . . . for your future. If you were my son, I would insist . . . expect and hope that you finish your education."

"I could live with Captain Waller?" James asked, confirming the terms.

"Yes. From Monday to Friday, you will board at the school. Edward and Anani live in Dorchester now, just a short carriage ride from the school." Sally replied, chasing after Thomas who seeing his mother preoccupied, decided to make a run for it.

"The Indian girl?" he asked.

"I . . . do not believe he thinks of her as such, but yes, she is half Indian. Her father was British. Though she is certainly no longer a girl. Edward tells me she has grown to become a beautiful young woman and well seeded in

Boston society. I am sure she would delight in introducing you to . . ."

"Two years, you say?" James interrupted, looking to Gregor.

Gregor left the window and stood beside his wife. "Two years. If you decided to stay longer, I am sure we can accommodate your . . ."

"Then I agree," James declared curtly. Realizing his rudeness, he softened his tone, "I accept your proposal. Please, I pray you think me not an ingrate. I do appreciate all that you have done for me." James bowed to Sally and Gregor and left the room.

After some thought and too long a silence, Gregor remarked, "He is an odd one, your brother."

Sally laughed. "However trying, I do believe his heart is pure, Gregor. We must trust he will do the right thing."

"And so, I believe, have we, my love. Now, let us turn our thoughts and prayers to our much wayward daughter. What can we do?" asked Gregor.

"Do? Do? Though it will break my heart to part with her, it is obvious what we must do. We have no option than to send her off to school as well, Gregor, as soon as she is of age. Lady Modyford suggested a school in London, a reputable institution whose sole task is to domesticate fearsome wild lionesses from the colonies. Miss Cupperfinch's School for Young Ladies. Frightfully expensive, but well worth every ha'penny if it will tame our Molly. They would teach her how to sew, to sing, and manage domestic duties. The very qualities that fine gentlemen of proper means look for in a young woman. I have done my best, dear Gregor, but she has such a strong will and has managed to navigate around our expectations."

Gregor looked surprised at his wife and wondered, *has she, truly, no clue that Molly is her exact likeness in looks and in manner*?

"Sally?" he asked nervously. "Do you think she has ruined . . . I mean, suppose one day she, by the blessing of some saint, finds the right gentleman. Do you think he'd be put off by . . ." Gregor could not bring himself to say it.

"I do not believe our Molly would ever settle for such a shallow man who would consider her ill-qualified to be a good wife because she lacks a single digit upon a hand she rarely uses!" Sally replied in a huff. "Tis nothing I say, Gregor, and we must project that sentiment in good faith around her so that, in time, she will come to believe it. Tis nothing!"

Over the weeks, visitors came from all over the island to wish James farewell and to check on the recovery of Molly. Molly quite enjoyed the attention. Her high spirits hastened her recuperation and before long, she was off again on explorative forays and misadventures, much to the chagrin of Sally.

However, there was a slight but noticeable limit to how far Molly would stretch her mother's patience. A tiny sense of reserved attitude and careful retrospect began to grow in Molly. She spent more time at home, caring for young Thomas, reading the few books available to her, and keeping a diary. She soon learned to move her afflicted hand in a graceful manner that concealed her finger's stump and scars. To make her missing finger less obvious, she wrapped her good fingers around some eye-catching distraction like a frilly lace handkerchief or some delicately convoluted fan of velum and whalebone.

James enjoyed a quiet peace in the weeks preceding his departure. He looked forward to living with Edward and to the challenge of preparing for studies at

Harvard College. He was confident that, with rigorous revision, he could match the ability and knowledge of those who had the advantage of attending school regularly. Gregor was particularly pleased that, at least for the moment, James seemed to set aside his desires to go pirating.

"It is impressive, James," Gregor noted, "that Massachusetts gives such high regard to the education of its citizens. I understand it is now the law that for every town of fifty families, they must provide a schoolmaster, and for a hundred families, a grammar school! That is progressive. In that regard, and in that alone, I believe Massachusetts has the better of us."

"Massachusetts cannot match us for the sun's warmth" James replied "and that is what produces wealth from the ground, not the education of its citizens. Their season is considerably shorter. I cannot imagine that the northern colonies will ever be able to produce the quantity of food they will need to feed their growing population," James replied.

"Ah," Sally added. "That is the very concern I have for Jamaica. We keep turning over our soil to cane, tobacco, and cotton that we cannot eat. That is why it is important to keep our seas open and free for commerce and our sons well versed in the knowledge of good husbandry!" Sally waved her free arm about while trying to spoon-feed a fussy Thomas with the other. Gregor and James looked to one another and rolled their eyes. They knew better than to tangle with her arguments. Sally noticed the exchange. "What?" she challenged.

"Well, it appears our James is packed and ready for this next adventure, Sally!" Gregor tried to change the subject.

"You have both done me so well. I shall want for nothing!" replied James, lifting little Thomas high into the air. The little boy screeched with delight and asked for more. Instead, James kissed Thomas tenderly on his forehead. "I shall miss you, my little beetle. Be a good boy while I'm gone!"

"Nero and Capt. Blake took the casks down the river on the rafts this morning," Gregor said. He looked to the sky and seeing the sun at its zenith declared, "They should be at the mouth by now, don't you think Sally?"

"Yes. And let us hope there is no one unexpected to meet them there," Sally added wishfully. James looked confused. Sally's eyes twinkled for a moment before she looked away.

"Those casks do not contain molasses, James, but logwood – in payment for your passage and comforts on this voyage," Gregor explained. James shot Sally a look of total surprise.

"Logwood!" he said. "You are shipping logwood? To Boston?" A broad self-righteous grin developed from his surprise. "So, my dear sister becomes a smuggler, now! And the recent edicts shall be ignored? Not a wonder Lady Cranston champions free commerce on the high seas!" James and Gregor laughed.

"Stop! The two of you!" Sally demanded, but clearly they could not. She let it go. It was a good moment, to hear her husband and her brother laugh together.

Behind his teasing, Gregor did harbor some measure of concern. A charge of smuggling would mean their end. Jamaica's insufferable Governor Lynch was determined to follow the letter of the laws of England as mandated in the Navigation Acts and did not tolerate the movement of goods to anywhere but England. The shipment of logwood from one colony to another was forbidden and a punishable offense. If caught, Sally and Gregor could face fines, revocation of their land grants, or worse. They stood to lose everything. And there was added fear of what would become of Nero and the old captain had they been caught with such contraband. However, this product had greater value than any monetary bribe to the captain sailing to Boston. That captain would most assuredly take good care of his cargo, both human and contraband, for he would not realize his greatly inflated profits until he delivered both safely to Massachusetts. If anything happened to James, Gregor was quite prepared to lay charges of smuggling on the captain. Even an unproven charge would destroy his reputation and career as a mariner. It would eliminate the possibility of him ever receiving another commission on a worthy merchantman. Extortion, it seemed, was a very tidy and effective scheme to assure James's comfort and safety. But the danger of discovery was real and the most vulnerable time was waiting for the ship to arrive just outside the mouth of the Milk River. Suspicious anchoring along the shores far from the harbor of Port Royal alerted patrolling British naval vessels to the possibility of smuggling and they had the right to board all vessels to search for contraband.

It was time for James to go. He said his farewells to Sally and Thomas, bowed and kissed the mangled hand of Molly and chased his young nephew around the house one last time. He left with Gregor on horseback to the Milk River. There they boarded a canoe and followed the swift water to the mouth where they met Nero and Captain Blake. They camped that night and at mid-morning the following day, they saw the ship sail past a spit of land to the east. There was little time to lose. They loaded the skiff with barrels of personal items first. Captain Blake and James took the first turn. Their careful tacking and timing was perfect and they intercepted the ship, unloaded the wares and James, and sent the skiff back with Captain Blake alone for the second load. This time heavy casks of contraband filled the skiff. Nero and Captain Blake sailed the skiff with great skill, unloaded the casks without incident and in no time, the merchantman pulled anchor, hoisted her sails, and was off. In all the rush, James realized he had not said his proper farewells to Gregor. He climbed the fore mast to the bottom of the fore sail, waved frantically, and shouted to the lone figure on the beach.

Gregor was concentrating on the returning skiff and waded into the water to help as Nero and the old captain beached it. He looked up in time to see the ship turn for deeper seas and thought he saw a man waving on the fore masthead. Hoping it to be James, he waved back. Gregor ran along the rocky shore, still waving, until the ship sailed off the horizon.

Two weeks after James left Windhaven, Sally finally approached Gregor with an idea that she had brewed for months.

"Gregor dear, what would you think about investing in property in Port Royal?" she tested one balmy night as they shared a moment of peace on the verandah after Molly and Thomas were tucked in their beds.

"Property? In Port Royal? Windhaven isn't enough to keep you and I occupied?" he asked.

"I was thinking of a shop. Not for me to run, of course, but to rent to a keeper of some respectable business."

Gregor considered Sally's proposition. The long silence grew awkward. "I think . . . ." he finally replied, then hesitated. As he dropped his head and rubbed the back of his neck Sally gathered her thoughts for a second round of rationale. Gregor cleared his throat and mumbled, "It's bound to be a good investment. Yes!" He looked up with a wide grin and declared exuberantly, "I think that would be an excellent idea, my dear! Yes, I do!"

For a moment, Sally was taken off guard for she fully expected to work harder at convincing him. Gregor laughed at her speechlessness. "I can think of no weighty objection. It is a good and solid idea. You would have to inquire, of course, what entrepreneurs might be seeking an establishment. Would you build your shop or purchase an existing one? What streets favor business and which to avoid? You would have to check the numbers. What are the current rates for such a building and what tariff would be tied to the shop? How much rent can you charge? How long would you hold the tenant? Would the shopkeeper require accommodation with the building? Might you rent rooms separately to tenants unrelated to the business of the shopkeeper?" he explained.

"I have already given much thought to many of your concerns and have done some preliminary study of Port Royal. My biggest apprehension is the amount of time this venture would require me to be in Port Royal, especially in the beginning. I cannot be away from Windhaven or the children for long. So . . . I thought of taking on a trusted partner, someone who lives in Port Royal and already has experience in running a successful business."

"That's very clever of you, dear. Have you someone in mind?"

There was a tense moment of silence as Sally tried to think of a way to soften the blow she was surely about to deliver. "Madame Jaclyn de Witt."

Again, there was awkward moment of silence as Gregor processed the name.

"You don't mean . . . this Madame de Witt, she is *the* Madame de Witt? Madam to several whorehouses in the Point?"

"And all highly profitable, Gregor!"

"Sally, I am afraid to ask, but how is it that you have become so familiar with this . . . woman?"

"She did me a kindness once and it was I who sought her for advice on this idea. She guided me through most of the inquiries you yourself have just now made. I believe her to be an honest soul, Gregor, and quite keen to diversify her . . . assets. She has already proven her gift for business and most importantly she is there in Port Royal to supervise the daily workings of the investment. I do not fear that my association with her would affect our reputation. In fact, Madame de Witt is well respected by many members of the community."

Gregor smiled, "I believe those particular members of our society would be exclusively male and most of them her clients, Sally." Sally was about to retort, but Gregor put his hand up. "You said Madame de Witt did you some kindness, and for that she has my gratitude. You said she is honest, and there is no one I trust more to assess a person's core values than you. You have already confided in her, before me, so I have little doubt that this woman has earned your trust. It seems, therefore, my dear wife; you have found a worthy partner."

Sally breathed a long sign of relief and looked at her husband with admiration. She reached out for his hand and he quickly surrendered it, wrapped it around her waist and pulled her close.

"We have found the perfect shop," she continued, "on Queen Street. It was formerly a bakery. The shop is now vacant and for sale. Jaclyn knows the owner and believes him to be desperate to make a quick sale. It has one large open room at the ground floor and two rooms above, and a substantial yard with a privy and storage shed. And, Jaclyn has found a potential renter. He is a young gentleman, a journeyman, a barber and peruke maker by the name of Benjamin Carter. He wishes to go into business as his own master and requires a shop with modest accommodation."

"Well!" Gregor declared. "I suppose we need to make plans to go to Port Royal and close this deal. A wigmaker?" he pondered. "Do we have one in Port Royal? There's the one I use in Spanish Town . . . Do you think he will succeed in a place like Port Royal? Yes, yes . . . I think you may be on to something, Sally, you clever girl! And, how did you meet Madame de Witt?"

CHAPTER 19

James could not believe his eyes. Imagining it a paltry colony of religious fanatics, Boston was, in fact, a formidable city. A forest of masts glistened in the morning sun that rose slowly over the bay. The harbor's deep water and wide berth for the docking of multiple ships made Boston a natural port.

"T'ain't like yer Port Royal, mate," a seaman warned in a throaty voice, "this here town be full of them self-righteous Puritans who don't rightly distinguish the law from the bible. Read that book, 'ave ya, lad? Well, they's soon as hang ya for any crime that's written in that holy book of theirs. Watch yerself there. They be short on tolerance for the wickedness we Jamaicans enjoy!" the seaman roared with laughter, then stopped suddenly. "Oh, nearly forgot why I come to ya. I'm supposed to tells ya, the captain wants to sees ya."

"Thank you. And for the warning!" James replied as he went astern to find the captain.

"Ah, Mr. Montague," the captain spoke in the same tone of kindness he afforded the entire voyage. "Safely delivered to Boston, as promised. I wanted to wish you well in your studies, Mr. Montague. It is a worthy ambition. See that you work on your patience for it. The colonies need home-grown educated gentlemen who understand both ends of an axe," he advised. The captain removed a folded paper from the small pocket of his doublet and handed it to James. "This is the name of an honorable friend. He's an Indian, a Pokanoket, but a gentleman who knows the King's language better than most ne'er-do-wells who call themselves Englishmen. He went to Harvard College. Look for him. He would be a good friend to have and an excellent tutor, should you need one. I trust few others in Boston."

James took the paper, opened it, and read the name. "Thank you, sir. That is most kind of you. I appreciate the introduction."

"Goodbye, Mr. Montague, and good fortunes!" The captain bowed quickly, and then returned to his duties.

A savage, James thought, *going to Harvard*! James returned to his cramped quarters below to pack the last of his belongings. It was a sunny, warm summer morning and he was anxious to put his feet on firm land again. He bade farewell to the crew and headed down the gangplank to the docks below. His first steps were wobbly. A few members of the crew watched from the rails, anticipating the difficulties James would have in regaining his land-legs. They howled with laughter. "Does the gentleman require a walking stick, then?" one of them mocked.

James laughed and sent a rude gesture back to the crew.

"Eh - eh, now, mate. Remember what I told ya about dat kind of wicked behavior. We wouldn't want to see ya hangin' from the yardarm, now would we?"

"No, no!" the rest of the crew chorused jokingly. Though not within his sight, James heard the captain admonish his crew, ordering them to get on with their duties. He laughed and watched as one by one they disappeared from the railings. He turned and once again tried to navigate down the dock. As he reached the street, a well-dressed man with a beautiful young woman on his arm approached him. He did not recognize Edward Waller, and nearly walked past the couple.

"James Montague!" Edward declared.

James hesitated, then embarrassed, he remarked, "Captain Waller! Forgive me! You are . . ."

Edward smiled and was gracious about the reference to his graying hair and broader figure. "You have grown older, too, James!" he joked. "We wanted to be here for your ship's arrival as, I confess, I felt the strong urge to see you the moment you set foot on our shores. Welcome! Welcome to Boston! Allow me to introduce my ward, Miss Anani Trapitt."

"Miss Trapitt," James acknowledged with a deep bow. "I am delighted and honored that you should meet me here at the docks. And I am pleased to see you again, Captain Waller."

"Please, call me Edward."

"And, as we will be living beneath the same roof, sir," the young woman chimed in, "I think it only fitting that you call me Anani. Papa has told me much about you. Your journey was pleasant, I pray?"

"It was without incident, thank you."

A sheepish man with his hat in his hand came from behind Edward. "Ah this is my servant, Henry. He will tend to your belongings."

James looked back to the ship at the end of the dock. He put two fingers between his lips and produced a piercing whistle. A crewman looked over the side rails. "This gentleman will handle my barrels . . . all *six* of them!" James shouted. The crewman waved in acknowledgement. To the servant he said, "They are full barrels, but give them a shake to be sure the contents have not been replaced with the ship's ballast." The servant smiled knowingly and nodded his head.

"Our carriage is waiting down the street, James. Henry will bring your goods along in a wagon. We are most anxious to hear of your voyage. How fares your sister and Windhaven?"

"Papa, let the poor boy start by shedding his sea-legs," Anani protested.

"Ah, quite right, my dear, plenty of time for questions," Edward offered his arm to Anani.

"Perhaps, Papa, I may service James's balance by walking beside him," she suggested. She put her hand gently on James's forearm, giving him the opportunity to admire her incredible beauty. He was immediately infatuated. Her pale azure eyes presented a striking contrast to her dark bronze skin. Though he knew her to be five years older than him, she was surprisingly small and delicate, almost child-like in stature.

"We've moved from Boston, James. Our home is now in the village of Dorchester, not far," Edward explained. "As soon as you are fit and ready, we'll come back to Boston and I will introduce you to Mr. Ezekiel Cheever, headmaster of the Latin Grammar School. You have been assigned rooms at the school where you can stay during the week. It's not much, I'm afraid, and you will have to share them with several others. I took the liberty to add some furnishings. At week's end you can come and join us in Dorchester."

"Thank you, sir. That is most generous. Tell me, Captain Waller . . . do you think I am too old to be attending this grammar school?" James asked.

"Edward, please. And no, not at all. I've seen young gentlemen, older than you, in attendance. Cheever offers tuition for the sons of colonials who have a good grounding and wish to prepare for studies at Harvard College, or even finer institutions across the sea. Your circumstances are not unique James, and you'll not be alone in your endeavors. The college is growing. They have recently started work on a four-story building. Harvard Hall, they are calling it. Quite impressive! I think you will be pleasantly surprised with the civil disposition and growth of our fair city."

James patted his pocket to check that the paper the captain gave him was still there. He wanted to ask about how it was that an Indian went to Harvard, but reminded himself that Anani was of mixed blood and thought it more prudent to leave the question for a time when Edward and he were alone.

Once his classes had begun, James found, to his amazement, that he was quite academically competent in the sciences and mathematics. But, he still struggled with languages, particularly French. By mid October, he realized he needed help if he was to pass his language exams. When he inquired about a suitable tutor, he was surprised when Headmaster Cheever recommended one John Sassamon for that job. James recognized the name immediately.

"I know this name, sir. The captain of the vessel on which I sailed from Jamaica suggested I introduce myself to him," James explained to the headmaster.

"And I see that you have not yet done so. Why?" the headmaster replied.

"I understand that he is . . . Indian," James said in an awkward tone.

"Mr. Sassamon is a *gentleman* from whom you would gain much knowledge, sir. He is well versed in several languages. Many students here have profited from his tutelage," the headmaster advised.

"Sir, where might I find him?" James asked.

"Ah, now that is a task. He often moves from our world to his and back again. Never long in either. He mostly stays near Lakeville, but comes to Boston regularly. Put the word out. *He* will find *you*, Master Montague."

It was less than a fortnight when a roommate announced to James that he had a rather unusual visitor awaiting his company. James rushed down the stairs to find not the image he had imagined, but a slender and tall man. Except for his dark skin and deep wrinkles, he could be mistaken for any gentleman of Boston by his manner and his dress. He was older than James had expected. His hair, long but neatly coiffed and tied back with a ribbon, was graying at the temples. He bowed slightly and said, "Je crois que vous avez besoin d'assistance à parler français."

"Yes, sir, I do need help with my French," James replied with a laugh.

"I am available for one hour, on this day of the week only, at this particular hour. Does that suit you?" John Sassamon said in a business-like manner.

"Yes, sir, it does!" James replied.

"And the fees?"

James had no idea what the charges were. He didn't want to ask for it did not matter to him. He suspected what he would learn from this man would be a great deal more than French.

"Yes, agreeable."

"Then let us begin without further delay. It is a fine day and the leaves are beautiful this time of year, do you not agree? Our first lesson will be there . . . under those maples," he said. John Sassamon placed his round, wide-brimmed hat on his head and immediately began conjugating in French, 'the leaves are turning yellow, the leaves have turned yellow, the leaves will turn yellow . . .'

Throughout the autumn and into his first cold New England winter, James looked forward to two events – Saturday and Sundays in Dorchester and his weekly session with John Sassamon. It took two sessions before James discovered his tutor and he shared a common tragedy. They both lost parents to the migration of the English to the Americas. Sassamon had lost his to the smallpox epidemic of 1633. At thirteen, he was the only member of his family and one of very few from his village to survive the disease. An English Puritan family living in the Plymouth colony adopted Sassamon and provided him with an education. He converted to Christianity and became a teacher and an interpreter. He was accepted to Harvard to study languages and the law in 1653.

"I hadn't even been born at that time, sir," James remarked.

"Then, along with French, I would be remiss if I did not teach you the history of Massachusetts before you white people decided take this land for your own," Sassamon replied in a light-hearted way.

As soon as his lessons were over on Fridays, James would hire a horse and ride to Dorchester to stay with Edward and Anani. Though she teased him mercilessly by calling him "boy" and "bookworm", Anani displayed no objections when he offered to escort her to parties, concerts, and other social outings. James savored every moment that he shared with Anani. He treasured most the quiet evenings when just the three of them sat around the great hearth fire. Anani sang or read to them. Her literary preferences varied widely from execution sermons to the poems of John Milton, all of which, she was certain, had some political agenda or hidden meaning worthy of discussion and debate. Aside from his studies, James had little to add to the dialogue except to share his conversations with his tutor. Eventually, it was what Anani and Edward wanted to hear most.

Early in December, just before the Christmas break, John Sassamon announced that he was confident James had mastered French to the level required by Harvard and would therefore benefit little more from the continuation of his tutelage. James was truly sad to end their weekly sessions.

"I must go to be with my people for a time," Sassamon declared. "I will check on your progress when I return in the early spring. Be well, James Montague, and mind your studies. Education . . . is a master key that can unlock any treasure chest."

James enjoyed the weeks of celebration and feasts with Anani and Edward and did not return to his rooms in Boston until the first week of January. The first day he was back, Headmaster Cheever summoned James and a few other students to his office.

"I have asked you here because each of you has had some association with Mr. Sassamon." The headmaster paused and slowly rose from his chair. "I am afraid I have rather sad news about him. He was found beneath the ice of Assawompset Pond and may have been there for sometime. There are few facts but, as is common in such matters, there are many grave rumors. A persistent one, though it has little in the way of proof or merit, speaks of possible motive and suggests that Mr. Sassamon may have been murdered."

James and the others gasped. He sensed the blood flow from his head and a flash of wooziness struck him. "Why would anyone murder that kind old man?" someone asked.

The headmaster cringed over the reference to being old at 54. "Mr. Sassamon had business with Governor Winslow about an impending attack on the outlying settlements of the Plymouth Colony and named

King Philip as the principal behind that assault. Mr. Sassamon disappeared soon after that. I do not know how to make sense of this tragedy. It is a terrible loss. Terrible!"

When James related this news to Edward, he jumped from his seat and paced the floor.

"Papa, what is it?" Anani asked, alarmed.

"King Philip. His real name is Metacom. He is the sachem of Pokanoket and grand sachem of the Wampanoag Confederacy. A ruthless renegade who has gained power by systematically eliminating his enemies. He has been seen, as of late, shrewdly building alliances of former foes. The death of John Sassamon is tragic, but I pray we do nothing to provoke this King Philip for I do not believe that we are strong enough to defend our villages against the forces he has gathered, especially during the winter."

"Surely our king will send troops to reinforce the militia," James said.

"*Our* king will do little to quell a local insurection, and considers the protection of our settlers the council's matter. We are meant to raise our own armies and the revenue to pay them, while *our* king takes our taxes to fill *his* coffers!" Edward ranted. The subject of taxes touched a nerve with him.

"Papa, you must calm yourself," Anani pleaded rolling her eyes in the direction of James.

"No, please!" James pleaded. "Do not stop on my account, Edward. I cannot believe how much you sound like my sister. I mean, in content of argument and the level of aggravation instigated by certain subjects, like taxes. On that Edward, you share her thoughts. Gregor fears she might one day be taken away in chains, as some of our aquaintances have!" James replied.

"Anani, you are quite right, as always, my dear," Edward said as he bent over and kissed her forehead. "It is a loss, James, the death of your tutor. A great and horrible loss to Massachusetts. Let us hope it ends with that."

But of course, it did not. In the spring of 1675, settlers concluded that Sassamon was not the victim of accidental drowning, but of murder, a fatal consequence of his conversion to Christianity and closeness to the governor. Some members of his tribe and others who did not know him, resented his learning the white man's languages and his belief in the white man's system of governance.

The idea of murder was loosely supported by an Indian with a dubious reputation. He claimed he witnessed three Pokanokets murder Sassamon and cram his body through a hole they created in the ice-covered pond. Though hardly credible, the eyewitness's account was enough to fuel a growing fear among the Puritan settlers who were convinced King Philip was surely behind the crime.

With only the circumstantial evidence, the accused three Pokanokets were indicted in June and quickly tried in Plymouth court. Despite the best legal counsel of Edward's friend, Richard Tucker and other reputable defenders, a mixed jury of Indian and whites convicted all three. The trial, and the rapid execution that followed, ignited smoldering feelings of mistrust and injustice among the Indians.

A single vicious retaliatory attack on an English settlement sparked a war between King Philip and the Puritans. Some settlers abandoned their village homes or consolidated for protection. Throughout the summer, constant harassment by the Pokanokets affected the production, maintenance, and harvesting of crops.

Too dangerous to harvest timber in his isolated forests, Edward concentrated on his cooperage on Cape Cod. In an effort to buffer the financial effects of King Philip's war he increased his trade of salted cod and whale oil.

Several times, James wanted to join the militia and each time it was Anani who talked him out of it. He finished his preparatory studies at the Latin Grammar School, Though his achievements were not outstanding, he passed his examinations sufficiently to warrant a recommendation by Headmaster Cheever to continue his studies at Harvard College.

During the course of his first year at Harvard, however, James developed a growing interest in the business affairs of Edward. He accompanied Edward to Cape Cod on several occasions, meeting up with his old friend, Twiggy Strangeway. He soon lost interest in extending his time in college and felt that he might better prepare for his situation if he apprenticed with Edward and learned the trades and craft of lumbering, carpentry, and the cooperage.

"But I am torn by your request, James, for I did pledge to honor your sister's wishes that you attend school. I cannot break that promise without her blessing. Write to her and Gregor. If they agree to your terms, then I would find it my pleasure to place you in the hands of Mr. Strangeway. No doubt, it would do him good to have an apprentice again. He has suffered many losses and heartache these past years." Edward said. He left the room and Anani took advantage of his absence.

"Yes, our poor, poor Twiggy! People have been unjust to shun him so!" Anani baited.

"Shunned? Mr. Strangeway? Why so?" James asked her.

"Ah!" Anani declared with an air of mystery. "There was that tragic ending for poor Mr. Tibbs. Did he not tell you?"

"He did. He told me Mr. Tibbs died during Morgan's raid on Panama," James replied.

"Ah, now see! Half truths! That is why you *boys* romanticize over the horrid ventures of these pirates. From their lips come much embellished versions of the truth. If you heard the *whole* story, you would not be so keen to admire those you call, The *Brethren* of the Coast," Anani scolded, "nor leave me in Dorchester to work for that old rascal!"

"And I suppose *you* know the truth?" James challenged.

"Indeed, I do! Papa told me. Did you know Twiggy and Barnaby followed Papa here . . . to Boston? They both shared a close partnership with Papa. But they became restless and greedy. They wanted high adventure and fast wealth. Sound familiar? They took their leave from Papa's business, burdening him with nothing but young apprentices to carry on the work. And Twiggy left his poor wife and two sons to run off with Morgan and his murderous thieves. Twiggy returned, but Barnaby Tibbs . . . *he* was left behind on the Isthmus."

"Yes, Twiggy told me as much. I knew several men that were left behind," James said, slightly annoyed that Anani knew more of the story than he.

"Ah, but I reckon Twiggy left out the details," replied Anani in a haughty way. "It was Twiggy who left Barnaby Tibbs. Did you know they *both* had a way of escaping the Isthmus? Twiggy abandoned his friend on the beach and never heard from him again. They say Twiggy is still racked with guilt. He never recovered from the pains suffered from deserting his friend. He blames himself for the death of Mr. Tibbs, as do many of his former friends."

"It seems his actions were limited. I am sure there is more to the story, more than you or I will ever hear," James tried to defend.

"Hmmm, that may be, but his grief was not sufficient to stop him from laying claim to Mr. Tibbs's property!" James looked at Anani in surprise. He had not heard this side of the story. She responded by raising her eyebrow and continued, "Twiggy said they each created a will in Port Royal. *He* claimed Barnaby Tibbs left all to *Mrs.* Strangeway. The probate showed little in the way of possessions and a substantial amount was owed to various people, in Nevis, Barbados, England, the Canaries, and Boston. Twiggy, thinking to honor his friend, happily paid the debts. After all was paid off, the small remainder was used toward the purchase of his farm on Cape Cod. You must surely have seen his farm . . . in Yarmouth?"

"Aye, we visited there, your father and I," James recalled.

"It was paid for with Barnaby Tibb's money! Oh, vicious tongues did wag, James. Some people believed there was some malicious purpose to leaving Mr. Tibbs on that beach."

"Not if they know the man. Twiggy would never do that!" James rushed to defend.

"Yes, *we* know that!" Anani went on. "Not everyone on Cape Cod is so charitable. He and his family suffered cruel treatment, the mean spiritedness played havoc on Mrs. Strangeway. She died of a broken heart."

"I thought she died of fever," James challenged.

"Yes, yes!" Anani agreed but with growing annoyance at James's attempt to correct her story. "She might have recovered had it not been for the scandal. Her death devastated poor Twiggy. Papa feared so for the man. He lives isolated now, on that farm. The twinkle in his eyes . . . gone! He is now quite a solemn, sad man," Anani dramatized.

"He is still and will always be a valuable partner in your father's business. And he is, as you claim, not alone but in the company of his two sons. And he still makes the most superb barrels in all of New England. Not to mention the fine furniture he produces. I did not see the good people of Cape Cod shy away from buying that furniture, Anani."

"Oh yes, he has enjoyed *some* measure of success, but his *soul*, James! His soul is haunted for all time, all because he wanted to pursue the life of a pirate," Anani moralized.

"Then, it seems to me, I would have much to learn from such a man," James surmised, toying with Anani.

"Oh, but then to apprentice with Twiggy Strangeway, one would have to *live* on Cape Cod, so far, far, far away . . . from me," Anani whispered in James's ear as she brushed past him. James caught her flirting with a seductive wink and cheeky smile. Before disappearing behind the door, she looked back once more and blew him a kiss.

CHAPTER 20

"James! James, lad, come quickly! Bring that spade," Twiggy shouted "and the hatchet. Those knives over there, bring them as well. And rope!" Twiggy beamed a wide grin, "We're gonna need lots of rope."

"What's happened?" James asked as he whirled around the shop, gathering the tools.

"Whales! Must be fifty of them blackfish. They've drifted ashore!" Twiggy said breathlessly. He grabbed a handcart, tipped the contents out onto the shop floor, and began filling it as he wheeled past the equipment he needed.

"Whales? Why have they come ashore?" James asked. In the time he had lived on the Cape, he spotted only spouts of whales lingering just off shore.

"No one knows why they strand the way they do. Some reckon the group of them chooses one to be the leader and the others follow. In this case, they chose a knuckleheaded piss-poor pilot who has sent them all to their deaths. And of course, there be those who figure it is some spiritual involvement . . . sending these whales ashore so that we might not starve through another winter. Me? I don't care the reason." He laughed rubbing his hands together, "I just knows there be fat on the fire tonight!" Twiggy was giddy over the sudden good fortune and hopped about the yard like a younger man.

Pushing the cart down the sandy track that led to the beach, James followed behind Twiggy and his two sons. Nothing prepared him for the grim scene he witnessed on the beach. The entire length of the buff-colored sandy strip was littered with long slender black whales. Their bodies, about fifteen to twenty feet long, were askew, some parallel to the shoreline, the rest at all angles. Some were completely out of the water while others struggled along the breakers. Most were still and appeared dead while others thrashed their sleek shiny bodies and struggled, not to return to the water, but to beach themselves further onto land. Most sustained damage with open sores that the gulls were anxious to pick. From those that still lived, gurgling sounds and bloody bubbles expelled through the blowholes.

What terrified James the most was the legion of Yarmouth villagers. Men, women, and children descended on the creatures, tearing and hacking at their flesh. The carnage turned the white crests of the waves pale red as the sea picked up the fresh blood that collected in the tidal pools. Boys, like Twiggy's sons, were leading draft horses dragging firewood while men and women set up large cauldrons over fire pits. Even the smallest children ran along the beach collecting driftwood for the fires. Like actors in a well-rehearsed play, each knew their part, though not necessarily a direct match to their occupation. Jonathan Wilkes was a preacher and a butcher of whale meat. Mary Harding was a seamstress and a renderer of whale fat. From much experience and practice, the flawless timing of the individual performances was neatly choreographed.

Twiggy took little notice of the terror and wonder in James's face. "Come along, lad. We 'ave to work fast. Tide's comin' in. Here, take this rope and tie it 'round that back fin over there," he ordered. "You lads," he shouted to some children waiting for instructions, "come help haul this one ashore."

The children giggled as they grabbed the loose end of the rope after James tied the other end around the narrow base of the fin on the tail. They all pulled and dragged the creature above the tide line. Twiggy untied the ropes and tossed them clear of the whale. He picked up his long handled axe, swung it over his head. It came down and landed a heavy blow in the side of the whale's head. The whale opened its jaw revealing its tight row of white teeth now stained with blood. It let out a short high-pitched muffled scream and jerked its body. It thrashed and shuddered. James looked into its frantic eye and noticed a thin outline of white around the rolling blackness. Several seagulls swooped down just above his head, trying to get at the newly exposed and bloody flesh. In that horrible moment, James saw the axe rise again into the air.

"Twiggy!" he screamed.

Taken off guard, Twiggy tried to halt the momentum of the axe, but it spun him around and he fell on the sand. Surprised, he looked about, then up at James. "What?" he shouted. "Holy Jesus, man, ya gave me a fright. I thought I was in danger of axin' one of the lads! What is it?"

"It's still alive," James managed with a dry raspy throat.

Twiggy grunted as he tried to right himself on the sand. "Well, of course it's still alive. A beast that size ain't gonna to keel over easy after just one whack," Twiggy shouted. It took him a moment to realize that James wasn't making an observation, but an objection. "Ah mate, it's not like I could deliver a thump on its head to knock it senseless. Look at the size of it, man! Besides, it's already a gonner. See them bloody bubbles comin' out the spout hole? These creatures ain't like them other fish. They breathe air. See there? See how its body moves up and down with each breath. Them bubbles mean it's drowned. There be water in its lungs. It's finished, as are the lot of them. No sense to letting good flesh rot." The gulls swooped down on them again, more aggressive than before. Twiggy swung his axe at them. "To be sure, mate, I'll not stand by and let all this go to the damned gulls! These blackfish are lean critters. They don't carry the blubber like the humpbacks. It takes just one of them humpbacks to feed half the whole Cape! No, these blackfish don't produce much, but the fat we manage to fillet from the carcasses is rendered, barreled up, and shipped off to England. That's good money to these here people, James. And the flesh . . . we'll salt that and put it up for the lean winter months."

Attracted by the thick acrid odor of boiling fat, a hoard of hopeful interlopers from Cape Cod towns farther away gathered at the top of the dunes. It was the job of elderly Yarmouth villagers to chase them off. James saw little difference between the actions of the humans and gulls. Each fought hard to defend their bit of whale meat.

"Ah, yeah," Twiggy nodded. "There be a definite order to the distribution of this here wealth. Not much different than The Brethren of the Coast and their division of plunder. A right pecking order, there is. See that group of nattering preachers over there? They'll get the first cut, and them two schoolmasters? This'll be their wages for the winter. A fair amount is stored in the church for the needy. Rather civil and smart of us, lookin' after the welfare of the needy without raisin' a single tax! See them caldrons over there? They be burning fat down at a low temperature, skimmin' it, reheating it, and skimmin' it again. It goes on like that until the oil is refined. Could take as long as a couple of days. Gives us plenty of time to prepare the barrels, fill 'em, and haul 'em in for shippin'."

"Who pays for the barrels?" asked James.

"Ah, now there ya go, lad! Thinkin' like a true cooper! No worries, there. Capt'n Waller, he'll gets what's owed 'im when we turn a pretty penny for the oil."

"How is it used, this whale oil?" James asked.

"The finest goes to greasin' clock works and other finicky workin' pieces. The medium grade, that's used in lamps and for candle makin'. Burns steady and long, that wax. The crude goes for tannin' hides and greasin' axles. Now don't ya forget to collect a few of them teeth for Anani. Make her something pretty with them. Get them quick a'fore them Hallet boys grabs the lot!" Twiggy pointed to the set of ruffian twins skillfully extracting teeth with one swift motion of a chisel and hammer. "When are ya goin' to ask Anani to marry ya, lad? Seems ya been courtin' her long enough." Twiggy asked with no regard to protocol.

James smiled, "I should object to your intrusion, but you're right. We have been . . . seeing each other . . . frequently, for more than a year. However, I am still unsure of my situation and as you see, I am *still* dependent on the amount of slush I collect."

"Ha! Slush!" Twiggy roared with laughter. "Nonsense, lad! You make a fair living workin' for the Capt'n. Not even this reckless war with King Philip has slowed the profits, least of all from the cooperage. Though many here 'ave been sorely affected by them war taxes and the loss of wages by those Yarmouth men taken by Capt'n Gorham to battle them Indians at Mt. Hope. Did ya hear, lad? Gorham got 'imself kilt after doing battle in the swamp. He left eleven orphans behind. Eleven, mind! Aye, I reckon Yarmouth suffered poorly by this strange war." Twiggy continued with his chopping and refocused. "Capt'n Waller, he has no sons, James. The cooperage would all be yours one day, if ya married Anani. Could do a lot worse for yer labors, and for a wife!"

"If I do marry her, it would be to profit my heart, not my purse! Besides, I had in mind to follow Morgan and thereby making my fortune by my own accord," James replied.

"What! Ya gone daft, 'ave ya? Did I not tell ya enough of the horrors?" Twiggy squelched through his clenched jaw.

"I do not doubt that you suffered greatly, Twiggy, but you have enjoyed the profits of that caper, have you not? And your sons, will they not one day share the farm that you provided for them from those gains?"

"Aye, and I'd give it all back if I could see me wife and Barnaby come walkin' down this beach once more!" Twiggy retorted. As he huffed to rhythm of his cutting, he was suddenly reminded of his wife as she beat that rug. "It's an evil plan, James. There ya have someone who will look after ya, treat ya well. Marry her and forget this nonsense that clouds your head so!"

James did not want to argue. He took the full wheelbarrow over to the fire pits and dumped the layers of fat onto a growing pile. He watched as a woman picked up a slab with a large hook and with a one graceful swing slapped it down on a plank. She chopped it into five smaller pieces while cheerfully whistling a shanty song. James studied her face and saw calmness and peace. She possessed a happiness that he found so difficult to achieve. She was boiling fat, a hot smelly job, and yet she seemed truly contented. *Why can't I reach such a blissful state as that*, he asked himself.

"Perhaps you are right, dear friend," James said to Twiggy when he returned to the whales. "It is time I wed and settled my fidgety soul."

Within a few days, the beach of slaughter was nearly clear of debris with hardly a morsel left for the crabs. Even the bones, after being picked cleaned by all sorts of critters, were hauled away. Every piece of the whale was used. Fuel, grease, food, bait, fertilizer, and even buttons. Though the butchering and processing of the stranded whales took every villager from their normal duties, it was, in the end, a profitable diversion. Several barrels of oil were shipped to England, payment of which would arrive in time for the spring planting, a welcome economic boost after the harsh challenges of a Cape Cod winter.

Chapter 21

The spring of 1678 brought a joyous occasion – the announcement of the engagement of James Montague to Anani Trappit. Lacking respect for protocol, James insisted the engagement be short. The ceremony at the Congressional Church on Cape Cod was simple but elegant and afterwards the wedding party traveled in open wagons, decorated with brightly colored bunting and spring flowers, to Twiggy's farm where festivities continued well into the cool June night.

"You have made me prouder than any father might be on such an occasion, James. I trust you will keep her safe and happy," Edward said.

"With all my powers, sir!" James promised.

"I have a little something for you both, though I suspect Anani will not be as thrilled." Edward presented a document, sealed and stamped. James cracked the seal, opened it and, upon examining it, grew elated. He tried twice to offer thanks, but found he was speechless. Instead, he ran off to find Anani. He showed her the contents of the document. She looked up at him, confused. James explained that Edward had just given them the deed to one hundred acres of woodlands in the highlands of central Massachusetts. Anani smiled and walked across the room to embrace her Papa.

"I am afraid it is a remote wilderness now, my dear, but may someday be valuable for its timber and land," Edward explained to Anani.

"Thank you, Papa," she said softly.

"I will miss you being by my side, my daughter, and the Cape shall seem as far away as England," he lamented with a shaking voice.

"Touch the water, Papa," she whispered in his ear.

By summer's end, Anani was pregnant. At first, she glowed with the richness and hopefulness of being a mother, but as the leaves fell and the winter gripped the narrow peninsula of Cape Cod in the worst season known to settler and Indian alike, Anani grew solemn and pale. She suffered nausea and vomiting right into her last months. Towards the end of her pregnancy, two village women who attended her insisted on complete rest. James built a bed for her next to the hearth in the keeping room of their little cottage, but even a well-tended fire did not spare her from the chill of the nor'easters that pounded the Cape one after another throughout the winter.

A storm in late March dropped over two feet of heavy snow and gale-force winds blew it into dangerous drifts that threatened roofs and blocked doors and windows. Most of the villagers remained housebound, unable to trudge through the snow banks and howling winds to check on each other or even to hunt. Food stores and firewood ran low. As the temperature warmed, the falling snow turned to a mix of ice and rain. It coated the snow-covered ground with a thick impenetrable glaze of ice. The air filled with cracking sounds of branches breaking under the strain and the ground shook from the thumps from falling trees.

By April, the spring sun had warmed enough to melt the snow and release the harbor from its ice packs. As soon as the bay was open, Edward sailed from Boston to Cape Cod to be with Anani in her time of confinement.

For weeks, Anani bore the tease of false labors. As persistent and regular pains gripped her, James would send for the attendants, who came no matter what the hour or the weather. But the delivery would not advance.

On the first day of May, Anani's waters broke and having been warned that this would be a true sign of impending birth, James sent Edward to fetch the midwives once more. Upon their arrival, both men retreated to the workshop to await the news. James tried to keep busy by finishing the baby's high chair that he started the month before, but he couldn't concentrate. He paced. Several times, they went back to the cottage, putting their ears to the door. Nothing. At sunset a misty chill blew in from the north. They built a fire in the stove and pulled up a workbench to keep warm. James thought of returning to the cottage to gather some blankets and food, but feared the wrath of the midwives. A wagon pulled up outside the woodshop.

"Thought ya might like some company and somethin' hot," Twiggy said as he presented a heavy crock with an iron ring that latched the beveled lid.

"Ah, Twiggy, you have saved us!" James opened the crock and a steamy scent of oyster stew filled the shop.

"How long now?" Twiggy asked.

"Since early this morning," Edward replied with concern.

"Does it normally take this long?" James asked.

"Oh, aye. Could take most of the night, too, being the first," Twiggy assured.

"She has had such a time of it," James reported. He found a couple of cups, knocked out the sawdust, and poured some stew into them. He handed one to Edward and the other to Twiggy while he sipped straight from the crock.

"Aye, that she did, but it'll all be over and forgotten soon enough," Twiggy assured the anxious husband.

The vigil did indeed go on. All three men found a place close to the fire and nodded off and on throughout the night. In the early hours of the morning, the door of the workshop swung open hard with the wind. Old widow Mortise Thacher was so slight; she struggled to close the door while juggling a lamp in one hand. James jumped up to assist her.

"Mr. Montague," the woman announced in a gentle soft voice, "you have a baby girl."

James exhaled heavily and grabbed the arms of his friend and father-in-law. "And Anani – is she well?" he asked anxiously.

"I cannot be sure of that yet, sir, for she did have such a hard time. But your little girl is well and whole."

"Can we see her now, Mrs. Thacher?" asked Twiggy.

"If by 'her' you mean Mrs. Montague, no!" the woman scolded Twiggy in a teasing manner. "She is not fit for visitors, Mr. Strangeway. But she does ask for her husband."

James pushed past her, yanked open the door and started to run towards the cottage. He spun around, however, and came back to the workshop to close the door.

"Thank you, Mrs. Thacher, thank you," James said giddily, shaking her hand. He left again, and again the door needed to be closed.

"Nasty winter we've had, Captain Waller," the widow exclaimed, "and now it looks as though we won't be havin' our spring."

"No ma'am. How fares my daughter?" Edward asked sincerely.

"Not well, sir, bless her soul. She lost so much blood and it flows from her still, though we packed her as tight as we dare. The babe . . . well, she was partially twisted inside Mrs. Montague. And when she finally came out, she had the chord tied tightly around her little neck and her little hand caught up in the tangle. She was blue, Captain. I thought it was just the dark color of the mother's skin. But no, the baby was blue and cold."

"But you said the baby is fine!" Twiggy challenged.

"Oh aye, sir, and that she is. That little lass opened her mouth wide and bawled like I never heard before. The more she cried the pinker and the warmer she became. No. That baby is a fine sweet girl, thank the Lord! Like so many of us, all she needed to set things right was a good cry! We must watch Mrs. Montague, Captain Waller, watch her closely this day to see that she recovers. I reckon she'll be too weak to nurse. Mrs. Miller . . . she's had a baby just this Christmas past and still bears plenty of milk. I'm sure she'll have enough to nurse the little one. I'll stop by her place to let her know about this baby," she said. She made her way to the door. "Nice to see you again, Captain!" she smiled and curtseyed. "Mr. Strangeway," she acknowledged, minus the smile and the curtsey.

When she had gone, Twiggy looked hard at Edward. "Think the Widow Thacher has an eye for ya, sir."

Edward said nothing, but went about putting out the fire in the stove. He and Twiggy returned to the cottage to find James holding the baby and looking anxiously at Anani. Mrs. Watson, the other midwife, collected the soiled bed linen, rolled them tightly, and placed them in a basket. Edward noticed that the basket was dripping with the blood of his daughter. Mrs. Watson tried to smile at Edward, but her heavy worried eyes revealed the truth.

"I will be back when the sun is up, Mr. Montague," she said to the doting father. As she approached the door, she whispered to Edward, "We've done all we can, Captain Waller. She's in God's hands, now."

Anani looked up and smiled at the three men gathered around her bed. "Is she not the most beautiful baby?"

"She is, indeed, Mrs. Montague," Twiggy offered. "I just wanted to wish ya well and I'll be on me way." Twiggy bowed and walked away from the bed. He stopped briefly to look at the baby, forced a smile at James, and left the cottage.

"James," Anani struggled to sit up.

"No, no, my dearest. You must remain still," Edward cautioned.

"James," she insisted. "I worry so about the baby. Is she still so cold? Could you gather more wood for the fire?"

James looked at the pile of logs stacked high next to the hearth. It contained more than sufficient logs to see them through another day, but to ease his wife's concerns he agreed. After gently passing the baby into the arms of her grandfather, he left the cottage to collect more wood.

"Papa," Anani whispered with a fierce urgency, "I fear I have not come through this as I had expected and worry that I will leave my baby girl without a mother."

Edward knelt beside her bed, holding the baby so his daughter could see her tiny arms failing about. Edward started to protest her worries, but Anani put her hand up to his lips to stop him. Even that simple gesture was an effort and her arm suddenly dropped.

"Please, Papa, listen to me before James returns. You must help him to look after our daughter. I am so sorry to burden you, but you must promise me this."

"Anani, you know that I will," Edward simply said. "I shall help you both with my granddaughter!"

James came in with an armful of logs. "There, my dear, this place will soon be as warm as Jamaica."

Just after dawn, Mrs. Watson returned to attend Anani's packing and bandages. She was alarmed to see the young mother's pallid flesh and red freshness of the blood. The bleeding had not stopped. Nothing further could be done. Anani was dying.

"I think it best if I take the baby to Mrs. Miller's house for the feeding, Mr. Montague. It'd be best for your wife, sir," Mrs. Watson whispered. She bundled the baby in swaddling, handed the infant to James and cocked her head towards the mother. James understood.

"Anani?" James whispered as he knelt beside the bed. "Our baby is going for her first adventure, over to Mrs. Miller's house for her breakfast."

It was a great effort for Anani to speak. "Let me kiss my baby goodbye, then," Anani puckered her pale lips as James held the bundle close to her face. He was quickly on his feet and away from the bed before Anani could see his tears. James returned the baby into the arms of Mrs. Watson who carried her out the door. He struggled to regain his composure before returning to his wife's bedside. He held her hand in his, while Edward looked on. The grim vigil did not last long. Within the hour, Anani took her last breath.

Though Anani and James attended the village's Congressional Church regularly and were even married in its chapel, the church elders would not consent to burying Anani in the churchyard cemetery due to her mixed race and doubts over her baptism. So, on a warm cloudless May morning, a large group from the villages of Sandwich, Barnstable, and Yarmouth boarded boats of all sizes and purposes to accompany Anani Montague on her last sea voyage. As her body sunk below the green cloudy waters of Cape Cod Bay, the villagers sang shanties and cast flower petals upon the water.

"I still remember," recalled James to Edward, "what Sally said after my father's burial at sea. I thought those words to be quite . . . poetic."

"I remember well, those words, James," Edward replied.

Edward stayed on the Cape long enough to see his granddaughter baptized Abigail Trappit Montague. He moved back to his home in Dorchester with the stipulation that if Twiggy saw that James was not coping or having difficulty, he was to send for him immediately.

Edward was in Dorchester only three weeks when he received a disturbing and somewhat encrypted letter from Twiggy urging the captain to return to the Cape immediately. As a precaution, he instructed Mrs. Watchit to find a reliable wet nurse in town.

Twiggy, much troubled and a bit vague on details, intercepted Edward at Yarmouth Port.

"He is a lost soul, is James. Lost in a swell of grief, Capt'n Waller," Twiggy started. "Me and my boys, well, we took the baby into our home." Edward could not disguise his growing anger and horror. "No, now," Twiggy continued, "the baby is fine. She's a bonny lassie, Captain. A bonny lass! She's eating well, she is. Mrs. Miller has seen to that. A kind woman, that Mrs. Miller. James . . . I suppose the lad is much consumed by his loss. He won't talk to me. Refuses to open his door to any of us." Edward's face turned red with irritation but before he could respond, Twiggy broke rank momentarily and gently put his arm on Edward's shoulder. "I knows the depth of that kind of grief, Captain Waller. I knows that kind of guilt. Before you took me back to this here cooperage, I wanted to . . . I planned to . . . well, after me Maggie died, I had in mind I should hang meself for her and for Barnaby's death." Edward swiveled in surprise. Twiggy's dark eyes looked deeply into Edward's. "You forgave . . . even when many others could not . . . especially me. And for that, you saved this miserable soul of mine. Can you not now forgive James for even less a crime?"

"Mr. Strangeway! I did not know . . ."

"Now, sir, let me finish for I find these words a mite difficult. Barnaby, well, we went back a ways, Captain Waller. He was me mate." Twiggy went silent. Edward intervened.

"I understand, Twiggy. I do. My first instinct was to run my son-in-law through with this sword!" Edward patted his blade. "I will spare him," he sighed, "but only for the sake of Abigail and . . ."

"And Lady Cranston," Twiggy finished. Edward again looked surprised. Twiggy ignored the look and continued, "James, he ain't a bad sort, Captain. A bit self-absorbed, but I reckon he'll come about in time, sir. Most young bucks do eventually, now don't they?"

"You are more charitable than I, Mr. Strangeway." Edward paused, then sighed from his weighty decision. "I will take my grandchild with me to Dorchester. But first, I must deal with my son-in-law."

Twiggy drove Edward to the small cottage at the edge of Yarmouth and waited on the wagon, while Edward approached. The stuffy cottage was unkempt and smelled of damp ashes and dirty diapers. The bed on which Anani birthed and died was still next to the hearth. The mattress was gone, but little attempt was made to check the flies and their specks covered every surface. The floor felt gritty beneath his feet. James sat in a chair next to the hearth and did not even show the courtesy of rising to greet Edward. Several empty bottles of rum lay scattered at his feet.

Barely able to keep his composure Edward challenged curtly, "What says you, Montague! Where is your child?"

"She stays now with Twiggy, sir," James replied flatly. "Captain Waller, I cannot go on like this. I sleep not, nor have appetite enough to sustain me. I see Anani . . . everywhere. She haunts me! I must go away for awhile, until this madness in my soul ceases."

"You think you are the only one who suffers so? And what of your daughter? Can you so easily abandon her?" Edward gripped the back of a chair. He inhaled deeply to gain his control, but the smell angered him more. "Go then, James, go find your soul . . . or whatever it is you claim to be lacking. I cannot say that I am completely surprised," Edward retorted cruelly. He turned his back to James and was about to leave when he remembered Anani. "What are your intentions? Where will you go?" Edward asked.

"I am not certain. To Jamaica, I suppose. God forgive me, but each time I see my daughter, I blame her for taking Anani from me. I cannot bear . . . to look at her. She is my daughter. I cannot burden her with this madness. Will you look after her, at least for a time?" James pleaded.

"It was my promise to Anani. Apparently, she knew you better than I. Of course, I will look after my granddaughter."

"Here, on the Cape?" James asked.

"No. She'll go back with me this very day."

"But, Mrs. Miller . . . she will not leave Yarmouth."

"No need. I have arranged for her care. Abigail will want for nothing, James. Go fetch your daughter but first, I insist you sign her care over to me, as Abigail's guardian and executor. And the hundred acres of land."

James looked surprised. Edward continued in the no-nonsense tone of a businessman, "I'll not have you gamble her inheritance away. I trust not your intentions nor feel assured you will ever come back for your daughter, but she is to have the benefit of that land, sir. You owe her that."

"I have every intent, sir, to come back. I just need . . ."

"Listen to you! *I* . . . *me*! It's always about you, James!" Edward's anger mounted and he feared losing control. "You will agree to my terms!"

James was about to protest further, but instead let out an exaggerated sigh and simply said, "Agreed. What do you need?"

"The deed, endorsed to me with a letter indicating you do this of your free will stating that the lands go to your daughter upon your death . . . or abandonment."

James finally rose and walked slowly to a writing desk across the room. He removed the papers that Edward requested regarding the land, searched among the debris for a quill and ink and having found them, penned his statement in the margins of the document. "I will be back, Edward. This is but a temporary arrangement, you understand?"

They drove off together to Twiggy's house and were met there by Mrs. Miller. The woman seemed genuinely distraught over losing her charge.

"She's a good baby, Capt'n Waller, and cries little. I packed up these diaper cloths for your journey. Would you be taking the cradle Mr. Strangeway made for the baby? It's a fine cradle and the familiar smell might sooth the little one."

"Yes, thank you, Mrs. Miller." Edward presented her a pouch of coins. "I do not know what you charge for your kind services to Abigail, Mrs. Miller, but I reckon this will more than compensate."

Mrs. Miller picked up the pouch and judging by its weight she said, "Oh, yes, Capt'n Waller, I am sure it will. Thank ya kindly, sir!" Dropping the heavy pouch into a pocket of her worn apron, she shot a disapproving look at James. She placed a small crock into Edward's hands. "This is a bit of honey water. If the baby gets a bit fractious, just dip this cloth in there and put it on her lips. She'll suck on it and, hopefully, it will appease her for a bit. Safe journey, Capt'n Waller."

"Before I take my leave, madam, might I ask that you and Mr. Strangeway stand as witnesses to this document?" Edward removed the land grant from his pouch and laid it on a table. "Mr. Montague is signing over some land to my trust for his daughter," Edward explained.

"I will be happy to, Capt'n Waller," and without looking at James, she signed her name and passed the quill to Twiggy. She gathered the baby and offered her to James to hold, but he backed away.

"I'll . . . carry the cradle," he said. He grabbed the cradle and quickly left the house.

Mrs. Miller looked at Edward and raised her eyebrow. Edward said nothing, but took Abigail into his arms. She stirred a little and he responded by talking to her in a way that only a proud grandfather could.

Before boarding the ketch to sail to Boston, Edward took his granddaughter by the water's edge. He removed her blankets enough to free her tiny hand. He held her over the water so the hand touched the top of the wave as it broke against the shore.

"That's right, Abigail, tell your Mama how much you love her and that you are safe now," Edward said with tears in his eyes.

CHAPTER 22

It had only been a month since Molly Cranston sailed away to England to attend Miss Cupperfinch's School for Young Ladies and a couple months before that, Peter Haywood finally returned to his family in Barbados. And so, Sally and Gregor, alone again, were looking forward to James filling the gaping hole in their hearts. However, James's sorrowful nature seemed to dominate every manner of his character. Added to his loss of Anani and the surrender of his daughter to Edward, was the sudden death of Sir Thomas Modyford on the second of September 1679.

"What he needs is a project to occupy his thoughts and hard labor to cleanse his soul." Gregor proposed to Sally.

"Perhaps he should go with Thomas's sons," Sally suggested. "They plan to cultivate cacao somewhere on the north side of the island. It is a risky enterprise but just the type of challenge James needs to pull him out of his doldrums."

"And have all three commiserating their grief? No, I have a better idea, and perhaps one that may profit Windhaven. I have long desired to build a turtle crawl near the mouth of the Milk River, but I never seemed to be able pull myself away from my duties on the plantation. Nero says there are turtles aplenty along our shores. Other turtlemen have scouted the Milk's mouth for years, but found it too removed from Port Royal to manage. It's not far from Windhaven. Anyway, why should others profit from what we could easily snatch from the sea? We just need to snag them, store them, and sell them to the turtlers of Port Royal. What do you think, Sally? It is the perfect task for James. I will ask what he thinks of the idea."

In early autumn, James went off down river to build the turtle crawls. He enjoyed the solitude and the labor. To be free of mosquitoes and menacing alligators, he built a small shelter on stilts along the narrow beach a fair distance from the river's mouth, but still close enough to catch the cooling sea breeze. He spent the next month gathering rocks and mangrove saplings. He fashioned the walls of the crawl by ramming the tallest saplings into the soft sand about four feet apart and connecting them with panels of woven reed. He lashed the walls tightly together and fortified the base with rocks. With some turtles weighing over 300 pounds, the enclosure had to be strong enough to pen them in and to keep sharks and other flesh-eating predators from entering. In contrast, the pen also had to be flexible to tolerate strong tides and storm surges. He went no deeper than chin height at high tide and no closer to shore than two feet of water at low tide. On the beach side, he designed gates for easy access into the pens.

When he was satisfied with the construction of four separate pens, he returned to Windhaven to collect Bo. Nero's son, Bo, was now twelve years old and an expert at hunting turtles. He knew their habits, where they congregated and nested, and what they ate. Bo's keen eyes could tell the best location for green turtle roosts from watching the dynamics of the surface water as it moved over clumps of submerged vegetation, rocks and reefs.

James and Bo rowed out together for the hunt. They sat on the water for several hours until Bo saw the first turtle. Amidst much commotion, Bo tied ropes around the front flippers while James dragged it into the flat bottom skiff. The pattern was set and they began to haul in about one turtle per hour. Out of water, the weight of a green turtle's upper shell would crush its lungs and for this reason, the turtles were flipped over on their backs. And to prevent the turtles from arching their strong necks and using leverage against the boat to flip themselves over, a small wooden block was placed under their heads. James covered their catch with a wet blanket to keep them cool. The skiff was soon full and they returned to the crawl to release the turtles into the pen. James stayed onshore to check for weaknesses in the crawls and collected turtle grass and beach vines to feed to their new captives while Bo continued the hunt.

It was a tough job for Bo to haul-in the turtles on his own, but repeatedly he came ashore with the boat loaded. By the end of the day, the pens were full. Bo stayed with the crawl while James returned to Windhaven. The next day, he mounted a fresh horse and went off to The Point to announce to the butchers that his crawl was packed. James sailed back to the Milk on the turtlers's ketch and helped them with the round up of the turtles. The turtles fetched a good price and James was confident that the crawls would last several seasons. He sailed back to The Point with the turtlers and helped them transfer the catch to crawls near the North Docks. Much like cattle in a stockyard, the turtles stayed in the crawls until the butcher was ready for them.

Instead of returning directly to Windhaven, James took the opportunity to visit his old haunt, the Three Turtles Tavern. Several old salts recognized him and invited him to join them.

"I believe, gentlemen, that you have not moved yourselves from this very table in all the years of my absence," he laughed and they welcomed him with several rounds of ale.

Two days later, James woke to find himself in the most popular whorehouse in Port Royal with no memory of the transactions that occurred during his lapse.

"Ah, come to light again, 'ave ya?" Madame Jaclyn said as she observed the awakening of James. "You've been passed out for a day and not exactly aware of your moral conduct the day before that."

"How did I get here?"

"Strange enough, ya 'ad the good sense to knock on the door of one of my own houses! The girls recognized ya and came and got me." Jaclyn enjoyed the look of surprise on James's face, but could not tease him further, "I am Madame Jaclyn de Witt and I'm pleased to meet the brother of my friend, confidante, and business partner."

"Oh, my apologies, Madame," he replied as he struggled to rise. "Sorry, did you say you know my sister?"

Jaclyn laughed. "Ah-huh. Your Mum told me you were back in Jamaica."

"Yes. I have been at Windhaven . . . a month now, catching turtles," James stumbled to the dressing table and dunked his face into the washbowl. He rubbed it vigorously hoping to clear his mind.

"And ya been hangin' out with that good for nothin' lot down at the Three Turtles!"

James could not tell if she was asking or telling. He said nothing, but accepted the towel she offered.

"Careful, laddie! Don't let those old farts put stars in yer eyes with their tales and lies. Most of them have salt in their brains!" she warned.

"I . . . have to get back, Madame Jaclyn. To Windhaven. Do I owe you any . . ." he started.

Jaclyn laughed hard. "In your dreams, laddie! Be on yer way, and if I was you, I'd avoid the Three Turtles. Understand you kicked up a few brawls while you were there. Go home, James, before I 'ave to confess to your sister what you've been up to." She went over to a bureau, opened a drawer, and retrieved a small pouch full of coins.

She threw it into James's lap. "You were shaking this in everyone's face . . . bragging about your turtle money! Lucky it was me who finally snatched it from your paws!" Jaclyn shook her head, but ended her riding. "See that you deliver my good wishes to your sister!"

"Thank you, Madame de Witt! And, how is it you know my sister? You did mean Sally? Lady Cranston . . . of Windhaven?"

"Go home. She'll tell ya all about it.

Gregor and Sally were pleased with Bo's reports on the turtle crawl and surprised by the generous price James got for the first load. But James only shrugged as he sat down for the midday meal.

"I suppose everyone is sick of salted pork," he said dryly. "You'd get a better return if you could eliminate the turtlers and sell directly to the butchers, but you'd need a ketch of considerable size for that." James played with the food on his plate.

"What troubles you, James?" Sally asked later when they were alone.

James shifted from one foot to another, determined to come out with it. "I am going away."

"Back to the crawls? But, you have only just now come, brother! Why not rest awhile here before ..."

"No!" James interrupted abruptly. "I mean," he said softly, raising his hand in an apologetic manner. "I intend to leave Windhaven . . . Jamaica."

Sally stopped, cocked her head, and narrowed her eyes to read him better. "You're returning to Massachusetts?" When James did not answer, she frowned as she gradually put the pieces together. She sighed, sat down, and put her hand to her forehead. "Oh, James, tell me you are not still determined to go off island with those . . . thieves? I understand that you still suffer from your loss, and appreciate that the death of Thomas Modyford must surely play on your mind, but this obsession to go pirating! I truly believe dear brother that you have seriously lost your direction and must take some time to recover, with us. You are just feeling . . ."

"Do not presume to tell me how I feel, Sally!" James snapped. He turned his back on Sally and checked his temper. When it waned he continued, "Had you let me go to Panama with Morgan's buccaneers, I would have been a rich man and could have cared properly for my wife and daughter. Morgan now has over 4,000 acres!" James paused. "4,000!" he repeated. "And all productive! I feel solely cheated that I missed that opportunity and find it . . . demeaning to live off the charity of my sister's husband."

"Panama?" Sally rose from her chair, her own anger mounting. "Panama! You bring this up, now? Good gracious, James, you were but a child, then. And I hardly think pirating is an appropriate means for supporting a daughter, my niece, who I have yet to meet! Panama, indeed! The better part of that crowd, those young Jamaican buccaneers who so blindly followed Morgan, have met their end, untimely and sometimes most cruelly. They're dead!"

"I was fifteen then, sister, and old enough. And some of those former buccaneers now live well; planters right here in Jamaica. In those first years, those *thieves* as you call them, protected this island, *our* holdings, and provided much of the capital that enables this colony to thrive well above all others. Instead, I was tied to . . ." James cut his words short when Gregor gaily entered the room.

"Sally, ah James, good, you are here! You must come and see the pumpkins! They are the finest we have ever grown! Absolute monsters!" He stopped and looked from one to the other. James was sulking and Sally was breathing heavily. The tension was palpable. Gregor inquired over the discourse, but Sally ignored her husband and confronted James.

"Tied, dear brother? You hurt me so! We never meant to tie you to anything but your dreams and your hopes. Charity! We have shared with you the profits of Windhaven, which you helped to build, and sent you off to receive the best education in the colonies. You do wrong to consider that a charity!" Sally stopped to calm herself. "But you are correct. At twenty-three, I hardly think . . ." She closed her eyes and took a breath. "We have no right to hold you back from pursuing whatever guides your restless heart. It is understandable that a young man, with your education and now a father with a child to support and nourish, would want to pursue something grander than Jamaica has to offer. But *pirating*, James?"

"What?!" Gregor bellowed. "What say you? Pirating? No, no, no. I forbade it then, and forbid it again!" he ranted. "I will not see you sail off to perdition, James!" Sally threw her arms up in exasperation and tossed a wicked glare at Gregor that stopped him cold while James strained to hold his tongue.

"A moment, husband! Please! Allow me this opportunity to speak with my brother! I'll come along to see the pumpkins, just give me this moment!" She waved her hands to shoo her husband back out the door. Gregor scowled. He puffed rapidly on his pipe and left a thin trail of smoke as he exited the room. When he was gone, Sally bit her lower lip and exhaled slowly through her nose. She sat on the settee in front of the gaping hole of the unlit hearth, smoothed the creases on her gathered skirt, and motioned for James to sit beside her. He obliged.

"Sally, I *have* to go," he pleaded.

Sally narrowed her eyes, turned to her brother and asked, "What is it you want of me, James? To give you my blessing? To wish you well as you board a shipload of murderous cutthroats? Buccaneering is a euphemism for theft! What of Abigail? Is she to lose her father as well? And Molly and Thomas? They adore you so. Will you have them mourn their only uncle?"

"It is for Abigail that I . . ."

"Oh, no!" she interjected, jumping to her feet again. "No, James. Do not dare to put this on her. What is it that you think she needs that you cannot provide for her with what is in your pocket this very minute? What? No, it's not the babe that sends you on this exploit. This obsession of yours has plagued you long before she was born." Sally was agitated. "And I sense you truly know that, had you gone to Panama, you would, most likely, be among those buried there. Remember what happened to Barnaby Tibbs? You loved that man. Do you remember? What future for those that follow this unholy path? A brutal noose, a cruel Spanish prison ship, some dreadful ailment, a combative drunkard, or marooned on some island forsaken by God?" Sally looked straight into his eyes. He quickly lowered them. She pointed a finger at him. "You know this, yet you still wish this upon yourself and your poor daughter! How can you burden us with such extreme worry? Do you not value your life more than this?" Sally recoiled with a sudden recollection of their mother's death and wondered if James was now making a similar choice. She turned away so that he would not see her tears.

James pursed his lips and sighed. He gestured several times with his hands as if to start a rationale, but words failed him. Finally, he stood and paced which was enough to loosen his tongue.

"There is some truth to your words of caution and you must believe me, I do suffer a measure of trepidation. Though I consider what these men do is not thievery, but an unconventional transference of the most extraordinary amount of wealth the world has ever seen. Starting with the savages that *steal* it from the Earth, the Spanish *steal* it from the savages, the English from the Spaniards, and the Dutch from the English. But I do not go to sea just for the riches alone. I go to rid myself of the wretchedness that I bear everyday."

"Wretchedness? What do you talk of, brother? What wretchedness?" Sally asked with genuine concern.

"When Anani . . . died, so did my soul," James continued. "There is nothing left of *me*. I feel like my heart has shut. There is no room in it for anything but this consuming grief, not even for my dear, sweet Abigail. Each day this awful woe grows strong while I grow weak. A grown man, that I am, but I cry each night and can scarcely muster the effort to rise in the morn. My temperament swings wildly. I battle it daily. I know that I should do better, but I seem powerless to tame this awfulness inside me. Thomas's death . . . yes, it *has* moved me. He should not have died so, Sally. They say he was not at all the same after two years in the Tower. The King's men had not the courage to lay charges on him because there was nothing to support such an indictment. Those accusations of corruption, they were nothing but shrewd ranting of jealous malcontents! Thomas acted to protect Jamaica. For the King to treat him so, throw him into prison like a criminal. He, a faithful royalist, who did much to return the sovereign to his rightful thrown! The dog that bites the hand . . . After such an act, can I now call myself a son of England? At least these buccaneers, with whom you are so quick to judge, live by a steady code of law . . . a sensible and fair code that holds to a higher honor than those appointed to uphold the law in the King's name!" His voice cracked with emotion and in that moment of silence, Sally interceded. She placed her fingers over his lips.

"I miss Thomas, too, and I wish I had known your sweet Anani. Gregor and I feel much pain to know that her loss has affected you so deeply. But your grief has stung your sensibilities, James, and clouds your thinking," Sally gently took her brother's chin and moved his face so she could lock her eyes to his. "Those at the center of your ideas can, in their artful manner, turn your words against you. Take care, brother, lest thy sharp tongue become the noose that strangles thee." Sally warned. "You thought highly of Thomas, as once did I. When you were young and so impressionable, I allowed your admiration for him to be so, thinking there could be no harm to it. He loved you like a son, James, and I thought then your desire to emulate a man of such influence might benefit you. However, I believe now, this faithful backing and abetting of him is not thoroughly just. I learned that he was not above using his bequeathed authority for personal gain. Respect him for what he tried to accomplish here, love him for the friend that he was, but do not imagine him to be faultless nor hail him as some misunderstood champion of good. He suffered not at all in the Tower and was allowed to purchase any comforts that he fancied while Elizabeth struggled here to keep the plantation running." Sally turned her back to James, stared out a window, and sighed deeply as she thought for a moment. "I think this world is actually shrinking, James. We now circumvent this vast orb as a matter of practice and *always* in search of the wealth we believe will help us to live longer or happier. Those that discover such treasures are then hated for being rich. However wealthy and influential they might become, they seem to always end up leading a pitied life that warrants the envy of no one. And there are those who have not made such discoveries, by being unlucky or lazy, and seem quite content to steal and even murder for it. And we, the bystanders to these crimes, what have we become? As foul and atrocious as these acts appear, we no longer look upon it as so very culpable an offence. We even invent ways to justify these crimes. In Port Royal, as anywhere I imagine, an outlaw might be held a man of honor while a wealthy honest man becomes a fair object to plunder." Sally shuddered and turned to face James. She could see that her rambling made no impression on her brother. She sighed, "What is to be done, then, brother? No doubt, I shall yield to your determination, as always. You have a way to create good terms with my easy nature. I have no power to challenge you, but as your sister, can only ask that you delay your decision until . . ."

"I cannot. I am sorry."

"Delay this decision a fortnight?" Sally begged. James did not answer. She looked through the window. Gregor was in the yard, still puffing on his pipe, bent slightly and waving his hands about as he engaged in some discussion with Bo, then throwing his head back in throes of laughter.

"You shall break his fragile heart," Sally tried.

James rolled his eyes and went to the window. "You must know, that is not my intent. You and Gregor have been gracious and generous to me. I know not how to repay you for this kindness."

Sally half-smiled, gave a short sarcastic chuckle, and shook her head. He heard nothing, she realized. "It is not payment we desire, but your company. He loves you. And your daughter . . . how much longer will you deny her the tender love of a father? You could settle here, at

Windhaven. Build a house at Moon Walk for you and Abigail."

"Abigail is safe with Edward. She'll want for nothing. I have seen to that."

"Oh James, you cannot believe that financial protection is all that a child needs," Sally said.

"No, but it helps. You, of all people should know that," James retorted. A slap across her face would have been less of a blow than that comment and he immediately regretted those awful words. In a softer tone he confessed, "When I look into Abigail's eyes, it is Anani that stares back at me. How might a child react to a father who cannot bear to look upon her face without such immeasurable pain? I glide about empty-hearted, cold and flat. I partake in and savor this morbid life haunted by my ghostly companion. Anani is a specter that never quits me. God help me, I welcome it, Sally, if that is all I am to have of her." He walked over to a table where Sally had earlier poured him a flagon of warm mulled wine. He emptied it in one gulp. "I grow more like the corpse my wife has become and forgive me, at times I fear it might be a better pleasure to join her. Those thoughts overpower me and destroy any desire to be happy with my daughter," James exhaled a long deep shivering breath as small droplets of sweat beaded on his forehead.

"You terrify me," Sally whispered. "I underrated the measure of sorrow. You must fight to quiet such blasphemous thoughts, James. Anani is dead, a dreadful tragedy, no one disputes that, but it is time to stop ruminating over this. You must pull yourself from these melancholies and stop imagining that pirating will bring an end to your woes."

"I trust the sea, Sally. It will serve to chase away this brooding insanity. I cannot say how I know this, but I am convinced this journey will profit my heart as much as my pockets."

"Would I had a farthing every time I heard *that*!" Sally whispered sarcastically. "You are hardly the first husband to lose his wife in childbirth. It is time to put the past in its place and look to your future, and to Abigail's!" Sally leapt from the chair and paced the room. She was hot with frustration but could see no further gain in pursuing the conversation. "Right then!" she resolved, "I promise not to think my brother a thief, if you promise to return safely and in one piece, dear brother. Yet still, I must ask, can you not give this decision a fortnight?"

"I promise and I cannot delay. I have already signed aboard the *Arabella*. She raises her sails for Skull Rock at Virgin Gorda in two days time. That island is . . . an opportune destination. I must seize this uncommon advantage and leave for Port Royal first light tomorrow."

Sally returned to her position at the window. "Let me break this troubling news to him." Sally solemnly faced James. "Take care, James. You must surely know that, in your absence, the mood for reckless pirating has sharply changed. Assembly members parlay in secret with Governor Carlisle. They covet his support for reform and these combative slave-owning sugar planters are gaining unprecedented power. Did you know Carlisle plans to return to England to plead the rights of the planters, albeit reluctantly? The King will not tolerate it, of course. He has declared enough times that, as colonists, we have no rights. And then, there is the problem of the French navy. As it grows in strength, this fickle assembly of ours may do the unthinkable and collaborate with the Spanish to protect Jamaica from the French. And who is the strongest proponent of *this* plan? Henry Morgan! If Carlisle leaves

Jamaica, Morgan's influence will grow. Your one time hero may fast become your nemesis, James."

"Morgan will never go against his buccaneers," James said assuredly.

"He has already! And he might again if their pirating activities threaten the shipment of goods from those 4,000 acres you were so quick to mention. He's the king's man now, James, and a popular member of this growing plantocracy. Besides, he is far too fat and old to return to his former profession!" Sally warned, "Care, brother, due care! The waters around Devil's Bay are familiar to those who may do you harm."

James wanted to argue and inject his political opinions on the matter, but thought better of it than to engage his sister. More words would only add to her apprehension and he knew he was no match for her political sagacity. Sally put her hand against his cheek and lightly kissed his forehead. She left the house to break the news to her husband. James watched through the window as Gregor's animated protests eventually quieted. He slumped, said no more, and dropped his head in resignation. Sally embraced him and they remained there, like that, for long time.

That night, Sally slept fitfully. It was still dark when she heard Nero bring the horses around to the front of the house. He would accompany James to Port Royal and return with the horses. Hearing the front door shut and the commotion of mounting the horses she could not resist jumping from bed and going to the window, half hoping James might waver and come to his senses. Against the faint orange glow of a sun rising she watched the silhouettes ride away. Sally closed her eyes and cried. She sensed Gregor behind her. She turned and fell into his arms.

"He'll be all right, Sally. He'll be all right." he assured, hugging her tightly and patting her back.

Nero dropped James off at Harry's Tavern in Port Royal and unloaded the packhorse.

"Your provisions will be safely stored here until you board your ship," Nero said. "You take good care of yourself out there. There are troubled times ahead!" Nero bowed and mounted. James handed him the reigns of the two other horses.

"Watch after my family, Nero, and yours," James pleaded. Nero nodded once and headed off.

The ruddy-face of Harry Burgess crinkled with worry. "Sure this be what ya want, lad?" he asked as he poured himself and James another cup of rum. James shot him a surprised look. "What? Think to keep a secret in this town? Ha! I knows ya intend to board the *Arabella* and I knows where she intends to go." Burgess bared his tobacco-stained teeth with a broad smile. "Ya stays alive, now, Mister Montague. Stays alive by trusting no man, especially among them lot ya be sailin' with. Not respectable folks, them, and there be rough waters about," he warned, "with strong appeals to the governor. The good citizens of Jamaica want to clean up these here waters. Them sugar planters, they 'ave an urge to shed Port Royal's reputation of being a tad . . . shall we say, lawless," he laughed long and hard. "Legitimacy and regulation! That's what they're after, and they don't mind who they 'ave to hang to get it. Watch ya don't get swamped by *that* wave when it reaches ya, lad," he cautioned.

"You sound like my sister," James said gulping the last of the rum. He placed the cup on the table and bowed slightly to Harry. "Good health to you, Mr. Burgess!"

"See that ya mind me words and come back to us lad," Harry shouted as James walked out the door.

The few hours left in the day were barely enough to purchase the supplies required to join the Brethren of the Coast: a month's rations of food and beer, medicines and toiletries, one gross of tapers, some sail cloth, and a sewing kit. He also carried with him a matchlock pistol, several good knives, a cutlass, his father's sword, velum, a spyglass, two pairs of shoes, a pair of boots, and extra clothes. As he repacked, he found the note and bouquet of lavender wrapped in an embroidered lace handkerchief that Sally had secretly stuffed into his duffle. James squeezed the handkerchief slightly in his hand to release the aroma before packing it at the bottom of his duffle. Wanting to save the letter for a quieter moment, he folded it and placed it in his breast pocket. James took one more look down Queen Street before heading towards the docks. He hired a boy with a handcart to help him load his goods on to the *Arabella* and presented him with a generous gratuity.

"Good bye to ya, sir, and good luck to ya," the scruffy cart boy yelled.

"And to you, good lad, and to you!" The *Arabella* sailed from Port Royal on the 17th of November 1679.

CHAPTER 23

The sweet perfume of delicate pink quince blossoms permeated the orchard as the paper lanterns, hanging on the branches, swung gently back and forth. The gentle movement of the lanterns gave each branch exaggerated grace and fullness as they swayed past one another. Along the fence, two fiddlers played a slow, soft, blissful melody as polished gents and coy young ladies in summer fashion airily danced the sarabande. Flower petals caught up in an unexpected breeze dropped like snow to create a pink blanket, while the rest, already on the ground, whirled about in a flurry among the dancing feet. Through a vortex of swirling petals, Sally saw the silhouette of a man leaning against a tree. His back was to her, but she was sure she knew him. His was dressed in a heavy woolen coat, not the formal costume of a gentleman attending this springtime occasion, and definitely not the fashion for the tropics. Sally called to him but he did not move. Sally looked at the fiddlers and gestured with her hands for them to play softer so she could be heard above their music. Anxious and confused by an overwhelming urgency to reach the man, she ran to him but instead of meadow grass, her feet, now in sand, were sinking and slowing her down. Finally she reached him and placed her hand on his back. "Madam!" He suddenly shouted without turning.

"Madam! You must come!" Nero shook the hammock on the verandah where Sally was napping. "Madam, wake up. The tobacco, it is not right."

"What is it, Nero? What is the matter?"

"The tobacco is not well, madam. You must come."

Sally scrambled out of the hammock and rubbed her face. She had only a moment to think about the strange dream before Nero brought the horses to the verandah steps. She mounted, leg over saddle, and they rode over to the south field where they met Mr. Watt and Capt. Blake. Mr. Watt held a plant in his hand and was in a crouched position examining a row of young tobacco plants not more than a foot high.

"Some foul wind hath imported a malady, Lady Cranston, the likes I have not seen before." Mr. Watt rose and held the plant out for Sally to see. Sally dismounted and took the plant from his hand and could not hide her disappointment at seeing the damage.

"I thought it be the work of insects," Mr. Watt explained "but I see none, not on the plant nor in the soil. It's affected my son's fields in the same manner. This pestilence attacks them lower leaves, drying them like parchment. They're dying curled and withered on the stalk. And these upper leaves, look how they be scarred. Tis strange, I tell ye. Not all are affected, mind, but a good number in this field, my lady."

"How will this affect our crop, Mr. Watt?" Sally asked the foreman.

"Ah, without these here younger leaves, the plant will not grow tall. The best of the old leaves, they are too narrow. Marked up like that, don't imagine they'd sell for much, if at all." Mr. Watt removed his hat and rubbed the sweat from his forehead.

"You said your son's fields have been so affected, what about other plantations? Is it widespread? Might we be able to remove the affected plants to save the others?" Sally asked.

"Aye, that be a good course to follow, my lady. The diseased here is still in clusters. If we cut out the diseased and several around the clusters, we may yet stop this cursed plague. As far as them other plantations, I can't say that I have heard. I can send Capt'n Blake to Kingstown to see what he might hear."

"We must try to confine it to these fields. Separate the tools, Nero," Sally ordered. "Mark those used for the affected and keep the others for all other purposes. Do not mix the tools, lest we spread this to other crops. Everyone washes feet and hands to the elbows in lye water. We know not the nature of how it spreads. I would not want to see another blight destroy us, Mr. Watt," Sally nodded toward the cacao walk.

For the next month, all working hands fought to save the tobacco. From the hill above the fields, Sally watched the circles of cleared plants become wider until only one quarter of Windhaven's tobacco crop remained.

"We needed this to be a hardy crop, Gregor," she moaned as they watched Bo and Nero pull the wagon of cut tobacco leaves on its final trip to the drying barn.

"Tobacco has never proven to be reliable, dear," he replied. "It is going to be a thin year for all. There is talk of mal air that blows across the island, carrying with it this newest plague on the tobacco. Windhaven is better off than most, but we cannot take another year of this or we may just see the last of Jamaican tobacco."

"Captain Blake has said as much, though I am less inclined to blame the air for its spread. This loss is bad timing, what with Jaclyn and me purchasing that Queen Street lace shop in Port Royal. I doubt that anyone will be interested in buying niceties like lace if tobacco fails and it will be a strain, now, to pay the mortgage on the other Port Royal properties," Sally sighed deeply. "Tobacco! It is a rather needy crop, is it not, my husband? It requires so much of our time and indulgence and is proving to be a risky enterprise," Sally complained.

"Ah, but it is highly profitable in a good year, dear. And we have had a few," Gregor reminded knowing that Sally was about to propose a plan. "And I shouldn't worry about your lace shop. If I understand the vanity of both sexes as well as I think I do, an inconvenient tobacco blight will not keep them from their fashion. Besides, we'll have the rents from the rooms above the new shop. And that barber, what's his name? He seems to be faring well. I see more wigs in town. No, I should not worry about the properties in Port Royal, Sally."

"What we need is a steady, consistent income from this plantation, Gregor. Tobacco is so fickle, as are some of the other crops. They are so vulnerable to the whims of nature. I have given it some thought, Gregor. Perhaps it might be wise to abandon tobacco. Or at least, dedicate no more time or land to its expansion. What thoughts have you on this?" Sally asked.

"The crop may be inconsistent, but the market is not. It continues to grow, Sally. As to acreage, I leave that to your good discretions, my dear." Gregor replied giving a quick little shrug. "We may have no choice but to reduce the acreage as we are much limited by our labor."

Sally tightened her lips. She appreciated his acknowledgement that when it came to decisions regarding the cultivation of soil or breeding of livestock, hers was more trusted. But her reputation and skill for good husbandry soon earned her the complete burden of the farm's management, one that she found increasing heavy. She was beginning to suffer the same fate as Elizabeth Modyford. Gregor kept inventory, the accounts, the payroll, attended auctions, and managed the correspondence and entertainment. He went hunting, riding, visited neighbors, and collected the rents and gossip from Port Royal. Sally, with the help of Nero and his son,

Bo, Mr. Watt, Captain Blake, and a few transient workers managed the farm and Moon Walk. Through experience and passion, she and Gregor reversed many of the customary roles of their positions, an act not fully accepted by some of their acquaintances. As she rarely made visits to the wives of other planters, she suffered their initial scorn. Thinking Sally to be unsocial and somewhat arrogant in nature, they fueled unkind gossip and referred to them as Farmer Sally and Socialite Gregor. However, over the years both she and Gregor earned the respect of their neighbors through their farming expertise and unselfish willingness to help others expand their plantations. They shared their knowledge and their cuttings, seeds, labor and livestock. Much of the development of the plantations in Clarendon and surrounding parishes were due, in part, to Sir Gregor and Lady Cranstons's generous nature.

Sally smiled at her husband, locked her arm around his and said, "There is an old English proverb: if you cannot beat them, join them!"

"We may attribute much to the English, but I doubt that proverb would qualify. Now, what mischief are you planning?" Gregor asked, raising an eyebrow.

"Pipes, Gregory. Pipes! We can recover our losses from this blight on tobacco by producing a pipe from good old Jamaican red clay of which there is plenty down by the Milk!"

"Impossible. The Guilds of London control the production and sale of pipes and receive the protection of the crown, Sally. Besides, is it wise to create a tool to smoke a plant that we cannot seem to grow?"

"Even if our Jamaican tobacco fails, I believe it will not have the slightest impact on the availability or demand for tobacco. I hear the northern colonies have already found a tobacco plant that can survive their colder climate. And I don't believe there will ever be a shortage of those who possess the desires of its smoke. Tell me Gregor, how so, this ban on native-grown pipes? The Arawaks have pipes, and good ones, yet we accept that they have not broken our laws, at least for that particular offense. And the Maroons, I have seen them smoke through pipes lacking an English hallmark. Surely these guilds in London cannot interfere with an individual's rights to create that which he deems so basic a need?"

"A home-made pipe is one thing, Sally, but if I understand you correctly, you want to enter the realms of commercial production. Hmmm. I know not, exactly, the hold guilds have on their industry. My simple understanding of this complexity is insufficient to offer you an adequate explanation and I worry my account of how they grip the industry may be full of inaccuracies."

"Please, do try, dear. I give you my full attention," Sally said as she sat on the settee, smoothed her skirts, placed her folded hands onto her lap, and nodded to signal her full attention.

Gregor cleared his throat, "Yes, well . . . um, the guild is a group of artisans, workers of clay and the makers of pipes. They consider their skills superior in all ways and desire to protect the quality of their product and, of course, their corner of the market. In doing so, they maintain a certain . . . control over the trade. They organize to create a shared brand, the hallmark. Now, let us say that you, my dear, make a fine Jamaican pipe. That's a worry to them. It's competition, so they can force you down or demand you become a member of their guild."

"Force me? Why should I bother with their guild? As you said, I make a fine pipe, perhaps one that is preferred. I've beaten the competition. How can they force me?" Sally protested.

"Ah . . . well, without the hallmark of true artisans, buyers will think your product inferior. In some trades, my dear, it is a crime against the crown to purchase such rogue products. You cannot compete with the makers of the king's goods." Gregor folded his arms confident his interpretation was correct.

"So then, how might I obtain the right to use this coveted hallmark on my pipes?"

"Ah, yes. Well, first you must become an apprentice and learn the craft from a master. The masters of the trade limit the competition through a rigid apprenticeship system. A master accepts only a few young gentlemen, perhaps just one, to become his apprentice. And yes, Sally, it *is* restricted to that gender. The apprentice remains in his service for many years, depending on how well he learned the trade. Only the masters of the guild determine whether the apprentice has succeeded in meeting the standards set by the guild. The apprentices, having completed their training become journeymen, thus worthy to strike their own torch. Even then, a journeyman must solicit a member of the guild to support and mentor him during the beginning endeavors of his business – get him off on the right foot, so to speak. If he fails in his endeavor, it is not just his reputation that suffers a blow, but that of his master and by association, the guild."

"Then, how and why is the crown so involved?" asked Sally.

"Let me think. The crown . . . it protects the rights of the guild by giving it permission to bring action against interlopers, even to the point of prosecution, and bestows upon them powers to regulate their numbers. In return for these royal favors, the guild is taxed, rather substantially, I believe."

Sally listened intently and was speechless at first. She huffed, "The process to me sounds like . . . like extortion, Gregor. Protectionism, at the least! And it must surely stifle innovation and improvements bred from the spirit of competition. This sort of controlling nonsense does drive a stirring in my blood! Ugh, that we must endure such yokes! It borders on tyranny! The crown fills its coffers by making craftsman pay for protection against free enterprise. And colonists are forced to buy only English-made products that carry not only those added taxes and unreasonable surcharges, but transportation costs as well."

"Aye, seems odd, but there is logic to the process, Sally. It prevents cheap and unworthy imitations of their craft and insures that the time-honored knowledge of the art is not forgotten."

"No, dear Gregor, it prevents inventiveness and ensures the treasury gets its share of the people's labors! Listen to my logic and compare. These pipes for tobacco draw smoke for how long a time?"

"The life of a good pipe? Hmmm, depends on how often it is used, but I would say on average, two or three months. After that, a cake thickens in the bowl and the bore hole, thus precluding a good draw."

"Ah, you see! If my pipe is half the price of an English pipe, then you could buy two pipes and be set for twice the time," Sally reasoned.

Gregor rubbed his head. "I am not sure I would buy a pipe without a mark of excellence."

"You would, sir, if that etching represented neither function nor form, but just another hefty duty," Sally huffed.

"How would I know this pipe would last, or draw correctly, or keep the leaves lit? It does take some design and skill, dear Sally. When I buy a hallmarked pipe, I need not worry about burning my tongue or constantly relighting the weed."

Sally thought for a moment. "If you smoked from nothing but a perfect hallmarked pipe, then how is it you know the disadvantages of a bad pipe?" Not waiting for his reply she said reflectively, "Our pipes would have to come close to the quality of an English pipe. Ah! I will design my pipes the way I design my dresses. I will simply copy the fashion of the day by examining closely the best English and Dutch pipes in your collection."

Gregor threw his hands into the air. "I can see that this discourse has fallen on ears closed and a mind full of new determination. And I suppose you perceive not, how this may be considered illegal and, by some, an act of sedition?"

"Sedition! Oh, Gregor, save faith! It is but a pipe! Perhaps our quality will exceed those of the Guilds of London and, they will invite *us* to join their organization – a colonial branch of the guild, if you will. Or better yet, I may see it in my powers to invite *them* to join our Jamaica Guild. How could the crown object? Who pays higher taxes than colonial merchants? I shall enjoy putting this Jamaican bee beneath their feathered London hats!" Sally snickered as she took the pipes her husband stored in a wooden rack by his chair.

"You say you will be using my pipes as your template? My pipes? You will take care, Sally? It takes me weeks to break in a good pipe." Gregor protested, but Sally was already off to search for Nero.

Throughout the weeks, Sally's pipe-making ideas proved more challenging than anticipated. She could copy the finest of gowns from the English court from a poorly done sketch, but could not piece together a simple pipe.

After scouting the bottomlands near the Milk River for appropriate deposits of clay, Sally went about surreptitiously gleaning information she needed from the pipe sellers of Port Royal. Under the guise of purchasing a gift for her husband, she learned to identify the nuances of English, Dutch, and Flemish pipes. The workings of the white kaolin clay were clandestine interactions involving a great deal of labor and time.

Sally discovered that kaolin was first packed into wicker baskets, allowed to drain, and then broken into clumps. To release impurities and improve the color and texture of the clay, the clumps were soaked in a series of water buckets. As the floating impurities were skimmed off, the remaining clay was too wet to be worked. It was necessary to add dry clay to make it firm enough to be kneaded like bread.

"It's much like making pastries, Lady Cranston," explained Port Royal's most knowledgeable pipe merchant, Percival Wickland. "If the dough is too wet, you have to add flour to knead it. Clay is the same. You have to add dry clay powder, called spew. And just like a good pastry cook, adding the right amount of spew is the secret to a good pipe."

Sally continued her inquiry and found that the spew was added in layers like a cake. The cake was chopped, mixed with a wooden paddle, and rammed down into one large solid mass. Workers of the clay beat the mass with a heavy flat metal bar first in one direction, then another. Once the mass was flattened, they chopped it into squares, each weighing as much as six stones.

The squares were then sent to the rollers. The clay was drier, but still flexible enough to be rolled and formed. A bowl is formed at one end, the stem at the other. No pipe seller could tell Sally how the borehole in the stem was made, only that the size of the hole varied little in pipes from different origins and that it was the diameter of the hole that prevented the pipe from burning too hot or not enough. Some countries used copper molds to form the bowl of the pipe, while others molded the bowl separate from the stem and attached them before firing. Key to creating an authentic-looking pipe, Sally surmised, was the size of the bowl, the length of the stem, and the diameter of the borehole.

Sally and Nero gathered the clay from the riverbank and, just as the artisans, left the clay to drain. They spent an entire month learning how to work with the clay. After many failures, Sally grew frustrated over the process of soaking the clay. It made the clay too sticky and for all their skimming, did not reduce a good deal of the impurities.

"What we have here, madam," Nero boasted as he threw a large chunk of raw river clay onto the table "is a lump of fine-textured red river Jamaican clay. It is already pure! We need to work it like we do for the crocks," Nero claimed.

So, they eliminated the complicated process of soaking and adding spew and instead worked directly with the raw clay. Nero carved wooden molds for the bowls while Sally perfected rolling the stems and giving them the characteristic subtle curve. The bowl was attached to the stem and to remove all signs of the joint, Nero smoothed the outside of the pipes with a thin wire. He adjusted the angle of stem to bowl against a template made from Gregor's pipes. When they had a collection of pipes similar in size and shape to English standards, it was time to fire them.

Firing the clay proved the most challenging step. Initially, all pipes came out of the kiln either cracked or broken. After days of modifying methods, timing, and the temperature, Nero settled on placing the worked clay pipes on a rack that he centered inside a long narrow lidded ceramic pot. He built the fire around the container so that the temperature within the pot was uniform. Though crude, the kiln produced pipes that were neither flaky, brittle, cracked nor broken.

"Look!" Sally declared to Gregor, holding out their first acceptable pipe. "Behold our Jamaican pipe!"

Gregor laughed and took the pipe from her hands to examine it. He held the bowl. "Ah, clever girl! You've given it a fine spur," he said referring to the little pinch of clay positioned at the bottom of the bowl, the purpose of which was to keep fingers from burning while holding the bowl of lit tobacco leaves. "The bowl seems right," he continued. "And the angle of the bowl to the stem, yes, yes. I think you have that right. And smooth, ah, like a baby's bottom!" Gregor lifted the pipe stem to his lips. His eyes widened. He removed the pipe and turned it long-ways to study it further.

"Well?" Sally asked impatiently.

"Yes, I believe it is a good pipe, my dear. Yes. But ah, there is one detail . . ."

"Yes? What is it? The texture? The length of the stem? It's the bowl, is it not? We had such difficulty with its formation and adjusting the angle without snapping the stem off," Sally replied anxiously.

"No. I was thinking more about . . . ah . . . well, it lacks the necessary hole from which to draw air."

"Oh, that! Of course, it lacks the hole, dear. We have yet to work on a hole. But the pipe, Gregor, what of the pipe? Is it to your liking?"

"As a respectable receptacle of tobacco, it is indeed a very good likeness, Sally. I must say, it truly is. As an instrument of pleasure, ah, I reserve my assessment until I might draw breath through it."

Sally was encouraged. It was now time to work on boring a hole with a diameter at its widest a mere three-eighths of an inch.

"I think we should roll the stem around a reed of grass, madam," Nero said, "then slowly remove the reed." The method failed. The reed stuck fast to the sides of the stem and produced a hole of inconsistent diameter. They tried greasing the reed with pork fat, but the residual fat in the hole burned too hot causing the stems to crack when fired.

"Perhaps we should not remove the reed, madam. Let it burn in the fire." Nero suggested. It seemed the perfect solution, but the reeds did not burn wholly or caused the stems to explode in the kiln. Other times, the reed would burn away and leave the hole clogged with ash that baked into the clay. While trying to remove the ash with a long copper wire, Sally stumbled on the best method.

"A wire," Sally said to Nero, "like a needle! We roll the clay around the wire. As the clay is fired, it will contract away from the wire and we'll remove it once it is cooled."

It took several rounds before they found the right gauge of wire to create the right bore. Removing the wire through the curved stem after the pipe was fired proved to be too difficult. Nero then decided it was best to remove the wire while the clay was still soft. When the improved pipes cooled, Sally and Nero proudly took their final product to Gregor.

"Ah, I think we should put this one to the test!" Gregor winked at Sally as he filled the bowl three-quarters with finely chopped tobacco leaves he kept in the small drawer beneath the tall-carved box that held his pipes. He used his index finger to gently tamp the tobacco to the correct compression. From the pipe box, he removed a partially charred burning stick, tapped it to remove the ash and lit it from a candle on a table by his chair. Gregor held the burning stick close to the bowl. Holding the pipe by the spur, he inhaled through the stem and exhaled out the side of his mouth in quick succession to draw the flame into the bowl just far enough to light the tobacco, but not far enough to inhale the heat. Smoke escaped from the bowl and as the tobacco smoldered, Gregor slowed his puffing and blew out the burning stick. He took a few more puffs before he nodded his approval. "Ah, it's good," he declared. "It is a fine pipe. A fine pipe!"

Sally grabbed Nero's hands in the excitement. "We are in business! Work with Mr. Watt, Nero. Tell him your needs to start production. We'll use the shearing barn as our pipe factory.

"One last detail," Gregor demanded. Nero and Sally froze. "Your hallmark, Lady Cranston!"

Sally beamed a smile. There was a twinkle of satisfaction in her eyes. She looked to Nero, "We need to add a stamp before firing, a mark just here," Sally pointed to where the bowl met the stem. "A single letter: 'W'."

"Windhaven!" Nero surmised.

CHAPTER 24

In the first months of 1681, the marketing of Windhaven Pipes did not progress the way Sally anticipated. As Gregor and Mr. Wickland predicted, shopkeepers seemed reluctant to purchase, claiming customers would not be interested in buying a local product when proper English pipes were readily available. They also feared the brick red color of Windhaven Pipes would be a detractor.

"If the clay holds up to a good fire and does not, in any way, interfere with the flavor of the tobacco, then why should anyone care about the color?" Sally argued, but to no avail. Shopkeepers claimed the clay would discolor the lips and fingers.

Two months passed without much activity. It seemed that Gregor and Percival Wickland were their only patrons. Gregor emptied his pipe holder of all pipes except for Sally's and openly flaunted the new pipes in the presence of his friends. Visitors to Windhaven were given two samples on speculation that if they enjoyed the pipe, they were to give the second to a friend or associate.

The slow progress of sales changed overnight after Madame Jaclyn de Witt started an outrageous rumor among the patrons of her brothels in Port Royal. She claimed that smoking a red clay pipe greatly enhanced sexual prowess. And as with most rumors in Jamaica, it quickly reached the ears of many. Demand escalated and it soon became acceptable, then fashionable, to smoke a Windhaven pipe. Within six months of its debut, Windhaven Pipes were all over the island, enjoyed by both men and women. As to Madame Jaclyn's claim, no one complained, or at least would not admit that the pipe's powers did not work for them.

Exporting the pipes was somewhat trickier. In violation of the letter and nature of the Navigation Acts, most colonial merchants ignored the restrictions imposed by London's Lords of Trade and managed to smuggle goods onto ships sailing to ports not claimed by the British Crown. If caught, one suffered a fine, but most offenders escaped prosecution with a feeble excuse and generous bribe. So it was in this spirit of willful disobedience that Sally risked asking Captain Edward Waller to help expand her trade outside Jamaica.

Edward was enjoying the success of his own business and sailed extensively throughout the Caribbean and American colonies, selling and filling his barrels. Sally knew it was not commerce alone that brought him to the shores of Jamaica and brazenly took advantage of his visits to advance her trade. Whenever he sailed from Jamaica, she made sure that a few casks of pipes were tucked in among his legitimate cargo.

Windhaven Pipes soon saturated the Jamaican market, but exports increased and the business grew faster than Sally predicted. The pipe-making skills of Nero and Bo were essential to the business, but to release them completely from their field duties would be detrimental to the plantation. She needed more hands.

Jethro McMann, an old planter who first came to Jamaica as a seaman with Venables and Penn in '55, died of old age. In his will, he freed all ten of his slaves. Sally wasted no time in hiring the four strong grown men of the group who were well versed in the working of cane and cocoa. Of the six remaining, five were women. She already had enough house staff and had no use for their skills; however, the last of the group was a young child about the same age as her son, Thomas. His name was Little Luke. None of the adults claimed him as their child and Sally feared what might become of the boy so she decided to hire him as well.

"He can work along side Bo making pipes," she explained to Gregor, trying to justify another expense against Windhaven's accounts. "Our first official apprentice, Gregor! And, of course, Bo and Thomas could use an extra hand with the turtle crawls," she elucidated. As his heart was even softer than hers, Gregor responded with a grunt of acceptance.

Experience taught Sally that, when given a fair wage and adequate lodging, freedmen worked harder for their wages than indentured laborers who often absconded to pirating or some other misadventure. The four laborers, having never enjoyed the status of a freeman, were happy with their accommodations in what Gregor called the long barn. Now compartmentalized into four two-room apartments, the long barn was first constructed for horses that Gregor had planned to breed. It seemed every year some other priority took precedence over the horses. Eventually the idea faded and Gregor decided to make better use of the building. It was far superior to the ramshackle hovels Jethro McMann provided for his slaves. Each man was given a horse, the freedom to come and go during off hours, and the pleasure of taking a wife, if he wanted. Two of the men did just that and married the women with whom they had been slaves, Matilda and Lizzie.

Little Luke stayed in the main house in a room next to the bathhouse. He had the lighter skin of a mulatto, soft wavy hair, and beaming black eyes. Matilda told Sally that Little Luke was the child of Jethro McMann and another of his house slaves who died of fever two winters past. High in spirit and quick to learn, Little Luke soon became an invaluable companion to Thomas. Their foolish shenanigans and earnest laughter brought richness to the plantation not felt since Molly left for London.

It was the task of Little Luke and Bo to collect the wood for charcoal used in the kilns. They cut down brush with stems too small in diameter to be useful for fencing and too large and firm for the weaving of mats or baskets. Nero referred to such brush as trashwood and if left to grow, it could fuel dangerous bushfires. With an axe, Bo cut bundles of the wood in lengths of about two to three feet while Little Luke piled the sticks tightly upon each other at an angle, using smaller pieces to fill the gaps. Once the height of the cone-shaped mound was up to their chins, they covered it with a thick layer of dry straw. Except for the peak, Little Luke and Bo encased the three-foot cone shaped mound with a daub of sticky soil mixed with sand, straw, and cattle dung. They left the mounds to dry slightly overnight. In the morning they set fire to the straw and twigs sticking out of the top of the mound. The fire burned down through the layers of wood, causing much smoke at first. As the flames reduced to a smolder, Bo made vent holes at the bottom of the mound to control the burn and to allow the tar, steam, and gases to escape from the mound while Little Luke used daub to seal the hole at the top of the mound. Eventually, the wood burned so clean that smoke could no longer be seen. It was a slow process. Depending on the wood used, it took the boys nearly a week to produce charcoal from one mound. Less than half of the charcoal was good enough to fire the kilns to the right temperature. The rest was used for the smoke houses and barbeque pits. The remaining ash was used for soap-making and the tar was collected for sealing leaks in buckets, rafts and skiffs.

Gregor managed the ledgers for Windhaven Pipes and was at his writing desk examining the figures when Sally walked into the room.

"My dear," he said to her. "I have some concern over the raw materials necessary for this venture. One kiln holds four racks of ten pipes. Yet it takes half a dozen mounds to produce enough charcoal for just one firing. At this rate, the boys will run out of the trashwood close to the shearing barn . . ."

"Pipe Factory!" Sally corrected.

"Yes, yes," Gregor dismissed. "My point is, if your company continues to grow, we will eventually run out of trashwood and may find it necessary to cut down more valuable wood or purchase wood from other plantations. And that, dear Sally, will nibble at anticipated profits."

"Nonsense, my sweet. Jamaica is covered with forests. I cannot imagine that the demand for pipes will ever give us cause to go too far afield for charcoal wood." Sally surmised.

Gregor said nothing. He squinted his eyes and tugged on his ear the way he always did when he questioned the judgement of his wife. "Perhaps we are not using the best methods for producing the charcoal or might I suggest building a proper kiln and therefore make more efficient use of the charcoal the boys produce? It is something I would like to investigate, Sally."

"What about the pottery in Spanish Town? They have brick kilns. And the kilns for making lime, I believe they are brick as well. Of course that old potter, Miss Hanover, is always so concerned about competition for her business, I dare say she would never let you near her kilns. But I think I know the perfect person to approach the old bat. Mary Elizabeth Morgan!" Sally was prepared for Gregor's predictable response. "I know, I know! The wife of a notorious pirate! But, Gregor, she is a sweet dear thing who no one can resist. She longs for a challenge and I for her company. I have played ombre with her and I can tell you she is quick of wit *and* cards. She won consistently against me and Madame De Witt. If anyone can cajole old Miss Hanover to give up her secrets, it'd be Mary Elizabeth! Yes, it would be a perfect task for her. Firewood! Who would ever imagine that we might see a shortage of wood. Oh, you are so clever to think of these practical things, Gregor. You fill the gaps where I am deficient."

"And you, my sweet, have the imagination and invention I lack," Gregor quickly acknowledged. Sally came up behind Gregor and bent down to gently kiss the top of his ear. "Oh, my dear," he declared, pointing to his ledger book, "Who would have thought . . . Jamaican pipes!" Gregor convulsed from the chills as her lips gently moved across the hairs on the back of his neck. She came down to his shoulder and he cocked his head to one side to accommodate her. "We . . . we just need to be sure this enterprise does not get away from us nor ask of Windhaven more than her lands may bear. Large tracts of Jamaica's forests have been felled for the sugar mills. I would hate to add to this island's woes," Gregor cautioned, while enjoying the tingles. He could stand no more and rose from the chair to embrace her. Sally responded. She closed her eyes and nuzzled her face against the folds of his waistcoat. With both hands, he surrounded her head, bringing her face to his. He kissed her, long and gently while he kneaded his fingers in the curls of her hair. He felt her breath quicken. She turned her head to kiss the palm of his hand then slid her lips to the tips of his fingers. She took his hands within hers and led him to the door and up the stairs. Gregor said nothing and happily surrendered to her completely.

CHAPTER 25

Months passed without a word of the exploits or whereabouts of James Montague. Rumors and stories of one raid or another bounced around Port Royal through the usual sources, but there was no way of knowing if James took part in any of them. The summer of 1680 produced the finest crop of tobacco at Windhaven. The leaves were wide, robust, and flavorful. The drying barn was packed so tightly; Nero feared there was not enough space for the air to circulate.

In early fall, Edward Waller came to Jamaica in time to transport Windhaven's tobacco to England along with other products he collected along the way. After unloading salted cod at Port Royal, he sailed his ship along the south shore and anchored at the mouth of the Milk. It was to be his last stop before sailing onto England.

He was not alone when he arrived at Windhaven. Riding with him was a strange dark man dressed in a sailor's clothes. Carrying a large duffle draped over the rump of his horse he looked much like a vagabond. Nero's wife, Ruth, greeted them at the door of the house and shouted the news of their arrival to all inside and out. Sally and Gregor welcomed them both. Before he was properly introduced, the stranger bowed and put his index finger into the air, gesturing that he needed a moment before continuing. He limped across the verandah where he found a chair to sit and relieve the obvious pain in his left foot.

"Sir Gregor and Lady Cranston," Edward announced, "may I introduce Senhor Soverosa, a Portuguese boatswain from the Spanish frigate, Santa Isabella." From his seated position, Senhor Soverosa bowed his head as he placed a hand over his chest. Edward continued with a twinkle in his eye, "He brings news of

James." Senhor Soverosa reached into deep pockets to remove a bundle of letters.

Sally could not contain her excitement. She unconsciously reached out her arms to receive the letters while Gregor verbally blurred one question after another.

"Please!" Edward tried to stop the attack. "This man has come far and has much to tell you, but . . ."

"Gracious! Oh, do forgive us. Ruth!" Sally shouted. "Bring drinks for our guests." To the men she added, "We've waited long for news of my dear brother, Senhor Soverosa, but I dare say that is no excuse to forget our manners. And Edward, such a pleasure to see you again!" Sally made a fuss over helping the Portuguese.

Thomas entered the room and greeted Edward with warmth and excitement.

"Thomas, this is Senhor Soverosa who brings us news of your uncle. Why don't you show him to the bathhouse? I am sure he would like to freshen before dinner and I believe a good soak is just what his foot might need," Sally insisted.

"Ah, so you have finished it?" Edward asked.

"The bathhouse was Edward's idea and my husband's design, Senhor," Sally explained. "You will see, it is a very large Waller barrel, one that Edward provided us on his last visit. Please enjoy it and rest for dinner."

Senhor Soverosa bowed deeply and, without saying another word, hobbled behind Thomas to the bathhouse. When he was out of earshot Sally asked Edward, "Does he speak English?"

Edward laughed, "He does, with difficulty. I found him in Port Royal, or rather he found me. He was looking for a way to Windhaven and Mr. Burgess sent him my way. He disclosed nothing about James to me, considering it a matter between you and him. I can tell you, he seems to be a man of honor, a gentleman, and is currently suffering from terrible gout.

"Ah, that explains his limp," Gregor surmised.

"Do you know, Edward," Sally asked, "is James at least safe?"

"Yes!" Edward confirmed. "At least when our Portuguese friend last saw him."

Sally suddenly thought of the letters. "Augh, why didn't I ask for them to read while he freshens?" Sally grimaced.

"Due course, my dear, due course. Now, Edward how goes it with you?" Gregor asked.

"Never better, sir. The warehouses of Port Royal are bursting, as are mine. If it were not so late in the season, I would be tempted to make another trip. But I have been gone too long from Massachusetts and miss my little Abigail. I could not suffer a winter so far from home."

"She is well, my niece?" Sally asked.

"She grows strong and fast. She skipped walking and took to running the minute she could stand." Edward bragged. "But, she is a lady, clear and through. Her hands are delicate and a face sweet and fair."

"Well, let's not keep Edward further, Sally. I am sure he would like a bit of rest before dinner. Do enjoy the barrel. I don't believe there is a finer bathhouse on the island!" Gregor crowed. "Ha, damn good idea, Edward. Damn good, I say!"

When the bathhouse was vacant, Edward jumped into the giant barrel and lowered his body into the cool scented water. He looked about approvingly at the décor – the walls of woven sea grass, the arbor covered with flowering vines, and the scattering of clay pots overflowing with colors only the tropics could produce. *Gregor has done a fine job with the bathhouse*, he thought. *We should obtain a royal grant for monopoly privileges on this!* He slowly slid deeper until his head was below the water.

To Sally, it seemed an eternity until dinner was finally announced. A new man entered the sitting room, shaven with his dark hair combed, drawn back and tied and sporting clean clothes, the Portuguese sailor looked years younger as he approached. He bowed deeply before his hosts.

"I am Edmundo Luciano Soverosa," Edmundo explained in fragmented and heavily accented English. "Thank you. I am very pleased with your kindness. James did not exaggerate your generosity."

Sally could not wait to ask, "How is my brother, Senhor Soverosa?"

"He asked me to tell you: he is still in one piece."

Sally laughed with relief. "Oh Gregor, he is safe!"

For the next hour, Edmundo explained how he met James, first his prisoner on the Spanish ship, *Santa Isabello*. The *Santa Isabello* was captured by the pirate ship, *Tigre*. The *Tigre* was the pirate flotillas' flagship and captained by the infamous Dutchman, Laurens de Graff. James joined the pirates and Edmundo, displeased with his Spanish captain, deserted and did the same. They befriended and spent several months together during which time they amassed a small fortune in booty. James taught Edmundo how to speak English and in return, Edmundo taught James how to throw knives. When Edmundo's foot swelled and reddened with gout, he decided to leave the *Tigre*. James, worried that he may be robbed of his earnings entrusted Edmundo to deliver most of the loot to Sally.

Edmundo pulled out a satchel from his duffle and presented it to Sally. Sally and Gregor looked at one another. When Gregor took the satchel, his arms fell suddenly from its weight. He untied the leather straps and peered inside.

"Oh, my heavens! Good gracious!" Gregor was giddy and could say no more. Sally looked amused and puzzled. Gregor tilted the open satchel so she could see inside. Her smile fell apart and she turned her face away.

Edmundo put his hand up. "Excuse me, por favor, Lady Cranston. James, he said this would upset you. But I must . . . intervene. James is most brave and honorable. He never committed an atrocity on another man. Never, Lady Cranston. There is no evil in his bones. He cannot be corrupted. James, he said for me to tell you, this," Edmundo exclaimed waving his hand over the satchel, "is all a big exchange. You understand?" Sally covered her smile and nodded. "James, he talked very much about his Abigail. He love that baby and will make a good papa someday."

An unexplained silence came over the party during dinner. The clanging of cutlery against plates, the gentle jingle of wine glasses was all that could be heard for an uncomfortably long time. Finally, Edmundo broke the silence.

"Lady Cranston, I do not wish to cause you and Sir Gregor pain."

"No, no!" Sally explained. "Oh, Senhor Soverosa, the news you bring to us is much appreciated. We've been so worried. I was just wondering . . . when this will end? When will James return?"

Edmundo lowered his head. "When first I met James, he was . . . careless. He took many risks, not thinking about his life. To me, such acts are blasphemy. But soon he changed. He talked more about his Abigail. He has now a will to live long. Have faith, Lady Cranston. I believe he will return to his Abigail soon."

Sally smiled and reached across the table to lay her hand upon his. "Thank you, Senhor Soverosa," she said softly. Suddenly the table came alive with conversation and laughter. Too soon it ended and after everyone retired for the night, Sally and Gregor turned their attention to the satchel. Gregor checked on the servants. Satisfied that they were alone, he dumped the contents onto the dining table. Silver, gems, pearls, and quite a few pouches containing hundreds of Pieces of Eight spread across the table. They stood silent for many minutes. It was Gregor who snickered first, but soon they were both bursting with stifled laughter. Gregor quickly stuffed the riches back into the satchel and tied the straps.

"Whatever do we do with this, dear Sally?" he asked.

"I want *nothing* to do with it, dear husband! We keep it safe for James's return. I will not to hear of it again, Gregor. Not ever. We tell no one of this, not even Molly or Thomas. It frightens me to provide haven for this tawdry purse of sinful gain. We shall surely be struck down for this." Sally exclaimed, rolling her eyes to the heavens.

"Poppycock!" Gregor protested.

"That thing!" Sally declared pointing to the satchel. "It goes away."

"You want me to bury it in the garden?" Gregor asked, only half joking.

"The bureau drawer will be adequate for now. The one that locks, Gregor. Then keep safe the key."

Gregor went to his wife and sat down beside her. "He is safe, Sally," he assured. "We now know at least that. And . . ." he struggled to keep a straight face, "apparently, he did well to provide for Abigail. That is thinking like a father." Gregor placed the satchel beneath a stack of loose papers in the third drawer of the bureau. He closed the drawer, locked it and placed the key in the top drawer. Sally shook her head.

"No Gregor that will not do. I would feel more at ease if that thing was put far from this room. Give it to me. I will place it beneath the floorboards where we keep our silver."

Gregor unlocked the drawer, withdrew the satchel, and surrendered it to his wife who, despite its weight, held it at arms length and took it up the stairs to their room with the loose floorboards.

Watching his practical wife ascend the stairs, Gregor suddenly regretted not having a closer look at the contents of the satchel so flush with pearls and gems. He knew that once Sally stashed it away, it would not be opened again until James returned from his misadventures.

CHAPTER 26

After avoiding stormy waters and pirate attacks around St. Kitts and Nevis, the merchantman carrying long-awaited letters from Molly finally anchored in Port Royal.

"Oh Gregor, these letters are *months* old. And look at their condition!" Sally complained as she sifted through the pile of musty water-stained letters. "This one, the latest from the looks of them, says she intends to board the ship *Valor* from Plymouth in late August." Sally declared after reading every word repeatedly. "If that is true, she must be well on her way by now."

"Aye, that she is, my dear. When I picked up these letters at Customs House, I checked with the master of the harbor. Word is, the *Valor* is due sometime next week, God willing. Frightful time to cross . . ."

"A week! Then, there is much to do!" Sally put the letters down for a moment and let out a dreamy sigh. "Ah Gregor, think of it! Our sweet, sweet daughter, seventeen and a woman now! It makes my heart feel quite . . . whole again to have her home. Thomas will be thrilled!" She read the letters once more to be sure the news was not a figment of her desires. She folded them carefully and placed the stack into the wooden box with all the others and cradled it against her breast. "She's coming home!" she sighed. Her eyes suddenly widened as the notion of the work involved in preparing for this great event struck her. "Oh, there is much to be done!"

After so many weeks at sea, Gregor knew the journey to Windhaven from the Point would be too much for Molly and he anticipated the post-celebratory condition of the homecoming guests would render them unfit to return to their homes in the night, so he rented all the rooms at Harry's Public House and Inn for the entire week. Gregor half-heartedly haggled with the tavern's owner, Harry Burgess, over the extravagant prices for copious merriment, food, and unlimited casks of wine. Surprisingly, Harry agreed, though reluctantly, to lower his charge for his dear old friend, but only after he inflated the initial cost to accommodate the expected favor. No matter the combination of different financial proposals Gregor presented, Harry artfully managed to get exactly what he wanted while leaving Gregor the satisfaction of having achieved a bargain.

Sally was busy with decorating a room at the tavern when Gregor came in.

"Ah, just in time!" Sally said as she balanced on a wobbly stool. "Can you toss me that bunting? Seems I have lost my helpers," she said, waving her hand in the direction of Ruth and Matilda who were sampling the food platters. "I cannot tell you how excited I am, Gregor! The most outrageous details of this homecoming occupy my every thought and I obsess over the smallest of things. However, all this decorating has busied my hands which makes this wait somewhat tolerable." Gregor helped Sally step down from the chair and examined the bunting. "What do you think?" she asked and not waiting for his reply, she interjected another thought, "Do you suppose she has changed all that much, Gregor?"

"Oh, my dear Lord, I do hope so! Otherwise our vast investment in Miss Cupperfinch's School for Young Ladies was poorly spent." They laughed together, but Gregor's nervous twitch gave hint to Sally that he was not wholly engaged in the decorating.

"What troubles you so?" she asked.

"Fishermen off Rio Cobre spotted the *Valor* offshore. She is making her way to port. I suppose I am just anxious. Our wonderful acting Lieutenant Governor Morgan is taunting pirates right off our coast," he said in a surly tone. "He is poking a stick at a hornet's nest, Sally, and just when our daughter sails these tumultuous seas."

"The ship, my lady!" Nero came running into the room. "It has arrived!"

Sally smiled at Gregor, "Such a worry wart! You see, she is here . . . safe."

It was not long before the ship was in plain view of the North Docks. Once firmly tied up, family and friends closed in on the portside as the seamen lowered a plank from her deck.

An impossibly tall, broad-shouldered young gentleman hovered closely behind Molly holding her skirts as she navigated the narrow steeply angled gangplank. Several sailors helped her as she disembarked and she was soon in the arms of her mother and father. While happy tears flowed, the gentleman trailing behind released the skirts and stood by nervously. Gregor looked at Molly and back to the lanky lad.

"Good day to you, sir!" the young man greeted in a pronounced manner. "You must be Sir Gregor. Molly has told me much about you. It is, indeed, an honor to meet you, sir. I am Harmsworth. Otis Harmsworth." As he repeatedly bowed deeply before them, Molly pulled away from her doting parents and took the gentleman's arm. "Mama, Papa, this is Otis," she announced loud enough for all to hear, for there were plenty of ears bent in her direction. "Otis has made a most generous and deeply romantic proposal and I have it in my mind to accept, if Papa thinks it to be a suitable match."

Sally and Gregor stood speechless while everyone else shifted uncomfortably. The crew of the *Valor,* stretching far over the rails, froze for the moment to listen for the reaction of Molly's parents. Finally, after a painfully long silence, Gregor bellowed, "Right, then! It's off to the inn, everybody, where I believe some wine and dinner awaits us." Grateful for an easy exit and never hesitant in accepting free drinks, the crowd quickly and merrily went off to the tavern. Meanwhile, the *Valor's* crew who bet on a more violent reaction paid off those who betted otherwise. Molly slipped away with the crowd, leaving a stunned Mr. Otis Harmsworth to face her parents alone.

Otis steadied himself against a loose stack of small dusty casks. He knocked several to the ground and tried fretfully to restack them in the correct order. The last one did not fit. He tucked it under his long arm and feigned an air of normality. Sally and Gregor stared at the cask. Suddenly acknowledging that the scene could easily be misinterpreted as an act of thievery, he wiped the cask with his sleeve before making an attempt to position it at the top of the pile. Now the whole stack threatened to tumble and he frantically waved his outstretched arms, ready to catch the first to fall. He held his hands close to, but not touching the casks as if to push the air and defy them to tumble. When he was certain none would fall, he stood back, dusted his coat, cleared his throat, swallowed hard and muttered, "I assure you, Sir Gregor and Lady Cranston, this is neither the scene we . . . Molly and I . . . so carefully rehearsed, nor was that the announcement I anticipated and I fear I cannot apologize for either, for it is that delicious, unpredictable spirit of Molly's that keeps my soul alit and in, as you see, a constant state of surprise. Truth be known, I *am* in love with your daughter and I have, indeed, asked for her hand in marriage and I do most certainly seek your blessings sir, my lady, to care for Molly as my wife." Otis stopped only because he needed to take a breath. He reached up to loosen his cravat and in doing so, managed to untie the ribbon that held it in place. He tried to replace the knot, but abandoned the idea. Gregor and Sally watched as the sea breeze took the ribbon and flapped it wildly about the young man's face. Without the ribbon to hold the cravat, it too fluttered beneath the now animated hanging locks of his carefully groomed wig. The punishment of the cravat beating against the wig released a fine cloud of powder before his face.

There was another moment of awkward silence. Gregor squinted. "You are surely not expecting an answer, here, on the docks of Port Royal, moments after our only daughter walks off a ship after being gone for three long years, now, do ya lad?"

Otis turned red. His eyes widened. "Ah, no. No, good sir. No, I do not," Otis muttered as he tried to tame the flying ribbon.

"Good, then come let's sup with the rest of them, afore the best of the vittles are gone!" Gregor demanded before storming off in the direction of the pub. Sally, trying to suppress her giggles at Gregor's discomfited attempt to make the poor boy feel at ease, lifted her arm. After an awkward hesitation, Otis took that arm and followed Gregor.

It was a grand party at Harry's with the playing of fiddles and joyous dancing. Several times Molly, still possessing her sea legs, was quite unbalanced. Feeling a need to sit down, she found that doing so worsened her condition and was convinced the tavern was bobbing up and down. Harry provided her with a welcome opiate and she soon slipped into a happier frame. Gregor and Otis helped her navigate the tall narrow steps to the upstairs bedrooms while Sally followed close behind. Once Molly was settled in a bed in her parents' room, Sally turned to Otis.

"She'll no doubt sleep through that ruckus below and be all right by the morn, Mr. Harmsworth," Sally explained. "I have not reserved you a bed but I am sure Harry Burgess can accommodate you. Speak with him, Mr. Harmsworth, and for now, we bid you a good night."

Gregor was surprised because he was, in no way, prepared to end his merrymaking so early in the evening. He was about to object when he felt a gentle pinch under his arm and recognized his wife's endearing way of silencing him.

"Sleep well, Mr. Harmsworth," he managed. Once the door of their room was shut he complained, "But dear we paid so much for those pleasures."

"Hush, Gregor!" Sally retorted. "Did you not hear? Our Molly intends to marry that man. What say you about this matter? Can we not take time to discuss this most important decision in our daughter's life?"

"Perhaps I should go back to the festivities to strike conversation with the lad so that I can better know him," he tried.

"Gregor!"

Gregor sighed. The party was over for him. He went to the door and cracked it open just a bit to have a last look. "Enjoy, maties!" he quipped sarcastically.

During the journey back to Windhaven and in the first weeks that followed Molly's return, Sally and Gregor attended to the pleasures of becoming acquainted with Molly's Mr. Harmsworth. Otis was delightfully intelligent, well mannered, and seemed highly ethical. His best quality was his genuine love for Molly. But that was not enough for Sally. She was determined to examine every detail of Mr. Harmsworth's character. She was not about to allow her daughter's destiny to fall upon the whims of her impetuous, free spirited nature.

Despite the public announcement at the docks of the engagement and the openness of their devotion, several sons of prominent planters came to Windhaven like bees to honey hoping to entice Molly from her intended, who was after all, not a member of the elite Jamaican plantocracy. Sally did little to discourage the promenade of potential suitors, until Silas Pringle made his move. Silas, or Silly as he came to be known, was the spoiled and lazy son of a sugar planter. Silly's father had, for years, claimed some childhood betrothal between his troglodyte issue and Molly and there were rumors that Silly had a mind to collect on the promise.

"What a monstrous fabrication!" Gregor objected when he heard that the assertion had been renewed.

"Ah, actually father," Molly announced with a wince, "I fear there may be a small . . . very tiny measure of truth to his claim."

"What! Lady Cranston, have your daughter explain herself!" shouted Gregor.

Sally was befuddled as she looked from Gregor to Molly who sat not six inches apart. She rolled her eyes, positioned her hands palms up, and raised her shoulders to her ears. "Daughter!" she said, trying to humor her husband, "Your father would like you to explain yourself."

Molly cleared her throat nervously, "I did . . . promise to marry him." Gregor jumped to his feet. "When I was but nine years of age . . . and under extreme duress! It was when I, and a group of friends, explored the depths of that limestone cave, the one over by Drew Norton's hill. Yes, the one that you forbade me to enter," she added to acknowledge her mother's look. "A sudden rainstorm caused the water inside the cave to rise. It rose so fast,

Papa, I feared we might all drown," Molly explained. "Silly Pringle claimed he knew the way out and would not show us until I promised to accept his hand in marriage when the proper time availed itself."

Though Gregor was furious, it was Sally's temper that fostered a slow burn. When Silly Pringle came to Windhaven to collect on that arrangement, Sally grabbed him by the ear and threw him from the verandah. His landing was off and he fell flat in the dust.

"I shall miss the friendship I had with your mother, Silas Pringle, but I must ask that you and yours never step foot on this plantation again. Goodbye, sir!" Sally shouted after him. The staff within earshot of the scene cowered from the surprising rage released from their madam, yet struggled to refrain from laughing at the young Mr. Pringle scrambling away from the house on all fours.

Later, as Sally related the incident to Gregor, she said, "To consider Molly with that despicable creature! It's unthinkable."

"Ah, Sally, you cannot fault the lads . . . so full of themselves. Where are they to find, on all of Jamaica, such a beauty as our dear Molly?" Gregor defended.

"You would think that gentlemen, even in Jamaica, might act in a more chivalrous manner. Their actions are simply vulgar! She is engaged," Sally protested.

"Aye, but such advances, however indiscrete and awkward, must surely be flattering to our Molly. And I did not see you protest their behavior until now!" Gregor laughed.

"It is not a funny matter, Gregor!" Sally insisted. Sally secretly wondered if Molly might not be better suited as a wife to a Jamaican planter. She was bred and born on the island and thus carried a wild, independent streak that Sally feared Otis would be unable to restrain. However, by her own doing, she put an end to all further quests of hopeful bachelors. As quick as the smoke from a burning cane field covers the island, so too did the news of the Pringle affair. No more would-be suitors came near Windhaven, drawing a close to the pursuit of the hand of Molly Montague.

Mr. Otis Harmsworth was unusual, to say the least. He was thin of frame, big of limb, and stood more than six feet tall. He was the fifth son of Sir Hugh Harmsworth, 2nd baronet of Aldridge, who sent Otis to London to study the law. While there, he learned to play tennis. It was a tennis match that changed the course of Otis's ambitions.

Being in a group of students with little or no money, objects of value were often presented to back a wager instead of coins. Otis won a watch at such a match and it fascinated him. He took it apart completely and rebuilt it in good working order no less than seven times. Each reassembly was faster than the one previous. That's when young Otis had his epiphany. He discovered his passion and took his ambitions in a new direction.

Against his father's objections, Otis ended his studies of the law and apprenticed himself with a French Huguenot who owned a shop in Soho. There, he learned the art of horology and mastered the trade well enough to receive an invitation, through redemption, to join the Clockmaker's Company. However, Otis found that the price of becoming a freeman with the guild was nearly as stiff as their rules. He opted instead to enjoy the creative freedom to dabble with the innovations of miniaturizing clocks without the restraints of the inefficient and expensive patent system. Under the tutelage of several French and Jewish horological craftsmen in Soho, Otis learned to make a keyless watch and several styles of alarm clocks and watches. His watch designed to chime on the hour and half hour is what brought Molly to him.

Molly, raised in the Jamaican milieu where time was not of high importance, was late for every engagement at school. After missing several classes, the bewildered headmistress at Cupperfinch's recommended that Molly purchase an alarm watch to help with her consistent truancy. Molly had her doubts about the existence of a watch that could chime but nevertheless went in search of one. According to Otis, the attraction was instant from the moment she entered the shop and their love grew stronger with every meeting.

"But, surely sir," Sally inquired as she and Otis walked through the cacao groves of Moon Walk one morning "another meeting with my daughter was not so easily arranged."

"No, my lady, indeed it was not. I shamelessly pursued her, to the point that the headmistress at Cupperfinch's threatened to have me arrested," Otis explained.

"What was it, specifically, about my daughter's character that attracted you so?" Sally probed.

"Her curiosity! Many people entered the shop. Most showed some measure of appreciation for the craft, albeit superficial. Molly . . . she entered the shop and uttered one word, magical to my ears; how?" Otis said.

Sally looked confused. "How? You base your devotion on a single word, sir?" Sally asked.

Otis looked puzzled by her lack of understanding, and then smiled when he realized the foolishness of his statement. "Molly asked me *how* I made the watch. She wanted to know all about the mechanical workings, the engravings, the embedded gems, and the gears. She was genuinely curious about how the watch worked and I knew I could not spend another moment of my life without her."

"You are certain, and you will forgive my bluntness Mr. Harmsworth, that you have not fallen for the compliment she paid *you*?" Sally pressed.

Otis stopped and faced Sally. "Upon my word, my lady, it is what stands behind that compliment that fuels our love – her drive for knowledge, her 'trust but verify' principle! Molly heard about a watch that chimed but did not believe it existed until she went forth to ascertain its validity using evidence gathered by own eyes!" Otis explained excitedly.

Sally failed to see how this could be a firm foundation for romance, but relied instead on her instinctive belief that Otis's devotion was not based on infatuation, and was truly caring and steadfast.

"I have little doubt, sir, that you have confidence in your trade and your skill, but do you believe it is sufficient to provide for my daughter and, God willing, a family?" Sally asked, suddenly worried that she might be intruding on Gregor's line of questioning.

"With all my trust, Lady Cranston. I believe it is the intent and the destiny of men to explore every inch of this world. Plotting a course for such an endeavor depends on knowing where you are. It is only with an accurate understanding of the time can a navigator know his exact location. But time is not constant, you see. We therefore need a device that will make this inconstant abstract relative and reliable, by measuring time and keeping track of it. And then there is the matter of the social importance of being *on time* and the consequences of *not* being on time." Otis stopped when he saw Sally look confused. "I believe, Lady Cranston, that everyone will soon need and want a timepiece."

"Ah," Sally replied, but said no more. She was satisfied that Otis appeared to be sincere, forward-looking, and honest, though his words often sailed past her comprehension. She gave the nod to Gregor and he, impressed by other more tangible elements of his character and prospects, gave his blessing to the marriage of their daughter. Gregor released the public announcement of the pending wedding of his daughter, Molly to Otis Harmsworth.

CHAPTER 27

In late summer, about the same time Molly returned to Jamaica, the profitable exploits of the pirate, Laurens de Graff, were so well known throughout the Caribbean that when complaints fell upon the ears of Henry Morgan, he felt obliged to do something in his official capacity as acting Lieutenant Governor. Morgan sent the frigate *Northwind* to hunt for the pirates, particularly the menacing Laurens. The *Northwind* was under the command of one-time Barbadian privateer, Captain Peter Haywood. It did not take long for this news to reach Windhaven.

Sally was shocked by the reports and concerned for James's safety. "Gregor! Does Peter know it is James that he hunts?" she protested.

"Peter cannot know that James is with Laurens de Graff, my dear," Gregor reasoned. "We don't know ourselves whether he is tied to this thief."

But James was with De Graff's fleet, and profited much by the victories of the pirate. They captured a Spanish galleon on its way to Cartagena whose manifest listed:

> ivory 2,236 lbs
> copper 1,680 lbs
> Brazilian redwood 1,544 lbs
> wax 107 lbs
> about 215 negroes
> other cargo

It was common practice for pirates to sell captured bounty quickly and share the profits among themselves according to strict rules of division. The captured Spanish crew was exchanged for a handful of pirates languishing in the prison at Cartagena. De Graff's men had barely time to enjoy the bounty from the galleon, when they encountered a French warship captured by the Spaniards, the *Princesa*. The *Princesa* did not give up its colors willingly and its clever Spanish captain proved masterful in warfare at sea. However, James was confident in de Graff's strategies of war. In one instance, rather than see the fleet battered and torn through extended battle, de Graff fortified his canons on the bow of his flagship *Tigre* and maneuvered her to come full speed straight at the *Princesa*. In the last desperate moment, just before the two ships were doomed to collide, the frigate *Tigre* fired her bow canons. The bowshot tore straight down the decks of the *Princesa*. The *Tigre* then dropped one of her anchors and pulled hard right rudder causing the ship to pivot sharply and giving her a good firing angle on the *Princesa's* port side. The *Tigre's* starboard, now fully exposed to the *Princesa's* canons, was too close to be fired upon without befalling equal damage to the *Princesa*. The *Princesa* fired no shots. Dead in the water and having lost five times as many men as the *Tigre*, the *Princesa* struck her colors.

The seriously wounded captain of the *Princesa* and his surgeon were put ashore. Ransoming the rest of the Spanish crew required tougher than usual negotiations. As the *Princesa* carried a payroll of 122,000 pesos in Peruvian silver for Puerto Rico and Santo Domingo, De Graff could well afford to off-load the Spanish crew for lower returns. After two good wins, de Graff's ships sailed for Petit Goâve on Saint-Domingue to refit their ships and celebrate their victory.

James was basking in his newfound purpose and wealth, though it did not come easily. The battles were fierce and bloody. On his ship several good men, whom he befriended, lost their lives or were badly maimed.

Though he had a burning hatred for the Spaniards, De Graff treated his prisoners with civility. When the battles were lost, the captain displayed no undue retaliation. The conduct of the victors was a far cry from the exaggerated rumors and myths James had heard from seamen in the taverns of Port Royal. De Graff commanded respect and received it from the men who served him.

There was a healthy undertone of serving not just a commander elected by brethren, but also each other and thereby the group as a whole. In contrast to this tight and rigorous communal existence, one man with a grievance had the opportunity to seek justice by a rule of law. That man's rank, his origin, or color of his skin did not matter. The brethren established a collective edict and the means to enforce it. Before hoisting sails, each member of the crew agreed to a code by making his mark on the ship's roster. The brethren voted on amendments to the rule and every member had an equal vote. One man, one vote.

The allotment of shares, however, was not an equal matter. Booty was weighted and distributed according to a man's importance to the mission and his acts of courage. Members wounded in the action of battle, on land or sea, were fairly compensated for their loss and hardship. Larger pieces of jewelry and ornaments were melted down or broken apart and shared out. With so much bounty on board, stealing from a member of the brotherhood was the most grievous crime and carried the harshest punishment - ruled by laws created by the brethren for the brethren.

James had plenty of advice from his shipmates on how to dispose of his shares. "Spend it quickly, lad, for the life of a pirate is a short one." "Spend it afore the Spaniards steal it back." "Buy a piece of land, find a fine woman, and forget about this." "Enjoy as many sinful pleasures as possible before they are denied you once you've taken a wife." "Invest it." "Stash it." "Give it away, and set your soul free." He thought the latter piece of advice was the wisest and was now grateful that he had unloaded the lion's share of his loot to his trusted friend, Edmundo Soverosa for delivery to Sally.

Every port, indifferent to the country to which it owed allegiance, offered a plethora of opportunities to detach a pirate from his money at tremendously inflated prices. As much as any man, pleasures and treasures lured James, but he put his practical sense before his temptations. He traded awkward, irregular, and heavy articles of his shares for coin, gems, and pearls that were easier to carry and conceal. He resisted the prostitutes, for the most part, and enjoyed a moderate amount of rum preferring instead to devour the fresh victuals and unsalted meats.

In remembrance to Thomas Modyford and with an understanding of their value, James searched for plants that offered novel flavors, foodstuffs, and medicines whenever they landed ashore. He started a collection of seeds and plant clippings. His botanical journal was full of sketches and records of the plants' natural histories, supported by pressed plant parts and dried specimens. His activities were often the target of much teasing from his crewmates; however, some covertly contributed to the collection and even offered water from their own rations to sustain the seedlings.

"Any one of these plants may one day start a whole new and profitable trade," he justified. *Perhaps there is a planter in me after all,* he chuckled to himself.

CHAPTER 28

With little more than his tools, his talents, and a barrel full of spare parts, Otis Harmsworth made good progress toward honoring his promises. Sally helped him find a small two-story shop in Spanish Town to rent and within the month he was taking orders and making repairs. Sally used her network of Windhaven Pipe clientele to spread the word of Mr. Harmsworth's services and by his first Christmas in Jamaica, his reputation for quality work and reliable timepieces was well established. Demand for his services increased. He took on two helpers, both sons of Irish indentured servants, who served him well. The loss of his sleeping rooms on the second floor of his shop to his helpers, however, forced Otis and Molly to look for a house to purchase.

Old Mr. Watson, a Port Royal baker, kept a lovely house in Spanish Town. No one understood why because he rarely occupied it. Watson died suddenly of black vomit fever and as he had no family in Jamaica, his death may have gone unnoticed except for that much-coveted house on White Church Street in Spanish Town. Probate of his estate settled quickly and his house was to be sold at auction. Molly liked the house. Though in need of minor repairs, it was roomy and only a short walk to Otis's shop on King Street. Most important to any house on the island, it came with a large cistern and a lovely open yard that caught the morning sun, but was shaded in the afternoon by a large blue mahoe tree. It did have one significant foible. Due to its long period of being uninhabited, rats had moved in. It would take some effort to be rid of them and correct the damages they left in their wake, but Otis and Molly were willing to do battle if the price was right.

With the supply of suitable residences in Spanish Town short, the bidding at the well-attended auction went high. However, Otis retained the highest bid and the house was theirs. All was set now for the wedding ceremony.

The summer of 1683 was full of excitement at Windhaven. Sally kept busy with plans for the Christmas wedding. There was much work ahead for Molly. Having mastered all the necessary accomplishments of writing, music, and singing, she still found the art of fashion an enigma. When she left for England, Molly promised her mother that she was going to gather, from the best seamstresses of the high streets, a ship load full of the finest dresses. However, she returned with only one modestly sized trunk, several barrels full of books, and a rather odd and awkward piece of furniture to hold them all.

Molly! I declare!" Sally had noted while unpacking the trunk, "You have returned to us with the same clothes you had the day you left. What kind of trousseau is this for a fine lady?"

"Aye, mother, tis true, but this collection of books is a far superior dowry for they contain tales that will surely outlast any threads. Beside, Otis likes that I am a reader. And I suspect that, after the wedding, he might be pleased if I wore no threads at all!" Molly laughed.

"Do not be so vulgar, daughter!" Sally squinted her eyes, the way she always did when trying to grasp the eccentric conduct of her unconventional daughter.

The wedding of Molly and Otis could not have been on a more beautiful December day. The ceremony at St. Jago de la Vega Cathedral in Spanish Town was followed by a perfect party in the meadows of the cacao walk at Windhaven.

"What a handsome pair they make, Sally," Gregor exclaimed with teary eyes as he watched them glide together in a merry dance. Sally said nothing but gripped her husband's arm tight and leaned her head on his shoulder. Suddenly she felt quite strange. The wind changed its direction blowing some of the dried leaves off the cocoa trees. Sally had goose pimples on her arm and she could not shake the feeling that the wind whispered a warning of some disquieting change.

"What is it, dear?" Gregor asked.

"I do not know. Tis nothing. The breeze. Perhaps I need my shawl."

CHAPTER 29

James's idyllic, violent, and profitable life as a pirate was about to be shattered by three important events. The first was the news that Henry Morgan, whom James once idolized as a child, was now hunting the buccaneers down and looking to crush the very force Morgan helped to build.

The second was an incident spurred on by de Graff's unwise decision to join forces with an insalubrious Dutch slaver, Nickolaas Van Hoorn and another Dutch pirate, Michiel Andrieszoon. After finding no ships to plunder off the coast of Cartagena, they decided to pillage the Gulf of Honduras. The pirates scouted the coast and found two Spanish galleons anchored. De Graff decided to hole up on Bonaco Island and careen his ships for repair while he waited for the Spanish to load the galleons before he attacked. However, the impatient Van Hoorn sailed straight into the harbor and assaulted the empty ships, ruining de Graff's plans. Fearing his numbers insufficient to win a counter attack, Van Hoorn sailed for Bonaco Island to join de Graff and Andrieszoon, but the angry de Graff turned Van Hoorn away. De Graff and Andrieszoon made plans to attack Vera Cruz, Mexico. Andrieszoon argued that they would stand a better chance with Van Hoorn's forces. De Graff baulked at the idea, but finally relented, a decision he would soon regret.

On May 17, 1683 James, along with eight hundred other men, boarded two captured Spanish ships that de Graff sailed into the harbor under the cover of darkness. The town, thinking the ships to be part of the Spanish Flota, lit fires to pilot them in. The pirates landed two miles from the town, slipped off the ships, and quickly took the town's defenses by surprise. Most of the soldiers and sentinels were asleep, keeping the losses of both sides to a minimum. By morning, the city of Vera Cruz surrendered, giving up two forts of twelve and sixteen guns.

Meanwhile, Van Hoorn's men, having landed further from town, came overland and joined the raid. Even though the town was already won, Van Hoorn's men attacked with a viciousness James had not before witnessed. Not finding gold and silver enough to satisfy their greed, Van Hoorn's men systematically tortured the most prosperous citizens of Vera Cruz. The violence spread and it was not long before the men under Captain de Graff joined the mayhem. What seemed more horrendous to James was De Graff's inability or unwillingness to stop the torture. When the Governor turned over seventy thousand pieces of eight as ransom for his people, Van Hoorn declared it was insufficient. He demanded more and to prove his sincerity, he rounded up several thousand hostages, locked them in the cathedral, and threatened to burn it down. The sighting of the Spanish plate fleet on the horizon, a flota of fourteen ships including several warships, was all that kept Van Hoorn from carrying out his unholy act.

The pirates packed their ships with bounty and more than a thousand hostages and escaped to Isla Los Sacrificios to await the ransom. None came. Van Hoorn grew impatient. Worried that the Spanish fleet would attack, Van Hoorn singled out twelve citizens of Vera Cruz. He bound their hands and beheaded two before de Graff could stop him. It was Van Hoorn's plan to send twelve heads to the Spanish in order to expedite the ransom negotiations. De Graff pleaded with Van Hoorn to show humanity and patience. Van Hoorn responded with insults. The argument between the two captains escalated to a clash of swords and ended when de Graff delivered a minor cut to Van Hoorn's wrist. After the altercation, the three pirate captains agreed to divide the treasure and part company, abandoning the hostages and any further hope of plunder.

James was surprised when the Spanish fleet allowed the ships to pass through their line without engagement. Seven ships under de Graff's command returned to Bonaco Island to divide the loot. James was sickened to see bejeweled rings still attached to swollen and decomposing fingers. Though his share of the loot was about eight hundred pieces of eight, he decided, at that moment, his days of pirating were over. Later, just before de Graff decided to sail for the Carolina islands, his crew learned that Van Hoorn's wound turned gangrenous and he died on board his ship.

The third and final incident that eradicated any thoughts of taking up pirating again came not as swiftly or as easy to identify as the first two events. Low morale sucked the drive and self-esteem from every man aboard de Graff's ship. It started slowly and increased its intensity until the communal framework of trust and integrity disappeared altogether. The crew constantly challenged the rationing of food and water. Fights broke out over trivial matters and were settled by increasingly harsher punishments. The crew carried out their duties with little care or attention and the ship suffered from that neglect. James thought about the warning of the old Port Royal innkeeper, Harry Burgess: stay alive by trusting no man. And that is exactly what James chose to do. He slept fitfully, ate meagerly, did his job, and looked no man in the eyes. With a ship full of other men, James was never more alone than on that long voyage to the Carolina colony. Once anchored, James jumped ship and eventually found passage on an English merchant heading for Bristol Port.

Faster than a crow could fly, rumors about the boldness of Lauren de Graff's escapades flew from one end of Jamaica to the other. Many feared his next target would be Port Royal.

"Lady Cranston!" Otis shouted as he burst into the great house at Windhaven. "Sir Gregor?"

"Here, Otis. What a pleasant surprise! Did you bring Molly with you?" Sally answered from the top of the stairs. She saw Otis and Nero standing by the front door. Otis's ashen face gave hint that this was not a social call. She lifted her skirts to accommodate the rapid descent.

"What is it? Is it Molly? Is she well?" Sally asked.

"Molly is fine. It's James. He's in trouble," Otis replied.

"James? How hear you this news? Where is he? Has he come home?" Gregor asked, coming in the foyer from the back of the house.

"Read this. It's being circulated around Port Royal. The news is all over The Point," Otis said annoyed.

"Shhh! Let me read it, then," Gregor pleaded.

"Otis, come, seat yourself." Sally demanded, trying to read over Gregor's shoulder. "Lizzie! Ruth! Bring some lemon water. Oh, you have rattled me, Otis. Gregor, do read it aloud!"

Two days ago, just as the fleet was leaving Port Royal, a fisherman came in from Caimanos with news that the privateer had taken Vera Cruz. About the middle of May VanHorn, Laurens, and Yankey sailed from Bonaco in the Bay of Honduras with seven or eight ships, five or six barques, and twelve hundred men. They plundered churches, houses, and convents for three days. On the fourth day, the flotilla of

fourteen good Spanish ships came to that port. The pirates made off with many shares of Pieces of Eight. VanHorn struck thirty shares of six thousand pounds for his own ship alone. A sloop that came in yesterday got this information from his men who deserted VanHorn. I have sent orders to the Point to prohibit all sloops from bringing persons or goods, for as we were not the thieves, we will not be the receivers. The council meets to give further orders tomorrow.

SIR THOMAS LYNCH, GOVERNOR, JAMAICA, JULY 26, 1683

"What is this, Gregor? What does it mean, Otis?" Sally asked.

"That same fisherman told several in Port Royal that James was among the pirates seeking shelter here," Otis explained. "There's no way to know if there be truth to this."

Sally stood up. "This is wonderful news. James is safe. The *Norwich* did not find him. Thank God!" Sally grasped Gregor's hands, "Oh Gregor, he is home!"

"No, no, Sally. This is not good news at all," Gregor surmised.

"As a pirate, he is considered by this council to be an outlaw," Otis explained. "If, indeed, he was with this gang and committed this outrage on Vera Cruz, then there will be a bounty on his head. If caught, he'll hang."

Sally gasped. "Who's to know?"

"What?" Gregor asked.

"He's been off island . . ." Otis started.

"Yes." Sally interrupted to repeat the lie perpetuated by the family. "James has been off island visiting his daughter and our dear friend Capt. Edward Waller in Massachusetts." Sally glanced at Otis, "This is the story Gregor and I have contrived during his absence and I see no need to change it."

"They are watching the port and denying entry to fishermen and seamen on ships other than merchants or navy," Otis warned. "I have put out the word to a few that I trust. If he is off our shores, perhaps we can intercept him. We must be careful as there are bounty seekers lurking about the ports like vultures. They wait for pirates who come to the Point or Kingston."

"Does Molly know?" Sally asked.

"Aye, she does," Otis said. "And is anxious for him and prays for his safe keeping. I know how you must want to see him, but not if it means hanging from a yardarm. You must be patient. Make no inquiries to his whereabouts. I will send word if I hear anything. Trust no one." He got up to leave.

"Will you not stay for dinner?" Sally asked surprised.

"No I must get back to Spanish Town. I do not want to leave Molly alone."

Months passed. Teasing tales persisted about possible sightings of James. Then, just after the New Year, Sally received a letter from an attorney in London. Mr. William Mosby claimed that he represented Robert Montague and requested instructions for the management of the still unclaimed property and investments.

"Gregor," Sally exclaimed as she re-reads the letter, "this letter claims that Uncle Robert left behind a substantial legacy and that I and James are beneficiaries to that estate!"

"Yes, dear, I read as much, but I suspect it may be a ploy by creditors to lure you back to London to collect your uncle's debts and to deliver an indictment for failure to pay your family's financial obligations." Gregor rubbed his chin. "Still . . ."

"Could it be a trap laid for James? What do we do?" asked Sally reading the letter a third time.

"Do? My better senses tell me we should take no action at present. If it becomes a pressing matter the lawyer, this Mosby character, will follow with another letter. Let us wait and see if my assessment is correct." Gregor suggested.

Rumors continued about the de Graff's pirates but a letter from London, dated February 1684 finally put an end to their worries. James was in London and intended to stay for a while to sort out some business affair.

"Business? I wonder what business . . . He says he wants to return to us for a visit," Sally announced to Gregor as she read the letter. "I had faith," she said with disappointment, "that he would, by now, tire of these misadventures and accepted his responsibilities as a father to Abigail."

"Though the lad has tried my patience, Sally, I still believe he will do right by her," Gregor assured, then chuckled while shaking his head in amazement, "London! I do say, that boy gets around! Perhaps he might have the time, whilst there, to investigate that lawyer, Mossy or Motley."

"Mosby, William Mosby," Sally recalled. "It is worth writing to James. Perhaps we can solve this mystery before he leaves London. As it may involve another elusive treasure, I am sure he would enjoy detangling the facts."

CHAPTER 30

The initial excitement of being in London quickly degenerated to mere curiosity. James had no real connection with the country of his birth and found divisions within its society more severe than the petty hierarchy of the colonies. He was just seven years old when he left and now, nearly twenty years on, he remembered little of the land or the people.

James spent most of his life imagining Britain to be some grand old matriarch, a mother country who, with her arms wide open, would embrace her long lost son. But what he saw was poverty and a pallid population skittishly scurrying about like ghosts, eyes cast down and necks tucked deep within their collars and shawls. Perhaps it was the weather, but James suspected the cause of such posturing to be, more likely, a fear of an uneasy political climate.

He found London a cold dark misty place and disliked the way the dampness pierced his clothing. No matter how many layers he wore, the cold found its way to his bones. Petty crime seemed as bad in London as it was in the back alleys of Port Royal. Once, at market, he caught a small child trying to pick his pocket of not just the coins, but also a watch that he only just purchased at great cost. A child and a thief! He smiled, thinking about Sally. "Getting a taste of your own freebooting!" she would say, wagging her finger.

He received Sally's letter, but a certain amount of edginess kept him from seeing his uncle's attorney until the latter part of his stay in London. Still believing it to be a case of mistaken identity or perhaps a more dangerous scam, he was reluctant to enter the office of William Mosby.

His caution was misplaced. The likable lawyer immediately exposed an ignescent persona that emitted integrity and wisdom. He sported a full white wig far too massive for his kind narrow face for it looked like the weight of it caused him to tip his head in an unnatural manner. Terribly apologetic, Mosby led James to a back room lit well by a window that extended from the ceiling to the floor.

After seating James and lavishing him with drink and cakes, the old attorney got down to the business of explaining his association with Robert Montague.

"Not five years after you left with your family for the colonies, your uncle struck it lucky at cards. He told me that, with just one precise hand and one extremely risky wager against a despairing fool, he indeed became a very wealthy man. And this touch of merciful providence brought about a sudden and much needed redemption of his soul." Mosby laughed. "Ah, you hear of such fateful turns in fortunes, but as I am with you this day, it was true! All true! A gambler no more, your uncle was able to settle his considerable debts and still left a sizeable balance to his estate. That's when he came to see me. He wanted to invest his money and to settle the matter of its distribution upon his death." Mosby's mood changed. The corner of his mouth drooped and he shook his head. "We were not to know that after he conducted his business with us, your uncle suffered such a set of unfortunate circumstances."

"The plague?" James offered.

"Yes," Mosby confirmed. "Ah, there was such chaos then. That mal air affected the contented lives of thousands of Londoners and it turned our fragile style of social order upside down. We know now that it was the quarantine that kept your unfortunate uncle a prisoner within this city and this is where he died."

"We received word of his death nearly a year after, but did not receive any news of an inheritance from your office or his wife. We assumed Uncle Robert had died the way he always lived . . . flamboyantly, but penniless." James explained. "What happened to his wife, and to his estate?"

"I am getting to that. More wine?" Mosby offered. James waved his hand and looked anxiously into the eyes of the lawyer.

"To complicate the matter, there was a terrible fire. It took many years to unravel each of our clients' financial affairs. Your aunt . . . well, she did not know her husband's fate immediately." Mosby's words caught in his throat.

James searched the face of William Mosby. He seemed genuinely moved, but James could not decipher whether it was due to the company's deficiencies or out of empathy for his aunt.

"Once we located your aunt," Mosby continued, "we saw to it that she lived comfortably on a generous allowance at your family's home until she died over a year ago. That's when I sent word to your sister in Jamaica."

"But, Mr. Mosby, your letter was vague."

"I thought it sensible to be discrete. I feared a more precise disclosure might compromise the safety of you and Lady Cranston. I hear that in Jamaica, people care a great deal about affluence and less about how they obtain it," said Mr. Mosby.

"Is it so different in London, sir?" James quipped without thinking.

Mosby seemed surprised by the witticism. He cocked his head even more and resigned, "Perhaps not. No, perhaps not."

"Dear Uncle Robert," James smirked, shaking his head in disbelief, "he was so bloody unlucky in practically every adventure, it seems unlikely that a single card game would set all things right. What of his estate now, Mr. Mosby?"

"Ah, I must again, Master Montague," Mosby said, "apologize deeply for the gross laxity of attention by this office. So many clerks, on whom we depended, died during the plague. And that horrible fire, nearly a score of years ago now, displaced many more. Such tragedy! It put our business into shameful disarray. Our offices burned to the ground, but we did manage to save some documents, like your uncle's will! Even now, I cannot fully explain the oversight. I can only guess that it was misfiled – for eighteen years! Shoddy and inexcusable of us! Though the will was lost, his accounts were still active. We have been managing his estate for all that time! Until your stepmother's death, no one had questioned why the funds were still unclaimed. I hope you can forgive this negligence."

"Mr. Mosby," James interrupted. "Perhaps if you stop apologizing and explain why *I* am here."

Mosby cleared his throat several times. "I came upon the will again quite by chance," he explained. "Though my encounter with your uncle was brief, I do remember him well. His circumstances were . . . memorable, if not extraordinary. He was set on the idea that you and your sister would return immediately to England and benefit from his new prosperity," Mosby explained. "Sad. So very sad! In his effort to put things right, he lost his life. But . . . not his fortune, Master Montague."

Mosby laid out several documents and a map of London on a table. "Here is what we know,' he explained.

"In late March of the year 1665, Robert Montague left his home in the West County for the last time. He traveled by coach from Bristol to London and secured lodging at a small inn located here in St. Giles-In-The-Fields," he said, pointing to an area on the map west of London, where the river turns south. "The inn is no longer there. It burnt along with most structures in that part of town. After we discovered your uncle's will, this office interviewed several innkeepers of St. Giles in the Field and were fortunate to find the keeper who attended to your uncle. He said that early in April of that fateful year, a patron of the inn succumbed to the plague and consequently, the inn was shut up and boarded from the outside."

James already knew that from the letter Sally and he received. He looked hard at Mr. Mosby.

"I know it sounds inhumane, but I assure you, Master Montague, we were all so desperate that the deadly malady not spread to the countryside. One by one, guests at the inn fell victim to the disease. The innkeeper remembered your uncle vividly because he had much hope for your uncle's recovery. His fever broke and he appeared to rally, but then his fingers and toes blackened, the fever returned, and within the week your uncle was dead. His corpse was collected and buried that same day. On the table in your uncle's room, the innkeeper found a letter. At first, he was too frightened to touch it. But he smoked the document and added to it, the time and place of your uncle's death. Though he was instructed to burn the possessions of the diseased, he bribed a nurse to take the letter and place it upon a ship headed for Nevis."

"How did innkeeper know to send it to Nevis?" James asked.

"Ah, the innkeeper said your uncle talked of nothing else but you and your sister," Mosby sighed. "I am sorry. There was no way for me to know that your poor uncle had suffered such an awful fate. He came here, completed his business, and left. The first we heard of his death was when we received this petition." Mosby pointed to another document on the table.

James read it. "I don't understand, Mr. Mosby. This claims my uncle abandoned his wife and property and it is dated 1675."

"Ah, you see, so many died in the city. Before the winter came, tens of thousands were buried in unmarked pits around the city," the lawyer dropped his head and shook it. "Such a sad time. You can still see the mounds . . ."

"Plague pits!" James suddenly remembered.

"Yes. The hasty burials resulted in inaccurate recordings of the names of those laid to rest in such a manner. Your uncle's name was not listed on the Mortality Bills. Your aunt suffered, like so many other families, from a lack of information. After a respectable time, a family could make such a claim to release property from probate. Your uncle's wife did what she had to do. And when she heard that your father and mother died on the passage, she tried to find you. She wrote so many letters, Mr. Montague, all to Nevis. It was only in the past years, when she lost her strength, did she ask me to help her with her inquiries. She died quietly in her sleep and until that moment, she never lost hope of finding you and your sister."

"How *did* you find us?" asked James.

"Ah, again, quite by chance. Our inquiries to Nevis failed. It seemed that everyone there who might have known about two orphaned children, had either transported to another colony or died. Then we had a fortunate encounter through our investments in a company that makes barrels in Massachusetts." Mosby paused to allow

James to process this information and then smiled when he saw James's eyes light up with knowing. He nodded and continued, "Captain Waller told us of how you came to be in New England and your sister in Jamaica. It was such a startling revelation! He also informed me of the great loss of your wife, sir. I am sorry. Mr. Waller asked me that if I had the great fortune to see you, that I relay a message from him – your daughter, Abigail, is well and is the most beautiful child either side of the great sea. You must be very proud."

James swallowed hard and dropped his eyes. He wanted to change the subject. "I am, indeed, sir. I am. What of the Montague house and property?"

"Sold after the abandonment suit. The house, the land, all of it. Until her death last year, your aunt lived off the profits of that sale and spent her last days in comfort. Not having issue of her own, the Widow Montague willed her sizable estate to you and your sister. And then, there is the matter of the investments that your uncle instructed us to manage when he first came to us. She never touched it, allowed it to prosper, and left it in your names. Your uncle's monies were all well invested by this office, sir, and I believe you will be pleased with the outcome of our efforts." Mosby presented ledger books and papers to James.

For the next hour, James sat with Mosby and read the will, reviewed the accounts, and examined the papers. The remains of Uncle Robert's estate were surprisingly rich. According to his uncle's wishes, the attorney was to invest the money "*until such time as my nephew, James Montague, heir to the estates of Montague, should make claim on this property, or upon his death, my niece, Sally Montague.*" Realizing the many ways the attorney and his firm could have cheated his family of the unknown assets, James developed a rare trust for Mr. Mosby and his firm.

"You invested well, sir. I see that the assets in these properties alone has tripled since my aunt's death." James observed while reviewing the ledgers. "Well done, sir."

"Indeed, Master Montague, you give me too much credit. It is not difficult to turn a handsome profit when the market is so rich with opportunities. The plague and the fire . . . that might have been the work of the devil as it did put the whole country in a dark hole, but only temporarily. Afterwards, the economic value of property holdings had nowhere else to go, but up!" The lawyer pointed to columns on the ledger. "I can liquidate most of these assets quite quickly and I can have something for you in a fortnight, perhaps, in a shorter time, if there is a need. However, I recommend, sir, that you retain these investments here and here. The property values along the King's Road in Chelsea have soared and your estate continues to gain considerable profit from the rents."

"And my family's debts? They have all been honored?"

"Oh indeed, sir, they have and with generous benefits to most of the debtors. They were all honored, in full, eighteen years ago. The fire created an inflated rental market and profits were high. I am happy to report to you, Master Montague, that with the sale of your family's estate in the West Country, some cautious but lucrative investments, and the rents . . . you and your sister are in very good standing. Those investments are solid, Master Montague, and seem to weather well the occasional fickle financial storms."

"The liquid assets you mentioned . . . the ones you can settle quickly, I see here on this ledger, they are in the amount of . . . over a thousand pounds. Is that correct? And that figure excludes the properties in Chelsea?"

"That is correct, sir, one thousand two hundred and thirty one pounds, seven shillings, and two pence." Mosby spouted the figure from his head.

"Then, sir, I wish to retain your good services and invest half of those stated funds and this!" James withdrew a sizable pouch from his breast pocket and removed the string that bound it. Onto the table, he emptied the pouch of Columbian emeralds, Venezuelan pearls, and Ecuadorian gold nuggets. Mosby was stunned into silence. The sparkle and shine mesmerized him. His unflinching stoic character failed him and he gasped loudly. He reached out a shaking hand to touch the gems, but pulled back.

"And I would like you to invest it in this company, to support this patent." James took several papers from his breast pocket and placed them on the table.

"How came you thus?" Mosby whispered, eyes still fixed on the sparkling gems. "No! No, no, no!" he cried giddily. He held up his hands while suddenly backing away. "I think it best that you not answer and I not hear."

James was tempted to be honest and say: *you see before thee the wages of a pirate*, but thought better of it. Though Mosby kept his distance, he could not pull his eyes from the table, so James picked up the papers and placed them into the shaking hands of the lawyer. Upon reading the patent, Mosby's left eyebrow raised sharply and high.

"Ah," Mosby said with surprise. He looked up at James, "Ah! But this . . . this is the Duke's folly!"

"I beg your pardon?" James asked, surprised and somewhat insulted.

"Forgive me, Master Montague, but that is what this venture is called among London's . . . shall I say, less adventurous. The Duke of Albemarle's Folly! Skeptics, I say! And hypocrites! A mere accident of fate has formed the financial turning point of many in this town, yet those who profit most by such quick turn-around of fortunes have themselves grown too cautious and much too conservative!" It was Mosby's pet peeve, and he suddenly felt that he had stepped beyond the boundaries of his representation. "In my humble opinion, sir," Mosby qualified, but he could not let it go. It was an opportunity to ring an alarm! "It was the plague, I say, and that dreadful fire. It burned the passion right out of a generation. Tragedy destroyed the confidence in our own spirited ingenuity. Unleashed, I believe there is neither boundary nor obstacle, present or imagined, great enough to stop the rule and influence of England. Like the Romans before us, we have the ability to . . ." realizing he had said too much, Mosby took up the paper again to study its content. "Do you trust this man . . ." he referred to the patent, "this William Phips?"

"Aye, sir, with my life, and have done so more than once."

"Then you have had a personal encounter? Tell me, Master Montague, who this man is that has so skillfully captured the interest of London's ne'er-do-wells and put others in a stir . . . this New Englander with excited wild hopes of discovering some lost Spanish treasure? What has he done to warrant such trust? Who is he, Master Montague?" Mosby asked.

"William Phips is a shepherd, sir, from the frontier lands of Maine. The youngest of twenty-six and all from the same woman, I hear! He is a doer and a dreamer. He left the frontier for Boston, taught himself how to read and to write, apprenticed himself to a ship's carpenter," James lowered his voice as if revealing a secret "and married a shipbuilder's widow who, though lacking in fortune and good looks, was well connected within the shipbuilding trade. Soon after his marriage and with just her nod, he received his first commission – a one hundred and seventeen ton ship. He opened his shipyard along the Sheepscot River in Maine, well populated by the members of his significantly extended family and near the lumber he sought to trade. Phips's first ship was just completed and ready for its maiden voyage. He was in the process of loading pinewood, cargo destined to pay off his Boston investors, when word came of a massacre by Indians not twelve miles from the shipyard. A young woman escaped with her life by running barefooted through the forest and swimming across a nearly frozen river. She alerted the settlers at Sheepscot and panic quickly spread. Phips off-loaded the pine boards, took on the fleeing settlers, and charged them naught for their safe passage to Boston."

"Extraordinary!" Mr. Mosby was on the edge of his seat.

"The hostiles," James continued, "were led by a Pokanoket Indian called King Philip. They burned Phips's shipyard and were looking to collect English ears for which the French Canadians paid a handsome bounty. It was a frightful time, I assure you, sir. I was there, in Boston, attending Harvard College. I remember well seeing the poorly trained but brave militia march out to roust the Indians, only to be slaughtered like lambs." James paused for a moment, sipped from his drink and shuddered.

"And what became of this King Philip?" the lawyer asked.

James looked at Mosby with surprise. Remembering how upset Anani was over the ghoulish display of the severed head of Metacom, Sachem of the Pokanoket, and Grand Sachem of the Wampanoag Confederacy, James cleared his throat, shifted his weight from one foot to the other, and simply replied, "He was captured and killed," and proceded with his story. "Meanwhile, with the Maine settlers safely in Boston, the tales of the quick and fearless action taken by the young ship builder spread throughout the town, but his bravery left no impression on Phips's investors. They demanded payment, all the same. With no lumber to sell to pay off his debts, and his shipyard destroyed, Phips's reputation was ruined. He wrestled with the courts to regain his good name and though he succeeded in staying out of prison, investors blacklisted him. The treatment he received by the ruling class of Boston was unjust! If he could not build the ships, at least he could still command one. So, he captained a sloop taking New England cod and pine boards to the West Indies and returning with molasses and rum. That's when he heard the tales, the stories of the old Spanish sailor. His and other accounts, some hear-say and some personal, planted the dream in Phips's head and through his uncommon charisma, he placed that dream in the minds of others."

"But, forgive me Master Montague, did not our king supply this man a ship, the *Rose of Algier,* to pursue that dream? And did he not return to England with her hull empty? I hear that his crew mutinied!" Mosby declared, with an air of reservation.

"Aye, you heard correct, sir. That is how I met William Phips. I boarded the *Rose of Algier* in the Caribbean after he rid himself of that mutinous and contemptuous crew. I sailed with him to the Ambrogian Shoals just off the Turks Islands. That is where the old Spaniard from Hispaniola said the Spanish Galleon, *Concepcion,* sunk in shallow waters in the November storm of 1643. The *Concepcion* was unfit and heavy with passengers carrying their riches. Just days after they sailed fully loaded from Puerto Plata, she and fifteen other ships traveling in convoy blew off course in a fierce hurricane. In the wind, the *Concepcion* separated from the convoy and was lost. She hit the reefs and took on water. She broke apart and sunk on the rocks . . . the rocks at Ambrogian Shoals! That old Spaniard claimed he was a survivor of the *Concepcion*. He clung for days on a raft built from the pieces found floating in the *Concepcion*'s debris field. He also maintained that before the ship broke apart, the captain stacked gold and silver on the highest of the rocks so that it might later be recovered. The old sailor was sure he could direct Phips to the location of the wreck."

"This wreck, Master Montague," Mosby challenged, "is now some forty years beneath the sea. And this survivor . . . if he was so sure of the location of the wreck, why did he not go forth to salvage it? In forty years, why has the treasure not been discovered? Are you truly willing to invest all of this," he swept his hand over the ledger, the gems, and coins, "on an old Spaniard's rambling tales? You believe Phips?"

James exhaled slowly and thought for a moment. "I believe *in* him."

"Why?" Mosby asked, not judgmentally or critically, but with a genuine sense of curiosity.

Again, James thought carefully. He could not possibly narrate the many adventures and trials he encountered while under Phips's command, so he told just one story – the account of the mutiny.

James ended his tale of terrifying escapades and the cunning maneuvers by the ingenious captain to regain command of his ship, but the old attorney was hungry for more. He re-examined the papers and said, "Not since the near-piratical exploits of Drake and Raleigh have I heard such reckless adventures." A shiver went down Mosby's spine and he convulsed in response. "I should counsel you otherwise, but come back Wednesday next. I will see that your interests are fairly invested in this company, Master Montague, and perhaps persuade a few of my associates to do the same, though I am not sure I am as able as you to distinguish the rash adventurer from the clear-thinking entrepreneur." Mr. Mosby gave a silly high-pitched giggle. "Such fables of sunken treasure make ordinary means of gaining wealth no longer fashionable. Why labor for profit when one might just as easily pluck it from the depths of the sea? Do you intend to crew for Phips again?"

"I had not, Mr. Mosby. My intent was to return to Jamaica, then on to Boston, to my little girl who awaits me there. But, alas, I find my restless disposition hard to ignore and with so much at stake, I think it best to seek the carpenter's post again, if Captain Phips succeeds in securing a ship."

"Oh, there is no doubt there, Master Montague. I hear talk that the good Duke intends to fit *two* ships for his folly. Now, sir, to another matter, and considering your next employ, a matter of grave concern, so to speak . . . our records show *you* have not secured a will."

CHAPTER 31

In 1686, Christopher Monck, the 2nd Duke of Albemarle, and other investors fitted two ships for the second of William Phips's expeditions to find the sunken *Concepcion*. The two hundred ton *James and Mary of London* was the largest with 22 guns and the smaller tender, the 40-ton *Henry of London*, had just 10 guns. This time Phips hired his crew on wages, not the customary and troublesome no-prey, no-pay compensatory agreement.

Being an investor and former crewman, James advanced to first mate of the *Henry,* a position that carried much rank and generous privileges. While readying the ship for departure, he spent time ashore working with a blacksmith in a clandestine effort to construct subsurface tools using ideas and designs from the first expedition. Though most of the work involved customizing drags and hooks, some time and expense was devoted to inventing underwater breathing bells. Experimental trials of this equipment proved less than satisfactory and, in the end, Phips believed the hiring of native divers was the preferred and, unquestionably, safer option.

In September, Phips again sailed to sound the waters off the shores of the Turks in search of the *Concepcion*. The *James and Mary* lay in anchor at Puerto Plata under the pretense of trading while the tenders, crewed by a few men, and Indian divers working from canoes, searched the water near the Shoals for glints of silver or gold.

It was getting towards the end of the season and Phips reluctantly prepared to return to England empty handed once again. Out on a tender, at the end of a long and fruitless day of searching, a crewman spotted a strange and brilliantly colored sea feather in the crevice of the reef rock. He ordered one of the Indian divers to fetch it for him. Squinting against the low sun's light, the crewman noticed that the diver swam *away* from the sea feather. Cursing, the crewman pounded the hull of the tender to signal the diver to return. Gasping for air, the diver needed help to climb onto the bow. The crewman cursed again when he saw the Indian had a silver fish in his hand instead of the sea feather.

"A fish! Ya brings me up a fish! Always thinkin' of yer stomach!" the crewman complained. The Indian, still unable to speak in his defense, threw the fish upon the deck. It landed with a clang. It was no fish. It was a silver ingot. After much jubilation, the Indian reported seeing many guns below and in no time, all divers and most of the crew went down to collect the treasure. They stayed as long as the fading light allowed, marked the spot with a buoy, and returned to Puerto Plata to break the news to Phips.

On the *James and Mary*, Phips grasped the silver ingot tightly in his hand and shouted, "Thanks be to God, we are all made!" The next day and several to follow, Phips loaded the two ships with treasures from the underwater wreck. Bags of coin coated with calcareous incrustations had to be broken open with irons. In all they recovered thirty seven thousand five hundred and thirty eight pounds of pieces of eight, twenty-five pounds of gold, and two thousand seven hundred and fifty five pounds of silver. There was much more below the waters but Phips, uneasy about the trustworthiness of the crew and fearing attack by pirates, decided to return to England in April 1687.

It was a wise decision. The riches of their cargo rankled the crew. Having been hired for wages, they now felt the contract of employment was unfair. Phips promised them, that upon safe return to England, a well-deserved bonus cut from his own shares would be added to their wages. The King's share of the treasure was one tenth while one sixteenth went to Phips. The rest of the profits went to his backers, paying off in some cases twenty-five times their original investment. James was now a wealthy man!

True to his word, Phips shared much of his personal profits with his crew most of who gladly signed on for a return trip to the Ambrogian Shoals. Though tempted, James was now determined to return to Massachusetts to be a father to his long-suffering daughter.

Phips's exploits resulted in fattening England's treasury and that earned him a knighthood just three weeks after his triumphant return. James attended the quiet affair at Windsor Castle on June 28th 1687 and was pleased to learn that the honor bestowed upon his captain was the first received by a colonist born in America. Before leaving England, James made several visits to William Mosby who was overjoyed by the fruits of his own modest investment in Phips's bounty.

"My dear wife" Mosby said with his high-pitched giggle "was none too pleased when I first told her of my intentions. Words came from her lips that I did not suppose she knew and I am still inclined to believe she could not possibly understand their meaning. However, she is a very happy woman now, Master Montague, she is indeed! And you sir, are a man of great substance."

"I wanted to thank you, Mr. Mosby, for all that you have done for my family. And you may be certain that the spirit of enterprise you feared was missing from the hearts of Englishmen is most assuredly alive. I soon sail again on the governor's ship to Jamaica, where I will enjoy a short visit on my way to Massachusetts." James declared.

On hearing that great news, Mr. Mosby smiled broadly and shook his head in approval.

"Then go with God, Master Montague, go with God," he said.

In September, a flotilla of ships sailed from England to return to the Caribbean to collect the remaining treasure of the *Concepcion*. Phips commanded the *Good Luck*, a four hundred ton ship fitted with special diving bells, modified versions of the "Bermudan Tub", and other improved salvaging gear. Accompanying Phips was the five hundred and twenty ton naval vessel, *HMS Assistance*. She carried the new Governor of Jamaica and a significant beneficiary of Phips discovery, The Duke of Albemarle, along with his wife the duchess, their physician, and a sizable amount of household possessions and personal attendants. Another naval vessel, the impressive fifty-two gun *HMS Foresight* was intended to protect the salvage vessels at the Ambrogian Shoals. The flotilla included the *James and Mary* and the *Henry* as before and two more vessels, the smaller *Princess*, and the duke's personal yacht, the *Boy Huzzar*. Crewing for the *Boy,* James befriended its young captain and relative of the duke, Thomas Monck, and was impressed by the way he handled the small yacht in open seas.

The return to the Ambrogian Shoals was unprofitable. The remaining treasure had been picked clean by smaller vessels of fortune seekers from across the Caribbean. With a disappointed Duke, the *Assistance* and the *Boy* split off and headed for Jamaica while the rest of the salvaging fleet stayed at the site of the wreckage to continue to search in hope for a morsel left unfound. It was the last time James saw William Phips.

After a brief stop in Nevis, one that was particularly profitable for James, he transferred over to the

Assistance. Aboard the *Assistance* was the governor's personal physician, Dr. Hans Sloane, who was also an avid collector and student of the natural sciences.

"Oddities of this strange new world are highly coveted back home, James," the young doctor explained. "It has become quite the fashion to display such specimens at dinner parties. They are stuffed or mounted or squeezed into bottles of preservatives, much revered and cared-for, but the owners of these prizes are completely ignorant of what they so flagrantly flaunt. They have no knowledge of the creature's natural history, or the plant's life cycle. To them, it is a freakish prize meant to cause the ladies to swoon and men to wonder. I intend to change that."

"How?" James asked.

"By making accurate observations and sketches of where each oddity occurs in nature, to record what it needs to live, what it eats, what eats it, and how it propagates. I want to collect living and non-living examples of the most eccentric things from this world and send them back – not in some nameless cask, but accompanied by a full explanation of what it is, where it is found, and what role it plays in this life."

"I'm afraid, Dr. Sloane, that the specimens you will find in Port Royal are unlike those you find in the back alleys of London," James laughed. "So, I must insist that you come to our plantation at Windhaven where you will discover the finest that nature has to offer."

"You do me a service, sir. To have such a base inland where I might pursue my studies! Yes, thank you!"

"I have a young nephew, Dr. Sloane, who shares your interests. Thomas attends school in Port Royal, but when he is not in classes, I am sure he would be delighted to show you the finer parts of Jamaica."

CHAPTER 32

The *Assistance* was due to arrive at the Point in mid December and the whole of Port Royal was abuzz preparing for the arrival of Jamaica's new governor. Everybody was in a celebratory mood, particularly the shopkeepers who were happy for any advantage that might put coins in their tills.

Jaclyn de Witt was not about to let this opportunity slide. She delegated a small army of her girls to make ready her two well-established houses and help with the newest procurement, the inn at the end of Queen Street. The Inn was a delicate and tangled acquisition crafted mostly by Lady Cranston and Jaclyn felt relieved that she could count upon Sally not only as a savvy business partner, but also as a friend. Indeed, without reservation, Sally was the only soul in Jamaica she trusted.

"We must have been mad to sink our hard-earned money into this worn out inn," Sally determined upon surveying the tavern and the rooms above. "It will take more than half as much to make the necessary repairs and to refurbish the rooms."

"Do I hear doubts?" Jaclyn asked.

Sally took in a long exaggerated breath, pressed her lips tightly the way she did when she allowed her tenacity to rule over common sense, and declared, "No! Port Royal has reached its capacity. There is no more room to build another structure. People are now extending upwards! I know little of constructing buildings, Jaclyn, but sometimes I question whether the foundations can support such heights. We *are* on sand, after all. No. No doubts, Jaclyn, this I believe is our finest investment. A building of this size and quality rarely comes on the open market. I say we did well!"

"Then, leave me to the decorations. By the time the governor arrives, you will not recognize it!" Jaclyn laughed but caught the look of concern on Sally's face. "What? You do not think me capable of presenting a respectable establishment? Why, darling, I can be as conservative and frugal . . . as a nun! Truly! Ah, now there's the vision – we want a look somewhere between one of my houses and a convent."

Sally bent over with laughter. "Something like that," was all she could manage.

"Then be gone. I know you want to prepare Windhaven for the arrival of James. I would ask one thing of you. Thomas. Will you permit him to come around after his schooling to help me?"

"Of course. I think any excuse to be out of his digs would delight him. I wish I could find him better accommodation, but so few houses will rent a room to a student," Sally complained. She gave Jaclyn a startled look. "You *were* suggesting he help with the Inn and not the . . ."

Jaclyn laughed. "Do you know, it has not been that many years ago that James . . ."

"I remember!" Sally interrupted to prevent Jaclyn from bringing up less desirable memories. "When James arrives, do try to keep him from your girls, Jaclyn. Thomas is to bring him along to Windhaven straight away! To have the family together again . . . it fills my heart so!"

"What do you hear from Captain Waller?" Jaclyn asked.

Sally frowned and wondered, *why would she mention him now?* "It's been months since Gregor and I have heard any news from Edward. Down at the wharfs, I have seen ships empty their hulls of barrels made by him, so I assume he and his business fare well."

"I meant, how does he feel about James coming back for Abigail?"

Sally flushed. "Oh. I . . . I should think he'd be happy. Don't you?" Until that moment, Sally had not contemplated any other scenario. *Is it possible that Edward would object,* she wondered? *James did undermine the trust Edward had in him.* Sally looked at Jaclyn.

"No, Jaclyn, Edward would not deny this reunion between father and daughter."

Jaclyn embraced her and said, "Of course he wouldn't. Who knows him better than you? Now, you must be off. The whole of Jamaica is raiding every shop in town of the best victuals for the celebrations. Go! Do your marketing before there is nothing left to buy!"

Gregor watched his wife fuss with the kitchen staff over complicated menus. "Remember," he said, "James is not staying for a long visit this time. It may not be wise to tempt him with such comforts."

"Oh, Gregor, do let me spoil him. Who knows how long it may be before we see him again. The Bay Colony is a world away."

"Then I will get out of the way of your planning, my dear. Nero was concerned about some cows that have gone missing. He seems to think they might have strayed up near the spring again. I'll ride up there and have a look."

"Take Captain Blake with you. You may need his help," Sally shouted after him.

"Aye, and I'll take Little Luke. It is time the boy learned how to wrangle up some cattle! Be back soon, love." Gregor walked across the barnyard and disappeared into the barn. When Sally heard the clump of the horses' hooves, she rushed out to the verandah to wave goodbye to the three. She stood there until they were out of sight and as she turned to go back into the house, a sudden wind rustled the bushes around the house and sent their tiny leaves flying into the air. It gave Sally goose flesh. She folded her arms close to her and looked again in the direction where her husband disappeared into the woods.

Port Royal was in full carnival spirit with Christmas celebrations and a new governor. What the parade lacked in grandiosity was more than compensated with the loudness created by full-hearted cheers and an odd assortment of musical instruments. The crowd pushed their way to the docks, anxious to catch a glimpse of the flamboyant governor and his infamous entourage.

Thomas was dockside, shouting his uncle's name and jumping in an effort to see over the crowd. James caught the voice above the mayhem and made his way to discover the source was a tall stalky good-looking lad. His eyes and face gave him away as being Sally's son.

"Thomas! Good gracious look at you!" James embraced Thomas then pushed him away at arms length to get a better look at him. James nodded his head in approval. "Ah, you are an image of your mother. Where is she?" He looked around the crowd for her.

"She's at Windhaven," Thomas explained, "and she has given me strict instructions to bring you forth immediately. A ferryman awaits us, Uncle. We cross the bay to Kingston. Mother knows well an innkeeper's wife there and they have two horses for us at the ready, sir."

"What?! Not even a moment to wet my whistle? After such a journey?" James protested.

"No sir, not here. Molly awaits your company in Spanish Town. We'll rest there for the night before traveling on to Windhaven. Molly is with child, her third, so she won't be coming with us. Otis is most anxious to see you and to hear all the news from London."

"Well, then, seeing that my sister wishes me to 'come forth', as you say, then I say, let us be gone from this wicked city, Thomas, in great haste!" James laughed as he grabbed his duffle, light on clothing, but full of gifts.

"Molly, you are beautiful and delightfully fat!" James teased, "and Otis, I hear you do well in your business endeavors. And I am so very thrilled to meet my grand nephews. How old are they now?"

Otis caught his oldest on the fly. "This one is Matthew. Tell great uncle how old you are," Otis summoned. Matthew held up two fingers before rushing off. "That would be three, actually. And this little character," Otis said proudly as he gathered the infant from its basket, "this little fellow who insists on demonstrating the capabilities of his lungs, is Michael. He's nearly two. How goes it in London, James?" Otis asked trying to comfort his son.

"Very well. I have a lawyer there who never stops bragging about how England is on some kind of precipice about to dive into a period of untold wealth and expansion! He does amuse me with his optimism."

"And, do you agree with his assessment?"

"Yes, I have to admit, I do. But I question . . . can a small island expect to hold a kingdom with such a wide berth? Will not such growth overpower its reach? As for wealth, there is little doubt that some have acquired enormous assets. But the distribution is unequal. Britain harbors a lop-sided society with the greatest portion being the miserable poor and dispossessed. How long will her citizens tolerate such an imbalance?"

"You speak with . . . a distance, dear Uncle," Molly noted. "Do you not consider that kingdom your own?"

James looked surprised. "I do, indeed. I am as British as you, dear niece. With all her faults, England is still the country I have pledged to defend. And I have, to a small degree, added to her treasury and fought her enemies. I am loyal to its king, even a Catholic king. There seems to be a growing concern over that matter."

Molly shifted her weight and added, "I ask because many who pledged their honor to defend the Brethren consider themselves separate from any nation. When asked to whom they owe allegiance, they reply Jamaica or Barbados . . ."

"Or themselves!" Thomas playfully interrupted and as always, Molly ignored her brother. She leaned closer to James's ear and whispered, "Some believe such thinking is seditious in nature."

James frowned. "I left the Brethren some time ago, Molly."

Seeing the painful look on his uncle's face, Thomas was happy to interrupt again, "Otis and Molly are thinking about returning to England, Uncle James, to Soho."

"For the sake of the children," Otis quickly added. "I must think about their education. There is such . . . turmoil in Jamaica and a considerable amount of lawlessness, especially in Port Royal. Perhaps the new governor can sort it all out, but . . . And then there are the storms. We have had some horrific events since you left, James. Terrible damage."

"And you think England will provide you peace of mind?" James retorted.

"Well, yes . . . rather. I think it will." Otis defended.

James looked at Molly. He stared at her swollen belly and watched as Matthew spiritedly clambered over

Thomas. "Yes, Otis, I think your assumption may be correct. The lawyer I mentioned, William Mosby, may be able to assist you. I will write to him to introduce you and to let him know you may be contacting him. He is worthy of your trust, Otis, and very well connected. He retains an office not far from Soho."

"Thank you, sir. That is most generous." Otis said with a bow and wide grin.

"When do we eat, Molly?" Thomas asked rubbing his hands together, while dodging another impish attack from Matthew.

James enjoyed his visit with Molly and her family and equally enjoyed the conversation with Thomas as they rode over much improved roads to Windhaven. As they approached the crest of the ridge just above Windhaven, they knew something was wrong. The smell of smoke filled the air and they could see trails of it drifting from several areas in the sheltered flat of Windhaven. Thomas whipped his horses into a full gallop with James at his tail. Before his horse slid to a stop, Thomas was off and running towards the house. James caught Thomas's horse by the reins, dismounted and walked across the farmyard littered with debris from the house and barn.

"Mother! Father!" Thomas shouted. The front door of the house was torn from its hinges and sharp edges of thick glazing jetted from the window frames.

"Sally! Gregor!" James shouted from the farmyard. His eyes searched the landscape. Across the field, he could just make out the figures of four women as they timidly poked through the brush along the edge of the woods. "Sally?"

It appeared that one of the women recognized the voice. She turned as if commanding the others to come out and then she ran at full speed to the farmyard. Thomas came out of the house and ran to meet his mother. James dropped the reins and followed.

Sally collapsed into their arms.

"Oh, my dear, what has happened here? Are you all right? Are you injured?" James picked her up in his arms. "Thomas, see to the others!"

Sally cried hysterically, but she did her best to relate the horrors that took them all by surprise.

"Raiders. I think they were Spaniards. I did not see them. Nero saw them. He said some wore the helmets of the Spanish, but most appeared to be scallywags. Nero came to warn us and we managed to run to the forest to hide." Sally grabbed the sleeve of her son. "They burned the drying barn, Thomas, and all the tobacco hanging within. Bo went to try and douse the flames."

"Tis nothing, Mother, we can grow more. Where is Father?"

"I don't know. He went to the spring . . . with the captain and Little Luke. Nero and the McMann men have gone to search for them. James, I am frightened. Can you go? He's at the spring, the one in the upper field. He went to hunt for strays. Please, James!" Sally begged.

"I'll go when I know you are well and safe." James was clearly shaken.

"I am now," Sally assured, struggling to sit upright. "Please go!"

"Thomas, will you stay with the women? They should not be left unguarded." James loaded and cocked his pistol and put it into Sally's lap. He laid his hand upon her scratched and soiled cheek. "I will bring him home!" he promised and left with the two horses. Thomas looked around. The servants, all women, huddled together and cried. Sally sat on a torn chair and stared blankly.

"Well, at least they did not burn the house or the barn," Thomas said. "Right! Let's sort this room, Lucy. Ruth, see what is left in the kitchen. Lizzie, check the well. Make sure it is not poisoned. The rest of you . . . see what you can salvage. We'll be running out of light soon. Mother, rest here a moment. I'm going to the barn to see if they left anything." Thomas carefully placed her hand on the pistol. "It's loaded and ready, Mother," he warned. "Just don't shoot me when I return!"

The livestock was gone except for one cantankerous old hen and a cow that needed milking.

"Too cunning and mean, were you?" Thomas asked to the hen. "Good for you, but I think your efforts were in vain. You may end up in the pot this very night. And you, dear," he said as he placed a rope over the cow's head, "were too fat! Let's see if we can relieve you of that milk." Thomas tethered the cow, found a bucket, and went about alleviating the beast of her discomfort.

"You sure you remember how to squeeze a tit?" Bo asked.

"Bo! Gosh, man, you did give me a fright. Where have you been? Have you seen my father? Who were these thieves? What's the news on the drying barn? Anything left?"

Bo shook his head. "Lady Cranston said Sir Gregor was up at the spring. My father has gone that way. These were murderous pieces of dung, Thomas. I'd hate to think what would have happened to the women if . . ." Bo stopped and nudged Thomas out of the way. Taking over the milking, he continued. "There's nothing left of the tobacco barn. Damn! That was our best crop, Thomas. But the leaves were as dry as tinder. There was nothing I could do. Why they had to go and torch it, I don't know. Did they not understand the purpose of raiding?"

"And you saw nothing of Little Luke?" Thomas asked.

"No." Bo wanted to say more, but hesitated. He handed the bucket over to Thomas. "Think that's all we're going to get out of this nervous nelly. Do you want that chicken for the pot, then?"

"Nah, let's leave it. Maybe she's a layer," Thomas replied.

Sally rallied the last of her strength to look about the house. It was gutted. Draperies, rugs, even the bed linens were missing as were small furnishings that were easy to carry away. Larger pieces like the settee were slashed and soiled. They smashed the crockery and windows and ripped the sconces from the wall. Scattered throughout the house were fouled food scraps from the kitchen and broken treasures of a personal nature. Not surprisingly, the guns, the powder, and the wine were gone. So too were their finest clothing, table linens and lace.

"The silver!" Sally made a dash up the stairs to the room with the loose floorboard. Though the rug that hid the flaw in the floor was gone, the loose board appeared undisturbed. She knelt next to the floorboard and tried to pry it with the tips of her fingers but managed only to rip her nails. She looked about and found a piece of metal to use as a lever. The floorboard held fast and then suddenly popped up with such a force it nearly hit her square in the face. There wasn't enough light for her to see. She found the remains of a candle but could not find the means to light it, so she slipped her hand under the floorboard and felt along between the joists. She touched something cold and smooth and recognized the shape of the silver teapot. Her fingers ran along the narrow stem of a candlestick and then brushed against the canvass rucksack that held James's loot. *It's there*, she rejoiced with a breath of relief.

The fools! They missed it Gregor! Thank God, our treasure is here! Gregor! Sally forced the board back and pounded it in place with the heel of her foot. She heard the front door open and rushed down expecting, with all heart, to see Gregor.

"Well, they've taken the horses and some of the livestock," Thomas reported. "I saw some cows down in the field, and that old bull, he's standing right near them, protecting them, I reckon. Bo and I will go down later to sort them out. They stole the finished pipes, Mother, but left the shearing barn unmolested."

"Bo? Is Nero back? Your father?" Sally asked, looking eagerly past Thomas.

"No. Just Bo. He's in the barn. It's getting dark, Mother." Thomas could not cover his fear.

Ruth came into the reception room with a pot of vegetables. "They was too lazy to dig roots, my lady. Left us some good ones. Should be enough here to whip up a stew. That'll keep us going. Do ya thinks the gentlemen will be back this evening?"

"No," Thomas answered, "I think they'll probably wait until first light now, Ruth. This will do nicely. And here's some milk." Thomas handed over the bucket. "Did you find any candles?"

"No, sir. Not a one. They done stole every last one of them tapers, Master Thomas. I'll make a fire and fix up some bedding."

"I think we had better all stay near the fire this night, Ruth. Gather up everyone. We'll stay together."

"It all happened so fast, Thomas. I keep going over the details, but everything seems so . . ."

"Trouble yourself not on details, Mother. We'll begin tomorrow to put things right."

Sally managed a smile. "It is I who should be comforting you."

Fitful sleep and wretched dreams fell upon all as the endless night wore on. Sally jumped at every sound. Sometime, just before dawn, she gave up trying to sleep and slipped away from the others. On the verandah, she curled up on the steps, and waited for the sun to rise. For the first time ever, she suddenly felt truly alone. She hated it. Her eyes grew puffy with the tears she would not allow to flow. Her throat was tight and dry.

This is nothing, she scolded herself, *just surface damage. Why, the wind has done as much. This bunch of rogues will not defeat us. Cowards! Too lazy and incompetent to work the soil themselves, they have to steal from others! When Gregor returns, we'll make a reckoning of our provisions and restock what they have taken. We will rebuild Windhaven, as we have done before.*

Sally suddenly thought of all the hapless victims of English privateers. Did some fierce action of James cause a Spanish woman to suffer a never-ending night? The soft roar of a distant Jamaican owl silenced the crickets and in the quiet, Sally finally closed her eyes.

She was startled awake by the small troop of wagons and horsemen that slowly made their way across the field beside the barn. Nero was ahead of the group on a grey that was crotchety and unruly. James, who led two smaller horses laden with bundles across their backs, followed him.

"Thomas!" Sally shouted. "It's James . . . and Nero. There're back!" She searched the others on horseback, but saw no sign of Gregor. She focused on the packhorses and let out a horrible noise, something between a moan and a scream. Stumbling down the steps, she ran towards the men. Thomas rushed to stop her. They stood frozen in the farmyard waiting for the blow that was to come.

A sharp pain of trepidation gripped Sally's heart so severely; she found it difficult to breathe. Nero stopped and dismounted. His eyes filled as he looked at Sally.

"He's dead, madam. Master Gregor, he's dead, and the captain, too," Nero cried. James dismounted and approached his sister.

"We found him at the spring, like you said. I . . . I am so sorry, Sally." The small band of servants, waiting and clutching each other on the verandah, began to wail. The other men in the group, the McMann four and neighbors they knew well, dismounted, untied the bodies, and gently laid them on the ground.

Sally knelt beside the crumpled corpse of her husband. It smelled strongly of horse's sweat, mud, and fetid flesh. It seemed so suddenly odd to Sally that Gregor, whose abilities and courage built Windhaven to be the finest estate, should find himself ended here in the dust of his farmyard. She tenderly brushed the dirt from his face. She picked up his head in her arms, pressed it to her breast and cried with a quiet dignity that expressed the deepest kind of love. One of the neighbors knelt beside Sally to comfort her. He gently pulled her away while others lifted the bodies carefully and carried them to the back of house.

"We met up with your negro by the spring, my lady," a stiff, tall, angular man related. It was Mr. Weatherstone, the sweet shy vegetable farmer. "Nero told us of your ordeal. Each of us here has suffered so, Lady Cranston. We found Sir Gregor and the captain not five yards from the spring. He must have pulled his pistols together for the powder blackened both his hands. Judging by the number of dead scoundrels sprawled about the place, they surely fought a gallant fight, my lady. Buried in the chest of one of them was the old captain's scythe." Mr. Weatherstone dropped his head and said quietly, "I believe, my lady, that your husband took several blows afore them blighters brought him down. It looked like the captain kept on fighting. His body lay over your husband's. Like he was trying to protect him."

"Why?" Sally asked. The gentlemen seemed struck by the simplicity of her question. They looked at one another in confusion. She repeated, "Why?"

"Sir Gregor was . . . I mean to say, my lady, he was most likely surprised by . . ."

Sally interrupted, "If they allowed themselves to be taken, would I not have paid gladly a ransom for their return, whole and very much alive? Why, then gentlemen, would they choose to fight and risk their lives?"

"These were murderous renegades, my lady, bent on taking no man for ransom," another replied. "A riff-raff bundle of poxy thieves and runaways. Scoundrels, Lady Cranston, determined to take the best, and destroy the rest. Exchange was not their plan. They were after the horses and loose riches to stuff their greedy pockets. And they took the negroes, not for ransom, my lady, but to keep them or sell them, I'd say. They touched neither cattle nor swine. They scattered them about, killed a few for sport, but they didn't want anything so heavy or cumbersome that would foil their cowardly but hasty retreat."

"They were not Spanish?" Sally asked.

"There might have been a few in their ranks, but these were freebooters, my lady, owing allegiance to no flag."

"Indeed," another chimed in. "They weren't too apt at minding the horses for most of them bolted free and headed for home. No, I reckon these were a loose lot and not our homegrown variety, either. Nero thinks they were too reckless to be Maroons. Maroons wouldn't leave the cattle behind. They would have captured the cattle and left the men."

"Aye," the Irish planter agreed, "we sent Thomas Saunders to Port Royal for assistance, but we'll not hold our breath waitin' for the help of this new Governor. We are headin' north to roust these rogues ourselves. It must be done 'afore they swell their ranks with others." The man shifted nervously. "Ah, but first, we wanted to bring Sir Gregor to ya, my lady, and to ask for your man, Nero. He . . . well, he knows Maroons who have, no doubt, suffered at the hands of these devils as well. We intend to solicit their help. A strange alliance, to be sure my lady, but necessary to strengthen our force."

Sally looked about. "Where is Little Luke?"

"We could not find him," James offered. "He was either taken, or he ran away. That's another reason why we need to make haste. Many of these men here lost property to these thieves, Sally. There may be a chance to recover some of it."

"But Little Luke is not property. He is not a slave," Sally said, more to the others than to James.

"Matters not, my lady. To a slaver, he's a negro boy," countered one of the men.

Sally looked to Nero. "If Nero wishes to go, he is a free man, gentlemen, and I expect you to keep him so. Go with God's speed."

"I'll be going with them, Sally," James said.

"We can manage here. I've got those McMann men and Thomas. It is my hope, gentlemen, that your success may relieve us all of this standing terror. And . . . I thank you . . . for my husband . . . and for the captain." Sally broke into tears again. "Please, James, find Little Luke."

Sally watched them mount and ride away. Mr. Willoughby, the owner of a large cocoa walk, was the last to leave. He only went a short distance when he stopped, dismounted, and walked back to Sally. He removed his hat and said softly, "He will be gravely missed. Gregor was a good friend, Lady Cranston, truly a rare and good man." He replaced his hat and said, "It might be wise for you to stay with your daughter in Spanish Town while we search for these renegades. It may take us some time, but we will get them. But in the meantime, it is not fitting or safe for my lady to remain here alone."

"I have Thomas . . ."

Mr. Willoughby shook his head and pointed towards the barn. Thomas was saddling a horse.

"Thomas!" Sally began. Mr. Willoughby grabbed her arm.

"Gregor was the boy's father, my lady, and that old captain was his friend. He just about grew up with Little Luke. You have to let him go."

Sally eyes welled again. "Please keep him safe, Mr. Willoughby. And may God keep you safe."

After the men had gone, Sally's brain began to reel under the fierce loneliness that was now leaping at her heart. She went to the back of the house where Ruth and Lucy and the McMann men were tending the dead. Gregor's body, already cleaned, was covered with a shroud of starched white cloth embroidered with pale pink rose buds, mint green leaves, and trimmed in a thin border of delicate lace. She recognized the cloth. It was her first creation of table linen.

"I found it in bottom of a cupboard, my lady. They missed it!" Ruth said with a measure of satisfaction. When the group finished with the captain, they left Sally alone to mourn. She crouched beside her husband.

"Look at this cloth, Gregor," Sally said. "The stitching is so poorly executed. It's not a wonder they didn't take it. Remember when I made it? I took it to the barn to be used as a cloth to wipe down the horses. But then, you had to rescue it. Remember? You put it out on the dining table. You ignored the uneven stitches and irregular trim. You said any fine lady in Jamaica would vie for the ownership of such beautifully worked linen. Do you remember?" Lost in her reminiscence, Sally smiled as her fingers lightly touched the embroidery. "For all my wild adventures, all my costly failures, you never criticized or berated my foolhardy endeavors."

Sally's roaming fingers came close to the head and she pulled her hand back quickly. She closed her eyes and whispered, *the face beneath this cloth cannot be Gregor's. They are mistaken. Tis not my husband!* She tried to clutch the edge of the cloth to pull it from his face, but her hand shook violently and her fingers would not bend. She need not look. Even shrouded, she recognized the familiar gentle curves of his profile. She gave way to her tears and collapsed over the body. For nearly an hour she cried until Ruth came and pulled her away.

"We gots to bury him," Ruth commanded. "Tis the heat of the day and we gotta be quick, my lady. Now you go on inside and let these here men start this sorrowful business. We'll come for ya when all is made ready."

"Beggin' yer pardon, my lady," one of the McMann fellows approached. "We was wantin' to know . . . where should we dig Captain Blake's grave?"

Sally was suddenly ashamed that she gave little attention to the other victim. "The captain was as good as family. His grave should be near my son and by my husband. There." Sally pointed to the little knoll surrounded by a low white picket fence, just behind the summer kitchen and beneath a large pepper tree. "There, somewhere in that sad, sad place where we buried Michael and the others."

It was late in afternoon before the funeral preparations were finally finished. The servants and field hands gathered at the graveyard where the bodies of Sir Gregor and the old captain lay at the bottom of their graves. Sally smiled and looked at the McMann men and nodded her approval. Each corpse was covered with thatching and flowers. Had the timing been different, Sally was certain that planters from all across Jamaica would have left their fields to come to give Gregor a more glamorous farewell. No one in the bereaved group except for Sally and Bo could read. Bo stood guard on the other side of the house, so it was up to Sally to present the eulogy.

She read brief passages from the Bible that she knew Gregor liked and when she finished, she bent down and took a handful of the dark gritty dirt piled high at the head of each grave. She was going to drop it over Gregor's body, but a haunting sound echoed in her head, "She should have said more. She should have said more." Sally was startled and looked about. It was *her* voice, as clear as if she had spoken aloud, yet no sound came from her lips. The small party gathered around the graves looked to one and other nervously.

"I want to . . . I should . . . say more!" Sally struggled. "A poem, perhaps. Yes, a poem." Sally thought for a moment, and then gave a little laugh. "It seems I have only one that I have put to memory. It is from one of Molly's books, written by a man named William Shakespeare. I like it . . . it reminds me of my father." Tears rolled down her cheeks. She pressed her lips together, wiped her eyes with her sleeve, inhaled slowly and recited:

> Full fathom five thy father lies
> Of his bones are coral made
> Those are pearls that were his eyes
> Nothing of him that doth fade
> But doth suffer a sea-change
> Into something rich and strange
> Sea-nymphs hourly ring his knell
> Hark! Now I hear them -
> Ding, dong, bell

As she repeated the last line in a whisper, she slowly spread the fingers of her out-stretched hand and allowed the soil to drop onto the body of Sir Gregor Cranston. She lowered her head in a final goodbye and repeated the act for Captain Wallace Blake.

CHAPTER 33

Due in no small part to the efforts of Thomas Saunders, news of the raids and killings spread quickly throughout Spanish Town, Kingston, and Port Royal. Otis and Molly arrived at Windhaven the following day and after visiting her father's grave, now covered with a blanket of fresh flowers, Molly sat next to her mother upon the broken chairs of Windhaven. Otis joined the others who feverishly worked at restoring the property to some sort of functional status.

For a long while, mother and daughter sat silent, reluctant to break the unspoken pain of sorrow. Molly was flushed and sweaty. Sally picked up the edge of her apron and tenderly wiped her daughter's brow.

"You should not have come, Molly. This heat! The baby . . ." she lectured. "Though I long to see the boys and want to hold them close, I am relieved that you did not bring them. As long as those murderous thieves are at large, the danger still exists, Molly."

"But the ranks of those who pursue them have greatly increased. Oh, Mama. How could this have happened?" Molly asked, knowing she would not receive an answer. She was angry – angry that the shores of Jamaica were still unprotected. And angry, too, that plantations and villages continued to be so vulnerable to such molestations.

The vigilante party returned five days after the raid on Windhaven. They did not disclose an account of their expedition, only the result. Thomas begged his mother not to inquire further.

"Trust, my lady," Mr. Willoughby assured, "that the immediate problem has been eliminated . . . completely!" They recovered a surprising amount of property but managed to recapture less than half of the missing slaves. The others most likely ran for their freedom in the mountains. I am sorry, my lady, Little Luke was not among the rescued.

"With luck," Thomas said on the side, "he may be with the Maroons."

Sally nodded, "I have to believe he is still alive."

Exhausted and shaken, Nero remained withdrawn for several days after he returned. He worked long hours to restore the barns and house without speaking and eating very little.

"He thinks he should have gone with Master Gregor, madam," Ruth explained after Sally inquired about Nero's melancholy. "He is sick at heart and blames himself for the deaths of Master Gregor and the captain and maybe poor Little Luke. Takes a long time to heal the wounds of the heart, longer than wounds of the flesh. He needs time, madam."

Now that the immediate threat was terminated, Sally insisted that Otis take Molly home to be with her children.

"Thomas and I will come for a visit soon," Sally promised. "Take care, my dears, and give the babies a hug from their grandmamma," Sally said. "Otis, do drive the wagon smoothly. Molly must not be shaken."

A certain rhythm of repeated events marked time in the weeks that followed the raid and a sense of normality crept back slowly into the healing lives of those that mended Windhaven. James extended his stay, but when news that a merchantman bound for points north was anchored at the Point he knew it was time to leave Windhaven and move on with his plans.

"So much has happened . . . I fear we had such little time to talk," Sally said.

"I do have news, Sally. I thought it better to wait for a more appropriate moment," he paused. "You must know, first, that I considered Gregor a father and a brother. I will miss him so and grieve deeply that I must reveal this news without him!" James sat beside his sister and took her hand before continuing. "Before docking in Jamaica, the ship on which I sailed from England anchored at Nevis. While there, Sally, I purchased a plantation from a Barbadian widow. She was on her way back to England and had intended selling it there, but I was fortunate to have intercepted her plans."

"A plantation!" Sally choked. "In Barbados?"

"No! The transaction occurred in Nevis, the widow was from Barbados, but the plantation is in South Carolina. Three hundred and ten acres of prime productive lowlands along the Ashley River! And it comes with a house in the settlement of Charles Town. I must confess, my bones have long feared another winter in Massachusetts. The climate in the Carolinas is much like Jamaica's. I have decided that Abigail and I will settle there. What do you think?"

Sally took a moment to process it all. "But why not here, brother? What about Moon Walk?" Sally asked, clearly disappointed at his decision to settle so far away. "I do not need to tell you, your presence at Windhaven now . . . ."

James cut her off as he always did when he didn't want to hear her rationale. "I cannot stay in Jamaica nor can I settle in Massachusetts. Carolina is a fresh start for Abigail and me. It's half the distance between Boston and Jamaica. Moon Walk . . . it's always been a part of Windhaven, Sally. I gladly give my Jamaican lands to you, dear sister. Have you heard from William Mosby, the attorney in London?" James asked.

"Mr. Mosby? No, not since the letter we received about Uncle Robert. What came of all of that?" she asked.

"Ah, now that, Sally, is a delicious story and I am happy to announce, one with a happy ending."

"A happy ending? Then, brother, I am anxious to hear it." Sally nudged him playfully.

"No, I wish only to tell it before a crowd of Cranstons. Let's go to see Molly and her crew! Thomas must come as well for it concerns him too."

The Cranston clan gathered in Spanish Town to listen to James's fantastic tale. The story of their newly acquired wealth changed everything and not in a way James had anticipated. Molly and Otis had now the means to return to England comfortably and they were even more committed to that decision after the raid on Windhaven. The once wild colonial free-spirited Molly had finally mellowed. She now harbored a valid concern for the lack of civility and law in Jamaica. And Otis was anxious to expand his craft and knew his associations in Soho offered a wider opportunity to develop his business. Thomas saw the opportunity to go to England to pursue his dream of becoming a doctor. And Sally thought of the newly purchased inn. Now she and Jaclyn would have the finance necessary to make it a grand establishment while still retaining sufficient funds to restore Windhaven.

So, in one afternoon, James succeeded, albeit indirectly, in dividing his family, the results of which meant that Sally would be alone in Jamaica.

"This was my way of paying my debts to this family and it did not have the outcome I had anticipated, Sally," James lamented.

"Do not fret so, James," Sally counseled when they were alone. "You have no debts to this family. And you have just announced the means to pursue so many of our dreams. What better outcome than that? I think I knew of Molly's intent even before she did. Each of us was too frightened to approach the other on the topic. This island has served Otis well. It provided an opportunity to build his reputation as an artisan, and not just with timepieces! Did you know he designs the most exquisite jewelry? To soar, he must stretch his wings further a field. And Molly, I think she wants more than Jamaica has to offer for her children. She was quite smitten with England whilst attending Miss Cupperfinch's School for Young Ladies."

James chimed in on the name of the school. It was said so often in the Cranston house, that it became a habit to turn the name into a chorus.

"And Thomas . . ." Sally continued, "He has the brilliant mind of his father and wants so to be a physician, James. A dream that he has had since he first saw Mr. Burgess pull teeth and stitch wounds after a tavern brawl. Thanks to your wild treasure-hunting expeditions, you have given him a chance to pursue that ambition! No, it is *we* who are indebted to you."

James smiled and took her hand. "Then say, thank you dear brother," he teased.

Sally laughed, "Thank you, dear sweet brother!"

"And say, you're the smartest most handsome man in all the kingdom!"

Sally's laughter turned to tears as she repeated the praise.

"Come with me to the Carolinas. I could use your wisdom on how to raise Abigail to be a proper English lady and a strong mistress of a plantation!"

"No," Sally managed when she recovered her composure. "No, I am not ready to leave Jamaica. I hope you understand." James studied the floor and thought for a moment.

"No, I do not understand. You cannot stay on this plantation by yourself!"

"I don't know what I can do, James, not yet. I need time to think things through. For now, at least, I have my family and friends here and a dozen staff to care for me at Windhaven."

"You are as stubborn and independent as ever! It pains me to leave you. I will be off to Port Royal in the morning. But before I sail, I want to visit a friend and invite him to Windhaven, with your permission. I would especially like him to meet Thomas, for I suspect they have much in common."

"Only if you promise to carry a message to Madame de Witt for me. I believe we are now able to . . . broaden our plans for the inn."

Though the parting was particularly painful for Sally, it was buffered somewhat by the knowledge that James was reuniting with his daughter and that he was, at last, planning to settle.

CHAPTER 34

Dr. Hans Sloane was in his element. Windhaven offered an appealing blend of natural landscapes and finely cultivated lands in which to explore and gather specimens. He reveled in the opportunity and with Thomas by his side they surveyed and examined all sorts of animals and plants for the doctor's collection. But after a week, they reluctantly announced to Sally that they had to return to their respective duties in Port Royal, Hans as physician to the governor and his wife and Thomas to his studies.

"Lady Cranston, Windhaven is a treasure! A utopian wonder of raw nature! My lady, you have rescued my sanity! I could spend the rest of my days cataloging the specimens found on just this plantation. And your son has an exceptional inquisitive nature that, I am certain, will benefit him greatly as a student of the sciences. It would be my pleasure to recommend him when he decides on the institute worthy of his quest of knowledge."

"Then you must return here often, Dr. Sloane. Please consider this your retreat from the woes of Port Royal, for I hear your challenges there are many. Jamaica does not possess a fair reputation for keeping our governors healthy and I understand this one is particularly difficult having not received the treasure he had hoped for from the Ambrogian Shoals. I pray you succeed in keeping him well so that you may enjoy our island for a long time."

"Your invitation is most generous, my lady, and I do indeed accept your kind offer. Perhaps, while Thomas is not attending his classes, he can share with me his knowledge of the local fauna and flora and help with cataloging our library of specimens," Hans replied.

"Oh, no doubt, sir, for I think you are two peas of the same pod," Sally laughed.

Dr. Sloane was one of many visitors to Windhaven in the weeks after Gregor's death. They came, paid their respects, offered their labors, or were just content to offer their company. Eventually, the visitations ceased and Windhaven settled back into its quiet routine. Sally, however, did not. So many times she thought she heard Gregor come through the door or she would make some observation and rush in to share it with him, only to find empty rooms, empty chairs.

She missed his distractions, those tiny disruptions to the humdrum of her daily account, those lovely momentary encounters of affection that added color and texture to her life. It would be so easy for her to slip into the realm of neglect. She called on those miseries before, after Michael died, and knowing the consequences of such melancholic episodes, she was determined to keep her head up and use the mechanics of her duties to fill the days and occupy her thoughts. However, the hectic business of farm management did not satiate the emptiness. No matter how hard she tried, she could not plug the hollowness nor resolve the restlessness of her soul.

Perhaps if I plan for the future, I might better visualize it, she thought one afternoon. On the long dining table, Sally rolled out a map of Windhaven and was disappointed to see how outdated it was for it failed to show the newly cultivated cane fields. Fortunately, the raiders did not burn the cane and despite other losses, the lower cane fields were producing a record crop. And Windhaven was looking to gain a sizable profit from the new cocoa trees. The farm was finally proving the potential that Gregor and she saw so many years ago. Scanning through the accounting book, she compared the figures against the topography sketched on the map.

Next year, she thought, *that meadow should be set to cane*. Sugar was the new gold in Jamaica and there seemed to be no end to its demand and subsequent price rises. The whole of Europe had an insatiable sweet tooth and Windhaven had the potential to be a major producer, but it was a labor-intensive crop. Cultivating one acre of cane required about one hundred and seventy two days of human labor. Gregor had worried that Windhaven's field staff was not sufficient to manage more cane. While other planters compromised and were driven to desperate terms, she and Gregor pledged they would never succumb to the unholy act of profiting from the work of slaves, even if it meant the downfall of Windhaven.

However, with her new windfall as security against the ambiguities of commodities, she was no longer under pressure to compete with other plantations. *Still . . . she* thought, *two fields of five acres each. We might manage that with the McMann men and perhaps two more.*

A couple of months after the raid, Sally called a meeting with her staff. When all had gathered on the front lawn, Sally came out of the house and stood on the verandah with Thomas by her side. The crowd seemed larger than she expected. There was Nero, his wife Ruth and son Bo, Lucy, Lizzie, Matilda, and the McMann four. Old Mr. Watt who, long since retired from farming, returned temporarily to lend a hand with Windhaven's recovery and to train the two new field hands that Sally had hired.

"After much discussion with my family" Sally began, "I have decided to move to Port Royal for a while." There was movement in the crowd and the anxiety was palpable. "I trust this decision will not affect the running of this plantation. Windhaven will operate as usual. Nero shall be your manager. He will give the orders and report to me.

Everyone will work his or her job as you always have and with Nero's nod, you will be paid as usual. I expect all fields to be tended, the pipes to be crafted, and the livestock to be well fed and cared for. We have two extra hands to help with the labors. Mr. Watt is returning to his family within the week and I thank you, Mr. Watt, for all the help you have given to us."

Mr. Watt bowed. "Twas nothin', me lady, nothin' at all."

"I will," Sally continued, "come occasionally to check that all is well." She thought she should say more, but could think of nothing to add. Thomas took her arm in his and led her back inside the house.

"I would like to be a fly in the kitchen on this day!" Sally giggled. "What must they be saying, Thomas!"

"You handled it well mother, but neglected to tell them that your family will quickly be deserting you," Thomas replied.

"Oh, please do not put it to such nasty words, Thomas! Desertion indeed! I cannot tell you how proud I am that you are continuing with your education. And, though it pains me to be so far from my grandchildren, I am pleased for Molly and Otis. Besides, I'll have Jaclyn to keep me company and many others: Mary Elizabeth Morgan, Mr. Burgess. Oh, and Nall and Haddie. You see, I am well served by many friends."

"But, Mother, Madame de Witt is . . ."

"A madam and a close and dear friend, the most sincere person I have ever met. And Mary Elizabeth is the wife of a pirate and Mr. Burgess is an innkeeper. They are all good souls, Thomas, and the prime reason for me to be in Port Royal. Windhaven is my blood, Thomas, but it is not enough to keep my heart beating."

"I hear tales that Mary Elizabeth has her hands full with Henry Morgan. It seems Jamaica' most famous pirate is gravely ill."

"Well, that's not a wonder, considering his excesses. I think the man has managed to eat and drink his fortune, and shamefully gives little regard to his wife. Poor long-suffering Mary Elizabeth. It will be my pleasure to offer what help and comfort I can give to her at such a time."

"I do not for a moment think you will want for things to do in Port Royal. What are you up to now? Six shops and one inn? Be careful Mother, you will make the governor's wife jealous."

Sally laughed. "Tell me, Thomas, is she as bad as all of that? Though I do not subscribe to gossip, my ears have heard such stories I find hard to believe."

"From what Hans has divulged, the stories are not just gossip. I suggest that whatever you have heard about the duchess is but a fraction of the horrors. She is a loony, Mother, and trust me, that assessment is kind."

Sally was ready to make her move in just under a week. It took a day to pack a single wagon with Sally's personal items, enough to fill comfortably the three rooms above her lace and linen shop in Port Royal.

"I am much relieved that those rooms are now without tenants, Thomas," she said as they drove along the dusty road. "I would not have liked to evict someone, especially when there is such a shortage of accommodations in Port Royal."

"And it will be easier for me, Mother. Tis a joy to imagine attending school without having to share one room with five other gents! And its only one street away from my tutor," Thomas said. "Peace and quiet – just in time for exams!"

"And home-cooked meals! And cleaned laundry!" Sally winked. "I have hired a dear sweet woman to help me a few days a week while we stay in Port Royal. Her name is Nora. She also works for Mrs. Burgess."

Thomas pulled back on the reins to stop the wagon. "Are you certain this is what you want? Perhaps it is too soon to make such a decision of this magnitude. It is quite a change. Port Royal is a raucous town! I don't imagine you will ever get used to the noise. There are frequent parades for every imaginable reason, and the changing of the guards is accompanied by a grand fanfare of drums and fifes and cannon fire, at all five forts! There are parts of Port Royal that never sleep. Molly is worried about you. As most sane-minded people, she believes the Point is a sinful, decadent town. The Sodom of the Indies, that's what they are calling it. City of Sin! The most wickedest city in the west! You could stay at Windhaven, Mother. After my exams, I could come back and . . ."

"And give up your studies? No Thomas. No, I want to do this. I long for noise! Let the merriment keep me company," she said smiling. "Perhaps, one day, the novelty of city-living will cause me to once again long for the quiet serenity of Windhaven, but just now . . . This is the tonic I need." She took the reins from his hands, gave the horses a bit of slack, clicked twice out of the side of her mouth and said, "Move on!"

Chapter 35

Lady Mary Elizabeth Morgan folded the note and quietly lifted the chair back from the table. She stood high on her toes and stretched her neck to watch her husband's chest. It rose and fell slowly. Henry was sleeping. Gathering her dress to keep it from brushing against the furniture, she tiptoed from her husband's bedchamber. Behind her, she shut the door and signaled to the servant standing guard at the end of the hall. He was a tall and striking man with graying hair and the upright position of a slave who had spent his long life under a master's roof and not in the fields. He bowed his head in acknowledgement and came quickly to her side.

"Ride to Government House and fetch Dr. Sloane," she whispered carefully pressing the small note into his slender wrinkled hand. "Make haste, I beg you!" she pleaded.

"Mumbling!" Henry shouted from his bed. "What is this? Stop your plotting behind that door."

Mary Elizabeth closed her eyes and inhaled deeply. She wondered how it was that he could he hear her whispers behind a closed door, yet fail to hear her much amplified words standing not a foot from his ear. She forced a smile, relaxed the furrows in her brow and returned to the sick room. Inside, the atmosphere was dark, raw and dank.

"I am here my darling. Rest easy now, I implore you. It is not good, all this shouting. Rest easy, dear Henry." She took the herbal soaked cotton from his ancient robust nurse, a slave they called Piety, and tenderly wiped the brow of her restless husband. Piety backed away slowly from the bed, gathering up the soiled bed linen tossed on the floor after the third change that morning. For a moment their eyes exchanged an understanding that all of Jamaica would soon come to know. Sir Henry Morgan was dying.

Mary Elizabeth shook her head and wondered what would become of her after he was gone. She had those same fears the night her father, Henry's uncle, died. Even in her younger days, she was no beauty. Marred by facial scars from a congenital imperfection of the upper lip and palate, she spoke little and when she did, it was often inaudible to strangers. Despite a generous dowry, promising relationships and marital matches remained elusive. Her marriage to Henry was one made out of pity, obligation, and convenience rather than preference. It was Lady Modyford who first suggested the match and after Mary Elizabeth's father died, it was Lady Modyford who assiduously pressed Henry to honor his duty to his cousin.

The union produced no flame of romance, they were not kindred souls, and no children resulted from the alliance. However, Henry did accept his responsibilities without compunction and Mary Elizabeth expressed her gratitude with devotion and hard work. He was off island for most of their marriage, but left her with considerable provisions and comfort. She wanted for nothing and was given much freedom to run their significant land holdings and great houses. Mary Elizabeth was well respected by the Jamaican plantocracy, not because she was married to one of the most powerful men in Jamaica, but for her honesty, hard labors, impeccable conduct, and her abilities to run the large estates profitably.

The front door opened and Mary Elizabeth jumped. She went to the hallway hoping it was the doctor.

"Oh, Sally, I thought you were Dr. Sloane. I sent for him," Mary Elizabeth exclaimed form the top of the stairs.

"Is Henry worse?" Sally asked.

"No . . . Yes, I suppose he is. Wait there, I'll come down." Mary Elizabeth turned and closed the door of the bedchamber and tiptoed down the stairs.

"So thoughtful of you to come. I welcome your visits. In all these years, you have been my most loyal of friends. Come," she said leading Sally to the bright sun-lit front reception room. "May I offer you some chocolate?"

"No, thank you and I won't stay. I just came by to see how *you* are."

Mary Elizabeth's frowned. "Do you know, in these past days, complete strangers have stopped me in the streets. They taunt me and probe me for information about Henry's hidden treasures. Can you imagine? I don't leave the house anymore, Sally."

"Oh, my dear. Those silly fools! Vultures! That's what they are. Ignore them, Mary Elizabeth." Sally could barely contain her anger.

"I confided to a woman we both know to be an insatiable gossip, hoping to snuff out the persistent rumors of treasures hidden. I said to her, 'there is no hidden cache and if there was, I would be the last to know its whereabouts.' Do you think that will stop the harassment?"

"If you are referring to the person I think you are, then the whole of Jamaica has heard your account by now. The best strategy is to ignore them."

"Where would they get such an idea? Why would Henry bury his wealth? His treasure is here, Sally, in all that you see and in three plantations. The acres of cane, the cocoa walks, the sugar works, and what we have in the warehouses of Port Royal. To keep these lands productive, we have one hundred and twenty two slaves, seven Indians, and eleven servants. This is his treasure. There are neither buried casks nor hidden barrels of pieces of eight stacked in some secret cave or hidden in some priest hole. I wish there were, I'd tap into it to pay off some of Henry's debts!"

"Henry is a legend, Mary Elizabeth. People love legends and I suspect that wild tales of hidden booty will tempt foolish dreamers and greedy speculators long after poor Henry is gone." Seeing how distraught her friend had become, Sally stayed with her until Dr. Hans Sloane arrived in late afternoon.

"Dr. Sloane, you are so kind to come, for I know that my husband has shown you much contempt these past weeks and has been the worst of patients."

Hans bowed and graciously took Mary Elizabeth's hand, but his concerns for her health distracted him from his manners. He glanced at Sally who immediately grasped his apprehension. Mary Elizabeth had grown alarmingly pale and thin with the strain of Henry's illness.

"I shall take my leave, Mary Elizabeth. Do try and rest today," Sally said.

"It is always a pleasure to see you, Lady Cranston, and to be of service to you, my lady," Hans bowed again as Sally left then turned his attention to Lady Mary Elizabeth. "I feel, my lady, that Sir Henry is now beyond my skills as a physician."

"Oh please understand, Dr. Sloane, my logic tells me that he is quite past all hope of recovery. I shall hold no malice to your practice as a physician, nor do I anticipate a miracle. But my devotion to him overpowers common sense and dictates that I do all that is humanly possible for him. In these past days, at his request, I have summoned the most questionable scoundrels who claimed their knowledge would cure him of his aliments. Witchcraft! One so-called healer, a negro from the mountains, encased his whole body in some sort of clay shroud. He chanted nonsense whilst the clay dried and then he left. He left! The servants had to take a hammer to set Henry free. Savage science! And to think, I sanctioned it. I fear it has only made him worse."

Hans gazed at the door as if to see through it and into the room where Henry lay. "My Lady, often I have thought my knowledge dwarfed next to that, which we call savage. The Caribs, Arawaks, and the Taino – they understand the properties of local medicinal plants. More than once their practices have proven to be more effective than mine. Do not condemn yourself for turning to such indulgences. By their hands, I have witnessed such astounding recoveries to diseases for which we physicians offer no cure through our modern apothecary. But alas, your husband bears the ills of many years of high living and neglect of his health and . . . "Hans stopped. There was little need to remind Mary Elizabeth of the sordid life of Jamaica's most infamous citizen. "Perhaps there is something I may do to ease his discomfort."

On entering the room, Hans found the bloated figure of a man with signs of dreadful dropsy. Henry Morgan no longer bore the evidence of great fame or of his true age. Once the most feared seaman in the Caribbean, he now lay disfigured and pitiful.

Hans put his hand upon the brow of Henry who woke with a start. "I will see them again in hell!" he labored in a rough, almost incoherent, voice. With ebbing strength, Henry grabbed the doctor's coat sleeve and with bulging yellow eyes yelled, "What then, man, what then?"

Hans said nothing. He eased his patient back on the pillow and, in doing so, noticed a strange foul odor as Henry exhaled. It was a metallic smell, like old armor or tarnished pewter. Henry's hands and feet were so swollen the skin had cracked open. Hans pressed his finger into the puffy purple flesh and smelled the bubbling yellow fluid that oozed from the cracks. The sickening sweet smell of gangrene gave clue that parts of Henry Morgan were already dead and confirmed that further treatment was futile.

Hans stepped back from the bed to observe. Unnatural sounds emanated from Morgan's barrel-shaped belly and his breathing was shallow, but labored. Yet some force within that rotted decaying hulk fought stubbornly on. *To what aim?* Hans wondered with a morbid fascination. *At what point does the soul decide to vacate its ruined shell, and what becomes of it when it does?* As a Christian, Hans was, from the time he could walk, taught an ecclesiastical answer to that question yet so often he saw those simple explanations conflicted with science. *And, what of the soul of Henry Morgan?* That powerful soul struggled against demons, even while parts of his body were already in hell. Hans rubbed his chin and thought, *No adventures, no amount of power or wealth can save Jamaica's most disreputable character from this frightfully slow and undignified death. No gold or glitter from this Earth can buy him a passage to heaven. No amount of bribery or corruption can save him now from this, his final atonement.*

Nothing in his handiness as a physician could undo this and so Hans left the room. Mary Elizabeth looked anxiously into his eyes and, reading the hopelessness, closed hers for a moment. She hesitated before returning to her husband, turned, and gave a nod of gratitude to the doctor.

On the 25th day of August 1688, at the age of 53, Sir Henry Morgan died. Funeral bells rang out from Christchurch in Port Royal the following day. Guns fired from all forts. Ships in the harbor fired their final farewell as mortal history found rest in Palisades Cemetery.

The will of Sir Henry Morgan was the most talked-about gossip on the island. Even before his burial, rumors of hidden booty and little bastards abounded from every tavern and shop. Port Royal buzzed with fantastic schemes and fabrications, but the will, though it represented substantial income and property, was quite ordinary. Sir Henry had no legitimate sons or daughters and no other children came forward. His property and wealth went to his wife and his sister's family. Of his three estates, one was sold to cover his considerable gambling debts. Distributed between his friends and servants were mourning rings, small amounts of money, and various bits of memorabilia. By Port Royal standards, the will of Henry Morgan was modest and common.

All the hoopla of Sir Henry's death had just begun to settle when the governor, The Duke of Albemarle, became gravely ill. Dr. Sloane, while treating the duke's dropsy, noticed the damp heat of the summer, poor diet, and excessive drinking aggravated his condition. The temperature also seemed to affect the duchess's deteriorating state of mind. Her behavior became progressively more bizarre as the summer warmth intensified.

In September, Hans cut down his time for exploring the island with Thomas and concentrated his attention on the increasing medical needs of the Albemarle family. The weather was now cooler and less sultry. While the duke seemed to respond favorably to the change, the duchess's state declined. Her rants and fits drove the duke away from the house and to the taverns and nightly parties of the planters. Drinking hard and long, he preferred the company of others to that of his mad wife.

Port Royal used any occasion to make merry en masse, but the announcement of the birth of the Prince of Wales put the town into a frenzy of celebrations that went on into the night. To mark the event, Hans was invited to dine with the Cranstons. He was in no mood to celebrate and arrived at the rooms above the shop looking haggard. Having little appetite at dinner he seemed preoccupied and agitated. Sally decided to draw his thoughts away from the Albemarles.

"Thomas has been telling me that you intend to write a paper to the Royal Society concerning an illness that you have discovered here, something of cassavas, was it?" she tried.

Clearly, Hans did not want to discuss the theory and seemed annoyed at the interruption of his thoughts. "Yes, yes!" he replied dismissively, then realizing his rudeness added, "I have isolated the problem of the vomiting sickness among the slaves. It is due to bitter cassava roots. The habit of planters to provide their slaves with market rejects appears to have only debilitated them. There is some chemistry involved in the fruit that makes them bitter and toxic to people. It turns them sickly. They cannot work. So the wise planter, who feeds his slaves swine slop, will also suffer from fields left unattended!" Hans was irritated. He threw his fork rudely onto the table and abandoned his normally impeccable manners. Sally and Thomas exchanged looks.

"What is it, Hans?" Sally pressed, "Is the duke much worse?"

Hans inhaled deeply, relieved to get his troubles out into the open. "Yes, yes he is. So is the duchess. One suffers illness of the body, the other of the mind. She becomes more insane by the day. Jamaica, it seems, is destroying the duchess and she, by God, is bent on destroying the duke. It is sinful of me and truly selfish, but I am not certain the loss of their health disturbs me more than the possibility that I may be forced to return to England too soon."

"Ah, so this island of ours *has* stolen your heart!" Thomas declared. "It has a tendency to affect its visitors so. I have heard some mischief about the duchess; that she travels upstream without two oars in the water. What is the cause of her particular . . . malady?"

"Thomas!" Sally reprimanded, "It's rude to speak of her so. The duchess is just delicate and . . . too refined to suffer the shock of colonial life. It is a harsh culture, is it not Dr. Sloane? Perhaps their retreat to England is the better option for them and possibly . . ." she lowered her voice and added, "better for Jamaica. These are dangerous times. We need a fit governor to protect our island."

Just like his father, Thomas cleared his throat before making a profound declaration. "Dr. Sloane, I know that your duty is to the governor and his family. If that duty takes you back to England, then so be it. But, if Jamaica is in your heart, why not come back to her. There is some fine land yet untaken and we can help you with getting it into production." Thomas shifted in his chair and looked pleased for coming up with the idea.

Hans was truly moved. "Thomas! That is a most generous offer. However, I know not what fate London will have for me if I fail to keep my charge alive." Hans shrugged off those thoughts and pushed his chair back. "Forgive me, Lady Cranston. I do this wonderful dinner an injustice. It may be better if I retire. You will think this strange, if not ill mannered of me, but I have observed one oddity. The duke is but six years my senior. We have the same stature. While we rode together, ate well and drank lightly, both of us maintained good health. He doesn't ride anymore. And now he drinks to excess, stays out far too late eating food too rich for the palate. I fear these celebrations honoring our new Prince may affect our governor poorly. We are all so quickly gone from our happiness of life, it seems strange to me that such men as great as Albemarle, Morgan, and the lot would knowingly hasten death's process by their actions. It makes me overly cautious, I suppose, about not falling into this manner of living. So, I bid thee a good evening, Lady Cranston, for I am off to sleep at a reasonable hour. It was an enjoyable dinner as always. Good night Thomas. I am truly honored and grateful for your generous offer to help me become a planter." Hans bowed and left the room at a pace. When his footsteps faded, Sally and Thomas could no longer suppress their laughter at the doctor's abrupt departure.

"It was a thoughtful gesture, Thomas. Thank you," Sally said. "The good doctor tickles my heart with his strange ideas. I will not be surprised if his self-imposed formula for long life will cause him to reach the age of Methuselah. And you, my dear son, should take heed of his wisdom! He once told me, 'You are what you eat!' and so your habit of chewing sugar cane may explain why you are so sweet, my son! It is also, no doubt, a fair explanation for your teeth rotting at such an age. This occasion does present a proper and private moment to speak frankly. Between the duke and his fare duchess, one or the other will likely necessitate Hans to return to England, and soon. And if that timing is appropriate, I want you to go with him."

Thomas was stunned and for a moment was unable to respond. "Go with him? But my classes at Oxford do not begin until next year. I cannot leave you alone here, in Port Royal, especially now with such uncertainties. You have only just recovered from Molly's departure and mine can wait," he protested.

"The pain in my heart is comforted knowing that Molly and Otis have gone to make a better life for themselves and my grandchildren. I think about your departure the same way, Thomas. Of course I will miss you terribly, but you must look to your future. And I will not deprive this world of its finest physician! Hans and I have spoken on this matter. The governor's convoy, whenever it leaves Jamaica, will be well protected. The duchess will see to that! I would feel more at ease with such an escort. Hans can help you settle before you start your classes and you may have time to visit with Molly and Otis and your three nephews!"

"Why not come with me, Mother, so our family can be whole again. Windhaven is properly managed. Nero has administered the estate well and will continue to do so, whether you are in Port Royal or in England. We can hire someone to oversee the shops and the inn. Madame de Witt can collect the rents."

Sally shook her head. "Ah, my dear, this is an adventure you must take alone." She placed her hand on his cheek, and then made a face. "Besides, I am quite certain I could never survive an English winter. I have in my mind taking on another project with Jaclyn. It's a very small warehouse on the corner of Bread Street and Lime. Do you know the one I mean? It used to be called Trog's Gate. Its owner has fallen on hard times and the warehouse is now quite rundown. We have taken a fancy to it, Jaclyn and I. If we can renovate the structure, we will lease it. What it lacks in space is compensated by its location. It may well suit us to one day demolish the existing structure and build something larger. It's a fine investment, Thomas. And Windhaven pipes are selling again! Percival Wickland told me that the pipes are flying from his shop like sparrows! He has doubled his order. You see, I am quite busy! My life is here, in Jamaica . . ." The words caught in her throat. She could not hold back the tears. She and Thomas embraced. "And I will be heart sick if you do not remember me in your prayers."

"Every day, dear Mother, every day."

In his room at the Governor's Mansion, Hans undressed, crawled into bed and slept soundly for the first time in weeks. It would be a short rest and the last peaceful one for many months. In the early morning hours, a servant came to fetch Hans. Albemarle had become gravely ill during the night. By mid-afternoon of October 6, 1688, the duke was dead.

CHAPTER 36

The fragile strings that kept the duchess linked to a small measure of sanity, snapped.

"This is outrageous!" she screamed at Hans. "You! You were hired to keep us alive, Physician! Always off to those mountains and fraternizing with those poxy natives and slaves!" She pointed her pudgy finger wildly at the doctor. "You tended your precious collections more than us!"

"My Lady, I cannot be responsible for a patient who neither takes my counsel nor accepts my advice," Hans defended, immediately regretting the challenge.

"Insolent creature! What of the bird pepper that other physician recommended? Did you administer that treatment to my husband? No. No, you applied no such treatment!" she screamed and suddenly lashed out at Hans, scratching his face. Her servants tried to restrain her and succeeded in calming her enough to take the opiate prepared by Hans. Having achieved the desired effect, the duchess, still mumbling, retired to her chambers with her servants.

Loud voices bellowed from the drawing room downstairs. Hans removed his kerchief from his pocket and dabbed the stinging wounds on his face. He was relieved the attack drew no blood, but he would not be able to disguise the welts. He scurried down the stairs to hush the council members who came to the governor's house upon hearing of his death. They were anxious, suspicious, and completely lacking any measure of sympathy.

Sir Francis Watson, President of the Council, rose and bowed to the doctor and to Capt. Monck, the duke's closest relative, though no one knew the exact nature of that relationship. Pulling on his pointed beard, Sir

Francis studied the marks on the doctor's face, shook his head, and then turned to face the members of the Council. He raised his hands to quiet them.

"I regret to inform you that our dear governor is dead," he decreed. His remark released jeering and displeasure by the council.

"For Heaven's sake, Francis, we *know* that!" a member retorted.

"Well then," Sir Francis replied nervously, "I suggest it is time to let the crier inform the good people of Jamaica. I call for the council to meet, say, in three hours time, at Lyttleton's Tavern. All establishments throughout the town will honor the mourning of our departed governor by closing their doors to business. God save the King!" As if on cue, the crowd repeated Sir Francis's tribute to the king in a low and somewhat unenthusiastic mumble. As they filed past Capt. Monck, they offered bits of sympathetic expressions and condolences. Before the last man had gone from the house, Hans heard the crier in the streets of Port Royal. Word of the duke's inconvenient death would soon spread to every plantation and town by riders on the fastest horses and by boatmen to outlying settlements along the coast.

"I am most grateful to you, Sir Francis," Capt. Monck whispered.

"No credit is due, Capt. Monck, for I have only beaten back the wolves. They will soon be at our throats again. How fares the duchess?"

"She is poorly," Hans volunteered, "and has been, even before this shock. She cannot be relied upon for good judgment, gentlemen."

"Hmmm. Capt. Monck, what plans have you?" Sir Francis asked, pulling at his beard.

"I wish, of course, to take her home . . . to England . . . to her father . . . as soon as I return from Boston."

"Yes. Yes, I think it best," Sir Francis replied absently until he processed what it was that the captain said. "No! Boston, you say? Oh no, sir. I mean, that would take considerable time, would it not, Capt. Monck? What takes you to Boston?"

"The yacht, Sir Francis. It is being refitted in Boston," replied Capt. Monck a little irritated. He had mentioned the refitting on several occasions and was annoyed that the president of the council now seemed so surprised.

"I will, of course, accompany the family to England, Sir Francis," Hans added, trying to hide his disappointment.

"Hmmm. Yes, of course. Jamaica will suffer a loss by your departure, gentlemen, but yes, of course. To England. Not until you get back from Boston, you say? That's the plan? Yes, a good plan, I suppose. The Council . . . they *may* go for that."

Capt. Monck took a step toward Sir Francis to protest, but Hans pulled him back.

"If you will excuse us, Sir Francis, we need to look after the Governor."

"Ah, yes, yes. My deepest condolences to you, Capt. Monck, and to her ladyship. A terrible loss. Yes, terrible." Sir Francis bowed deeply before Capt. Monck. He went for the door, hesitated, and then came back. "I beg your forgiveness, but I must speak with the duchess regarding the arrangements for the funeral. The people of Jamaica would want to pay their last respects. We must permit them this."

"She is most distraught, Sir Francis. Return within the next hour. We will address your concerns before your meeting at Lyttleton's," Capt. Monck commanded.

Sir Francis once again approached the door and turned before exiting. "Forgive me again, dear sirs, but might not the yacht be picked up on the way back to England?" he suggested. However, upon reading the impatient glare on Capt. Monck's face he corrected, "No. No, perhaps not. After your return, then. Yes, that's the plan."

Once out the door, Capt. Monck turned away. "Impudent fool!"

"No matter, Capt. Monck, you handled it well. In such desperate times, they will be thinking of themselves and their reappointments, I fear," Hans interjected. He looked in the direction of the duchess's rooms, dreading the questions he would need to ask her. He looked back to the captain.

"Aye, Doctor, we best get on with it, then."

At midday, three hours past the scheduled time of the council meeting, all members finally gathered at Lyttleton's tavern. Despite the mourning decree, food and drink were plentiful.

Sir Francis entered, threw his hands up in utter despair and began immediately, "Gentlemen, this is a grave matter indeed".

"So to speak!" one member said, generating much laughter as he played on the pun.

"Ah, quit being the alarmist, Watson!" a planter interrupted, "'Tain't like we 'aven't been through this before."

"Aye!" another added. "If ya want a short life, be the governor of Jamaica!" This brought more laughter.

Sir Francis ignored the rudeness and continued, "Dr. Sloane and the good Captain approached the distraught duchess concerning the burial arrangements of our departed governor, The Duke of Albemarle. Gentlemen, she refuses to have the man buried."

That statement silenced the room immediately. The lull lasted only a moment. A rush of astonishment and protests quickly followed it.

"What does she want to do with the body, then, Watson? Drift it out to sea, or something of that nature?" The planter got his laugh and Sir Francis raised his hand to plead order.

"She claims it is the duty of the poor doctor to somehow . . . well, preserve the body . . . so she may take it back to England."

"Ah, saints *preserve* us!"

"Disgusting!"

"The woman is loopy!"

Sir Francis raised his hand again to silence the council. "And on that command, dear councilmen, the good doctor informs me that there is a measure of reasoning and precedence. He does, in fact, fear for her sanity and reckons conciliating the woman's demands may be the best option. May I point out, fellow councilmen, that the duchess is the daughter of William Cavendish, Duke of Newcastle-upon-Tyne, Earl of Ogle, Viscount Mansfield, and Baron Cavendish of Bolsover. She has the power to ruin anyone of us here!" Sir Francis paused to allow the crowd to think about the implications. The members went silent. When he was sure they understood, Sir Francis nodded his head and continued, "Let no man here doubt, each of our positions is precarious. Her connections and her money are no match for any of us. It is dangerous to speak so freely, but I am concerned that the deterioration of her mind and soul may threaten the safety of Jamaica. What do you think would happen if the Spanish learned that a crazed widow occupies the King's House? We must act, gentlemen, quickly and with one mind to preserve our good colony." Sir Francis's usual soft and shaky voice now rang out with clarity and purpose. "I propose, if there are no objections, that I take on the responsibilities of acting governor until a replacement is named by the king. A vote gentlemen?"

"Aye, aye" was the dry, quiet mumble from all the council.

"Can you do that mate? Appoint yerself, I mean. Don't the king have some say in that matter?" a yeoman asked.

"Ah stuff it, Jack. Ya thinkin' 'bout takin' on the job yerself, then?" A roar of laughter settled the matter.

"Thank you, good councilmen," Sir Francis acknowledged. "The first order of business: I shall talk with Dr. Sloane and Capt. Monck. Whatever the duchess wants, the duchess gets. We must humor and oblige the widow so we may return her safely to England . . . and soon!"

"Ya mean, be rid of 'er, don't ya, mate?" someone gestured and the crowd laughed.

"How will Sloane accomplish this bizarre act . . . I mean, preserving the body? Sounds like the devil's work," a member shouted.

At this, Sir Francis threw his hands up again. "I do not know, nor do I wish to know." Sir Francis's mood turned somber. "My sense of wisdom tells me that this is clearly something that should be kept just amongst us here, gentlemen. If word of this reaches our more pious citizens, they may strike a call to burn her as a witch." Sir Francis glared at the company around him. "Let's make it our pledge, then gentlemen, we keep this matter to ourselves."

"What about the funeral?" someone asked.

"We'll have it," Francis declared, "and then afterwards, the good doctor can preserve the body or whatever he is meant to do with it."

"He better do it quick, in this heat . . . if ye gets me drift," a member said holding his nose.

"Hey now," a council member queried, "Capt. Monck told me a fortnight ago he'd be heading to Boston to collect the duke's yacht. That still true?"

"Yes, gentlemen. The duchess will not return to England without her yacht. And she believes Capt. Monck is her only ally on this island," Sir Francis explained wearily. "She'll leave neither behind."

The council members stopped their jeering and looked to one another. Finally, one stated the obvious in a solemn tone, "That'll take months to put that together, Acting Governor Watson. Months!"

At that, Lyttleton's tavern ripped with protests and cries of outrage. Sir Francis declared an end to the meeting, though no one at that point was paying much attention to him. He positioned himself at the forefront of the rowdy crowd just near the tavern's door to remind all who passed of their pledge of silence. However, he knew in his heart that within moments of their departure, the whole of Jamaica would be buzzing with gossip about the insane acts of the dangerous and demented dowager.

It was a short distance from Lyttleton's to Sally's shop. Thomas stood at the doorway smoking his pipe as he watched the noisy crowd tumble out of the tavern. As a dejected Sir Francis came by, Thomas joked, "Ah, Sir Francis! You've come to ask if I would be governor of this fine island?"

Sir Francis managed a smile and said, "I may yet, Sir Thomas, I may yet! As it is, the council has voted me to be the unfortunate stand-in. I need Dr. Sloane's good counsel, if he is about."

"Hans!" Thomas shouted up the stairwell, "A very somber Watson is here to see you!" Trying to make light of the matter, Thomas smiled behind his pipe. "There, there Watson. It's not your end. Jamaica has a new governor on average, I'd say, every two years or so. Your burdens will soon be lifted, no doubt."

"Not funny, Sir Thomas! Some of our councilmen did mention the notably short longevity of our governors. It's not the loss of the governor I fear most, or of me taking his place." Watson lowered his voice and moved closer to Thomas, "It is his ranting wife. She makes my hair stand on end!"

Dr. Sloane came to top of the stairwell. "Come up, Sir Francis! Lady Cranston is cutting a lovely cake to sweeten your palate after such a sour encounter."

"Ah, my good doctor," Watson started as he struggled up the narrow stairwell. "I bring to you the news of the council: simply, that we should hasten the departure of the duchess. The sooner she is back in England, the safer Jamaica becomes for us all. We must honor her request . . . about the deceased, that is . . . unholy as it may be."

"I think I may have a solution to that. I have been reading this book on preserving wood," Hans reported. Sally entered the room with the cake nicely sliced on a platter. The men became silent. Sir Francis nervously pulled at the point of his beard and Thomas cleared his throat.

"It's all right, Sir Francis, I loaned him that book. The talk of this matter does not offend me, so please continue, Dr. Sloane."

Sir Francis bowed. "I am grateful for your gentle disruption, my lady, for it is *I* who do not wish to hear the ghoulish details. I hope that does not offend, but I do find the idea of this most . . . well, I worry that some may consider this blasphemy. Just do it quickly good doctor, I implore you. It is urgent that the duchess and her entourage get off this island!" With that, Sir Francis took a slice of cake from the platter and smiled with satisfaction. "Lady Cranston, you should think about converting that old warehouse into a bakery! This is . . ." he crammed the rest into his mouth, brushed the crumbs from his beard, and blew a kiss from his lips. "Must depart!" Sir Francis bowed. "My lady, Doctor, Sir Thomas," he acknowledged while grabbing another slice.

When he had gone, Thomas and Hans exchanged quick glances. Sally shook her head, laughed, and mumbled something about Sir Francis's gift for drama.

"As I was saying," Hans continued, "I believe I can preserve his body through the same process as preserving wood. And a man's body cannot not be entirely different from the many other creatures I have preserved." He looked up from his book to study Thomas's face. "What is the urgency . . . about getting the duchess off island?"

"Politics," Thomas replied simply.

Hans had no interest in discussing the politics of the council. He put his nose back into the book and concentrated on his macabre task. During the evening following the elaborate funeral, he worked on the embalming plan and the design for a coffin and sent several of the duke's servants to collect the materials he required. With little regard to the time of night, the servants woke shopkeepers and merchants who scrambled to cover the strange catalog of goods. Though Hans told no one of the purpose of the midnight caper, not even the servants, everyone assumed it was for a common goal of ridding Jamaica of the depraved duchess and went to extraordinary lengths to help expedite the process.

When, at last, he assembled the materials, Hans dismissed most of the servants except for a few he knew to be most loyal to the duke. He asked Thomas and the Rev. Heath to assist him in the preparation of the corpse.

Upon the first incision, an odiferous and quite audible expulsion of gas made them all swoon. The Jamaican heat had already taken its toll.

"See this advanced state of decay? It proves that our duke suffered gravely while he still breathed," Hans concluded. To continue, the men covered their mouths and noses with cloths soaked in extract of vanilla and mint. Hans removed the entrails and placed them in a bucket. The air filled with the smell of excrement. He took a moment to study the condition of other organs.

"Look at this liver, Thomas! The Duke lived thirty-five years, yet his inners are more like that of an older man." Hans declared, shaking his head. "See, how enlarged it is? And these patches of pale tissue, they come so easily apart with even a gentle touch." Hans reached high into the chest cavity to remove any soft viscera that would come with a good tug. "Ah, now I see. When I listened to his heart it seemed strained and muffled. It must have been impeded by the constraints of this yellow layer of fat. Perhaps it reduced the room for which to beat."

Rev. Heath took several steps back from the body. "Please, good doctor, spare us your analysis and press on with this morbid deed or you shall not have me present."

Hans regretted that he did not have more time to study his patient post mortem. He gutted the corpse completely, cleaned the body's cavity with salt water, dried it the best he could, and began to paint it with thick heated pitch.

The smell of flesh searing at the touch of hot pitch made the reverend collapse and even Hans began to question the morality of this folly. When he recovered, the reverend began to quote his prayers loudly as if to assure his Lord that their caper was somehow holy . . . or, at the least, for the well-being of his good servants in Jamaica.

After a sufficient coating of pitch, Hans stuffed the cavity with cotton soaked in coconut oil and with a large and long needle, sewed the flaps of flesh together. He wrapped the body with strips of muslin cloth, soaked in oil, from the neck to the toes. This proved to be a difficult task physically for every go-around, the body had to be lifted by Thomas and the reverend.

"He looks like a rag doll," Thomas noted.

"I am copying an ancient technique used by Egyptians," the doctor explained.

"That is simply unholy," the reverend protested, trying to hide his awe and curiosity.

"How so, Reverend Heath? Do *we* not believe in some form of after-life?"

"Aye, for our soul, not the flesh," he replied.

"Then there lies the difference, Reverend. Perhaps they believed the body was the vessel of the soul. The better the vessel is preserved, the better the chance the soul had in reaching its destiny in the after life. Ah, but how I wish I read the words of that study with more intent on remembering them."

"You mean, you are doing this from memory? You do not have their formula for such . . . shenanigans? This is your invention?" the reverend gasped.

"Formula? No, good reverend, I don't believe anyone possesses a formula for such a process. I am using what is logical and available locally and what has worked before in the preservation of specimens I have collected. This is the same pitch we use to seal the cracks in our ships and the same oil used to preserve wood. What is wood, but the flesh of the tree? What is good for one must surely be effective for another. This is not new science, gentlemen," the doctor explained. "I have actually seen a mummy in a collection in Amsterdam. The skills of preservation were not committed by barbarians, but learned men of science of a great and noble past." Dr. Sloane sighed long and hard. "Be it so, pray louder, Reverend, just in case."

"What about his head?" Thomas whispered, as if speaking louder was somehow disrespectful. "Is it not most important to preserve that for the sake of the widow?"

"I confess, gentlemen, there I am at a loss. What do we do with the head? If I alter it, and the duchess makes the discovery, it could be my doom. If I do nothing, and it decays, I might equally be doomed. I know not how to remove the contents of this skull without molesting the face. I rely on your good judgment and learned advice. What should we do with the head?"

The reverend and Thomas looked at one another with puzzlement. Finally, the reverend offered, "Perhaps the oiled cloth is sufficient. I say wrap it, unaltered."

"Yes, unaltered." Thomas agreed.

Hans continued with the wrapping until he encased the entire body in oiled cloth. In another room and with fierce urgency, a carpenter and his apprentice finished the constructions of two bullet wood coffins, one smaller to fit inside the other. The wood was heavy, thick, and not prone to attack by insects. Pitch sealed the cracks. The men put a layer straw on the bottom of the smaller coffin and placed the body inside. They packed straw around and over the body, and then nailed the lid to the smaller coffin. They laid that coffin gently into the larger, packed straw around the edges, and sealed it shut.

"I can still smell death," Thomas noted.

"Aye, it is a persistent smell. Perhaps a day or two of airing," Hans said as he strained to lift the end of the coffin. "I believe the weight of this coffin must surely sink the ship that carries it," worried Hans.

The Reverend made the servants and carpenters swear their silence in the name of the king. By daybreak, the deed was done.

The duchess, of course, demanded to know the details of the preservation process. Hans related a much-modified version of the truth and was thankful she did not inquire as to the whereabouts of the duke's entrails, for he was uncertain of their fate. He did notice, however, that a bucket very similar to the one he used, sat empty outside the pigpen.

CHAPTER 37

For a while, the Dowager Duchess of Albemarle seemed pleased with her treatment and busied herself with plans for the return trip to England. Captain Monck sailed to Boston to collect the newly repaired ducal yacht, refitted now for heavy cargo and the voyage across the Atlantic.

However, in the ensuing weeks, the dysfunctional duchess's mental state deteriorated into a sullen cloud of confusion and suspicion. She accused Sir Francis of wanting to evict her from the mansion so he, like some conqueror, could move in and take over the duke's furniture and property. Then she feared an attack by pirates. Convinced that there were Spanish spies in Port Royal, which undoubtedly there were, she tried to have the port closed to all ships, lest the spies report that she was alone and unguarded. Rumors bounced through the Caribbean and Jamaicans became ever more anxious to have the mad woman out of Port Royal.

In a fit of paranoia, she announced one day that she was going to move to their country home in Liguanea, in the gentle rolling foothills on the northeast side of Kingston. She demanded from Sir Francis a militia to accompany her.

"She wants what?" Sir Francis had taken about all the demands from the sick woman that he could. "She has exhausted much of this colony's treasury and certainly the tolerance of the council!"

"This is a manifestation of her illness, Sir Francis," Hans tried to explain. "The poor woman is convinced everyone is plotting to attack her – the servants, slaves, pirates, Jews, even the townspeople."

"Ha! Of that, my dear doctor, she may have warrant!" Sir Francis interjected.

"She trusts no one and now feels that she will be safer in the country, *away* from the sea and Port Royal."

"Aye, and away from us! That may be in our favor, but I cannot dispatch men from the fort and leave this port defenseless for a . . . personal escort. The woman is . . ." He stopped short of slander, even to Hans. Sir Francis sighed. "What exactly is wrong with the duchess, doctor?"

"I am not sure," Hans sighed. "I thought perhaps this lunacy may be a manifestation of syphilis but, lately, I am more inclined to suspect the paint she wears on her face. Captain Monck mentioned that the madness seemed to start not long after her recovery from the pox. A woman who lives near Bridewell Prison concocts the cosmetic. To prevent it from caking and cracking on the flesh, a considerable quantity of lead is added. I have treated two others who use that same paint to cover facial scars and they both share the same symptoms as the duchess – loss of hair and teeth, no appetite, confusion, memory loss, stomach cramps, and irritability. Some time ago, I ordered the other two to stop using the cosmetic. Their symptoms abated and their health improved to some extent."

"Did you not tell the duchess of what you suspected?"

"Of course, and the duke. She put her vanity above logic and refused to stop using the paint."

"Such turmoil, and all due to a woman's facial mask!" Sir Francis mused.

"That is only my conjecture, Sir Francis. She could just as easily be suffering from some other ailment of body or mind."

Sir Francis's face softened, "I will present her request to the council, but I fear I already know their answer." Exhausted, Hans turned away from Sir Francis and began to walk out the door. "Dr. Sloane," Sir Francis beckoned. Hans inhaled slowly and braced himself for further complaints from the man who was speaking for all of Port Royal. "Dr. Sloane, your loyalty to your charge is laudable. We recognize your task must be . . . difficult. A small militia may relieve you of your most urgent burden. I will speak to the council with favor."

Hans did not reply, but instead bowed and left. Over the past days, he developed a new desire . . . to return to England. He wanted little other than to be finally relieved of the disconsolate heiress and to be back among all that was familiar and once enjoyable to him.

The council granted a minor militia to guard the influential widow while she remained in Jamaica. It took weeks to transfer her innumerable servants, hundreds of tons of furniture, her personal treasure, her Chinese porcelains, and of course the coffin to the house in Liguanea. For a while she seemed appeased, and all of Jamaica breathed a sigh of relief. But it was short lived. News came from England of the dethroning of King James II in London but with no word regarding who now ruled in his place.

Fearing a defenseless position in the countryside if her militia was recalled, the duchess decided to return to the governor's mansion, now occupied by Acting Governor Watson, where she would wait for Capt. Monck's return from Boston. Without knowing who had power in England and with growing apprehension over the duchess's influential family, Sir Francis thought it prudent to tolerate the disruption from his unwanted guest.

Captain Monck returned from Boston five months after the death of the Duke of Albemarle and much to the delight of all of Port Royal, preparations began for the duchess's final departure from Jamaica. It took over a fortnight to load the ships with every belonging of the duchess plus Dr. Sloane's hundreds of curiosities, plants, and animal collections. Sally, too, prepared several barrels and a duffle for Thomas's departure. Every ship in the convoy was loaded to the gunwales.

"We are ready at last," Hans declared to Thomas and Sally one evening. "The captain of the *Assistance* told me that we leave this very night, trusting the cover of darkness will thwart the attempts of thieves. It is short notice, I'm afraid, but we seem to be carrying a tempting cargo for the buccaneers!" Hans saw the sadness in the face of his kind friend. He took Sally's hand and bowed low. "How can I ever thank you, my dear lady, for all your kindness you have shown me since I came to Jamaica? Your laughter gave me strength in the very worst of times. I will always remember you and be forever in your debt, Lady Cranston."

Sally wept as she kissed Hans's hands. She embraced Thomas who remained speechless. "All this time to prepare, yet I feel so unprepared to bid thee farewell, my son. God grant you safe passage! Make good your studies, Thomas, and in everything else – moderation!" She pressed her head upon his heart and wept. "Take care, Thomas. Look after him, Hans."

As they left the house, Nora rushed out with a large package neatly bundled in beautifully woven sea grass.

"I pack you up some Jamaican fruit to keep you from goin' bad on the sea. They be coated with candle wax to keep 'em fresh. Fare thee well, Dr. Sloane! Fare thee well, Sir Thomas!" Nora face streamed with tears.

There was much bustle at quayside as Hans and Thomas boarded the *Assistance,* a full-rigged, 48-gun fourth rate ship of the line. The duchess was already on board. Captain Monck sailed the yacht from the harbor the night of the 16th of March 1689. The *Assistance* and thirteen merchant ships followed, heading for the Windward Passage.

After their first week out to sea, a convoy of merchant ships from England passed near the *Assistance*. As was the custom during calm seas, the captains exchanged visits to obtain news, carry mail, and trade goods. Captain Wright of the *Assistance* learned that James II was indeed, dethroned and exiled to France. The English parliament supported the Protestant daughter of James II's first marriage, Mary and her husband William of Orange and thus, with minimal bloodshed on either side, the English people rid themselves of their disliked Catholic king. With this confirmation, the captain of the *Assistance*, being a reactionary Stuart loyalist, set his sails for the shores of France and to his king, James II.

The duchess panicked. Fear of landing on foreign shores led her to the desperate demand that she and her belongings and servants be transferred to her yacht.

"This is madness, madam. A dangerous act mid-ocean! You and yours will surely perish, if not in the transfer, later once the sea kicks its mighty fury. That yacht cannot hold you!" Capt. Wright raged.

"Then will you at least drop us onto English soil before sailing for France?" the duchess pleaded.

"And have my ship fall to disloyal hands? Never! I follow my king!" he demanded.

"And have the French rob me of my gains and my husband's body? Never!" the duchess fired back.

With this, Capt. Wright retreated to his cabin. He slammed the companionway door and gave orders to his mate that he would not return to the deck until the duchess was off his ship. He would neither condone the transfer nor stop it. As captain of the king's frigate, he was answerable to his king and to his king he would sail.

Hans was not happy with the duchess's decision to leave the *Assistance*. Like the captain, he feared the smallness of the yacht and the brewing storm that threatened the seas. There was no reasoning with the woman, nor could any soul convince her to part with a single possession. As the sea was rising, the dangerous transfer of the Albemarle family, servants, possessions, coffin, and the doctor began. Crates, casks, livestock, barrels, and all sorts of household items made their way across to the yacht by way of ropes, chains, hooks, and tackles and pulleys. More than once, the ropes and chains broke as the choppy seas tossed the bucking ships apart.

Reluctantly, Thomas decided to stay with Hans. The sailors rigged a rope chair and with a raging sea below, Thomas dangled between the two rolling vessels believing the prayer he shouted above the wind would be his last. When it was her turn, the duchess remained surprisingly calm. Not so were the servants, most of whom screamed in terror and continued to do so even when landed safely aboard the yacht.

The transfer took the better part of a day and owing to the skills of the crew of the *Assistance*, not a single life or crate was lost to the sea. True to his word, Capt. Wright of the *Assistance* did not appear on deck until the duchess was off. Now free of his burden, the *Assistance* alone headed for France.

By the next day, the sea was quite ugly and rough. Many suffered terrible sickness and the yacht took on more water than the crew could manage. Captain Monck finally convinced the distraught duchess that she and much of her possessions would have to transfer to one of the merchantman, the *Generous Hanna*, before they were all lost to the sea.

Once again a perilous mid-sea transfer occurred. Because the merchantman was itself full of cargo, it was necessary to transfer some its load to a third ship in the convoy to make room for the duchess's goods and the retinue of servants. The hands of all ships involved were skilled and the second transfer might have transpired without incident had it not been for one the duke's personal slaves. According to the others, the ancient gray-headed negro declared he had faced his greatest fear during the first transfer and knew he could not do so again. In the confusion of moving the human cargo, the old man climbed over the rails and jumped into the churning sea. One sailor leaped in after him and managed to retrieve the broken body of the old slave, but seeing his eyes wide open with no signs of life, the sailor allowed the sea to claim its victim.

The duchess reacted furiously. With no appreciation of the risk the sailor took, she grabbed a length of knotted rope and swung it at the hapless rescuer. It took several others to remove the rope from her grasp. They tied her to the rope chair and sent her off the yacht to the *Generous Hanna*. Though Dr. Sloane went with the duchess, this time, Thomas declined to follow and stayed with Capt. Monck to help crew the yacht.

At the end of May, the convoy arrived just outside Plymouth. Still unsure of the political climate, Capt. Monck ordered a skiff ashore to seek more information. Thomas accompanied two crewmen on the skiff and as they approached land, they came across some fishermen. Thomas hailed them.

"How goes the king?" he shouted.

"Which King would that be, friend? King William is well and the other has run off to France!" was the reply.

The convoy decided to sail on to Portsmouth and was surprised to see the *Assistance* riding at anchor in the harbor. Apparently, as Hans later discovered, Captain Wright had time to reflect his position and, wisely, chose to swear his allegiance to King William and Queen Mary.

Having delivered his charge to the family of the Duke of Newcastle, Dr. Hans Sloane was once again a free man and, at twenty-eight, was ready to make his mark on London. But first, he wanted to settle a debt and a promise to Lady Cranston. He introduced Thomas to several of his colleagues from Oxford, scientists and physicians like himself, who in turn introduced him to men of stature at Oxford University. Being from the colonies, Thomas was put through a battery of entrance exams, both oral and written. He did brilliantly on all, at least to the satisfaction of his examiners. Oxford declared Thomas up to the standards of their rigorous academic challenges and invited him to begin his career as a student of philosophy and science.

Sally was pleased of the news of her son's admission to Oxford. In his absence, she suffered terrible loneliness, but had a welcome reprieve with the visit of Edward Waller in October. Having just accompanied James and Abigail to their new home in South Carolina, he decided he could not travel so far south without coming as far as Jamaica.

"Edward, do tell me, what is it like . . . James's plantation?"

"Ah, it's quite large, Sally. He acquired an adjoining property and it is now over 500 acres. Untamed lowlands now, but I believe James will have a splendid

estate in no time. The house in Charles Town is impressive
. . . exquisitely furnished and very comfortable. Even in
September, the climate felt tropical, very hot and sticky
without the advantage of a sea breeze. I understand that it
is cool in the winter, but nothing like New England and
snows only rarely. Flowers are everywhere and gardens to
rival the best of England. There is an air of fragrance like
no other place. And Abigail, ah Sally, she is such a beauty!
How James dotes on her. All those worries we had that he
might never be content or settle in a profession. Well now!
There he is! A finder of treasure, a superb father, and on
his way to being a successful planter in South Carolina!
But, I do go on, and have yet to ask of you."

"I thought I would die when Gregor left me. But,
I couldn't die. I had Thomas, Molly was about to give
birth, Windhaven and all my new enterprises here in Port
Royal. I just didn't have the time to die, I suppose. Ah but
then, my children left. First Molly, then Thomas and I
thought I would die all over again. I keep busy. You must
come and see what Madame de Witt and I have been up to
since your last visit!" Sally replied with a twinkle of pride
in her tone.

"Madame de Witt? *The* Madame de Witt?"
Edward asked mockingly.

"The very same! She has an eye for profit and a
keen sense of interior decoration. Our inn is rapidly
becoming the smartest on the Point!" she quipped. "At
least that is the hope, for it was a terrible gamble, Edward!
I fear I have a bit of my Uncle Robert's blood in me after
all."

"I am sorry I missed Thomas," Edward said.

"I received a letter from him just days ago. He's
been accepted at Oxford, doing well and is very happy.
Han Sloane also sent a letter to confirm that Thomas is

well seated. Seems the duchess made an unexpected recovery and has retained the services of Dr. Sloane." Sally bent close to Edward's ear the way she always did when she delighted in some bit of gossip. "Hans decided her influence in London's society weighs heavier than his sanity. He is staying at her house in Clerkenwell. How long can you stay, Edward? Do you have time to visit Windhaven?"

"Aye, I do. I have not yet secured my passage back to Boston. I am here on reconnaissance to see what manner of goods I can market in New England. Boston grows in size and, mark my words, it will soon take the lead over Port Royal. The smaller settlements that surround Boston have expanded such that the gap between them is disappearing. One day, it will all be a massive city like London, Sally."

"Well, then, Captain Waller, seeing how the only respectable inn in town is being renovated, I insist you stay here. You can have Thomas's room."

Edward gave a look of surprise. "Wouldn't be proper, now, would it? You being a widow and me still a bachelor!"

"Poppycock! This is The Point, Edward. Trust me, no one will question it. I could ask Jaclyn to stay as chaperone. Now *that* would make a few tongues clack!"

Their time together was full of happiness, so much so, that Sally left her shops completely under the care of her hired keepers and went off to spend time with Edward at Windhaven. But by the end of November, Edward was concerned about the winter storms in the north and was eager to make ready for his new trading enterprises gleaned from Jamaica, Nevis and St. Kitts.

Sally didn't want Edward to leave, but could not bring herself to reveal her true feelings because she wasn't sure herself what those emotions were. She dreaded being alone again and convinced herself that her desire to cling to Edward was based on that fear and nothing else. When Edward finally left Jamaica, instead of suffering the pains of loneliness again, Sally felt an unexpected rejuvenation. With a youthful vigor, she continued to work on the inn, sold more pipes than ever, especially at Christmas, and had a banner year at Windhaven! For the first time since Gregor's death, Sally had a firm sense of hope for the future.

CHAPTER 38

Percival Wickland drew up the bucket of water from the cistern in the yard behind his shop. He poured half the contents into the scrub bucket and the rest over his head. The water felt cool and refreshing.

"This incessant heat," he muttered to himself. "For months, it's been thus!" He looked skyward. There was no sign of rain. Even the mountains remained cloudless. The rains failed in the spring, and it would be a long while before the short rains provided relief from this summer's heat.

As the water dripped down his back, Percival spread it about his neck with his large rough hand. In the only sliver of shade left in the garden, he sat on an old crate and gazed past his shop to the docks across the way. Throughout Port Royal, the hot June air released the protocol of formal dress. Merchants and seamen alike wore loose cotton shirts and breeches with neither waistcoat nor hat. Many shed their silk stockings and shoes and some servants were content to wear even less. Half-naked slaves were down to ragged breeches with knee gatherings torn open to allow a hint of wind to blow up their bottoms.

And they be the wiser, Percival chuckled to himself. He had spent the entire morning in his shop cleaning the pipes and polishing each onion-shaped blue wine bottle, making sure the engraving etched in the glass faced outward for his customers to examine. He arranged the local Windhaven red clay pipes in neat wheel according to the length of the stem and the angle of the bowl. The Jamaican pipes did not match the artistry or craft of the white clay pipes from London and Bristol. However, most of his patrons were not discerning. They favored function and price over quality. The margin of profit on the reds was greater than the whites and he was pleased to see so many Windhaven pipes go out the door. Percival kept the finer hallmarked pipes behind the counter in a drawer and displayed them only upon the request of his most trusted customers who were not concerned so much about the price or the heavy tax laid upon them. What mattered more to them was to be *seen* in the possession of the very best.

Rocking on the crate to create momentum, Percival pushed on his knees and struggled to his feet. He straightened his back and sucked in his portly middle, making it easier to pull out his watch from the waist pocket of his breeches. It read 11:30.

"That cannot be right!" he whispered. He tapped the watch with his index finger, held it to his ear, and was relieved to hear it ticking. He bought the watch from Otis Harmsworth before the watchmaker left for England and it had not failed him once. *Seems far too hot to be morning still*, he thought, *and this the first week of June!* He returned the watch to his pocket and then collected the laundry hung out to dry earlier by his wife, Mattie. She got up early to scrub and hang it before the baby woke. Mattie managed the family's laundry herself for Percival could afford neither servant nor slave. Over the yard wall, he saw two young lads in the alley pushing a cart with a large barrel strapped inside. He recognized one of the boys, Timothy Trevor, the coppersmith's son.

"Come up from Fishers' Row, Tim?" he shouted.

"Aye, sir. Littleton's Wharf."

"What ship, there now?"

"The frigate *Swan*, Mr. Wickland. That and another, a fifth-rate Dutch warship. Careened for repair, they are. The Dutch ship, she's gettin' refitted with English guns. This barrel of salted pork comes from her. We're pushing it over to Harry's Tavern."

"Ye picked a hot day for such a task. Make sure Harry Burgess gives ya a good helpin' of that pork, now! Good day to ya, boys!" Percival waved.

"Aye. And to you, Mr. Wickland, sir." Tim waved back.

With one hand full of dried laundry and the other clutching an iron poker, Percival stoked the few embers remaining beneath the brick oven in the cookhouse. He threw a loaf of bread into the oven to warm for the midday meal, grabbed the scrub bucket, and headed for the backdoor of his shop. As he entered the room, he noticed the strong smell of citrus. Earlier he squeezed the rinds of lemons onto the freshly chopped tobacco leaves. Much to the chagrin of the vicars, many women in Jamaica had taken to smoking a pipe and preferred their leaves lightly fragranced. Percival was the only merchant in Port Royal selling lemon-scented tobacco.

His wife, Mattie, was sitting on a stool and had a firm hold on the leading strings of their toddler's apron. Percival set the bucket down and tossed the laundry on a table. He pulled up a stool to play with his son, but the child saw the scrub bucket and made a dash for it.

"He grows like a weed, Mattie!" Percival complained proudly. He watched his son pull hard on the leading strings just short of the bucket. He tumbled, rolled on his back, and laughed. The pudding cap tied securely beneath his chin provided a soft cushion against such self-inflicted assaults. His mother knelt down for the rescue and presented the baby with a rattle to take his attention away from the bucket. She cooed and cackled at the boy and he responded with shrieks of joy.

"I put some bread in the oven, my love. Can ya check it in a moment to see that it does not toast?"

"That was thoughtful of you, dear. I'll check it in a moment," Mattie replied. "Going in the shop again, are you?"

"Aye, more to be done. Not many shoppers today, though. Must be the heat."

By the time Percival Wickland reached the front room of the shop, he felt a sudden uneasiness, a strange dizziness, not too unlike the feeling he got when he returned to land after too long at sea. He wondered if he had over-worked or perhaps the day's heat was playing tricks on his balance.

"Tis odd," he whispered as he put both hands on the counter to steady himself. It was moving. Vibrating. The pipes on the counter were dancing up and down like marionettes. The ground rumbled and a low loud bellow came from the north.

"What was that?" his wife yelled from the back room. Percival watched the pipes settle again. "Must have been an earthquake." It was all he managed to say for in the next instant the glass in the window shattered outward and from the boughs of the Earth came a loud long hideous groan. The shop floor rose, then split down the middle. The gap widened, following the herringbone pattern of the bricks. The sidewall facing the alley fell inward sending a plume of dust and bricks into the shop. Another window shattered, spraying tiny shards about. Seeing that the roof could not possibly hold, Percival tried desperately to reach his wife and son just as the whole shop tilted at an impossible angle and plunged forward towards the street. Percival's body catapulted and landed hard on the cracked and ruined street.

He could feel the building breaking up behind him and summoned all his strength to reach his family. The roof of the shop collapsed. Percival screamed for his wife and child. The Earth continued to moan and shake as the ground below him buckled high then dropped vertically by several feet. On his hands and knees, Percival watched as water seeped through his fingers. The sandy ground converted to a wet sludge. He screamed and in panic he did the wrong thing. He attempted to right himself but each time the ground beneath him gave way and his feet sank deeper into the mire. The slushy quick sand gobbled his legs. Percival cried for help as he struggled to keep from sinking further. But in seconds, it swallowed him to his waist.

As suddenly as it began, the ground stopped shaking. Percival wiggled back and forth to free himself, but to his horror the oozy ground began to set, cementing his legs and hips. Geysers of sand exploded around him as if shot from a canon below the surface. Frantically he pressed hard with his forearms against the unyielding ground, but it no longer mattered. At the sound of another, yet different, monstrous roar he stopped struggling. A dark shadow covered Percival and he looked up to see the dripping head of a giant white bird. Fate spared him long enough to recognize the bird. It was the figurehead on the bow of the frigate *Swan*.

As the Earth heaved and Port Royal slid into Kingston Harbor, the sea responded and rose in a giant wave. It tore ships from their anchors and moorings and pushed them ashore like giant battering rams. They tore into warehouses and wharfs along the waterfront. The debris-laden wave moved inland, crashing its way through the town's interior. It ripped and tore, killed and maimed all within its path. The initial thrust stopped and the water receded, not gently but with equal ferocity and more destruction. The ebb-waters took everything – debris, bodies, and frantic survivors. It scoured and leveled as if to remove evidence of the two disparaging assaults, first by shaking land, and then by flooding waters.

By noon, two-thirds of the nearly two thousand buildings that crammed the fifty-acre sand spit were gone; pulverized, dismantled, burnt or washed to sea. The sandy foundation on which the town was built dissolved and the northern edge of Port Royal vanished into the harbor leaving just under half of the original landmass. The quake and resulting gigantic wave killed thousands in an instant and left hundreds more injured and stranded. Within minutes of the first wave, two smaller waves pounded the new and raw shoreline. Only a few rises in the land and the rooftops of the tallest lasting structures were spared the destructive forces of the floodwaters and there the remaining survivors huddled.

It was the second smaller wave that broke apart the debris dam on which Tim Trevor's cart was caught. He couldn't remember how he managed to hold onto the cart or what had happened to his friend, Philip. Riding the wave, he traveled far across the town, right past St. Paul's Church. The rushing water whipped the cart around like a top, bumping and scraping against floating debris. The wheels tore from the axles until all that remained was the backboard, the bed, and one handle. Tim wrapped himself tightly around the leather straps that earlier tied the barrel. As the wave returned to sea, it carried Tim, his cart, and all the loose debris of the ruined town into the harbor.

Miraculously, the cart partially floated like a raft. Tim debated whether he should stay with his cart or swim for something larger. All around, he heard screams and cries from people thrashing in the water. He saw a small fishing boat with two men rowing towards a group of people clinging onto what looked like a bit of roofing. Tim shouted to the rowers and waved his hands. He cupped one hand to paddle towards the boat while clinging to the straps with the other. The boat reached the people, but in their panic, they rushed to the side. Tim saw the battering arms of the desperate swimmers reach from the water and catch the side of the boat. It tipped. Too late, the rowers tried in vain to push the survivors away with their oars. The water rushed in and the boat sank within seconds. Worried that the frantic survivors might try to swamp his own lifeline, Tim back paddled away from the scene.

He maneuvered his body, careful not to lose his grip, and raised himself to look out over the harbor. He wasted much of his strength just trying to stay upright long enough to get his bearings. The normal landmarks were gone and he couldn't make out the shoreline. Thames Street, where he and his father lived, was gone. It looked as though the entire Point was missing. The turtle crawls and the docks were nowhere to be seen. The larger buildings along the shore, which before he could easily identify from the water, were not there – the North Dock warehouses, the forts James or Carlisle, and the Customs House. Tom's legs were cramping from the strain. He nestled back into his half-submerged raft, held the straps tightly, and took quick inventory of his situation. He was a long way from shore. Unlike most of his friends, he had the advantage of knowing how to swim, but the shore was too far even for him. His swollen fingers and bruised arms were painful. He was cut, bleeding, and bruised everywhere. He panicked when he thought about how his blood and that of others would soon draw in the sharks.

The cart was holding up surprisingly well. It floated, though just below the surface. He looked about the water, gathered more floating debris, and with the leather straps, lashed what he could to the cart. It was hot. Tom looked up at the sun. *How odd that the sky be so blue at such a dark hour as this*, he thought. He reckoned it to be just past midday. He was thirsty. He was thirsty before this all began, but he had taken comfort in knowing that Harry would give him and his friend each a flagon of beer.

"Poor Philip," he said softly. "I wonder if he made it?"

With swollen fingers, paddling to shore in the heat of the day would be a challenge. He knew the tide would be with him, at least for a while. Time and the heat were against him. He needed to start paddling while he still had strength and before the tide pulled him further offshore. He picked up a straight flat board that was floating close by. Though short, it would make an adequate oar. There was a bit of paint on the board and Tom recognized it as being part of a sign. He turned the board over and rubbed his fingers across it. Carved deeply into the wood and painted in blue was the word Harry's. Tom gasped. He half-chuckled and looked about with the need to share this bit of irony with someone, but there was no one. He rubbed his hand over the lettering again. Harry's. Tom looked to shore, understanding now what this debris implied. It was then that he noticed the silence. He cocked his head to focus on sound. He vaguely heard some ruckus on the water to the east and thought he heard a church bell from shore. Around him, it was quiet. No more screams, no cries for help. He sighed deeply and through quivering lips whispered, "What mischief has the devil bestowed upon us? What punishment, God?" He had been so busy trying to live; he had not stopped to question what it was that he had managed to survive. With agile and painful manipulations, Tom crouched and balanced on his knees on the cart. He tied the free end of a leather strap around his waist, took up the board, and paddled towards the unfamiliar shoreline of what used to be his home.

Madame Jaclyn de Witt moaned as she pushed the weight off her legs. She could not see. She lifted her wet skirt and used it to clear the mud from her eyes. Her left eye was tender and swollen completely shut. Her nose was torn, bleeding, and numb. From her good eye, she discovered that she was sitting in the middle of the road two streets away from where she was having her midday meal of turtle stew and crumpets.

The Earth rumbled again. It was less severe than the previous three shakes but it sent people running and screaming. The juddering brought down an unstable building nearby and filled the air with dust. Those who ran into the street fell and remained prostrate until the shaking subsided. When it was over, they rushed back to search for those who were buried and trapped. Some ran right past Jaclyn, not even looking at her. She tried to speak, but her jaw ached and she choked on the blood in her throat. She raised her hand to those who passed, but they did not stop to help.

Nor will they, she concluded. *They have others to see to.* She would have to fend for herself and see to her girls, if any survived. Trying to rise to her feet, she felt her right leg tingle. It did not want to bend. Jaclyn raised her skirts to look at her leg.

"Where are my shoes?" she asked aloud. Bloody mud caked her shredded stockings and sticking out of her inside calf was a splinter of wood at least the size of her foot. Jaclyn vomited. It was not so much from the sight of her damaged leg; she had seen worse after a brawl in her brothel. It was the coppery taste of blood mixed with salt. Jaclyn quickly covered her legs. She would not be able to move without help. She looked about and could barely decipher where she was by the tattered remains of the buildings. Through the ruins across the street, she could just make out the top of her three-story brothel. There wasn't much left except for the common wall shared with the adjoining house. Most of it was gone, too. Jaclyn looked around and gasped. All the houses were in ruins. The pile of debris that lay around the buildings did not seem to account for all that went into their construction. *Where did all the furniture go,* she wondered. *What has happened here?*

She twisted her head wildly around until her good eye caught some strange movement. A black shadow scurried along the ground and was coming her way. Rats. A pack of rats, more than a hundred strong, ran past her. Jaclyn screamed. She tried to keep her reason, but terrorizing thoughts of a rat pack chewing her flesh while she still lived was too much. She needed to move. A section of the brick road that had buckled high above the floodwaters seemed unblemished, dry, and oddly free of debris . . . as if someone had just swept it clean. Jaclyn used her arms to drag her lower body over through the muddy water. She cursed aloud at the pain, but finally felt the bricks beneath her hands. She hoisted her bottom up onto the raised walk. With her legs dangling over the edge, she had better access to the splinter. It needed to come out. She tugged at it, but her strong sense of self-care prevented her from inducing more pain. She squinted through her good eye to see if there was anyone within shouting range. She called for help, but no one responded. She sat for a moment, trying to comprehend what had happened. She recalled sitting at a table, complaining that her porringer of stew was not hot enough. She heard the sound, felt the awful shaking, and shouted for everyone to get outside. She thought she moved toward the stairs to warn the girls and their guests. But then, how did she end up here, so far away from the brothel? She looked around. Something in the flooded road twitched . . . then another, and another! Jaclyn gasped when she discovered what they were. Fish! She looked down at her sodden dress, picked up its hem and sniffed it. "It's seawater!" Jaclyn declared aloud. She became anxious and scared. She believed the dangers of this disaster were still imminent and felt a need to move.

"Jaclyn! Madame Jaclyn!"

Jaclyn twisted her head as she struggled to see who called her name.

"It is me, Athena. Oh, you are hurt, Madame!" the woman struggled to wade though the ankle-high water.

"Athena! Thank God. What has happened to us? Where are all the others?"

"I have found not one of us alive but you, Madame. Maggie, Rosamund, and Bess - they are dead and buried under the rubble. At least, I think it is them." Athena crossed herself, moving her lips in some silent prayer. "The others, I cannot find," she continued. "The wave . . . it has taken the dead along with many of the living, I fear. It took the whole building, the beds, everything. There is nothing left. I thank God, it did not take you, Jaclyn, though I was sure that it had. Come, I will help you up."

"No! No, please!" Jaclyn begged. She moved her skirt to reveal the splinter. Athena gasped. "It has to come out," Jaclyn said in a commanding tone. "Can you do it? What wave? Athena, what has happened to us?"

"Earthquake, Madame. It happens often in my country and also the big wave that follows the movement of the land."

"I do not remember a wave, just the ground shaking. Is it over?"

"Hmmm . . . Smaller quakes, perhaps for many days, sometimes months. But the sea, it is calm now. Three waves came, each lesser than the first. I cannot believe we will see more. I saw you in the first wave. It took us both to the shore and brought us back. I called to you, but . . . I thought we were dead, Jaclyn." Athena could not control her reactions as she examined the splinter in her madam's leg. She spoke Greek as she turned the leg and peeled away the stockings to see how far the splinter penetrated. "I think I can get this out. It is not as deep as it looks. I need to find someone to help me. I will come back."

Before Madame Jaclyn could protest, Athena was gone. She watched as Athena went from person to person. They pushed her away or shook their heads while they continued to dig through rubble. Finally, Athena returned with Mr. Howard, the butcher whose shop and home was further up the street.

"Right," Mr. Howard said to Athena. "I will hold her leg steady while you pull that wood. Mind, pull it quickly so it comes out in one piece. Ya cannot leave pieces to fester." Mr. Howard spread himself over Madame Jaclyn's stomach while pushing hard on her right knee. "Pardon, dear lady. Must be done. Do it now, Miss!"

Athena pulled, but stopped when Jaclyn screamed.

"No! You cannot stop now!" Mr. Howard shouted. "Keep going, lass. Nearly there, dear lady, it will soon be gone."

Athena shut her eyes, crossed herself again, and pulled on the wood with greater force. This time the splinter slid from the flesh with ease and surprisingly little blood.

"That does it, then." Mr. Howard declared as he helped Jaclyn sit up. He looked at the wound. "Looks like it just slipped under the skin. You should be all right. I must be gone. You see, I cannot find my Bess and I . . ."

His voice broke and he slushed back to the pile of bricks that was his home and his shop.

"God bless you, Mr. Howard." Athena shouted after him. "We will pray for your dear wife." She got down on her knees again and tore the bottom of Jaclyn's skirt. She roughly reconnected the torn edges of flesh and wrapped the cloth tightly around Jaclyn's leg.

"It bleeds, but only a little. This is good! No vessels have severed," Athena declared.

"Athena," Jaclyn looked confused, "I cannot find my shoes."

Athena looked hard at Jaclyn. "What an odd thing to say, to worry about shoes at a time like this?" Athena scolded. "You must be brave and try to stand, Madame. The blood flowing to your wound . . . it will keep the flesh alive. I am sorry, I do not know what to do for your nose."

"My nose? What has happened to my nose?"

Athena did not answer. Gingerly touching her face, Jaclyn stomach turned as she realized that a portion of her nose hung loosely from a narrow piece of skin just above the bridge. Athena wrapped a narrow strip of cloth around Jaclyn's head and over the damaged eye and dangling nose.

"I am so sorry, Madame, I know how it must pain you," Athena apologized.

"Mercifully, it hurts little. Do you suppose it will drop off?"

Athena said nothing. She waded out into the street to an overturned table. She raised her skirts and kicked at one of the legs of the table until it finally broke loose. She picked it up, examined it for a moment, and returned to Jaclyn.

"Here," Athena instructed. "Put your weight on this while I help you to your feet." She put her arms beneath Jaclyn's and they struggled. Jaclyn cried out, but persisted. Her leg throbbed beneath the tight bindings and she felt quite dizzy, but once up, Jaclyn took a few hobbles on her own. It was then that she looked down the street at the destruction.

"What place is this, Athena? I recognize it not."

"Madame Jaclyn, I must leave you here. We will be doomed if I cannot find fresh water. The waves breached the cisterns and fouled the drinking water with all manner of filth. Keep safe until I return."

"Athena . . ." Jaclyn stretched out her hand.

Athena took the bloodied hand and brought it to her cheek. "I will come back, I promise."

Athena left and Jaclyn wondered, *What now? How far is the damage? How many killed? How many injured? What still remains? What of her shops and the house on High Street and the girls there? Is the inn still standing? Sally! No, she's at Kingston. Perhaps they have been spared.* She smelled smoke and saw flames dancing behind a standing brick wall.

"Rats, now fire. What more? A plague? Starvation?" she complained aloud. Because she could not see well from just one eye, she thought for a moment her vision was deceiving her. From the height of the walk, she could see over the rubble of collapsed buildings across the street.

"Dear God!" she cried. "It's the sea!"

"Whore!" the woman approached Jaclyn on her blind side. Jaclyn pivoted and lost her balance. She fell hard on her bad leg. Frantic and in great pain Jaclyn twisted her head to see who it was that called that name.

She did not know the woman but her wild, depraved look frightened Jaclyn.

"You and your pestiferous whores! You have poisoned us all with your sins!" the woman screamed. Pointing to the sky she raged, "His wrath is upon us! And He hath destroyed our city, just like he destroyed Sodom. It is written in Ezekiel: Now this was the sin of your sister Sodom: she and her daughters were arrogant, overfed and unconcerned; they did not help the poor and needy. They were haughty and did detestable things before me. Therefore I did away with them . . .' He punishes us for *your* sins, whore! He condemns us because of *you* and your wickedness! Condemned us to hell! Condemned, we are!" The woman bent down, picked up a dead fish and threw it at Jaclyn. With her depth perception off, Jaclyn reacted poorly and the fish hit her squarely on the wrappings of her mangled nose. She screamed in pain and covered her face with one arm while still clutching the table leg with the other. Thrashing the table leg in the direction of the woman Jaclyn shouted, "Go away! Go away!" When silence gave her a sense that the assault was over, she slowly lowered her arm. There was no sign of the woman, but others in the street were now staring in her direction. She had seen such stares before. Her profession was an easy target for blame. Punishing enablers of indulgences was less complicated than revealing the identities of the actual sinners.

Fearing the hostile crowd, she shifting her weight onto her good leg and swung the table leg again to threaten the on-lookers. She limped over to the remains of a wall and put it to her back.

Blame, she thought to herself wiping the fresh blood from her lips, *they would seek to blame someone for this . . . these pious pedantic peddlers of Port Royal. I can count on no one to defend me, lest some blame be cast upon him. Where is Athena? Where is that girl?*

CHAPTER 39

Sally Montague Cranston was nervous about leaving the shop in the hands of the boy she had newly hired. Her fears were at the very heart of the appointment she made in Kingston. She was certain the boy was stealing from her. The accounting of monies taken did not equal what she had inventoried. Something was amiss. She ruled out all other possibilities. He had to be stealing from her; however, his methods of underhandedness eluded her.

She was tempted to be rid of him at first suspicion had he not been the son of the woodworker who made her spools. Her lace-making business was prospering and she needed those spools to hold her cotton thread. Yet, every reputable woodworker was far too busy with the fitting of ships and other more prosperous assignments. She found it difficult to find someone who would turn her spools and he was the only one who agreed to meet her needs in a timely manner, though even that turned out to be an untruth.

"The apple falls not far from the tree!" she concluded. It irritated her that necessity required her to handle the woodworker's fraudulent son with tact and discretion. That went against her grain! The boy did not deserve such leniency but it would be imprudent of her to anger his father. So, she decided to seek the thoughtful wisdom her friend and former shopkeeper who suffered similar circumstances.

Sally wrote to her longtime confidant, Nall Wilkins. For years, Nall kept a leatherworking shop on Fishers' Row and rented another shop to a coppersmith on High Street. She trusted him and was sure she could count on his generous counsel. Years back, Nall contributed greatly to the success of Sally's pipe business by smuggling them in with his legitimate exports. He offered her critical advice when she first opened her lace shop and suggested the warehouse might be coming onto the market. He would, no doubt, know exactly how to discover her young robber's scheme. After Nall's wife died, he sold his shops in Port Royal and retired to his plantation near Spanish Town. On nearly every trip from Windhaven to Port Royal, Sally would stop over at Nall's house for a restful night. Over the years, Nall became content to stay at home and rarely ventured beyond the boundaries of his plantation. In his return letter to Sally, he declared he desired never again to plant a foot in 'that sinful port' and suggested they meet halfway at the Wigstan Inn in Kingston. She knew the Inn well for her good friend Haddie married the innkeeper there and was happy for the opportunity to visit. Sally took passage on a small sloop to Kingston and enjoyed Haddie's hospitality for two nights while gaining valuable guidance from Nall Wilkins.

Before Sally caught the ferry back to Port Royal, she and Haddie had breakfast together in the courtyard of the inn.

"Did he help?" Haddie asked of Mr. Wilkins.

"His suggestions have always been a great help to me. Nall Wilkins is as shrewd as he is clever. He did indeed have a plan that might just help me to snare my little thief and still have my spools. But Haddie, you look pale and not your happy self. Are you in good health?" Sally worried.

"Yes, of course. I am just . . . getting used to this state of matrimony. I mean, it is quite . . . a change, really . . . isn't it? I find it a bit challenging, to be two when before you were just one. Before, I was of my own mind, made my own decisions. Now I must mind my husband's wishes. Sometimes we do not agree." Haddie looked off towards the sea. It bothered Sally to see her friend so unsettled. *Was she unhappy with this marriage?* Everyone thought it was a bizarre match. Haddie radiated enviable energy and had a reputation for being vivacious and fun. Her husband, on the other hand, was a dour old stuff who rarely smiled and had an annoying habit of wanting to control everything. He fussed over unimportant details. It upset him if a hanging picture was crooked, or the linens were not tucked into the bed a certain way and he had an unnatural interest in the alignment of utensils. On the shelves, he outlined all the items in chalk so that when they were removed, they could be returned to their exact spot.

Out of respect for their friendship, Sally learned to ignore the man's strange eccentricities, but it did rankle her when he was openly hostile to Haddie. She couldn't understand, with all her endearing qualities, why Haddie did not have a stronger backbone and stand up to her husband. Sally did not press for further details and instead, thanked her for her kindness and left the inn for the docks.

She sailed back to Port Royal on a sloop she shared with two other passengers. It was a beautiful hot day with clear skies and calm seas and one passenger spread himself carelessly across more than his share of the boat. He smelled of stale wine and snored loudly as he slept in the sun, but was otherwise finely dressed in white silk stockings and clean polished shoes. The other passenger was an older stout woman, short on words and busy with her needlework. Sally struck up a conversation with the master of the vessel and their topics jumped from politics, to weather, to where to buy the best bread in Port Royal. He was mid-sentence when he suddenly stopped. Sally read both terror and puzzlement in his face and could see his fingers whiten as he gripped the helm tighter. At the same time, the sleeping passenger stopped his snoring and although he did not move, was now awake and staring intently into the eyes of the master at the helm.

"What is it?" Sally asked the master. The old woman put down her needlework and looked about, puzzled.

"Shhh!" the ship's master replied. He stared at the water and turned his ear to the shore. They all heard it . . . a low humming that filled the air, penetrated the flesh, and vibrated bones. The snorer sat upright and cupped his hands behind his ears. He moved his head from side to side trying to hone in on the source of the sound. He stopped with eyes gazing in the direction of the Point.

"What is it?" Sally repeated, more frantic than before. The master did not reply, but removed a spyglass from his belt and aimed it at Port Royal. The noise increased in magnitude. They all covered their ears against the piercing whistle.

"Look there!" the master yelled. Even from their distance, they could see with unaided eyes the buildings falling and the great plumes of dust billowing against an otherwise perfect blue sky.

"What blow is this?" the master whispered. "Are they being attacked? I see no signs. What . . ." he stopped as they witnessed the seafront suddenly and wholly fall. The wharfs, warehouses, and buildings disappeared beneath a boiling sea.

"Dear Lord!" the snorer exclaimed. "What evil is this?"

The lines on the master's forehead smoothed and he rounded his eyes with fear and sudden recognition. "I think it's a landslide."

"From what cause, sir?" Sally asked. Her breathing was rapid and she felt a cold sweat beading on her forehead.

"Earthquake, perhaps." The master and the snorer locked eyes. Together they realized the implication and sprang into action, dropping the mainsail and securing the jib.

"What is happening? Will someone tell me what is amiss?" demanded the older woman, stuffing her sewing into her bag.

"The land," the snorer explained in a heavy accent, "the land went into the sea, and the sea, my ladies, will surely balk at that. We must make ready."

"Ready? Ready for what? Are we in danger? What is happening?" the old woman was growing frantic. She clutched her bag tightly to her chest. Sally put her hand on the arm of the distraught woman in an attempt to calm her, though she failed to hide her own fears.

"I would say the port is in more danger than this craft," the snorer said. He did not stop his labor, but occasionally freed his hands long enough to animate his explanations. "The land sliding into the harbor will raise the seas. A wave, my ladies, a wave! It'll be a big one but should threaten us not. We will but bob on top of her like a piece of floating driftwood. Those poor blighters in port, if the crest is behind them, they will be taking a sleigh ride right into land. It's the return of the wave to the sea that is our threat. The wave will want to carry back the shards of its destruction. We might be just far enough away that . . ."

"Listen!" the master interrupted, stretching out his hands to signal silence. "That moaning whistling sound, I hear it no longer." All four strained their necks and ears to see and listen for signs of the quake.

"It must have ended." Sally whispered. "Thank God, it is over."

"No madam," the snorer warned, "I fear it has only just begun. See there!"

They watched helpless as the sea retreated far from the beach, baring its naked sand and sea grass bottom. It then rolled back furiously as frothing water covered the sandy point. No obstacle on land seemed strong enough to withstand its force. From their view, it looked to them like the water passed over the entire spit, shaving all structures to the ground. Sally raised her hand over her mouth, as she was sure she heard screams.

"Dear God," she whispered, "have mercy on their poor souls!"

"But it does not look to be very high, that wave," the old woman remarked.

"It's not the height so much as the rate of motion that causes its destructive force," the snorer replied.

"Look there, now. The water recedes again." The master observed. "She comes our way. Look for strong holds. I cannot tell how fierce she'll be."

"But I see nothing." Sally said

The returning wave was of little significance to them. It raised the sloop high on its crest and set her gently down in the trough. It was a smooth journey. Sand and mud clouded the water but remained free of the debris that cluttered the surface closer to shore. The ship's master hoisted his sails and set-to for the broken shore.

"What are you doing? Surely, we must return to Kingston." The old woman demanded. The others stared at her. "Well, the port is clearly shattered," she defended, "and we will land amidst disaster. Who can tell, the port may still be unsteady and the sea may rise again. We must return."

Sally glanced quickly at the master and seeing that he made no gestures toward turning about, she addressed the woman softly. "I live here, in Port Royal. My businesses are here, as are my friends . . ." Sally's eyes filled with tears. She could not finish.

The master intervened in a commanding tone. "This ship docks at The Point, madam, and to The Point I steer her."

"Or, to whatever is left of her," the snorer added while looking through the master's spyglass.

"May I?" Sally held out her hand to the snorer signifying that she wanted to look through the glass. She tried to focus on The Point, but could identify only a few familiar landmarks. "I could never make use of these things," Sally dismissed as she handed it back to the snorer. She had, in fact, seen correctly. Her home, her shops, and the inn were gone!

As the sloop approached the new craggy shore, survivors in the water shouted for help. Sally and the snorer reached out to them by extending the oars and a grappling hook. They were too weak to climb aboard a moving vessel. Instead, they clung to ropes the snorer tied to the cleats and threw over the sides while others held the yawl tied to the back of the sloop. One way or another, they picked up fifteen men, women, and even a child. The snorer was able to pull the child aboard. He was barely conscious. Those that hung on fought collisions with floating debris. They had horrible wounds and were too weak and thirsty to answer the many questions put to them. Several begged for water, but when offered, they were too frightened to let go of their hold long enough to accept the drinking vessel. Too injured or too exhausted, the men who tried to hoist themselves into the yawl, failed. The ship's master kept from sailing full wind for fear of crashing into the floating debris. For the sake of the survivors, he believed the best option was to sail them into shore as close and as fast as he dared.

"I know not now the depth of these waters, nor what lies below the surface. I fear going in closer, but I cannot anchor too far off shore. I trust not that these poor souls will have the strength to swim the distance. I am going in. I'll beach her and be done with it."

But before the sloop reached the beach, it caught on sand with water about her and its master moved fast to take down the sails and drop anchor.

"This sand is fresh and still shifts. It'll hold for now, but the tide is bound to free her and pull her out," the master warned.

Sally and the snorer helped the survivors ashore through water thick with shattered timbers, thatch, the contents of ruptured privies, broken furnishings and the dead. The old woman continued to sit in the boat, waiting for someone to carry her ashore. When that did not happen, she reluctantly and without grace, struggled over the side and made her own way to shore with her skirts billowing like a sail in full winds. Once ashore, she kept walking away and never looked back.

Sally and the snorer gently carried the wounded boy to shore and laid him on the sand. The young lad had no flesh on his knees. His fingertips were black, his lips blue and he was covered with bruises and cuts. The dark purple flesh below his ribs and grossly extended stomach gave hint to the extent of his internal injuries. The poor boy moaned in pain but did not open his eyes.

"I fear" the snorer said quietly "we have brought him back to land only to bury him. He is badly broken inside."

Sally walked among the rescued survivors who now lay on the beach trying to regain their strength.

"Does anyone know this boy? Can anyone here claim this child?" No one spoke. She knelt in the sand beside a woman who was lying on her back. "Please, I have seen you before. You are from Port Royal? This child here is hurt," Sally pleaded. "Do you know him? Do you know his family?" The woman struggled to sit up on one elbow and looked over to the boy.

"Can't be sure, his face is so swollen, but he looks to be the Trevor boy. Tom Trevor." The woman collapsed on her back again.

The snorer put his hand on Sally's shoulder and helped her to her feet.

"It matters not," he said.

"I cannot leave a poor child unattended. Someone here must know this Tom Trevor."

"No, it matters not because he is dead."

Sally gasped. Not believing the snorer, she knelt over the boy to check his breathing. The child's eyes were half open and staring directly in the sun. She reached down and pulled his eyelids shut.

"What do we do?" asked Sally.

The snorer gave a long sigh and said, "Reckon we leave him here. Look!" He pointed to the bodies that lined the shore and floated among the debris in the water. "There must be hundreds. Nay, thousands! I suggest, dear lady, we get off this beach."

Sally stood up and looked at the destruction around her. She would have screamed, but the smell prevented her from gasping the air necessary to do so.

"This is not the beach, sir. We stand in the *middle* of Port Royal," Sally said, but when she turned, the snorer was gone. He waded back to the sloop once more to talk with its master who remained onboard. The master threw Sally's bag and several other items over the side and into the arms of the snorer. The snorer and the ship's master had further conversation and judging from his waving arms and the just audible shouts, the master did not appear happy. The snorer dipped several times into his pockets and handed the contents to the master before wading back to Sally on the beach.

"Your bag, madam. And our friend kindly provided us each with a flask of water. Protect it and use it sparingly. Hide it within your bag for I have no doubt, it will soon be more valuable than gold."

"Who are you, sir?" Sally asked.

"Ah, tis true. There were no introductions on our sail. I do beg your pardon, my lady, and trust you will forgive my rudeness. I am Josiah de Torres, at you service, madam," the snorer replied, bowing deeply.

"Josiah de Torres, I am Lady Cranston." Sally was not in the mood to follow protocol and did not curtsey or lower her head.

"You said you lived here. May I escort you to your home?" he asked.

"I could be confused about our position, sir, but I fear that I am not. It therefore appears that I have not a home, an inn, nor any of my shops, for I clearly left them there!" Sally pointed in the direction of where Queen Street once stood, "As you see, there is nothing but water."

"I need to go to Fishers' Row," Josiah said. "My business was with a warehouse there. I must see what, if anything, can be salvaged. Might you show me the way, Lady Cranston? Actually, I must insist for I fear it may not be in your best interest to travel alone. Look there." Josiah pointed down the shoreline where several men were walking along, seemingly going from one body to the next.

"Are they identifying the dead?" Sally asked shielding her eyes from the sun.

Josiah shook his head as he loaded up with their baggage and belongings. "They are *robbing* the dead. And,

I suspect, profiting dearly. Who among us does not believe that the only secure place for cash is in our own pockets? We best be moving, dear Lady, before they reach this beach and extend their enterprise to more than the dead."

"What about the others?" Sally looked around at the prostrate survivors they pulled from the sea.

"We have done our best for them."

"Wait, please, Mr. de Torres, Sally begged. She went to the water's edge and shouted, "Listen to me, please! Thieves are headed this way and may do you harm. Get up! Go inland!" Some responded while others were still too weak to move.

"Come, now, Lady Cranston!" Josiah implored, grabbing her arm. They climbed over the debris and made their way to the south side of upper High Street. Most of the houses and buildings along the north side were destroyed, but some structures just the other side of the road, though windowless and cracked, remained remarkably intact. Bodies, not just of people but also of all types of barn animals, butcher carcasses, and even corpses of those long buried littered the road. Some houses, while surrounded by floodwaters, were burning. Everywhere people were searching for their families and friends buried in the rubble or floating in the water. Unbelievably, they came across gangs of young men and even some women who carried in their arms loot from unattended shops.

"It is my hope that what I am about to say will not cause you to doubt my honest nature, Lady Cranston, but if the opportunity arises we must do the same. The cisterns are most likely tainted with saltwater and I believe the taverns of Port Royal may not open their doors for some time," Josiah remarked. "Is there shop where we might obtain some food along this route?"

"Sir, what you propose is outrageous. These keepers are my friends. I know these people and will not steal from them. They are my neighbors!" Sally protested.

"Look about you, my lady. The keepers of these shops are probably dead and we the living have our needs!" Josiah retorted.

Sally led him down an alley just off High Street to Randolf's greenery. Though sporting a gaping crack down its middle, the shop stood whole but abandoned. Sally gasped, "Look, it must be the only building whose windows are not broken!"

"Ah, well, I am about to change that, I am afraid." Josiah picked up a loose brick from the street and threw it into the window. The panes were small and reinforced by lead. It did not break on his first attempt. He was about to try a second time when the front door, that Sally had tried to open, fell straight off its hinges.

"Good thinking, my lady."

Inside, the goods Mr. Randolf had kept arranged so neatly on the shelves were now scattered across the floor. Looters had already been there and scavenged the best. Josiah dumped the contents of his bag and filled it with dry edibles, cheese, and crocks of dried fruit, potatoes and carrots that littered the floor.

"I suggest you do the same. When hunger strikes, a bag full of lace is not going to help."

Sally took a step back towards the door of the shop. "How do you know the contents of my bag, Mr. de Torres?"

Josiah stopped the looting and stared at Sally. "I know not what your bag contains, Lady Cranston. I merely suggest that what women normally carry in their travel bags may be of little use in this crisis."

Sally accepted the explanation with reservation. *How is it that Josiah de Torres seems to know about robbing the dead, carrying cash in pockets, looting, and surviving such a disaster as this,* she wondered. Sally emptied her travel bag of the lace products she took to show Nall and Haddie and filled her bags with food that was not likely to spoil quickly, a few pharmaceutical jars, a heavy crock of ginger jam, and two flasks of wine.

"This is dishonorable, Mr. de Torres."

"Confess that to your god later, dear lady, we must make haste." With bags full, they ran down the alley and cautiously returned to High Street. They didn't walk far when they came across a crouched woman with little left of her face.

"Oh my dear God, it is Jaclyn!" Sally cried as she dropped everything and went to her side. "Jaclyn, can you hear me? Thank God, you are alive."

"Of course I can hear, my ears are still on my head, are they not? I believe I have lost an eye and perhaps, my nose. Sally, I thought you were in Kingston. Is she struck as well?"

"I don't know. I was in the harbor sailing back here."

"My lovely whorehouses, all gone, Sally, and the shops. And the inn! All our investments – gone! Athena was here, but she left me and has not come back. It was hours ago. She promised to return. See that fish lying there? Someone struck me with it. They all want to blame me for this, Sally."

Sally looked up at Josiah with eyes that expressed her wishes.

"No, Lady Cranston. This is not possible. Look at her leg. She cannot walk."

Sally stood up to face Josiah.

"Madame Jaclyn de Witt, this is Mr. Josiah de Torres. He has been kind and correct in his direction, so far. I regret that we must part our ways for I truly appreciated his company and protection. Mr. de Torres, I cannot leave her. I will not. She is my dearest, selfless friend."

Josiah raised his eyebrow as if to challenge the possibility that such a refined lady might have for a friend, the likes of this woman.

"Josiah? Josiah." Jaclyn repeated. "After they crucify us whores, they will go after you Jews for this. You must know they will. They always do. I can walk, Sally, with aid of this table leg. I know it I must look like the devil himself ate my face, and I seem to have lost me shoes, but I can walk, sir. I can walk!" And as proof, Jaclyn rose to her feet with Sally's help and hobbled with her make-do cane. "Wherever we go, I hope it is in the direction of the mainland before they close off the Palisades. They have done that before, after the great storms, fearing the spreading of some pestilence of sort. They have the means to cage us on this sandy spit and by my troth, they will. If you thought the port was lawless before the quake, wait until the devil grips those who survived."

Sally turned pale. She had a good idea how fast the social structure of the peninsula would deteriorate. Had she not herself become a thief herself just minutes ago?

"I have seen enough of the town to learn that my business here is cancelled," Mr. de Torres explained dryly. "I arranged for the master of the sloop from which we sailed to meet me again at the spot of our debarkation. We must return there now if we are to make it in time with this crippled woman."

"But, my shops? My goods?" Sally slipped, not meaning to say it aloud.

"There is nothing you can do, my lady. All is gone. Now think about your life," Josiah snapped.

Sally gave Josiah a hard look. He was unbearably so matter-of-fact.

"Let us go, then," Jaclyn interjected, "the sooner we go . . ."

Hearing Jaclyn's voice reminded Sally that Josiah was also generous to accept the challenges of taking on another when he could so easily abandon them both. She heard clearly Josiah say *me* . . . 'the master of sloop would meet *me*'. The master would not expect to board two others. But walking the distance to the mainland across the Palisades would prove too great for Jaclyn. And two women traveling alone, there was little doubt of their vulnerability.

"Thank you, Mr. de Torres. Bless you for this," Sally whispered.

Josiah offered to take her travel bag so she might better help Jaclyn.

"Thank you, but no. This bag acts as counter to the weight of Jaclyn and helps to keep my balance." It was a lie and she figured he probably knew it was a lie, but she did not fully trust him and did not want to provide the opportunity for him to run off with her illicit stores and water.

The air was already heavy with death. It was difficult to breathe. Twice the ground rumbled, forcing them and all others to run out of the way of falling debris. Obstacles confronted them with every step. Walking was painful for Jaclyn, but she complained little, even when they fell. When once they lagged behind, Jaclyn whispered, "So, when did you meet this Mr. de Torres?"

"On my honor, it was not until this very morn on the ferry," Sally replied.

"You do not know this man?" Jaclyn asked, surprised.

"No, not at all!"

"You trust him?"

"No. Not wholly." Sally explained, "Just now, I think we are better off with him, than without. We have nowhere to go, but back to Windhaven. Shhh. He comes."

"Would you like some water, Madame Jaclyn?" Josiah asked.

"Thank you, dear sir, I would." Jaclyn gulped from the bottle.

"Sparingly, please, dear lady. We know not if the sloop's master keeps his word."

"You have doubts?" Sally inquired.

"Aye, such trips across the harbor will undoubtedly be highly desired. Difficult times produce the greatest opportunity for profit. I am certain a place upon that sloop will go to the highest bidder. I confess, to reserve my spot, I paid the man less than I now wished I had. Paid only for my passage, not yours, I am afraid. If it comes to it, that we are offered only one seat, then I shall bequeath that seat to our poor Miss Jaclyn. I believe she would not make it otherwise."

Sally swallowed hard. Could she have been so wrong about this man? She started to say something, but Josiah put his hand up to halt her words.

"Come, now, we must continue if any of us are to have a hope at leaving this cursed peninsula." Josiah came close to Sally's ear and whispered, "Do not doubt, dear lady, that self preservation may yet take me over and I change my mind."

Sally's eyes widened in disbelief. *One moment he is a saint, and the next moment he speaks as if possessed. This man is an enigma,* she thought, *and I must reserve my trust in him.*

CHAPTER 40

The newly carved beach smelled worse than the town. The afternoon heat was working on the open flesh and excrement of the dead, and not all of it was human. The quake and the landslide destroyed life within the sea and their remains washed ashore to add to the malodorous collection of debris and death.

To their surprise, the sloop was still anchored offshore. Josiah hailed its master. Sally's heart sunk when four heads rose within the boat. As they waded out to the boat, Jaclyn whimpered from the stinging salt water. Sally had no option but to give her travel bag to Josiah. He held the bags high above his head to keep them dry as Sally struggled to keep Jaclyn upright. Every time she slipped below the surface, the blood from Jaclyn's nose ran hideously over her lips and down her chin.

"The payment was for one!" the master shouted as soon as Josiah was within range.

"Indeed it was, sir, indeed it was. However, circumstances have dealt me a different and somewhat difficult hand. Can you oblige us, sir?"

"Can you me, sir?"

"One moment, if you please, gentle master." Josiah, still holding the bags above his head, waded back to the struggling women. "If you have cash in your pocket that we talked about earlier, now would be the right time to show it forth, my lady."

"I am sorry, I have none," Jaclyn whispered. "Sally, you must take me back to shore. I will catch the next boat."

"Do not be absurd, Jaclyn. I will not leave you. Take her, Mr. de Torres. My purse is firmly fixed to my . . . my thigh. What sum does the sloop's master require?"

"I do not think the man is in the mood for negotiations, my lady. It is all or nothing at this desperate time. Make sure he sees you strip the purse from your leg and leave him no doubt that you are indeed presenting him with all you have."

Sally removed her purse and held it high for the master.

"And what of the other?" he shouted.

"This should cover the three of us nicely, sir," Sally shouted back.

"If there is no truth to that, you'll be thrown over, you understand? It's business, madam . . . my *own* business, not the company's. You understand?"

"Oh, aye, I do, sir. A man has to make his living!" Sally tried to sound genuinely sympathetic.

"Hurry onboard then, I mean to sail her 'afore she be swamped by others."

It was difficult to hoist Jaclyn over the side without her crying out. The master of the sloop twice threatened to leave her. Eventually, with the help of the others in the boat, they rolled her over the side and she was in. Josiah helped with the sails and the sloop was under way.

Sally sadly watched the scraggy coastline disappear. It occurred to her that there was no reason to return to Port Royal. So, to herself, she bade farewell a dream.

"Hey, I know you," said a fat passenger crouched in the bow, "that meat-face there, she is Madame Jaclyn. Madam to the two best whore houses in Port Royal."

"You are quite mistaken, sir!" Josiah protested with convincing anger. "This is my sister, Violet." He quipped with such speed and confidence that other members of the boat dare not challenge him. The fat man had no recourse than to stand down. Sally caught the smile on the sloop master's face.

Kingston's port was chaotic with post-quake commotion and the town was filling with refugees from the Point. The master tried twice to dock at one pier only to find it overcrowded and sailed to another. Upon Josiah's first stepping onto the pier, a boy rushed at him and tried to snatch his bag but received, instead, the back of a fast hand.

"Cheeky little bastard!" Josiah shouted as he helped Jaclyn out of the sloop. "Well now, Lady Cranston, Miss Violet, that being our first welcome to Kingston, where to now?"

"I thought . . . you would want to be well rid of us by now Mr. de Torres." Jaclyn said between heavy breaths.

"Ah, truth be known, I know not a single soul in Kingston. I came here only to drum up business. I am expecting my ships to arrive back here in a couple of weeks."

"Ships, Mr. de Torres. Ships – as in more than one? Who are you, sir?" Sally asked.

"A merchant," was his only reply.

Sally waited for more, and when nothing came she offered, "Well, I do know someone in Kingston and it is our good fortune, she and her husband own an inn. You would do my conscience a good deed if you relied on my direction for a change," Sally said.

They staggered up the long hill, stopping often to allow Jaclyn to rest. They finally reached the white painted Wigstan Inn above Kingston Town. The front door to the inn was slightly above grade over a stone cellar. Sally climbed the brick steps to ring the bell. The servant girl, who served Sally that very morning, came to the door.

"I am sorry, miss. This inn is full," the servant said, her eyes fixed to the floor.

"Lotty, it is me, Lady Cranston. What's going on? Is your mistress here? I would like to speak with her, if I may."

"Yes miss. Please wait, miss." The servant, not opening the door more than just a crack, closed it completely.

Sally turned to the others, surprised and puzzled. Some time passed. "This is very strange. I cannot imagine . . ." The door opened and again, just a crack.

"I am sorry, miss. The Mistress cannot see you. My master told me to tell you this inn is full." While she was speaking, she slipped a note through the crack. "I am sorry, miss," she whispered and closed the door.

Sally was mystified. She unfolded the note and read it aloud.

"Forgive me, my dear, dear friend. Word of Port Royal and of your arrival came to us by way of our servant, with whom you shared passage. He informed my husband that the man with whom you travel is a Jew and the woman, a whore. My husband will open his door to neither. I do remain your trusted friend and ask your forgiveness,

Haddie

"How do they know . . . that I am a Jew?" Josiah asked, visibly shaken.

"The same way they know old meat-face here is a whore." Jaclyn replied. "Small island, this!"

"No matter," Sally decreed, crumpling the note. "We'll go on to Spanish Town. Nall Wilkins will take us in. His plantation is in on the way, about a half day's walk." Sally looked at Jaclyn's leg. "Or, perhaps longer," she added.

"Then let us find suitable accommodation beneath the stars, my ladies. Look. Look how beautiful the skies are. Though the Earth be shattered, the evening sky is whole and shall no doubt display brightly a lovely sunset. Come!"

"Mr. de Torres, you sound like a poet!" Jaclyn said.

Josiah started walking, then stopped. "Lady Cranston, will you lead the way, if you please, for I find myself on unfamiliar ground." He bowed deeply.

Sally pointed in the direction of Kingston. "The road leads from the town's center at the bottom of this hill," she said. Josiah took Jaclyn by the arm for going down the hill seemed more difficult for her than the journey up. Sally turned and looked once more at the inn. The door was slightly opened and Haddie's face peered through the crack.

"Sally," she beckoned with her hand. "Sally, please stay. We will gladly put *you* up."

Sally stared back and was neither surprised nor judgmental, only deeply saddened to lose an old and once trusted friend.

"From this day, Haddie," Sally said softly. "I ask that you direct thy feet where you and I henceforth may never meet!" Smirking, she turned from the inn and thought, *Mr. de Torres is not the only one who can do poetry in a crisis!*

Just outside Kingston, on the Spanish Town Road, Josiah found a clearing well off the road in which to rest for the night. The fire he built was comforting and they huddled together to share some hard biscuits, cheese and wine.

"Has ever a simple meal tasted better?" Josiah asked.

"I cannot taste and find it somewhat painful to chew. What of my nose, dear Sally, tell me honestly, do I still have one?" Jaclyn asked.

Sally stuttered for the right words.

"Miss Violet," Josiah interjected "it is time we dealt with your wounds before they fester." He crouched beside Jaclyn and slowly removed the bandage from her face. "Hmmmm . . . though I believe it is seriously broken, you have a nose, sister Violet. The flesh wound is not deep and is not so terribly raw. I believe it may heal with time. If you can stand the pain, it would be good to clean your wounds before the flesh heals over the dirt." He reached into his travel bag and pulled out a round ball of soap. He sniffed it. "Lavender! At least we thieves have class. Only the best for my ladies!"

"Lavender! Oh, now *that* will make a difference! Mr. de Torres, I do not know who you are, but if you are willing to tackle the foul job of cleaning my fetid flesh, I say you are an angel," Jaclyn praised.

"I saw a pool of water by the road. I will fetch some and make you as good as new. I will be back, I promise!"

When he had gone, Jaclyn confided in Sally.

"Those words, Sally. The same words Athena said to me before she left me to die."

"Be kind to Athena, Jaclyn. You do not know what unforeseen event kept her from returning. I only hope she is well, along with the others."

"There were three buried in the rubble of one house. Athena found them."

"I am sorry for them and for so many others. I left a child on the beach, Jaclyn. We plucked him from the harbor, but his injuries were too great. Poor lad. How many more?"

"Me. I *am* going to die, am I not?" Jaclyn asked.

"Of course not! You are much too stubborn to die or you would have done so by now, Jaclyn."

"Will he return?" Jaclyn asked nodding in the direction of the woods.

"Yes." Sally looked over to where Josiah stashed his travel bag. It was gone. She swallowed hard and replied less assured, "He was only going to the road."

Over an hour later, Sally paced around the fire. Josiah had not returned. They were alone. Jaclyn was sleeping fitfully, snoring loudly as she struggled to breathe through her mouth. Sally was sick with worry. *How am I going to manage to carry my crippled friend all the way to Nall's plantation*, she wondered. *And then what? We can't walk all the way to Windhaven and I have no money for ship's passage. Nall might help us, but then, perhaps he cannot. Kingston did not escape the terrors of the earthquake, perhaps Spanish Town is affected as well.* Sally heard rustling in the bushes. She stopped pacing. The noise grew louder. It was not the sound of one man's footfall. Sally looked around for a suitable weapon and picked up a smoldering log. Jaclyn sat up suddenly.

"What is it?"

"Shhh . . . it's coming from there." Sally motioned using the burning log. The sound increased and now she could just make out the movement of the bushes. She raised the log high ready to thump the intruder, man or beast. When she could wait no more, she lunged forward and yelled as she swung the log back and forth.

"Woe! Woe there, my lady! You mean to do me harm?" Josiah objected.

"You!" Sally declared breathlessly.

"Aye, tis me. You were expecting another?"

"You said you would be back without delay. You said you would return." Sally clenched her teeth.

"Aye. And here I be. I return with this." He pulled a rope. A reluctant donkey came out from the bushes into the light of the fire. "Well, what do you think of my friend?"

"Splendid!" Jaclyn laughed.

"That she is, sister Violet, thank you," Josiah said with a bow.

"Where did you get it?" Sally demanded.

"I stole it."

Sally shot him a look.

"Of course, I did not *steal* it! At least, not the donkey. I paid good money for the donkey. What I mean to say, the payment was honest but the money I used came not by honest means. I stole that, the money that is, from the shop in Port Royal."

"You took money from the shop? I thought we were only stealing food?" Sally asked with hands on her hips.

"You stole the food?" Jaclyn gasped, looking at Sally.

"Sinners all!" Josiah declared with a shrug. "Now, sister Violet, I have not only good water, but medicinal herbs and some unguent. I met a Frenchie who sold me this donkey and was eager to part with his medicines, but only for a fine price."

For the next two hours, Sally brewed herbal infusions of wintergreen and oil of roses. Made of egg yolks, turpentine and chocolate, the unguent was a thick sticky paste. Sally stirred oil of roses into it to make it a smoother consistency and thus less painful to apply. Josiah meticulously reopened all wounds to clean them of dirt, sand and even fish scales. Aside from the tangled threads of the bandage sticking fast to the opened flesh, the leg injury did not seem so severe. However, the broken and torn nose proved to be a challenging fix and most painful to Jaclyn.

Sally was relieved that she did not toss her needles out with the lace. She carefully unraveled her silk camisole. Using the fine threads, Josiah stitched the flesh of Jaclyn's nose back to the skin on her face, trying to match the margins of the torn flesh to make a perfect fit. He bent the needle slightly to work it into and around the curvatures of her face. Through it all, Jaclyn cried tears, but not once did she cry out.

"There! Tis done, madam." Josiah examined his work. "I regret I do not know how to fix the break. The nose is soft and is not the same as bone. It cannot be set as such. At least this nose, once again, is wholly attached and if the blood finds its way back to the tip, may remain so. The eye is less swollen, can you see from it at all?"

"No. Nothing, though it is easier now for me to focus with one."

"Miss Violet, you are the bravest woman I have ever had the pleasure of torturing. We will soak these bandages in the herbal infusion and allow them to drain over your wounds this night. Try to sleep without much movement, if you can, so they remain in place."

They positioned themselves around the fire. Josiah kept a respectful distance from the women, but close to the donkey, lest it had a mind to run. Sally could not sleep. The horrible scenes of Port Royal invaded her restless dreams causing her to toss on the hard ground. Discomfort woke her and worries over de Torres kept her from returning to her sleep. *Who is this man with skills and knowledge of a physician and the cunning of a hunter*, she wondered. He spoke with an accent she could not identify, but had the vernacular of an educated man. He could be sharp-tongued, witty, and even rude one moment, soft and compassionate the next. Honest and truthful, then evasive and deceptive.

Sally sat up from her fitful sleep. Her stomach was raw and she decided to settle it with a bit of ginger jam she had taken from the shop. She felt through her bag and found the heavy flat-bottomed stout iron stone crock with the wide cork stopper. Sally scooted closer to the fire for light. She had difficulty in opening the jar and had to bury her fingernails deep into the cork to create the leverage needed. When it finally gave way she did not find ginger jam, but a linen cloth stuffed firmly within. She tried to pull it out, but it was stuck fast and too full for the crock. Full of coins! Sally manipulated the coins, gave a firm yank, and the linen pouch was free. She opened it. The flames bounced off the polished gold pieces. She gasped loud enough to cause Jaclyn to stir. Sally froze and looked over to Josiah. He slept on his side with his face away from the fire. Sally quietly returned the coins to the pouch, folded it tightly, and stuffed it down her bodice. It stuck out in an unnatural way, forcing her to adjust the coins while trying to stifle the jingle of metal on metal. She looked over to Josiah again. He did not stir. She breathed a sigh of relief, crawled back to her makeshift bed near the fire, and resolved not to sleep for the remainder of the night.

In the morning, the heaving shrieks of the donkey woke Sally with a start. She was instantly angry that she fell so hard asleep and surprised to see the sun had already crested the trees.

"I think he bellows for his breakfast," Josiah said squatting next to the fires. "What manner of food doth this creature consume?"

"You do not know?" Sally asked feeling for the pouch between her breasts. It was still there. "It is, perhaps, the only redeeming feature of a donkey. They are not terribly particular!"

"Did someone mention breakfast?" Jaclyn said removing the herbal cloths. Both Josiah and Sally stared at her face with astonishment. There was an awkward moment of silence.

"Please, at least tell me that my nose still remains *somewhere* on my face." Jaclyn finally said.

"Oh, forgive me, Jaclyn, but you do give me reason to stare," Sally explained.

"That bad?"

"No, no. To the contrary! Though both eyes are now quite colorful, the swelling has decreased. Considerably! How is your vision?" Sally asked.

"Blurred. But I see from both eyes. I feared I might wake without an eye or a nose. And my leg! It no longer pounds with every beat of my heart."

"Perhaps our dear little donkey can assist you in your efforts to walk, today." Josiah said as he tried to move the beast. "My ladies, I will leave you to freshen. There is a flask of water there, with some bread. I left the unguent next to them. It may spare your wounds from turning septic, Miss Violet. I will lead this animal – or he, me – to the road and wait for you there." Josiah explained.

"Mr. de Torres" Jaclyn called to him, "thank you, for my face."

"Good fortune is with you, dear lady," Josiah announced. "You are about to embark on a new adventure, a new life, with a new name, and a new face. Providence provides, just when we need it most!" He bowed and left, struggling to pull the donkey through the bushes.

When he was gone, Jaclyn struggled to her feet, gathered her skirts and squatted, awkwardly and painfully, to relieve herself. Sally did the same.

Still squatting, Jaclyn remarked, "He is deliciously strange, Sally. Who is this man?"

"On my soul, I tell you the truth. I did not know Mr. de Torres until yesterday. I know nothing of him. I must have lost my senses to have given him any measure of trust, but I fear more our travels alone without him." Sally adjusted her skirts, took a swig from the flask, rolled the water around inside her mouth, and spat.

"Well, I think he is a gem. And as for trust, if he wanted to do us an evil, he would have done so by now. We have nothing but our lives to offer. We lost all, dear friend. Lost it all." Jaclyn looked at Sally. "What? Why make such a face?"

"True, we have lost a great deal. Everything in Port Royal. But, I would not say we left Port Royal without a sixpence to our names!" Sally smirked.

"What do you mean?" asked Jaclyn.

Sally looked around, then dipped her hand down her bosom and pulled out the linen cloth drawn tight with string. Again, she looked to the bushes and listened. Satisfied that Josiah was out of range, she took hold of Jaclyn's hands, cupped them in the shape of a bowl, and dumped the contents of many gold pieces in her hands.

Jaclyn was speechless for a moment. "I cannot see well, nor can I smell, but I know the touch of gold! How came you of this?" she asked.

"I stole it," Sally confessed.

"What? You *stole* this gold?"

"True. I did. I took a crock from Mr. Randoff's shop." Sally picked up the pieces of gold, one at a time, and returned them to the pouch. "Jaclyn, it said Ginger on the crock. *Ginger*! I assumed it was ginger jam, though I did, momentarily, wonder why it was such a heavy jar. Who stores his gold in a ginger crock?"

Jaclyn laughed but winced in pain. "Half the citizens of Port Royal! I take it good old Jeremy Randoff was not *in* his shop when you were robbing him of his gold."

"Oh, please, I beg you not to put it in quite those terms. I can already feel the noose around my neck as they hang me at Gallows Point! Of course he was not in his shop!" Sally declared.

"Yes. And for good reason. At least his reasons were good for me. He was getting' his mid-day jollies with one of me girls. Miss Nell, I believe it was. Ever wonder why he closed his shop between 11 and 1? A standing appointment, so to speak. Ever since his wife died, well . . . the man had his needs."

Sally gasped. "You mean he –" Sally gasped again and placed her hand over her mouth. "I presumed he was taking his meal or an afternoon nap." They both laughed.

Jaclyn turned somber. "I am quite sure he'll not be accusin' ya of stealin' his gold, Sally. He was in the house, upstairs, when it collapsed."

"Oh no! I have stolen from the dead!"

"That can hardly be a crime, then. Sally, you have no idea, do you?" Jaclyn held one of the gold coins close to her good eye. "This isn't just gold. These are five guinea coins!"

From a distance, Josiah called.

"Tell him nothing of this, Jaclyn, swear to me!" Sally pleaded as she scrambled to replace the coins back in her bosom. "He must not know."

"By my life, *no one* shall, ever!" Jaclyn promised.

They headed through the bushes, back to the road.

"Sally," Jaclyn said softly. "I have taken Mr. de Torres suggestion to heart . . . I mean, about a new start. I believe from this day, I would like to be called Violet."

Nall Wilkins was a saint, at least to Sally. He was quite certain he recognized the Point's most famous madam, even with Jaclyn's altered appearance and alias. And Josiah de Torres was a complete stranger to him. Yet, Nall did not hesitate to welcome the motley crew into his home and into his big heart. They stayed three days while Jaclyn's wounds healed enough to continue the journey to Windhaven.

It wasn't until their last evening with Nall as they dined well into the night, that Sally learned more of the nature of Josiah de Torres's business. He said he owned eight ships that carried finished goods from the Commonwealth to the colonies of New England. There, he filled his hulls with salted pork and cod and lumber that he traded in the Caribbean for rum and molasses for the markets of England.

"Good gracious, Mr. de Torres, that is a substantial fleet," Sally declared.

"It is, my lady, and I have been blessed with honest partners and the strangest of good fortunes," Josiah said.

"Strange fortunes? How so, sir?" Nall asked.

Josiah hesitated, as if searching for the right words. "Near misses," he explained. "A series of near misses. A hurricane off the coast of southern Florida scattered the other ships in our convoy across the Bahamian Banks. However, my ships sailed straight through it with their crew and cargo intact. The other ships were so badly damaged, two were taken apart to refit the others. And once, my ships left New Orleans just before the town was quarantined for Black Vomit Fever. So many mariners died that the ships that were still at port could not find crews sufficient to sail and remained trapped in the harbor. Then there was a foiled attack by pirates near Gibraltar. And now, this."

"But how do you consider this event to be fortunate, strange or otherwise?" Sally asked.

"My business here in Jamaica was in Kingston and Port Royal. An associate in Kingston invited me to dine with him. So, you see, I spent an unscheduled night in Kingston. Had I not, I would have taken a ferry to Port Royal the day before and would have conducted my business at the King's warehouses just when that land sunk and disappeared beneath the sea."

"Indeed!" Nall nodded. "Providence has something in store for ye, lad."

"Perhaps it was to rescue me and Miss Violet." Sally proposed.

"Then he chose a worthy emissary," Nall declared.

"That is what I do not understand, sir. Why me?" Josiah asked thoughtfully.

"Hmmm, Perhaps that is not for *us* to question," Nall speculated.

When it was time to go, Nall offered a calash drawn by two fine horses and completely loaded with supplies.

"I cannot ever repay you for the kindness you have given us, Nall," Sally said.

"You do me wrong to credit me, Lady Cranston. It is I who pay a debt to you," Nall replied.

"A debt? How so, good sir?" Sally asked.

"Wallace Blake was my wife's brother," he replied.

Sally gasped. "He said he had no family. Why did you not tell me this years ago?"

"I made a promise to Wallace. He was ashamed and wished to spare his sister the pain of knowing the man he had become. Though I believe he came to Jamaica to be near her. I saw him once, in Port Royal. I wanted to take him home with me, but he refused to go and made me promise never to tell my wife of his condition or whereabouts. I suppose it was easier for him to keep away. What you did for him, Lady Cranston, was a good thing. I am beholden to you. My wife, Annie . . . Well, I broke the promise I made to Wallace, just before my wife passed on. You see, she believed Wallace had died at sea. Knowing he was well looked-after gave her peace."

Sally could say nothing. She laid her hand on Nall's cheek and kissed the other. He helped her board the calash and with a crack of the whip, they were off to Windhaven.

CHAPTER 41

The aftermath of the earthquake was burdened with as much tragedy as the event itself. News of Port Royal reached Sally and her two traveling companions through the tales of witnesses they encountered who like themselves, sought refuge in the interior of the island. When they reached Windhaven, Sally barely had time to dismount the calash before Nero went into a raging discourse. He related how the count of those who died from the quake and the floods was over two thousand.

"And as many as that have died since from their injuries and sickness that ravishes those that still live on the Point," Nero accounted. "There be all kinds of preaching men claiming that this is the voice of God and that it is God that arises to shake terribly the Earth and if we don't mend our evil doing, the Lord will smite us all down again. These preaching men blame the people and the people are passing the blame onto others, madam. They hung the Jews and they tore up their burial grounds, what was left of them. Then they hung the free blacks and then they hung their own slaves. They blame the pirates, madam, and they hung some of them, too. They hung so many people they ran out of yardarms. Tis terrible, madam, what those people do. And what is left of The Council, all they did was to declare another holiday. The seventh of every June from now on shall be a day of fasting and humiliation to remind us of the Lord's wrath. They said we are not deserving of the Lord's mercy if we do not learn righteousness. That's what they say. The Council, madam, have done nothing about no water and they have nothing about no food." Nero was breathless. "Damn, Miss Jaclyn, what'd you do to your face?"

"Why, thank you, Nero, you do know just how to flatter a lady, now, don't you? And Nero, I am called Miss Violet now. You tell the others. Miss Violet Longfellow. That is my name. Understand?"

"No, Miss Violet." Nero shot a glance at Sally who nodded inconspicuously. "I'll get Miss Lucy. She'll know what to do," Nero said softly as he helped Jaclyn into the house. "Good you changed your name, Miss Violet, I hear tell they be hangin' the likes of you, too."

"Then you do understand, Nero," she chuckled.

"Yes, Miss Violet."

Once inside, Sally felt safe and the inner qualities she gathered to build her strength and resilience in the past days fell away like leaves from a tree. She began to shake uncontrollably. To stave her pending breakdown, she went straight to the bookshelf and removed Thomas's book of bound papers from the Royal Society. She leafed through the papers but the tears welling in her eyes blinded her and made it difficult for her to disguise her building emotions. She finally found the page she wanted.

"It's utter nonsense," she announced with her lower lip trembling "and just plain ignorance of the facts!" Josiah and Miss Violet exchanged look of confusion. "Here," Sally insisted, "in this paper by Robert Hooke, he clearly states that 'quakes are eruptions of fiery conflagrations enkindled in the subterraneous regions of the Earth'. And another where he states a cause may be the sudden shift of the planet's center of gravity. I will not believe this gibberish that this natural occurrence is some type of punishment from God! If that is true, why did he wait so long?" Sally demanded.

"God is patient," Violet answered as she propped her sore leg on a stool.

"And if He truly wanted Port Royal to be smitten, why did He not sink it all?" asked Josiah.

"God is merciful," Violet answered again, smiling beneath her broken nose.

"Poppycock!" Sally protested while trying to suppress the surge of sobs. "God created a universe that operates by the natural laws. And we with all our sinning have no influence on those laws. We cannot subjugate or interfere with the laws of nature anymore than a rock or a cow."

"Careful, Lady Cranston," Josiah warned. "It is that very lack of power and control that puts fear in the hearts of men and makes them react so irrationally at such times. We all like to think we have some autonomy over our lives and surroundings, but we are quick to lean on higher powers when events are not so easily explained. Thus some greater power, we believe, must surely be acting for our common good. I would be careful, my lady, about contesting such firm beliefs."

"Madam's shops?" inquired Nero giving a sideways look at Josiah.

"Gone, Nero!" Miss Violet offered. "The inn . . . everything on Queen Street. It seemed a whole part of Port Royal simply slipped into the waters of the bay. It pains me to recall those images. You felt nothing of the quake here?"

"Oh yes, Madam, we did. I was down at the turtle crawls and heard what sounded like canon fire from the east and the north. The ground shook so that it knocked me off my feet. The waves washed away the wall and we lost most of the turtles. But Bo is there now, fetching them back," Nero answered.

"Is that all?" Sally asked. "Everyone is safe? No damage to the buildings?"

"Everybody is well, madam, except for Matilda. She was in the kitchen when the earth shook. It frightened her so that she just keeled over. I do not know why. Frightened to death, I reckon. It is only Lucy now in the kitchen. We buried Matilda out there with the others, madam."

"I am sorry to hear this news, Nero. Poor Matilda. Can Lucy manage on her own?" Sally asked.

"Yes, madam," Lucy said as she carried a tray full of drinks and cakes, "I done manage this whole house and I done managed it well enough!"

"Lucy, I have no doubts. And it is good to see you so well. Our guests will be staying with us for a while. Will you show Mr. de Torres to the bath house and put Miss Violet in the front room?"

Lucy applied a cool cloth to Miss Violet's face and turned to escort Mr. de Torres from the room. "Yes, madam," Lucy continued. "That big barrel, it sprung a leak, madam. All that shaking around made them staves move about. Nero, he bunged up the gaps just fine with some pitch. I think it'll hold water now. Give me some time to fill it, madam. We's all pleased you're back with us. I told you not to go to dat town. I told you. You can't go back to dat town, madam. It's a bad town. A bad town!" Lucy continued her rant even as she left the room with Josiah.

"She's right, Jaclyn. We cannot go back there," Sally sighed. "Least not for awhile."

"It's *Violet*, dear, and I never want to go back, Sally, never. I am through with it. I have never been one to listen to those raging preacher types, but many others do. There was a moment, when I was alone on the street, that I thought they were going to stone me dead. Or at least whack me to death with a fish or two. Since then, I cannot shake the feeling that I have been given a second chance. A chance for a different life! I am fixing to ask Mr. de Torres if I might obtain passage on his ship when he sails for Boston."

"What would you do? Boston! I hear the people there are rather . . . devout." Sally asked.

Violet chuckled as she took note of her broken body. She put her hands on her face and gently patted its fractured texture. "I suspect this face will no longer fetch much bounty. My whoring days are over Sally, and I wish not to manage the affairs of others in that way. I chose that way when I had nothing else to keep me from starving. It took years, but I learned things, Sally. Now, I want . . . respect. Have ye not heard, my dear?" she mocked. "Miss Violet can read and write and sew. She has managed property and investments and fancies opening a shop of her own. This Miss Violet . . . she'll do all right on her own!"

Sally removed the pouch of gold coins still lodged between her breasts and placed it in her friend's lap.

"You must promise me, Violet, to name your shop after Jeremy Randoff," Sally said.

"No. I will not take this, Sally. You need this to cover your losses."

Sally placed a finger over Violet's lips to stop her from saying more and shook her head. She winked and said, "I have Windhaven. Besides, this is due you. I believe Mr. Randoff did not pay you for his last service." They both laughed, but the outpouring of emotion released the pent-up tears; tears for the loss of so many friends, for the destruction of Port Royal, their businesses, and for the end of a familiar way of life.

Word soon came to Windhaven that Josiah's ships had finally returned to Jamaica and were docked at Kingston harbor. He and Violet said their farewells to

Sally. Josiah delighted in accompanying Violet to Kingston and took great pleasure in supporting her well-contrived story of the mysterious Bermudian widow, Mrs. Violet Longfellow.

"Why Bermuda?" he asked.

"What are the chances that the shadow of another Bermudian would ever cross the widow Longfellow's toes?" Violet reasoned.

Violet hid her disfigurements behind a veil of black crepe. Kingston was full of women in mourning, so the veil drew little attention. No one challenged the loss of her disembarkation documents. Josiah was prepared to vouch that they arrived on the same ship, that while in Jamaica she visited with friends, and now was planning to return to her home in Boston. Though a seemingly perfect fabrication, it was not necessary. Kingston was far too chaotic and the administrative infrastructure too broken for anyone to be troubled over one person's displaced documents.

Kingston's port was not well suited for docking in bad weather and could handle less than a half dozen ships at one time. With Port Royal's defenses in disarray, Kingston was now vulnerable to attack. Captain Kent of de Torres's company flagship was anxious to unload his cargo and be off to deeper seas. He planned to thread the Windward Passage north to the Caicos Islands and join a convoy of other merchantmen.

"I've been to the Point," the captain related to Josiah and Violet, "and it is a scene of terror. The death toll grows higher as those who survived the quake now fall to terrible sickness, hunger, and unspeakable violence. No one attempts to remove the dead and the dogs and the birds feed on the corpses – the dogs that are left, that is, for many have been slaughtered for a meal. And I've heard worse tales, Mr. de Torres. Even the highest of society must compete for a small space in slave quarters for those are all that remains standing. Shortages have turned civil men into savages. Such conditions, Mr. de Torres! I pray my eyes never again fall upon such suffering."

"I had in mind to take a ferry across to the Point while your ship unloads, Mr. de Torres," Violet admitted, "but on second thought, I think I do not wish to cloud happier memories of the Port Royal that was. With your permission, I would like to stay aboard your vessel until we make sail."

"I would want it no other way, Mrs. Longfellow," Josiah replied and gave orders for several crewmen to help settle her below. Just as she was about to maneuver down the companionway stairs, she noticed a familiar brand across the bilge of the barrels being off-loaded. Violet gasped when she recognized the name – Waller.

"Mr. de Torres!" Violet exclaimed. "The name on those barrels . . . I believe I know well the distributor."

"Captain Edward Waller, from Boston?" Josiah asked.

"There can scarcely be two," Violent laughed as she returned to his side. "He trades all manner of goods in barrels he makes at his cooperage on Cape Cod?"

"The same. I have been doing business with Captain Waller for many years, now. A good man!" Josiah pointed to the net holding several Waller barrels and being pulled across the rails by the block and tackle. That shipment contains groundnuts, from his son-in-law's plantation in the Carolinas."

Violet put her hand to her mouth in an involuntarily gesture of surprise at the irony. "A good man, indeed! Tell me, Mr. de Torres, has he now . . . a wife and perhaps . . . a family?"

Josiah looked puzzled. "Aye, the Waller I speak of has a family. The son-in-law I mentioned and a granddaughter, but no wife. He had a daughter but she died in childbirth some years past. She was a pretty thing, had some native blood. She married a planter from Jamaica, I believe, by the name of . . ."

"Montague!" Violet finished.

"You know this man, Montague?" Josiah asked.

"Yes, I do. And you, sir, know his sister, Lady Cranston!" Violet replied.

"Sally! Tis a small world, Mrs. Longfellow! I know little of Montague except . . . some scandal involving his child, Edward's granddaughter . . . Abigail. Yes, that is her name. Rumor had it this Montague fellow ran off with pirates and came back for his daughter years later after coming into much wealth." Josiah thought for a moment, and then added, "I remember Edward was quite cut-up about giving up that little girl. After that, he became quite reclusive . . . doesn't take to the sea much anymore," Josiah explained.

"So that's why Edward has not come!" Violet whispered to herself. To Josiah, she asked, "And how do you come to know Capt. Waller?"

"Through a mutual friend, Richard Tucker of Dorchester. Mr. Tucker is an associate and this company's largest investor. He is also the father of my wife, Alicia."

"Your wife! In all this time, you did not tell us that you had a wife, sir!"

"You, Mrs. Longfellow, failed to ask. But what is this all about?"

Violet laughed long and hard. She wrapped her arm around Josiah's elbow and said, "My dear Mr. de

Torres, I do hope this is a lengthy voyage, for I have a rather long and heartbreaking tale for your ears. It is a love story! One that has taken more knocks than the King's chopping block, but a tale that, with our good graces and proper timing, may end happily for two misguided lovers."

Though Windhaven was a welcoming retreat, it took weeks for Sally to get back into the rhythm of farming. She missed the pace of Port Royal and the company of her friends. She slowly came to accept that her time on The Point was a sidetrack, a temporary detractor, albeit a gutsy attempt at making it as a merchant and investor. She took some satisfaction in believing she was defeated not from poor management or unwise ventures, but by a catastrophic act of nature. She was home now and busy again with the tasks of planting, harvesting, and pipe making.

It wasn't long before Sally realized that her beloved plantation had lost its sparkle. It wasn't as much fun when there was no Gregor to please with an over-sized pumpkin or an exceptional pipe, though she still found herself running about the house searching for him. There was no James to nag to rise from his bed. No Molly to pick up after, and no Thomas to read to. No grandchildren to spoil. No Little Luke to tutor and tease. Nero's wife, Ruth, had joined the others in the graveyard this summer past and Bo, grown and managing his own farm, spent fewer days at Windhaven. The plantation was short on life and laughter.

To his credit, Nero did a fine job at managing the estate and had strengthened the productivity of every field. He made improvements not imagined by Sally and he did it all without the labor of slaves. Sally lacked the innovative spirit and passions of her younger years and faced the harsh reality that Windhaven no longer needed her. The workings of the farm continued to fill her days and checked her tendency for loneliness, but she conducted her tasks with stolidity and worked through each day waiting for the next.

By September, the economic aftershocks from the quake hit Windhaven and other plantations throughout Jamaica. Though the docks of Port Royal were partially restored, disease and lawlessness kept many ships away. Kingston as a trading center was a poor and dangerous substitute. Its shallow waters and craggy shoreline made docking too risky for ships laden with heavy cargo. Provisions and infrastructure onshore were scant and unreliable. Ships avoided Jamaica altogether, causing severe shortages and backups in what remained of the warehouses.

Though the first harvest after the quake was bountiful, markets were not. Jamaica suffered its worst recession since the plague of 1666. Nearly half of Port Royal's capital wealth sank in the harbor in waters too deep and too murky for even the most talented divers to recover.

Jamaica's slaves suffered most horribly. Vegetables and grains could not compete with the highly profitable cash crops of tobacco, cane, and cotton. For years, Jamaican planters had abandoned their traditional edible crops for more lucrative, but labor-intensive yields. Unable to find sufficient food for their slaves, masters abandoned their care. Those who did not run away, starved. Other planters allowed their slaves to keep small vegetable patches to provide sustenance, but it was not enough to keep them healthy. On an island once considered the Garden of the Caribbean, emaciated souls struggled to survive. The rains that failed the previous spring produced stringy, bitter yams and caused the leaves to drop from the cassavas. Even the monkeys, who like the Maroons sought refuge in the mountains, came down from the hills to raid the pathetic gardens of the slaves.

Thunderclouds rumbled across the island throughout October, but again no rain came. Wildfires destroyed cane fields before they were ready to harvest. Rivers were so low that river rafters found them difficult to navigate. It seemed, to many, that God was now getting around to punishing the rest of Jamaica. Some planters gave up and moved to other colonies or headed back to England.

Nero and Sally kept Windhaven going, but only at the subsistence level. The clay along the riverbanks was too dry to dig and there was a large inventory of unsold pipes. So few ships came to Jamaica that every inch of cargo space was reserved for merchants who could pay the greatly inflated prices. Windhaven cotton was very productive, but Nero lost his pickers, the four McMann men, to the higher wages offered by the builders in Kingston. It was impossible to replace them with the wages Sally could afford. Roving herds of monkeys destroyed the vanilla vines and a persistent blight reduced the production of valuable cocoa at Moon Walk. By spring, Windhaven was in trouble.

"Nero," Sally said after reviewing the accounts, "I have to sell those two lower cotton fields. We haven't the hands to pick it. Mr. Weatherstone expressed an interest in the purchase of the larger of those fields. I do not think it will be difficult to sell him the other, especially with such a high yield."

"Master Gregor, he would not like it that we carve up Windhaven, madam. But there are only those two field hands and I." As the gravity of the situation settled into his mind, he sighed long and hard. "And the taxes, madam . . ."

Sally smiled. After so many years, she and Nero had an easy working relationship and could often read each other with just a look or a sigh.

"I will ride over there tomorrow, then. Perhaps Mr. Weatherstone will have heard some happier news," Sally replied. Nero left but Sally continued to study the ledgers. She flipped the pages back to the beginning. "I can't deny these numbers, Gregor," she defended. She took other ledges from years passed from the shelf until a pile of twenty-eight ledgers was stacked upon the desk.

"Twenty-eight years!" she remarked aloud. Reverently, she caressed the stack with her hand, each book triggering a happy memory of that year. She froze for a moment and noticed her hand. She lifted it from the books, held it out at arm's length so she could focus her eyes on the detail, and studied it. *When did my hands get so . . . wrinkled,* she wondered. Sally left the books on the desk and walked through the open doors to the little graveyard on the hill behind the house. She read the names carved into the narrow slate markers. Sir Gregor Cranston, Bart.; Michael Cranston, infant son; Matilda, housemaid; Captain Wallace Blake; and Ruth, wife of Nero, mother of Bo. With tears in her eyes, she knelt beside her husband's grave.

"Oh, Gregor, here is a right mess we are in! I cannot see how we can manage, with so few of us. I just haven't the . . . the strength. Please believe me dear, I never imagined that I would be anywhere but beside you, here at Windhaven but . . ." Her sobs came heavy. "I'm not ready to join you, Gregor. Forgive me. I want to see Thomas and Molly. I want to see my grandchildren!" Sally could say no more. She stayed there, sobbed and said goodbye.

CHAPTER 42

"Don't be a stupid fool!" Violet Longfellow raised her voice in a way that was both shrill and sweet.

Edward Waller cringed at the sound. "This is a pursuit," he protested, "that can only end in mutual . . . heartbreak. I am certain she has moved on, the way she always does after a crisis. And what would I offer her . . . a life here, in Massachusetts . . . after living in the tropics so many years? She would not survive the first winter, Jaclyn. Forgive me, Mrs. Longfellow!" Edward protested.

"At least give her the option to choose. You have loved that woman for three decades, Edward. Where is it written that a man and a woman who have such affections cannot enjoy the rewards of being together in their final years? She is alone, Edward, as alone as you!" Violet pleaded.

"I could not agree more, old boy," Richard Tucker chimed in, "We can't have you here growing old and crotchety. Retire from this work here, Edward. Go . . . find this woman!"

"Et tu, Richard?" Edward said to his friend.

"Edward, she did show a measure of courage I thought not possible in a woman," Josiah added. "Even so, I fear the circumstances in which we left her may have declined drastically since we parted. The reports from Jamaica have not been favorable. I fear for her safety and intend to rescue the Dowager, Lady Cranston, on my return trip from England – with or without you. I encourage you to come with me on this venture."

There was a deafening silence in the room. Edward paced. He stopped in front of the large hearth and stared at the flames. Violet and Josiah looked at each other and then held their breath as they watched him anxiously.

Edward, keeping his back to them, put out his arm and held onto the mantel. He dropped his head, so low that his chin rested on his chest, and remained that way for quite some time. Then, with one quick motion, he suddenly turned to face them and asked Josiah, "When do we sail?"

Mid-May was not the best time, but Josiah decided to sail four of his smaller merchantmen half loaded with lumber from New England to the Carolinas. There he would take on cotton and join up with two other merchantmen and a ship of the line on their return voyage to England. Edward planned to travel with Josiah as far as Charles Towne, visit with James and Abigail, and then find passage to Jamaica.

About ten years before, Charles Towne moved from the original settlement along the west banks of the Ashley River to the marsh-fringed peninsula where the Ashley and Cooper Rivers merged. The harbor, now the mercantile center of the colony, was full of coastal traders in small ketches and larger merchantmen. The sound of hammers announced the bustling growth of Charles Towne as seasoned settlers from Barbados, Virginia, and New Amsterdam mingled with the newer immigrants from all over Europe and even refugees from Port Royal. The mix of customs, races, and languages created a light-hearted cosmopolitan atmosphere.

The Montague townhouse was a large three-story red brick home not far from the embrasures where cannons aimed at the Ashley River and the mouth of Old Towne Creek. Edward knocked on the door. A young negro boy, dressed very properly and sporting a spotless white wig, answered. He bowed slowly.

"Captain Edward Waller to see Mister James Montague," Edward announced. The boy opened the door wide and in an exaggerated well- rehearsed gesture bowed again, swinging his arm low in a deep arc nearly touching the floor.

"Edward! I am so pleased you arrived safely," James declared as he came to greet Edward. "So good to see you!" James backed away slightly before bellowing in a thunderous roar, "Abby! Come see what the tide has brought us!"

An angel of beauty descended the broad curved stairs. Abigail was about the same age as Sally when she and Edward first met and for a second, there was an uncanny resemblance. She was quite the grown young lady and she took Edward's breath away! The little girl was gone and in her place, a lovely princess. Upon recognizing Edward, however, the refined proper lady fell to the wayside as Abby lunged into Edward's arms. It was a moment Edward wanted to savor forever. How he missed her!

There was not a moment to rest. Abby insisted that he try every exquisite taste of Charles Towne and meet every notable family, most importantly the family of Nigel Pelham whose oldest daughter, Rebecca, James proposed to marry. South Carolina was every bit as hot as the West Indies, and unlike the islands, there was no relief from a sea breeze. The heat lingered long into the night. Insects hummed so loudly, it disturbed Edward's sleep. As the sun rose above the dunes, Abigail was there every morning to roust him from his bed, refusing to waste a moment of his visit.

Edward's days in Charles Towne were an endless blur of parties, dinners, and trips up river to see the plantation, the grand house, attractive gardens, productive fields, and the neat rows of tiny cottages of the slave quarters.

"What do you call this plantation of yours?" Edward asked. James looked at Abigail and they both smiled.

"Anani-on-the-Ashley!" they both replied in unison.

"That is touching," Edward acknowledged, nodding his head, "Yes, she would have liked that." Edward waited until Abigail left the room to bring up the matter of slaves. "How many slaves have you working the fields?"

"Field hands? Thirty-two now, and half as many working the barns and the house. But I lose too many to fever. It's a stiff price we pay for all the advantages of planting this low country. Plenty of water-rich soil, but the swamp air attacks the health of even the strongest here. Fortunately, they breed up fast and I hope to have a strong, new crop come next year."

Edward's head whipped suddenly in the direction of James in an involuntarily reaction to the insensitive words he just heard. "Are you referring to your slaves or your plants?"

James looked puzzled for a moment until he remembered his words. "Oh, I see. Well, I suppose I hope for both to produce in abundance."

"James, you . . . treat them well?" Edward asked, but he was uncomfortable with the question and knew in an instant that he offended James.

"What an extraordinary question! They represent a considerable investment, Edward, not just in money, but also in labor. The plantation is wholly dependent on their labors. I cannot operate without them. Of course I treat them well."

"It is just that . . . the Barbadians," Edward interjected, "are growing in numbers here. They are known throughout the Caribbean to practice a code of slave management that is unnecessarily harsh. Their measure of punishment is . . ."

"I agree," James interrupted, "though not completely, and I have heard the rumors, as you. We Carolinians recruit experienced planters in much the same manner as Modyford did for Jamaica. However, we are not about to let Barbadians dictate the administration of our domestic affairs in the Carolinas!" James paced the room, and then stopped before Edward. His face took on a worried look. "These slaves . . . they outnumber us now, Edward," he continued. "If they had a mind to organize . . . a slave revolt is a genuine concern of all planters in this colony. If our punishments of those who display rebellious tendencies seem harsh, it is to keep the others in their place. The alternative is . . . untenable."

Edward shot him a look.

"What?" James asked.

"I just remembered hearing those very words . . . when I was a very young lad at the siege of Colchester," Edward explained with a distant stare.

"From the lips of whom, a Roundhead or Royalist?" James asked.

"Does that matter?" Edward replied, appearing confused.

James grew impatient. "I have heard much about this anti-slave rhetoric coming from Massachusetts, particularly among the Quakers who, after stirring those in England well enough, now seek trouble in the colonies. Ironic, considering they support the shipment of slaves. Not directly perhaps, but through their financial investments, they make the movement of such cargo possible. Hypocrites! Your New England farms are smaller, Edward. Your soil is richer, the production per acre greater and all within a shorter, milder season. It is not surprising, I suppose, that you misunderstand the needs of our southern plantations. Can you imagine a white New England farmer stooping to pick the prickly cotton all day in this heat? Do you think a white indentured man would bend over to dig the groundnuts from dawn to dusk? Cotton is the fruit of this new world that will put gold in the treasury of an empire, Edward, and we cannot accomplish this without slaves. They are as valuable to us as the soil we cultivate."

Edward was now desperate to change the subject. He cleared his throat and interjected, "We must discuss your production of ground nuts and cotton, James, but first, I wish to talk about another matter of importance. It is more than trade that brings me south, James." Edward was suddenly jolted by the gravity of the topic he just introduced. Perhaps, he thought, the topic of slaves was less contentious than what he was about to reveal. "I . . . I intend to call upon Sally . . . to ask her to marry me. I had hoped to receive your blessing, being her closest kin."

James was stunned, but only for a moment. A beaming grin covered his face, followed immediately by a puzzled look. "In England?" he asked.

"England? No, I wait for passage to Jamaica," Edward replied, equally confused.

"Forgive me, Edward. I am delighted by this announcement, though for the life of me, I cannot understand why you have delayed so. And of course, you have my blessing, but my dear man, Sally is no longer in Jamaica. She left for England two months ago." James stated.

"England?" Edward repeated, his throat turning dry.

"She wanted to see Thomas and Molly and the babies. I . . . thought you knew. I am certain she wrote . . ." James stopped and rubbed the back of his neck. "Thomas has earned himself quite the reputation as a physician in London, but decided to leave it all for the colonies. He has accepted a post at the new university just built in Virginia. I believe they are naming it after the sovereigns, William & Mary. He's planning to come this fall to take up his position there." James was beaming with pride, but his voice softened and his face took on a somber look. "Sally had a terrible time of it, after the quake. Windhaven . . . well, it fell on hard times. She has money in England, but refuses to use it, giving it all over to Thomas and Molly. She sold off some Windhaven acres to pay her debts and used the money I gave her, the dirty pirate money as she calls it, to pay taxes in advance for the next ten years. She thought it just recompense, using those ill-gotten gains to pay off unfair taxes. You know how she feels about taxes. She signed over a hundred acres to Nero in payment for looking after Windhaven and Moon Walk. Her letters, Edward, have recently had a sad, tired tone. I am not sure she intends to return to Jamaica. I invited her to come to live with Rebecca and me, but she has yet to reply on that matter."

"England?" Edward said again. "I thought . . . Do you think . . .? I am sorry James, but I fear I must return to the docks immediately!" Edward took a breath. "Pray de Torres has not yet raised his anchors. I must be off if I am to catch her in England! Abigail?"

"Abby!" James thundered. Abby came running and was quite distraught to learn the news of her grandfather's sudden departure, but was comforted when she learned the reason.

"Perhaps you and your father will come to Boston for our wedding, if it be my good fortune," Edward said.

"Indeed!" James replied, "Only if you promise to return to these shores for mine, sir!" Upon their return to Charles Towne, James gave orders to the house staff to prepare for Edward's abrupt departure and then hurriedly scribbled short notes for Edward to deliver to Sally and his old lawyer, Mr. Mosby.

Josiah de Torres was quite anxious to be underway, but relieved that Edward caught up with him before doing so. He lost two men to desertion and one to a fatal brawl over the price of ale. The other three merchantmen in the small fleet did not fare better, forcing the captains to cancel all further shore leave. The crews grew restless and angry over their confinement within earshot of the delightful distractions of Charles Towne. Josiah was growing weary of containing them and was thankful to hoist the sails and be off. During the misty twilight hour of the morning, when the clouds were pink and there was adequate light to read the shallows, the ships pulled anchor and left Charles Towne Harbor for the open seas.

In August 1693, London was besieged with a steady flow of casualties returning from the battle at Neerwinden. Though King William boasted otherwise, the English, Dutch, and other allied forces were soundly defeated by the French army. Some 19,000 allied troops were killed or imprisoned and thousands of wounded were transported back across the channel in a hasty retreat. London docks were so overwhelmed that many wounded had to remain on the anchored ships. Countless did not survive the ordeal. The injured, dying, and dead lined the dockyards.

"Have you ever known a time when England was not at war?" Josiah asked Edward cynically as they made their way through the lines of writhing men crying on the docks. "Look about and see how our colonial taxes are spent! We toil to support these petty disputes. The royals of Europe sit in the comforts of their castles sparring like spoilt children while these poor blighters suffer the consequences. Think about the good that *could* be done with the revenue from the colonies, yet, here we are . . . This sad, sad tale never seems to change." Josiah stopped once more and turned around. He lowered his head and slowly shook it.

Even though they walked several blocks away, the smell from the docks permeated the air. They arrived at a small, but crowded coffee house on High Street, not far along the Pool of the Thames. "Here is where we must part, Edward. My business is with these men inside. We sail on to Jamaica in a fortnight and will expect you, but if your plans lead you to another destination, I am certain I can find passage for you and Lady Cranston aboard another vessel if given a few days' notice."

"Josiah, you have an undying confidence that I will find Sally and that she will, indeed, agree to come with me. I appreciate that faith, sir, because it is stronger than my own."

"Ha! Not as strong as Mrs. Violet Longfellow's! Go find her, Edward. When you do, you would do me a great honor to arrange a time when I might see her again. The proprietor of this house is a trusted man. I will keep him abreast of my whereabouts. Careful of this town, Edward, she harbors a greater wickedness than Port Royal! May good fortune go with you, sir!"

"And with you!" Edward bowed and walked away heading west on High Street toward the Tower.

According to Josiah's directions, he headed north to Leadenhall Street. Otis Harmsworth kept his shop on the fashionable Threadneedle Street near the corner of Leadenhall and Bishops Gate. The large and imposing building was their place of residence and business. The shop was on the ground floor and family residence in the upper stories. From Violet, Edward learned that Otis had expanded his wares beyond watches and clocks to include fine jewelry and spectacles. His ties to the Caribbean provided a steady stream of raw materials, probably gotten through questionable means, and he used his skills to smelt down the incriminating swag to transform the metals and gems into lovely works of art. His first shop was so successful; he opened another across the river on Dover Street.

Edward peered through the leadlight next to the door. The tall lanky profile of Otis could not be mistaken. He wore a craftsman's apron and was sitting on a high stool. Bent over a counter, his hands were busy manipulating the workings of some intricate device. There were two other men behind counters. One was displaying a box of something to a customer. The other suddenly looked up and towards the window. Edward pulled back, not wanting to be seen. As he stepped back into the shadows of the portico, he caught his own reflection in the glass. An old man stared back with hair graying at the temples, sagging jowl, and broader face. He was fifty-seven and suddenly unsure of his intent. He and Sally had retained a deep friendship throughout the years and he was frightened to risk that relationship.

Edward threw a fist of one hand into the palm of the other. *I have not thought this through at all*, he muttered to himself. As he paced before the shop planning his retreat, a carriage pulled up. The driver pulled the reins while the footman jumped from behind. He placed the footstool near the door, opened it and reached in to take the hand of a woman to help her from the carriage. She kept her head down to watch her footing on the small and somewhat wobbly stool. When her feet were firmly on the ground, she adjusted her skirts and raised her head to look directly into Edward's eyes. Ignoring the footman's hand and the stool, a young boy jumped from the carriage and brushed past the woman. When he saw that she did not follow he stopped, looked up at her, then followed her eyes transfixed on Edward.

"Grandmamma, are you coming?" the boy asked. "What is the matter?"

The woman blinked and broke her stare. "Nigel, I don't think you have met him before, but this is Captain Waller," she said. "Captain Waller, this is my grandson, Nigel Harmsworth."

Edward bowed deeply and the boy mimicked the action.

"Edward, this . . . is a wonderful surprise! What brings you to England?" Sally asked.

"A common acquaintance, my lady. Josiah de Torres. I came on his ship," Edward explained.

"Josiah, here?" Sally asked excitedly looking around.

"He is off doing business, but has expressed his desire to see you, if that would be convenient, my lady."

"That would be delightful! But here, we mustn't chatter so out in the street. Do come inside, Edward. Otis and Molly will be so pleased to see you. Nigel, run up and tell your mama to expect a surprise," Sally instructed the boy with a sparkle in her eye. She laid her hand upon Edward's to escort him into the shop, but he planted his feet firmly. His fingers encircled her hand, held it firmly, and looked at her intently. A commotion at the top of the stairs prevented Sally from responding to his touch.

"Captain Waller!" Molly yelled. "Captain Waller, this is an unexpected surprise! Do come in. Mama? Did you know the captain was in England?" Molly rushed down the stairs, tapped on the shop window to gain her husband's attention, and curtseyed to Edward.

"No, Molly, I did not. I met him, just here, on the street," Sally replied. Edward bowed before Molly and followed her up the wide stairs to the large but cozy rooms above the shop. Otis ran up the stairs to join them and instructed his oldest boy to fetch Thomas from his lodgings. It was a happy reunion, well celebrated with a fine meal.

"That is quite an exquisite piece of silver on your hand, Molly," Edward declared.

"Isn't it grand!" Molly showed off the ornately carved and bejeweled silver finger, perfectly formed and ingeniously fastened to the end of her stump by a series of fine rings. "Otis designed it for me," she said with a glint of pride. "Now tell us, dear Edward, what brings you to London?"

Edward was dumbfounded. He had spent so much time on what he wanted to say to Sally, that he had not thought to contrive any other excuse for being here. He didn't know what to say.

"Mother?" Molly was concerned. "Are you all right?"

Edward looked over to Sally and noticed her face was flushed. He stood up abruptly and said to Sally, "Perhaps, my lady, some fresh air. I would like very much if you would walk with me to the Royal Exchange. I have yet to see its new construction."

"New construction?" Otis looked confused, as the current building had been standing for years. "Oh, I see, you mean since the fire. Shall I accompany you?"

"No!" Edward and Sally replied in unison. They both looked surprised and laughed at their lack of subtleness.

"Ah, I see," Otis replied sheepishly after receiving a playful thump from Molly.

Once outside, Sally linked her arm around Edward's and mused, "I believe I can hear their tongues wag, even from this distance!" she laughed. "How is Josiah and how came you to know him?"

We've done business for years, but a mutual friend of ours, Jaclyn de Witt, who now calls herself Mrs. Violet Longfellow, brought us together for another reason," Edward replied with a wink.

"Jaclyn? Oh, do tell, Edward, how is my dear old friend?"

"She is well and moved on to the small village of Concord, just west of Boston. Her plan was to live the secluded life of a widow, but of course we are talking about the former Madame Jaclyn and her seclusion did not last long. Our Mrs. Longfellow is, in fact, well known by every citizen there."

Sally stopped walking. "No!" she said in horror, putting her hand over her mouth.

"Oh no, no!" Edward laughed when he understood the misconception. "Not in *that* manner. Apparently, Mrs. Longfellow has quite a talent for good penmanship. She scribes wills for the magistrate and writes letters for just about every settler from Concord to Boston. As such, Violet knows everyone's business, but has cleverly insured that no one knows hers. She has played her hand well, Sally. Even if a sliver of truth were revealed sometime in the future, no one would ever believe it of their beloved Violet Longfellow and would defend the poor widow with their lives."

"I have heard such shocking details to the contrary, Edward, I mean about the nature of the citizens in Massachusetts. It's all the talk around London. I understand they have staked and burned defenseless women on trumped charges of witchcraft in Boston!" Sally scoffed.

"Hung," he corrected. "And it was Salem, not Boston. And it was men as well as the women. Fanatic Puritans, again! But have no concerns about our dear Violet. She is counted among the most respectable widows in all of New England!" Edward replied with a glint in his eyes. Then, he turned solemn. "She and Josiah told me of the great hardships you suffered during and after the quake. I am sorry, Sally, sorry that I was not there for you. Josiah says he never saw such courage, in a man or woman."

"Courage?" she quipped. "What courage? I just had a sudden recognition that there was something more important than fear. Life! If I struggled harder than most, it was because I was so desperate to live. Self-preservation! That's all it was." Sally stopped walking and turned to Edward. "You once told me you would never step a foot onto English soil again, at least not past the docks. And though you frequently came upon the shores of our islands in the Caribbees, you avoided returning to this land of your birth, so what brings you here and now, Edward? Is it your business? Are you doing well?"

"You!" he answered without hesitating. "It is you. I have come to ask you . . . to consider . . . I want you to be my wife, Sally." Edward bit his lip. Those were not the careful words he prepared.

There was an awkward silence broken by her simple question, "Why?"

Edward felt deflated. "It seems quiet inadequate . . . that is, to say these words now and I muddle my thoughts, so the words do not come easy," Edward paused to gain control of his tongue and his thoughts. "I love you and have always, from the first time I saw you in Bristol. I loved you when I left you in Thomas's care. I came back for you, to marry you. I was too late. While I let my ambitions tangle my foolish heart, you found another." Edward swallowed hard. "Gregor was a fine man, Sally. I was honored to have him as my friend. He gave you much joy and company and two lovely children. But now, he is gone and we both face . . . a different time. I do not wish to spend a moment of *that* time without you. Marry me?"

"Oh Edward, I cannot. I have the children . . ."

"They are grown and have made their own path, with great success. I will always care for them and their children. That, I promise you!"

Sally nervously twirled the hair dangling from her bonnet, just as she did when he first met her. She began to pace back and forth.

"I must have time to think, Edward. I have spent this past year weaving a plan. Now you ask me to unravel it and re-knit something that is strange and new." She stopped, looked directly at him, and giggled, "I had not expected this - truly!"

Edward laughed, "What says you, my lady? We have a great history, you and I. And I believe we have many more adventures to come. Marry me! Do not let your plans tangle *your* heart!"

Sally laughed with him. She grabbed his hands and in an instant, they were together, in the middle of the busiest street in London! But just as suddenly, her laugher died and her smile faded. She slowly let go of his hands as she stepped back away from him. "Windhaven," she whispered.

"Windhaven? Windhaven will not come between us. Whatever the complications, we can resolve them, together. I would never presume to ask you to give up what you spent your life building. And I understand, more than most, how a piece of your heart will always remain in Jamaica."

"Nor can I propose that you sacrifice your businesses in Massachusetts to share my life in the tropics," she countered. Her head dropped as she started towards the Exchange again. Edward followed and she reached out to tuck her hand in the crux of his elbow. No words were exchanged, no words could be.

When they returned to Otis's shop, Edward decided to take his leave from Sally at the door.

"Will you not come up? Where are you staying? I am sure Molly expects you to stay here with us," Sally asked.

"Thank you, no. I have . . . some business to attend. If I may, I would like to return tomorrow, if you are free."

"Wonderful! Yes please. I would like that. Say, around midday?"

"I'll be here. Midday." Edward took her hand, bowed deeply, and gently pressed his lips against her fingers. He froze in that position beyond what was required of him as a gentleman, but he was afraid that if he let go, he would lose her again, forever. "Midday then," Sally said as she backed away to break his hold and ascended the stairs.

He lingered in a daze for a moment until he locked eyes with Otis through the leadlight of his shop.

Otis put his finger up and mouthed the word, "Wait!" He removed his apron, and spoke to a younger man behind a counter. He opened the door to the stairwell and ran upstairs to retrieve his coat and Thomas.

"I thought we might have a drink together, Edward," Otis suggested. "There is a respectable inn just around the corner. Have you time?"

"She did not say yes," Edward blurted. The two men looked astonished at first. Then smiled at each other, completely understanding Edward's position.

"Come, let's talk on the way," Otis directed. "You do understand that women need a bit of time over such matters?"

"I think perhaps she might have considered my offer were it not for our ties," Edward went on.

At the inn, the three sat for hours mauling over the problems and offering one solution after another until Thomas came up with a radical but feasible plan.

"Keep your respective holdings," he submitted. "There is no rush to disperse with either. Start anew in neutral territory, somewhere half way! Say, in Virginia, or the Carolinas. From what I hear, the winters are not as harsh as New England and the summers are at least as hot as the Caribbean. It's a perfect compromise!" Thomas construed.

"And Virginia is a growing colony, Edward, full of promise with its tobacco and cotton," Otis reminded.

"You would be nearer Abigail and James, and soon, me! I'm off to Virginia by summer's end!" Thomas added.

"Yes, I did mean to congratulate you on your assignment, Thomas. This sounds like a good compromise," Edward mused. "Fair, yet still challenging. I think she might consider such an offer!" Edward rose suddenly from his chair with goblet in hand and new hope in his heart, he offered a salute, "I feel as giddy as a school boy! Thank you both"

CHAPTER 43

The air had a chilling bite that April morning as the *Tempest* sailed close to the western shore along the Chesapeake Bay, past Elizabeth City, and on up the James River. Long strings of smoke escaped from the chimneys of homes in the tiny settlements along the river. The smoke poked through the low fog and rose straight up before unraveling to mingle with orange streaked clouds. Watermen hailed as they sailed past the *Tempest* on their way out to the fish-laden waters of the Bay. Their cheerful cries broke the silent morning fog that hugged the water's surface.

Abigail Montague convulsed with a sudden chill and Rebecca removed her shawl and placed it over the shivering shoulders of her stepdaughter. "Do be careful not to catch a chill, Abigail," she mothered.

"Are you not cold in this morning air?" Abigail asked.

"No, not so much," Rebecca fibbed. "The sun is rising and will soon be upon us. It already carries much of its promise of summer warmth."

"We'll soon be there," James declared. "Not far now."

The *Tempest* entered a narrow cove and tacked carefully into the small port of Middle Plantation. There was a crowd at the dock, headed by a grinning Professor Thomas Cranston who waved with carefree abandon.

"I half expected the happy groom to show up in his cap and gown," Abigail mocked in a kindly manner.

"Ah, he does look well," Rebecca noted. "And look, there she is!"

James squinted. "Is she *with* him, or waiting for another ship to dock, perhaps?" he questioned. He shielded his eyes against the glare. "No, she *is* with him! Look there, how their arms are locked. Hello! Hello!" he shouted.

Once on shore, there was a hubbub of excitement as they all reunited and met for the first time the bride to be, Miss Margaret Dundee. Thomas brought around the open buckboard colorfully decorated for the wedding in bunting and flowers. It was a tight fit, but they were soon seated for the short ride to Thomas's house on the outskirts of the settlement. As they drove through Middle Plantation, people on the street waved and congratulated the happy couple. James remarked about the extensive building and construction going on in the town.

"And this is only the start, Uncle James. The House of Burgesses has just elevated Middle Plantation to the status of Capital of the Colony of Virginia and with its new status, a new name: Williamsburg! And there, in the College Building," James pointed to the largest structure, "is where I teach my ingenious scholars, all natives of this colony. That is also where the Indian School is housed, the one I wrote to you about, Abigail. And those grounds over there between the College Building and the church are where the May Day celebrations will take place."

"What goes on in this . . . Indian School?" Rebecca inquired.

"Education!" Margaret offered.

"There are only a handful of students so far," Thomas explained, "and sadly, some of them are diplomatic hostages to insure peace with the Indians. But we are hoping the tribes will choose their brightest to come and study with us," Thomas turned around and mockingly whispered to them, "to learn the ways of an Englishman!" He righted himself and took on a determined demeanor. "It is our hope that someday, these children will return to teach others of their tribe and we will become one people."

"Might that be construed as arming an enemy with intelligence?" James asked.

"If by intelligence you mean literature and science, I believe it will benefit us all, Uncle James," Thomas replied.

James shook his head and sighed, "You sound so like your mother, Thomas!"

Thomas smiled at the compliment and continued his tour with a hint of pride. "There is our May Pole. Shorter than most, but we had a time convincing Rev. Blair that there should be one at all. But then he believes all dancing is unholy and a remnant of pagan rituals."

Margaret laughed and said, "I believe the scheduling of our wedding for the day after May Day helped to mellow his objections. What you see there is a pole shortened greatly by cleric compromises."

"Tomorrow," Thomas continued, "we will, no doubt, all suffer through many dull May Day speeches around that pole, but there is at least one that I think you will enjoy. A student, one of several who presented the idea of moving Virginia's capital from the Jamestown settlement to Middle Plantation, will extoll the highlights of his thesis. By invitation of Governor Nicholson, all members of the House of Burgesses will attend this May Day celebration. I am eager for you, Uncle James, to meet them." Thomas pulled back on the reins and turned to face the ladies in the back. "I am so pleased you were all able to make it for May Day and our wedding! It means so much to me and Margaret!"

Though Dogwood House was a short distance outside the village, it was not a torturous trip as the road was in good condition and heavy dew mercifully dampened the dust. They finally arrived at a gated lane lined with dogwood trees. White petals fell like snowflakes as the buckboard made its way down the lane. The motion of the wheels sent grounded petals wildly into the air only to cascade slowly down again in the wagon's wake.

Abigail stretched out her hand in failed attempts to grasp a single petal. "It's lovely!" she giggled. "I feel like we are Romans returning from a great battle and the citizens are showering us with flower petals!"

Two large chimneys framed the substantial boxy three-story red brick house at the end of lane. An old, terribly wrinkled but smiling negro servant, sporting a neatly curled wig that perfectly set off his bright white stockings, waved from the deep front porch. He ran out to grab the halters of the horses to steady them while Thomas helped the women from the buckboard.

"Oiy, Masta Thomas!" the negro had a wide grin with a distracting gap between his teeth. "Welcome Miss Margaret! Welcome everybody!"

"Greetings Patrick, is all well?" Margaret asked.

"Yes 'em, it is, Miss Margaret." Patrick nodded. "I'll takes dis pretty wagon over to da stables, Masta Thomas. And Millie, she done fix up a fine meal for ya all. Ya jist give her a holler, Miss Margaret, she's a bakin' back there in da summer kitchen."

While Thomas escorted the women inside, James stood outside for a moment to study the house.

"Well, what do you think?" a familiar voice asked.

"Sally!" James whirled around. Hounds of various sizes, shapes, and dispositions surrounded her. One growled at him as he approached her.

"Pip! Now, is that any way to treat my brother!" she scolded.

They embraced and teased and laughed.

"I couldn't stand waiting for you anymore, so I took the dogs for a walk to pass the time!"

"Ah, it's been too long, Sally!"

"Since your wedding, dear brother. Much too long! Well, what do you think of our Dogwood House?"

"It's striking, Sally. You've done well! Yes, very grand! Before we go in, I would like to pay my respects to Edward."

"Then come, he's over here." She took him by the hand and led him to a grove of cherry trees under which was the stone marking the grave of Edward Waller.

"I wish you could have seen this place a month ago, James. Every branch of these trees was covered with delicate scented blossoms. Edward planted them even before we built the house and they have already started to bear fruit. Quite sour to my taste, but Millie has a way of turning them into the most scrumptious pastries. I think he rests well in this spot."

James looked at his sister and struggled for words.

"I know, I know," she tried to comfort. "But these past five years brought us both such happiness, James. We were so contented. And here I am; twice now a widow, yet I am embarrassed to admit, I still have a belly full of energy and much curiosity about what's to come. Edward . . . he restored that in me." Sally wrapped her arm in his and led him towards the house. "It's a new century, James, and this is a brave new colony full of hope and prosperity. Don't you wonder what it will be like in the years to come?"

"I *fear* what will come of these colonies," he replied.

"Always the pessimist!" she teased.

"Hmmm. I know you dear sister! What are you up to now?"

Sally looked about as if she was to divulge a great secret. "After the wedding, I am off to Boston. I have decided it's where I would like to be. There's much to sort out, the properties and businesses, and I find the disposition of that city much to my liking."

"Sally, don't be ridiculous. It's too far away. Who would protect you?" James protested.

Sally ignored his concerns and continued. "As a wedding gift, I am giving Dogwood House to Thomas and Margaret." Sally stopped and turned to him. "James, I am glad for this moment alone because there is something I want to tell you before I greet the others. Edward left the properties and cooperage in Massachusetts to me, but with the stipulation that when I die, the properties will be divided between Thomas and Molly. The cooperage goes to Abigail. It's what Edward and I want."

"That . . . is extremely generous, Sally. Abigail, I'm sure will be delighted. But . . . what of Windhaven? Will you ever go back to Jamaica, Sally?"

"I don't know. Perhaps, one day. We have all benefitted by Nero's good management, James, but he grows old, as do we. What then, dear brother? We must think about that, but not today! Today, we celebrate this happy reunion!"

James hugged his sister.

"Oh, there is something else," she added while straightening her bonnet. "Before he died, Edward was soliciting Dutch ships to export his goods. These wretched Navigation Acts were set to strangle any colonist bent on making profit! The Dutch tariffs were digging too deep into his profits so, Edward's good friend in Massachusetts, Richard Tucker, talked him into purchasing an English merchantman, the *Swift*. It lies at anchor in Boston's harbor waiting for your instructions, dear brother. The *Swift* is your, James. He wanted you to have it."

James was dumbstruck. "A ship!" he finally managed. "I have a ship?"

"The *Swift*! I'm sorry, I don't know much about it except what Edward told me. It's a solid stable ship, not very old, has been refitted to hold more cargo, and has a dependable young captain who stands at the ready. Hugh Haywood."

"Haywood?"

"Yes, Hugh is Belle and Ned's grandchild! Can you believe it? He has captained for Edward this past year and has proven to be accomplished and trustworthy. Equally important, he has a flair for choosing a reliable crew. The problem is, he is a Catholic and as such, he's been thrown out of Massachusetts. The condition Edward set forth is that you must take him along with the ship and sponsor him in Charles Town until he is able to stand on his own. Do you agree to the terms, brother?"

James was silent for an instant and then let out, "Sally, I own a ship!"

Sally nodded with a wide satisfying grin. "Yes, you do! I would say we've done quite well for a couple of orphans!"

"But won't you require a ship for the cooperage?" he asked.

"Not for now. Mr. Tucker assures me there are other less complicated options. Now, go in and tell the others. I'll come along. I just want a moment . . . with Edward."

James gave Sally a long hug, then held her out at arm's length. He smiled warmly, nodded and went inside the house.

Sally watched until she saw the door close. She turned and went to the cherry grove. "Well, Edward. That's that. At 52, I suppose the practical thing would be to stay here and let the family see to my needs." Sally looked over to the house and frowned. "I didn't know you would leave me so soon." She sighed deeply to stop her tears and reached down to remove a weed. "Patrick promised to look after you. He's a tough old goose, but he's a proud free man who knows a thing or two about keeping the land looking nice." Sally stood tall. "You'll be all right, Edward." Looking straight ahead she declared, "So will I."